THE HOSTILES: STORM AREA 51

TOM ASHTON

Copyright © 2020 Tom Ashton.

ISBN 978-1913762353

A catalogue record for this book is available from the British Library.

Edited by John Wait.

www.blkdogpublishing.com

Also by Tom Ashton:

Lemonade
By Tom Ashton

Peter Lemon and Aidan O'Sullivan are the proud co-owners of Grenton Groceries, a successful fruit and veg retailers in Grenton Village, Cumbria. However, commercial bliss is thrown into disarray when Aidan's brother Norris arrives at the shop, having been recently released from prison.

Soon Norris begins to drive a rift between the men, and, following the advice of a neighbour, it becomes clear to one of them that there is only one solution.

Lemonade is a story from Ashton's Grenton Village Collection, and has been described as 'Cosy Crime', a subgenre of Crime Fiction in which the crime takes place in a small, socially intimate community, often described using dark humour.

CHAPTER ONE

'*Jason Carlton Wins General Election.*'
  '*Can Jason Carlton's Words Stop Bombs?*'
  '*New PM Carlton Announces Priority Shake-Up.*'

The headlines were similar, below Harold's game of Patience. He continued to digest them as he laid the King of Hearts on top of the fourth little pile. A knock at the door broke his reverie, causing him to scatter the Hearts across the table.

'Good morning, Professor,' came the sultry and familiar female voice.

Harold scooped up the cards and struggled to jam them back into their packet, as his assistant crossed the room to the window and drew the blinds.

'Good morning, Anne-Marie,' he replied. 'I didn't know you were in yet.'

She held a crisp white envelope and his 'World's Greatest Boss' mug, neither of which dangled a degree in her grip, as she swivelled and walked towards him. He held out his hands for both, but instead received an expression of suspicion, and then her green eyes dropped to his laptop and the 'Penis Enhancement' ad visible on the screen. He slammed it shut, and pulled it towards him, as though frightened she might steal it and show it to everybody he knew.

She smiled, thin-lipped, and set down the envelope and mug on the desk.

'What's this all about?' she asked. A blue, manicured fingernail, tapped the words 'Top' and then 'Secret', which were emblazoned in bold red across the top of the envelope.

He read the words. Then picked up the envelope and re-read them. Any amorous fantasies he enjoyed about his administrative assistant were dissolving, replaced instead by a desire to be left alone to read.

'Are you a spy?' Because if you are, I think you'll agree I'm due a generous bonus for Christmas, in exchange for my silence.'

So that was it.

'I don't think so,' he said, 'it'll be some drivel from HR. Probably some consequence of the election. This new bloody liberal government... anti-nuclear, you know? Probably harbouring some animosity regarding the A1 project.'

She bit her lip and rolled her eyes. 'I see you're not going to let me in on the act Mr Bond... maybe a Vodka Martini some time might loosen your tongue.'

She laughed, that saccharine laugh, and left him to shake his head at his letter. The girl was about fifteen years his junior and an avid reveller in social media scandal. He would not have his indiscretions laid bare online, and risk his marriage again — certainly not while sober.

As soon as the door clicked shut, he wiggled the paper halfway out of the envelope, but then felt a sting and released it. He stuck his thumb with the blossoming red bubble in his mouth and unfolded the letter with his other hand. Why did paper cuts hurt so much?

The letterhead read 'National Defence Engineering Systems.' With a little bloodstain beside it.

'Dear Professor Harold Dunn.' It said in biro, before transitioning to type.

'We regret to inform you that all production and research associated with the A1 programme will be terminated with immediate effect. We advise you contact human resources to discuss your redundancy package. Please be aware that this is a parliamentary decision, and by no means reflects the desire of the company.'

Harold dropped the letter a second time and stared at it as though it might explode at any moment. Twelve years of research. A place in history. Anne-Marie. All gone. Just like that.

Could they do that? They couldn't do that.

Impossible.

Harold picked up the phone and speed-dialled number five for HR. His heart rate quickened in a manner that further unsettled him as he listened to the dial tone.

'Good morning,' came a female voice, 'NDES Human Resources. Molly speaking.'

'Hi, this is Professor Harold Dunn. Maybe you've heard of me. I'm the man who's just spent over a decade developing the biggest nuclear warhead the world's ever seen, for you, and I've just opened my bloody notice of dismissal!'

Harold glared down at the letter, as though it was re-offending, and listened to some muffled conversation from the other end of the line. A more dominant female voice spoke.

'Ah, Professor Dunn, hello. We're incredibly grateful for your service, and we think that's reflected in your redundancy package set at £60,000...'

Harold spotted a few strands of brown hair dangling in front of the glass of the door.

'Marie, go back to your desk!' he said and then tried to speak in softer tones, in case her retreating shadow was a deception.

'I don't want a bloody redundancy package. I want my job. You can't treat people like...'

'Ah, Professor, I do empathise with you, but unfortunately new government policy takes a focus to political solutions to our global conflicts, and has made programs like the A1 obsolete. Now they're demanding we put our engineers to different tasks, building trawlers, supply planes, and such, and we just don't think your niche expertise...'

Harold jabbed the grey button and terminated the call. What on Earth was happening? He would go down there. He would make them see reason.

He moved through the adjoining office, almost toppling the ridiculous potted plant Marie had brought in, 'to oxygenate the place.'

'For England, Harold?' she said. But he ignored her and wrestled his way through some youths in the stairwell. Probably film students on their way to the studio on the third floor.

They swore at him as he stuck out his elbows. He hated them, and they knew it. They'd caught his glares as they smoked out front and drank their coke in the downstairs lobby. A man of his stature should not be sharing a building with the likes of whom probably voted for Jason bloody Carlton. He had hoped upon completion of the A1 program he could expect to move to an office in a more affluent area. Now he might as well move into a bloody tent.

A further irritation awaited him as he crossed the lobby to the revolving front door, and it was called Mrs Partridge.

'Oh, Professor Dunn,' she said stepping into his path.

Why now? And what was it this week? Had there been explosions heard from his office again? Maybe he'd been spotted dumping nuclear waste in the recycling bin? Or were people still getting ill because of the gamma waves he omitted? Why didn't she nag those bloody film students?

'What is it, Mrs Partridge?'

'A man has just arrived to see you.'

She pointed to a well-dressed man in one of the cushy chairs beside the long street-facing window. His suit looked tailored, and the thirty-two-tooth smile he threw his way made Harold suspect the man was a lawyer of some sort.

'I was just about to pass the message onto that revered administrative assistant of yours — though I'm not convinced she can answer a phone. Still, that's not why you hired her...' She said, giving him a glance over her withered, green-blazered shoulder as she clicked back to the desk.

Once she'd outrun his glare, he turned and found the man in front of him, hand outstretched.

'Professor Dunn?'

Harold took the hand but made to move past the man, puzzling only for a moment over the American accent, 'Hello, yes, I'm in something of a rush, so perhaps you can have Mrs Partridge make you an appointment with my administrative assistant. I can assure you, she does know how to answer a phone, now if you'll excuse me…'

'There's nothing to be negotiated regarding your job with the N.D.E.S, Professor Dunn, it's all over.'

Harold stared at the man, still holding on tightly to his hand.

'How do you know about that? Do you work for N.D.E.S?'

'No.'

'So what are you then? An employment lawyer…?' He froze, 'Press?'

'Wrong on all accounts,' said the man, 'please, come over and have a seat.'

Harold followed him and plonked himself into the leather armchair.

The man sat down in front of Harold and ran a hand over his bald scalp.

'My name is John, and I work for the US Government.'

'The US…?' Harold gulped. Was he being extradited to Guantanamo Bay or something?

'Am I in some kind of trouble?'

'I suppose that depends on whether you find your sudden unemployment troubling?'

'Of course.'

'Then yes, but fear not, for I think I have the solution: a new job, with a generous salary, far better than what you're used to at N.D.E.S.'

Harold let the air rush out of him, as though he were a balloon deflating. This guy was a recruitment agent, and this was salesman talk. These buggers moved fast.

He began to feel annoyed again, now caused by the stress this John had put him under.

'What kind of job? Where?'

'The advisory kind, in Nevada, USA. It's your AI project we want. Unlike your new liberal government, we intend to have a response when the Russians start firing.'

Harold looked at his watch, if he left now he could be at N.D.E.S in twenty minutes, there might still be time to make them see reason. He realised John had stopped talking.

'Look,' he said, 'my research… my knowledge… is all bound up in the Official Secrets Act.'

John smiled that toothy grin of his.

'Carlton has already sold us your research.'

Harold gawped and forgot all about his stampede to N.D.E.S.

'You're the reason I lost my job?'

'Of course not, your unemployment came about because your new Prime Minister believes Great Britain should set an anti-nuclear example to the world, and men like you do not fit into that picture.'

'I'm a scientist,' Harold said.

'A scientist who engineers devices that kill millions of people.'

Harold fidgeted, as he always did whenever reminded of this.

'I have a life here. I'm married.'

John settled back in the chair, frowned up at the halogen bulbs, and removed some shades from his pocket.

Shades, indoors? How American.

'And how are things at home?'

Harold processed the man's tone. He couldn't possibly know about Helen and he, could he?

'They're ok,' he said, 'but I don't think she'd be up for moving to… where did you say?'

'Washington initially, then after the four or five years we suspect it'd take to finish the build, we'd move you and the project to a secure location in Nevada.

'Where in Nevada?'

'A very secure location.'

Harold grinned in spite of himself.

'Not Area 51?'

John glanced round at the other people loitering in the lobby.

Harold composed himself. This guy was clearly nuts, and something about the opportunistic nature of his visit made Harold feel uncomfortable. That and the way he flicked his tongue over his lips every few seconds.

'My wife definitely wouldn't go for it,' he said and stood up.

John stood up as well and reached out to grasp Harold's hand again.

'Discuss it with her and call me,' he said and placed a white business card, blank, save for a telephone number, in Harold's jacket pocket.

CHAPTER TWO

John watched Harold Dunn hurry on through the revolving glass doors and let his tongue taste the air, as the man disappeared from sight.

He took his cell phone from his pocket and dialled.

'Bartonville Fruit and Veg, Illinois,' came the young girl's voice, 'can I take your order?'

'2835, John, 091019.'

'Just a moment please, sir.'

There was a crackle of static as the line was transferred.

'John?' MJ1 sounded concerned, 'the Brit?'

'It's a negative. Something to do with Dunn's wife not wanting to relocate.'

MJ1 murmured something at the other end of the line.

'Sir?'

'You can't take him by force John, the last thing we need is for the UK to catch us absconding with one of their nationals.'

John replied he had already considered that and added Dunn's advice throughout the remaining months of the A1's construction would be reserved if he were there under duress.

'I could give him a few days to change his mind?' John suggested. 'Maybe find some way to facilitate the process?'

'What were you thinking?'

As John rolled some ideas around his head, his tongue slithered out and caught the smell of something unpleasant, light and warm, like urine. He hung up on MJ1 immediately, and strode towards the door and into the street.

Valk cursed the Agent's incompetence in convincing the human to move his operations to Area 51. The Americans needed to be ready to respond to the Russians. There needed to be a war.

He flung down the newspaper and glowered at the image of the new Prime Minister, Jason Carlton on the front cover. Peace lovers like him weren't making things easier either.

He exhaled and relaxed into the comfortable chair to consider a new plan of action. It would not do to relay what had happened, to Leader Atherpock without one.

From what he'd overheard, Dunn's wife was the problem, so the obvious solution was to remove her. However, humans were weak hearted creatures — would Dunn be too grief-stricken to work if she were to disappear?

A clacking of heels distracted him, and he spotted a young brunette approaching reception, who used the words 'Professor' and 'Dunn', before being drowned out entirely by the din of some passing students, whom he would have enjoyed skinning alive had he had the time. Valk rose, folded the newspaper, and fell in line behind the girl.

'I'm sorry,' the old crone behind the counter was saying to the young woman, 'your... employer... left. Shan't imagine we'll be seeing him or you for some time now, what with the new government coming in and everything. Antinuclear, you know? And isn't that what he's embroiled in?'

The brunette whipped her hair from her face and over her shoulder, 'where did he go? He's not answering his phone. We need to discuss this.'

'I've no idea. Perhaps he felt he should discuss it with his wife first? You knew he had a wife, didn't you?'

'What are you implying...?'

'Excuse me, ladies,' Valk said, and both women glared at him as he pushed the folded tabloid onto the counter, 'thanks for the paper.'

He winked, contented Dunn's devotion to his wife might not be as absolute as he'd first suspected.

Tom Ashton

CHAPTER THREE

Harold was still reeling from his dust-up with HR, as Helen ladled some blackened chicken onto his plate. He'd encountered Molly first and questioned how a girl who was barely more than a temp could give him his marching orders. He'd felt very foolish after he'd said it. And of course, it resulted in the calling of a superior, who'd turned out to be the other woman he'd spoken to on the phone, Veronica.

If Molly's empathetic prattle had been passive aggressive, Veronica's blunt utterances were directly assertive. 'That's the offer.' 'Lower your tone.' 'Leave.' 'I can call security.'

He'd left before the door-thugs could reach him so he would retire with at least a little dignity, and a sordid cheque for sixty grand, which remained folded in his pocket with his letter of dismissal.

He turned over a piece of meat.

'What's wrong with it?'

'Nothing,' he lied, 'I met a man today.'

During the hour he'd been home he'd been turning over ways to tell her in his head, but then his mouth had just begun speaking on its own accord. It did that sometimes.

Helen swallowed her food.

'You're leaving me?'

Harold dropped his fork onto his plate, and they both stared at one another.

'…because you're gay.' She said, her eyes widening.

'Oh, yes, very funny,' Harold said, 'no, he approached me about a job in the US.'

She began chewing again, cheeks flushed. 'Are you looking for work in the US?'

'Well, no, but…' His autopilot failed, so he took the letter and cheque out of his pocket, and slid them over to her.

She opened the cheque first, and a look of joy, Harold had not seen for a long time, passed over her face.

He sniffed and pointed with his fork towards the letter, which she opened with intrigue. The intrigue turned to confusion then to horror in under a minute.

'You lost your job?'

He nodded.

'Why didn't you tell me?'

'I'm telling you now.'

'Yes, but what are you going to do? What are we going to do?'

'I dunno.'

Her own fork went clattering off the table and the flush spread across her entire face, as her intakes of breath grew more numerous. The slim, five-foot-one woman was like a puffer fish when entered into a hostile situation — she could give the impression of being much bigger than she actually was.

'Well, what did you say to this American?'

'I told him no.'

'Why?'

'I don't know. It didn't feel right, I thought I might be able to sort something out with N.D.E.S, but it's this new bloody hippie PM we've got. My research is useless nationwide, at least until the next election.'

'And this guy wants to use your research?'

'He wants me. It's an advisory position.'

'So take it. It's an easy choice, throw away the last ten years of your life and embrace unemployment, or relocate and be successful. I can't believe you said no.'

'But what about you?'

'They have retail over in America too you know?' She glowered and then broke into what looked to be a reluctant smile. 'This might be a good opportunity for us, Harold. A new environment might do us some good.'

Harold felt a little bit stupid. Now that he'd discussed it with Helen, the whole thing didn't seem so suspicious. The simple fact was he was being headhunted by a rival institution, a big one at that. Things like that happened to people all the time.

'So you think I should give this guy a call?'

'Absolutely.'

'Unless…' She said eyes fixed on him, 'there's some other reason you don't want to leave the country. Someone else? Like that little administrative assistant of yours, perhaps?'

'Don't be ridiculous,' he said, eyes diving into his mashed potato

'Is it so ridiculous, darling?' She said, and although he wasn't looking at her face, he knew her eyes had gone all squinty, and the smile had grown so thin her lips had disappeared.

Harold found John's card, took out his mobile, and dialled.

It rang once.

'Professor Dunn,' it was not a question.

'How did you know it was me?'

'Don't be naive. Now, I'm assuming you'd like to meet?'

'Say I'm coming too,' said Helen.

'And your charming lady too?'

'Yes.'

'How about Aspire in an hour? It's a little cocktail bar on Sidney Street, do you know it?

'Aspire… in an hour. That's half seven?' Harold said looking at his wife, who gave him the thumbs up in that emasculating way of hers, 'Yeah that sounds fine.'

At a quarter past seven, they turned the corner from Woods Lane onto Sidney Street Their hands touched for a second before Harold's dove into his pockets.

It was a chilly night. The frosty pavement sparkled in the streetlights.

'Quiet tonight,' he said, seeing only a homeless guy

snoozing on a bench in a blue sleeping bag, and three kids drinking cider outside the town hall. 'I remember when this street used to be bouncing. I blame the economy — everybody's too scared to spend anything.'

'Oh, Harold, do shut up.' Helen dropped back a pace and busyied herself on her iPhone.

It was all very well, for her to accuse him of infidelity. He'd found her Tinder account last week. Then there was that other month when she'd stayed out until nine am, after 'crashing out' at a mate's. And the condom wrapper he'd found under his own bed — some foreign brand he'd never even heard of. She'd claim it was all revenge if he confronted her about it, so why bother.

Wouldn't it be funny, he thought, if I just got on the plane with this John and left her behind?

Though he knew he wouldn't, for the same reason he would never confront her about her hypocrisy. The only thing he feared more than being with a woman, was being without one.

As they got closer to the bar, he composed himself for the meeting. He felt a breeze on the back of his neck and looked back over his shoulder.

Helen looked too, and they both saw a purple Ford Ka, prowling along the road behind them. Was it John? Harold doubted he drove a Ford Ka somehow. Perhaps it was some curb crawling youths. The reflection of the streetlights on the windows made it impossible to tell. As he considered stopping to see if the car would roll past, the driver's window descended, and a man in a cheap, hooded tracksuit top, leaned out.

'Professor Dunn, you are going to work for the Americans, da?'

Russian? Harold thought. News of his dismissal had travelled fast and far indeed.

'Why should we tell you anything?' Helen said taking a step towards the car, and Harold rolled his eyes. The minx always seemed to throw him into some test of manhood whenever they went out together.

'Because Russia has a message for you and those American pigs.'

The man leaned back, and sparks burst towards them.

'Get down,' Harold said, as the air filled with the noise of screams, and shattering glass, and metal casings bouncing off concrete. Then, it ended, and the car accelerated away. Harold looked up from the pavement and saw a shadow rush out of the bar and fire a single shot into the bodywork of the vehicle before it screeched around the corner and out of sight.

The chavs had vanished and could be heard hollering down the other end of the Town Hall car park somewhere, but the homeless man bounded past in his sleeping bag like some Olympic sack racer, and it was he that brought Harold' attention to his wife, bleeding beside him.

'No,' he said, as a black, American saloon pulled up and John arrived at his side, trying to pull him into the car.

'You did this,' Harold said, springing to his feet and giving him a shove, 'you fucking killed her.'

'No, Professor Dunn.'

Harold swung two punches, both of which John caught at the wrists. Around them, residents were beginning to appear, in their dressing gowns with their smartphones held aloft, and sirens could be heard in the distance. Harold kicked John in the knee, who hissed with pain, and then head-butted him unconscious.

Harold awoke with a smarting headache. He pushed himself back off a dashboard, saw it was John driving the car, and noticed a gun resting in the man's lap, pointed ever so slightly in his direction.

'Professor Dunn. I am not your enemy,' he said.

'You killed my wife.'

'You know I didn't,' said John, 'I was waiting for you in the bar.'

Harold glared at him and rested his head in his palms.

'Did the shooter say anything to you?'

Harold returned his eyes to the windscreen and half-watched the road markings and houses flash past. He remembered the car pulling up beside them, the window rolling down, and then the gunfire.

'He spoke in Russian,' said Harold, he said that he had a message for 'you American pigs'.

'Then the Russians have discovered we've tried to recruit you and wanted to stop that from happening,' John said.

Harold noticed that the houses were familiar. They were turning onto his street.

'You're taking me home?'

'It would be proper to give you some time alone to come to terms with your wife's death, but you're no longer safe here. You need to pack. We're on a flight in two hours.'

He rolled to a stop but put a hand on Harold's arm as he made to exit.

'My partner went ahead of me. He said that they burgled your house before they came for you. Might he have found anything that might jeopardise our proceedings?'

Harold sighed, reached into his pocket, and revealed a polythene bag containing eight pen drives and an external hard-drive, 'my research goes everywhere with me.'

John nodded, though something in his face said that he wasn't done talking.

'Professor Dunn, I'm sure your wife's death is something of an emotional challenge for you right now but… '

'It's fine,' Harold said, 'I'll go pack.'

And as he tottered up the garden path toward his front door, Harold realised it was fine because a nasty part of him was glad to be free. What a loathsome bastard he was.

CHAPTER FOUR

(11:00 AM, Wednesday, September 4th, 2019 – Six years later.)

Restricted Area! Deadly Force is Authorised Beyond This Point!

The signs grew more threatening and more difficult for Harold Dunn to ignore as he continued down the dirt road towards one of the most secure military installations in the world. Soon he began to spot sound masts and CCTV towers, hidden lazily in amongst red rock piles and cacti, and as he reached out to pat the laminated visitor's ID badge, on the cotton lanyard beside him, a large white 4x4 rolled to a halt and observed him from the slope ahead.

The sweat cascaded down his neck, and his heart rate quickened, and he was forced to remind himself that his Google research had told him to expect this. He continued his course without changing speed, past the 4x4 atop the hill, and found another parked across the centre of the road, with four armed men in black and beige camouflage waiting in formation beside it. As he braked, the other 4x4 rolled into the path behind him.

'Freeze!' Said a moustachioed guard, 'This is a restricted area!'

All the other guards broke out in frenzied repetitions of what the Moustache had just said.

Harold lifted his palms in clear sight. In the weeks

leading up to his arrival, he'd watched several YouTube videos featuring these uncompromising security guards, most of them manhandling UFO nerds scoping out the base. They were known online as 'Camo Dudes', and the nerds were self-proclaimed Ufologists preparing for #StormArea51, a trending hashtag, and event due to take place on September 4th.

'I've clearance!' He yelled through the open window, feeling his stomach churn in request of an Imodium tablet.

'Put your hands on the wheel!' ordered the Moustache, prompting all the other guards to mimic him again.

He complied, of course, and the guard approached, filling the oval driver's side window of the rental Audi TT with a broad chest atop a broader gut. Harold turned and saw a meaty face descend, skin burnt scarlet, and a thick moustache bristling on the upper lip, like some enormous caterpillar sizzling in the heat.

'Don't recognise your plate!' He said in an Alabama drawl, 'Let's see your pass!'

Harold managed to unglue his hand from the wheel and reached down to the passenger seat, which caused a flurry of raised weapons from the onlookers. Slowly, he lifted the lanyard in plain sight and trembled it into the steady palm of the guard.

He grunted, took several steps away from the car, and began gabbling into a walkie-talkie, as Harold continued to glance nervously down the barrels of the four assault rifles.

This is it. Harold thought, a dangerous fart erupting from his backside. My pass is going to be inexplicably denied then I'm going to be water-boarded and thrown in a cell for the rest of my life.

His pessimism was cut short by the return of his ID, which struck him on the chin — the guard grinning, perhaps hoping to prompt an act of disobedience. 'You check out. Follow me.'

Harold wasn't stupid enough to rise to the bait, though he could feel the small nick on his chin throbbing, as the Moustache and half the guards, got into the 4x4 ahead of him, and accelerated into the distance. He stalled the Audi and then wheel-spun up the next dune, as the guards in the other truck watched, sneers below black shades.

After about half a mile, the dirt road became tarmac, and Harold caught up to the 4x4, which led him to a fifteen-foot wire fence, topped with razor wire, beyond which were a dozen unremarkable looking concrete buildings, and a long, dusty runway. They rolled to a stop in front of another 4x4 parked across the road, blocking the entrance.

The Moustache got out and was approached by a skinny guard with a mullet. The two had a long conversation, with some pointing towards the Audi. They both shared a few laughs, while Harold remained sitting there, his fingers drumming the steering wheel.

The Mullet swaggered over to Harold and said. 'Don't recognise your plates! You got your ID?'

'I just showed it to your colleague.'

The Mullet raised his rifle at once, prompting the Moustache to do the same.

'Alright... alright...' Harold said, trembling again as he offered his ID up a second time.

Both men lowered their weapons, and the Mullet took the ID, turned away, and began to speak into his walkie-talkie. The Moustache's gaze locked on Harold's, his sneer now an expression of concrete ambivalence and Harold couldn't help but avert his gaze. Fortunately, he did this just in time to spot his ID flying back in through the window and caught it.

The Mullet chuckled. 'Fast learner... Go on through, you're clear.'

Harold was so eager to be away from the pair he nearly hit someone as he accelerated into the compound, and was forced to slam-on, hard. The car stalled a second time, he bumped his chin on the steering wheel right where his ID had broken the skin, and, worst of all, his near-victim turned out to be a beautiful woman.

He stuck his head out of the window. 'Sorry!'

'Professor Dunn?' She said.

'Yes?'

'Professor Dunn, my name's Dr Tsai, I'm to give you a tour.'

'Oh...' Harold said, dissecting the girl in a second. She

was slim, with straight, jet black hair, all the way to her waist. She was professionally dressed, but cut a nice figure in a long black skirt and a button-down white shirt. She was of oriental descent, probably Chinese.

He shamed himself away from further sordid analysis, restarted the car, and, feeling many eyes upon him, carefully pulled forward into a parking space.

She approached the car and waited as he fumbled his suitcase over the seats and opened his door, nearly hitting her with it.

'Welcome to Area 51, Professor Dunn.'

He shook her hand, cringing at how sweat-free it felt compared to his own.

'Call me Harold.'

'Lisa,' she said, over her shoulder, as she wiped her hand on her skirt, and began walking towards a black door in the side of one of the buildings. He hurried after her.

'Chinese?'

'What gave me away?' She said, 'I look so Caucasian, and with a name like Tsai… you're wasted as a scientist.'

Harold frowned, unable to tell if she was being standoffish or playful. He decided to be optimistic.

She swiped her ID card through a reader, which beeped for a second before the door swung inwards to permit them entry. Harold decided he liked the sharp angles of her face, and the flick of her mascara.

He followed her down a generic office corridor, of potted plants, wooden doors, and cheap ocean canvases, until they reached another security door. She paused with her card above the reader.

'Brace yourself and stay close,' she said.

Harold nodded and prepared himself for whatever was beyond the door. Giant, man-eating rats, perhaps? Or scorpion robots with laser beams for stings?

It was neither, merely a lobby with many exits, containing a huge crush of about two hundred scientists, dropping papers, spilling coffee, and yelling into mobile phones.

Despite her warning they instantly became separated in the swirling current, and Harold swore many times as his heels were trodden on, his ribs were elbowed, and his head was bashed with a metal tripod.

He heard someone call his name over the din, and spotted her beckoning him towards an empty corridor on the east side. Teeth gritted against further assault he waded to the edge of the crush and tumbled out. His brown leather shoes he'd polished that morning had been scuffed beyond redemption.

She cocked an eyebrow at his shoes, turned, and then led him away from the chaos, which gave him the impression that it was all normal procedure.

'I was raised local, as it goes, right here in Nevada,' she said, 'Vegas.'

'Vegas, huh? I've always meant to check it out.'

'Some people find the roads around Vegas a little... challenging,' she chuckled.

He rolled his eyes in mock exasperation but felt a little uncomfortable that she had, in fact, not forgotten about his haphazard driving.

Time for a salvage operation, he thought.

'Well if you're such a good driver, a Vegas local, and my de-facto tour guide, then maybe you should take me and show me around.'

Her smile drooped, and Harold realised in the fray he'd just fought his way through, he'd not seen another person nearly as attractive as Lisa. She must get lame pick-up attempts a few times every day.

'Unfortunately, I'm a scientist, not a tour guide, and your tour with me is limited to within the base.'

Harold felt the full force of the cold. 'I know — I was just saying...'

He bartered with a higher power for a witty way to redeem himself before the hostile silence passed the three-second mark from which there would be no return.

'So... what are the chances of me seeing an alien around here?'

Her glance was disconcerting.

'Hey, where better than Area 51, right?'

'Mmm.'

Like the petulant child, too naughty to go to the fair, he

sulked, listening to Lisa's heels clack steadily along the laminate floors. After awkward minutes that seemed like awkward hours, they arrived at a door, much like the one through which they'd entered the base. In fact, all the doors were pretty much identical, except this one was labelled 205.

Lisa spoke with an authoritarian tone.

'I'll come and get you for lunch at 13:00 hours. You've an en-suite should you wish to freshen up, and if you need anything else, just dial 'hash' and my assistant will help you.'

As she handed him a key card, their fingertips touched.

'Take it with you if you decide to take a stroll, but you might prefer to wait until I'm with you. You've seen how it can get down there during rush hour.'

Her softer countenance had arrived too late. Harold had already worked his way into a humiliated mental fury.

'Never mind all that. When will I get to see my A1?'

She sniffed.

'It will be on the tour,' she said, 'see you soon, Professor Dunn.'

Harold scraped the panels around the reader three times before he found it with the card, ensnared by the retreat of the standoffish woman.

His room was unremarkable but comfortable — small bed, small wardrobe, small bathroom. He showered vigorously, to rid himself of the dust from the dirt road, but became distracted, once again, by the memory of Dr Tsai's retreating bottom, resulting in his shower lasting far longer than it should have.

When he eventually wrapped himself in a towel and padded from the bathroom, feeling a little ashamed of himself, he picked up his tattered pack of cards off the dresser, then set them back down again, and took to exploring the drawers instead. In the third one down, he found a pair of green binoculars, marked in Sharpie down one side: **Andrews.**

As he wondered if there was a Lost Property section he could give the binoculars in to, he lifted them to his eyes, gazing out the small window. The vista led him to inally fully comprehend he was in the mythical Area 51. The view itself was obscured by a thick whirl of sand, but he could see a long runway beyond the initial blocks, where he suspected they conducted the test flights. Suddenly, his observation was interrupted by the two white 4x4s hurtling through the compound towards the gate.

Off to star in another YouTube video?

As his eyes began to sting and the idea of a power-nap grew in its appeal, he spotted a group of men, scuttling in ant-like formation across the concrete square, towards a small western building. It didn't look big enough to fit six men, let alone a dozen.

It must be a stairwell to an underground hangar. Perhaps his A1 is down there?

All of a sudden, he was disturbed by a sharp rap at the door. Seized instantly by an intense weariness, he shot his watch an exasperated glance. 12.45. His curiosity had gotten the better of him, and now his opportunity to nap had vanished.

'You're early!' he said, as he opened the door, only to discover a man's face, where he'd expected to find Lisa's.

The man smiled. 'Professor Dunn, my name's Agent Steve. I'm here to show you to the canteen.'

Harold snorted at the black trilby and trench coat combination. If anyone could tell him about UFO crashes and alien bodies, he reckoned it was this bloke. Although his tone seemed uncomfortable — reserved — like he found speaking a chore. Perhaps, he was not the man to ask, after all.

'Won't you follow me, Professor Dunn?'

Harold shut the door behind him and fell in with Agent Steve, who set a leisurely pace.

'Good flight?'

'Yes, not bad' Harold said, 'We had quite a bit of turbulence over...'

'Good drive in?'

'Uh... Yeah. No trouble renting the car. Though I think I'll end up paying for some damages. The roads around here are...'

'Just hell, aren't they? Hope security didn't rough you up too much at the entrance?'

'They're pretty intense. Though I suppose when you're

charged with guarding a military base as high profile as this one you'd have to be something of a…'

'Yeah, they're pretty thorough. Ha-ha!' His laugh had an eerie ring to it, which prompted several passing scientists to look round with curiosity. 'So, see anything of interest with your binoculars?'

Harold slowed at this, filling with derision. 'You were spying on me?'

'Not at all, Professor Dunn,' said Steve, without breaking stride, 'You were merely noticed by someone outside, and they mentioned it to me in passing conversation. A spot of bird-watching, was it?'

'I was checking out the compound,' Harold said.

'I see.'

Steve stared at Harold as they walked, and would've walked straight into several scientists had they not spotted him and stepped out of his way.

'What's that building to the west, out of interest? Is it the entrance to an underground hangar… housing my AI perhaps?'

Steve came to an abrupt halt so Harold passed him and was forced to stop and turn to look at him. The Agent's body remained still, eyes locked on Harold's face, and then he revealed a peculiar tick. His tongue wriggled out from between his lips and began to flicker.

'Alright… 'Silence of the Lambs',' said Harold, 'What are you doing?'

Steve sucked his tongue back in, rolled it around inside his mouth, and then said, 'That building is beyond your clearance, Professor Dunn. There's nothing of value to you in there.'

Harold shrugged. 'Just wondered.'

Steve nodded, turned, and set off back the way they'd come.

'Hey, I thought you were showing me the canteen?'

'So did I,' said Lisa appearing from an adjacent corridor. 'Thought we were meeting at your room? I was just on my way to get you.'

Harold pointed at the shrinking figure, 'He turned up and said he was taking me… I dunno…'

Lisa followed Harold's finger and spotted the Agent before he disappeared into the crowd of scientists surging towards the canteen.

'What did he want?' She said.

'Nothing really, I found some binoculars in my room, and was having a look round, and then he turned up wanting to know what I was looking at.'

'What were you looking at?'

'Nothing, just that little building over to the west.'

She shook her head. 'No Harold, Professor Dunn, Hangar 18 is beyond your clearance.'

'I know, he said that,' said Harold, his ears getting hot, 'I only glanced at it. I thought my rocket might be down there.'

'No.'

Harold didn't speak to her again until they'd made it into the busy canteen and secured their place in line.

'Who was that weirdo anyway?'

Lisa replied out of the corner of her mouth, her eyes sweeping the room. 'He's an Agent. They coordinate a lot of the security on the base and deal with external PR stuff as well. Not too sure. Not much is known about them. Just rumours.'

'What kind of rumours?'

'Rumours that they're not to be messed with,' she said, accepting a plate of sloppy pie from an unshaven man, in a dirty apron. 'Try the pie, Harold.'

Although he felt irritated by her evasion and condescension, he decided to drop it, eager not to do further damage to their relationship.

He felt his mood lighten as the cook scooped the pie, mashed potato, and peas onto his plate. He was surrounded by some of the most brilliant minds in the world, and they were all dining as though they were still at school. With a wry smile, he fought the urge to flick peas at a miserable looking bunch on the front table and followed Lisa to a table at the back of the hall.

'Hi Lisa,' said one of them with more enthusiasm than the others — enthusiasm which faded as he clocked Harold. 'Who's this?'

'This is Professor Harold Dunn. He's just visiting, and

I'm giving him the tour.'

'How nice.'

One of the others butted in, 'The same Harold Dunn who designed the guidance system for the A1?'

'The very same,' Harold said.

They murmured to one another, save for Lisa's admirer who rolled his eyes.

A boisterous bald man with a large, ginger moustache and bushy eyebrows to match, announced himself. 'Professor Dunn, it really is a pleasure to meet you, my name's Jasper, Dr Jasper Hennimore,' he cleared his throat. 'Can you tell us anything about the magnetic guidance system of the A1? Most sophisticated I'm told.'

'Classified, no doubt,' said Lisa's admirer, 'I'm sure Dr. Dunn can't tell you a thing.'

'Professor.' Harold corrected, staring hard at the man, thinking that he'd quite like to meet him alone in a bar one day.

'He can only say no, Kowalski,' Jasper said.

Harold swallowed his mouthful along with a threat he had ready for Kowalski should he continue in his abrasive manner — the pie really was very good — and waved his hand. 'Guys, guys, I can tell you in the simplest terms without disclosing anything too technical...'

They fell silent, and even Kowalski's fork hovered in front of his mouth.

'The missile was designed for the express purpose of destroying the Russian's new nuke...'

'The Satan 4,' said a thin, spectacled man at the end.

'Yes, the Satan...'

'Nuke on nuke action,' said Jasper.

Harold paused at the vulgar remark, forever wary of tabloid journalists who could be anywhere at any time, ready to print a headline to the tune of 'Eminent Professor revels in the thought of Nuclear Holocaust.' Though, perhaps not at Area 51, he decided.

'In addition to the usual systems, the A1 can lock on to something as small as a chemical compound or a metallic particle, from fifteen thousand feet, and will instinctively avoid all incoming bogeys. There hasn't been one of our test ballistics that's successfully countered it thus far. Ergo, once we send it up, it can only be stopped if we deactivate it.'

Harold was almost relieved when Kowalski interrupted the flurry of questions that followed.

'So, I saw you talking to an Agent on my way in. What was that about then? Are you a spy?'

'If I told you that…' Harold said with a grin, allowing time for Kowalski to register irritation at the colloquial threat, '… no, it seems someone saw me checking out the base from my window and the Agent, Steve I think his name was, wanted to know what I was looking at.'

He digested the concerned expressions around the table.

'What were you looking at?' said Kowalski.

Harold chewed his last piece of the pie, swallowed, and decided to lie. 'I was watching those Camo Dudes whizzing around. Was there a break in or something?'

The table relaxed and Lisa raised an eyebrow but didn't say anything.

'Ufologists at the gate… constant nuisance.' Jasper said. 'Even more than usual, preparing for this ludicrous 'hashtag Storm Area 51' nonsense.'

'Braver men than I,' Harold said. 'Those Camo Dudes are intense.'

'Not as intense as those guys,' said Jasper, nodding towards the group at the front, who were staring hard at their food, eating slowly and in silence. 'Hangar 18 guys, don't you know?'

'Time we went down to Hangar 7 for this long-awaited AI discussion, don't you think? Since we're all so desperate to go,' said Kowalski.

Harold shrugged, stood, and pulled on his jacket, as Kowalski hurried over to Lisa, offering to take back her tray. If his skin could crawl, it would.

He followed the pair from the canteen, and as Kowalski yammered on and Lisa pretended to listen, a glint of light blinded his right eye. He stopped, waited for the blue circle to dissipate, and then spotted the source — a plastic ID card reflecting the sunlight from the window. The ID card was lying on the table where the Hangar 18 guys had been sitting and they'd all been first out of the canteen. He looked up to call after Lisa but noticed she was a dozen paces ahead. Resigned, and alone, he slipped it into his pocket, determined to hand it into the first security guard or Agent he saw. The binoculars too.

Harold failed in his second attempt to build a card tower, and resolved to read his book, propped up by doughy pillows. He failed at that too. The book was '*Fear and Loathing: in Las Vegas*' by Hunter S. Thompson, and the scenes remained mere ink blots on soft wood, denied a mind willing to decipher them and hallucinate accordingly.

His speech, in Hangar 7, was well received. They particularly enjoyed it, as scientists of that sort always did, when he announced the A1 was nine thousand times more powerful than the bomb dropped on Nagasaki in 1945. They applauded.

When he announced the A1 was two thousand times more powerful than the Russian's Satan 4, he'd been forced to smile through a display of ape-like hysteria. Maybe he should be flattered, but such incidences made him a little nauseous. He was helping to build a weapon of unfathanable mass destruction, after all.

He closed the book and read the blurb.

Raoul Duke roared down the desert highway to Las Vegas with his attorney, the Samoan, to find the American Dream.

The American Dream? He wasn't sure what it was, but Duke was more likely to find it in Vegas than Dunn was on the base.

He dumped the book and looked at his watch, and saw it was a little after six pm. He could be in Vegas just after eight if he drove like a maniac and the traffic was kind. Perhaps the American Dream was blackjack, party girls, and enough liquor to erase cold women like Lisa Tsai from one's short-term memory?

He reached for the cordless phone propped up on his bedside table, and dialled the hash key.

A young female voice answered, 'Professor Dunn?'

'Yes, I was wondering if I might be allowed to leave the

base for a few hours.'

'I see… could you just give me a moment?'

'Sure,' he said, but from the fluctuating static on the other end of the line, he knew she'd already pressed the receiver to her chest so that he couldn't hear her discussing his request with someone else. Such a common action, amongst administrative assistants and receptionists, but Harold always found it patronising. It felt like he was being told that he was about to be criticised, so could he please just cover his ears so as not to become offended? Why hadn't she just stuck him on hold and let him wait in ignorance?

'Yes, Professor Dunn, that's fine', She said, as though it'd been her who'd made the decision, 'I'll clear that with the gate — just remember to take your pass with you.'

Harold slammed down the receiver.

As the Audi grumbled over the last dune, Harold spotted a commotion over by the Restricted Access sign. It was a boisterous mob, an eclectic display of obesity and anorexia, who seemed unfazed by the six large Camo Dudes, armed with gas-powered rifles, and threats of an untimely demise.

'They can't stop us all!' Chanted the group and tried again to spread around the Camo Dudes, and enter the base. 'Storm Area 51! Show us the Aliens!'

Nutters, Harold thought, and continued slowly down the track, hoping all involved would remain concentrated on their respective task at hand.

Then, as he rolled over a raised part of the road, one of the soldiers lost patience and fired a shot. It was a wild one into the sky, and it had the desired effect — the group scattered.

It also prompted Harold to accelerate at the worst possible moment — just as a man ran out with his arm stretched out behind him, right in front of Harold's car. It was a 'Naruto run', popularised by a Japanese manga series, which the nerds insisted online would help them evade the bullets of the Area 51 security.

'Shit,' he said, and spun the wheel so he missed the man, but then found his windshield obscured by a white placard, with the words #StormArea51 scrawled in luminous green upon it. Next, he heard, and felt, the car clatter over a boulder, and knew he'd left the road.

He gave the wheel a half-turn right and then a full-turn left, as he jolted over more rugged terrain, which sent the placard tumbling and allowed him to rediscover the road. The screech of a metal chassis connecting with sandstone continued to ring in his ears, as he drove away from the crop of jagged rocks he'd swerved through and the commotion around them.

His security deposit was definitely something he could forget about, but the car was still moving, and there was the exit to Route 375 up ahead. Good old German engineering, he thought… then the vehicle coughed.

'Only a light cough… barely a child's cough,' he told himself.

It coughed again — not a child's cough — a sixty-a-day spinster's hack.

'Oh, come on, you son of a…' Before he could finish the insult, the dashboard lit up like a pinball machine, and then went blank.

Rolling to a stop, he realised he couldn't hear the engine. Turning the key off and on again did nothing to change that.

He sat for several minutes, massaging his temples and preparing for an abrasive discussion with the Camo Dudes as he walked back to the base, when he heard a tap at the window. He opened his eyes and found himself surrounded by flashing cameras and X-Files T-shirts.

He sighed, knowing walking back to base with them trailing him was hardly going to help his cause, and rolled down his window. 'Hi, guys.'

A pimpled, ginger-haired male waddled towards him. 'You're from the base!'

'Just visiting.'

'Do they really have aliens in there?' Asked a thin, hunched woman, with jam-jar glasses, who reminded Harold a little of a Praying Mantis by the way she positioned her hands.

'Yes, it's me. I'm an escaped alien.' Harold said before he could stop himself, and regretted it immediately as their eyes nearly popped out of their heads.

'I'm yet to see an alien up there,' he said, 'Hey, you don't know someone who could help me with my car do you?'

'You should ask up at the bar in Rachel,' said the fat man, 'We can all have a drink while we're there.'

Harold smiled, knowing that if he went to the bar in Rachel, a long line of irritating questions awaited him. Still it was better than sitting in his room on his own. He'd just have to be very careful that liquor didn't make him say anything he shouldn't.

'Come on guys! Party's over!' Yelled the fat man, and his army, grumbling a little, retreated from the Camo Dudes and their live ammunition.

Harold followed them up the track, and accepted a lift to The Little A'le'inn, in Rachel — a small ET-themed motel and bar, with a model flying saucer outside. He found the place quite endearing and had never encountered a clientele like it.

'It's all classified,' he kept repeating, grinning from behind his third glass.

'But the Roswell crash…?'

'Classified.'

'The alien bodies…?'

'Classified…'

'The abductions…?'

'Cla…'

A long-haired man at the end of the bar snorted and shook his head.

'Problem, buddy?' Harold said, feeling derision boil up in him, in the way that alcohol facilitates primal aggression.

The man glared at him, skulled his short and stood up from the bar stool, stumbling a little as he approached the table.

'I worked in that facility for twelve years. Why don't you ask me your damn questions?'

The landlord, a chubby but broad-shouldered, balding man, came round the side of the bar. 'Come on, Andrews, leave them alone.'

'Those Agents ruined my life. I've seen things,' he gestured wildly, knocked a beer out of someone's hand, and over the landlord's apron.

'Right, Andrews, get out. Come on,' he yanked the drunk over to the door.

'Hangar 18. It's where they took the Roswell ship. You… Area 51 jerk… take photos of Hangar 18 and post them on my site… stormarea51.net. You need proof out there before they paint you as a psycho.'

'Out!' The landlord yelled, hurling Andrews into the parking lot.

The group had already recommenced their discussion, which Stacey, the Praying Mantis, was leading. 'Ever heard of Reptilians, Harold?'

Without waiting for a reply, she plunged off on a tangent about Alien reptiles, though Harold had already become distracted by the reopening of the door. The return of the drunk?

'Lisa?'

'Whey, Lisa.' The geeks chorused, grateful, perhaps, for the presence of another woman.

'Security said you'd gone off with this lot and that I'd find you here. I nearly ran into your car at the turn-off. What's going on?' She said, eyes flicking over each of the group.

'Have a drink.' Harold said, pouring a fresh glass from the pitcher, 'Stacey here's just telling me about how certain members of the British Royal Family are in fact extra-terrestrial lizards in human suits.'

Lisa smiled, glanced towards the exit, and then resigned herself to the seat next to him. Their forearms touched and tingled, for half a second.

Harold screwed up his face, dragged back to consciousness by the glare of the security light outside his window. He knew he would not be able to sleep again until he shut the drapes. Regardless of a headache, growing in severity, he took a swig from the wine bottle on the bedside table and then swung himself out of bed, smiling at the tousled-haired, red-eyed rock star, in the mirror, with whom he was very impressed. As he replaced the bottle, the light shifted and caught the ID card, half hidden beneath one of his socks.

The man on it was a pasty fellow, mid-thirties, whose

eyes wandered to the left of the camera lens, betraying some awkwardness.

If awkwardness was a shared characteristic of all those who worked in Hangar 18, then any strange behaviour by an unauthorised visitor might not look so strange at all.

The drunk's tirade, Andrews, from the bar, swam back into his mind. He'd said he'd seen something in Hangar 18 — the infamous Roswell craft? And that following his capture the Agents had ruined his life. The latter he could believe but the former…?

Harold continued to stare at the ID glimmering in the light. Why speculate? Well, because if he was caught, he could well end up as Andrews' new drinking partner. But if he could just sneak a look without getting caught…

He ignored the nagging voice telling him that the idea was alcohol inspired idiocy, and felt himself begin to work on some automated level. Rising, he crept across the room to the white coat hanging on the door hook. It was a little tight and a little short, though he doubted anyone would notice at a glance.

Next, he took a passport photo from his wallet, licked the base, and secured it over the scientist's face. He shook the ID a few times, but the photo remained where it was.

Back at the mirror, the rock star was now an Area 51 scientist, and then he felt his nerve slip. The idea was ridiculous, and likely illegal, moreover, he had a beautiful woman in his bed, albeit, asleep. He took up the wine bottle again, walked to the window and took a long draw. The illuminated compound was empty, with not a Camo Dude in sight. Plus, he looked the part, so anyone monitoring the cameras wouldn't think it unusual to see a scientist walking around. They worked weird hours.

His indecisiveness continued on his journey through the deserted building and intensified as the first gust of air washed across his face, and he heard the growls of 4x4 engines amplified by the ocean of rock formations out in the desert.

As he walked, other reverberating ghosts dogged his progress, snippets from telephone tirades about his audacity, orders for him to be executed on sight, the sound of running footsteps…

There it was, looming out of the darkness, hardly a hangar at all, more a concrete shed, then he was there in front of the silver door, and his hand was in his pocket, fumbling out the ID card and running it through the reader. Nothing happened.

Fear overwhelmed him. Of course, the ID had been reported missing. He'd set off an alert, and now they were coming for him. His whole career had been thrown into jeopardy because of his damn curiosity. How could he have been so stupid?

Then the reader beeped, and the door slid open.

He took a step into the hangar, finding that it was not as musty or decrepit inside as he'd expected, but clean and smelling of disinfectant, like a hospital. Its sole feature was a steel spiral staircase in the corner. A compulsion took him, to graze the rough, concrete wall with his fingertips as he stepped forward — a sensory reminder what he was doing was real. He hovered his foot over the first step, and allowed gravity, rather than independent thought, to bring it down again. Despite his attempts to keep the rest of his descent more subtle, each footfall created a clang so conspicuous he was unsurprised by the attention it eventually drew.

CHAPTER FIVE

T he guard frowned and looked up from his Kindle, as the stranger stumbled down the stairs.

'Burning the midnight oil, huh?' He grunted through the hole in the plastic screen.

The man didn't reply as such, just gave a compliant chuckle and stood there rubbing his eyes.

'Clearance?'

He held up an ID card.

'Ok, on you go then,' said the guard pointing towards the double doors,'… freak.'

Harold longed for an inhaler, as his breaths grew ragged and he became increasingly nauseous. Vomit… or worse, either, and he would be exposed. Catch 22, he thought, as he felt the guard's eyes on the back of his head, and he ran the ID card through the reader. Fortunately, the set of double doors opened more quickly than the ones up on the surface, and he was able to escape into a sloping corridor, ending with another pair of identical doors. The relief at feeling the guard's scrutiny vanish, with the closing of the doors behind him, was momentary, as up ahead there was an ominous black CCTV dome in the ceiling, reminding him that his actions were still far from private.

Ahead of him was a short hall terminating in an elevator. There were two doors, one on either side. Straight ahead was an elevator with a retinal scanner.

Just as he was taking it all in, the elevator doors started to swoosh open. Knowing this would be his only chance, he rushed to the door, and managed to be standing next to the retinal scanner when the doors opened.

Two men in white lab coats stepped out. One glanced at Harold, who gave him a slight nod as he moved into he elevator without hesitation. 'Just act like you belong here' Harold told himself under his breath.

There were no buttons. As soon as the elevator doors closed, the elevator started to decend – very rapidly. When it stopped, the doors obediently opened revealing another short hall and another door, although there was no apparent security lock.

From beyond this next set of doors, he could hear a buzzing noise, much like that of a powerful concert amp. They must use a hell of a lot of electricity, he thought, I wonder how they account for it all? For that matter, who are they even accountable to?

He opened the doors, and the spectacle was revealed.

It was an enormous, metal, stingray, levitating several metres above the ground. A dome sat on top, and there was a sealed compartment in the belly. The buzzing noise seemed to stem from the craft's constant vibration.

Anti-matter distribution? Harold thought, and then Andrews' words filled his ears, as though he were in the hangar with him. 'Take photos… you need proof out there before they paint you as a psycho!'

He fumbled out his iPhone, dropped it, tapped in the wrong password twice, accidentally set it to video, and then managed to take six pictures. He had the frame of mind to take the last one in 'HDR' to ensure the quality; determined not to have some 32-year-old virgin, in his mother's basement, slate the validity of his claim due to any graininess. Though, he was sure he'd never actually put them online. The pictures were merely his bargaining chip should the Agents discover him, and so far, he had gotten away with it. He decided it was time to leg it.

CHAPTER SIX

Agent Steve's eyelids peeled themselves apart as his hand slithered under his pillow to where his semi-automatic Glock 40 slept. His roaming pupils settled on the blinking red LED atop his phone, which had just emitted a second loud beep. He reached over to his bedside table, coaxed the phone into his palm, and swiped the icon on the screen, which simply read: 'ALERT'.

He squashed his fingerprint against the screen and was taken into Security App 2, where the words 'UNUSUAL CONDUCT' were flashing across the top of the page. Below the banner was a profile for a 36-year-old man called Hector Kaepernick, and a note to say he'd just entered Hangar 18.

Steve frowned. Kaepernick was a name he'd committed to memory ten years ago, an employee with the highest clearance level, who worked exclusively in Hangar 18, though never after 18.00 PM according to his 'Recent Movements'. The current time was 12.51 AM.

'Outstanding report, Doctor?' Steve said, clicked the Home button, and returned to the main screen, from which he accessed Security App 1, giving him access to every CCTV camera on the base.

It took him several seconds to find Kaepernick, standing in the central laboratory in front of the craft, with... was that a phone?

As the fingers of one hand closed around the cool, steel

handle of the Glock, he zoomed in on the face of the man with the other. He realised that it was not Kaepernick, though it took him a full minute to identify the face.

He was, however, fully dressed by the time his partner, John, burst into his room, brandishing his own phone.

CHAPTER SEVEN

'The existence of a craft does not prove the existence of extra-terrestrial life,' Harold whispered, as he sat wheezing on the edge of the bed. Saying it aloud was a comfort, but his heart continued to race, as he examined the image on his phone.

His attempt to reduce graininess with his phone's 'HDR' function proved laughable as the craft's perpetual vibration gave its hull the appearance of black haze, rather than metal, save for the glass dome on top, which retained its clarity. He wondered if it sat on an independent mechanism, from the rest of the craft, to keep it stable, while the distorted fuselage acted as a disguise from any onlookers below.

Harold could hear the voices of a father and son, walking across a field, or a beach, and the boy looking up and spotting the craft.

'Daddy, what's that in the sky?'

'Why that's nothing but a puff of smoke, son.'

Was this American technology? Or had they stolen it from someone else?

He heard a soft grunt beside him and glanced at Lisa, who fidgeted under the covers and then went back to sleep. His eyes moved to the empty wine bottle. How he wished he had some left.

What if the craft was proof of alien life? What if he'd hung around — would he have found bodies?

He looked down at his phone, typed stormarea51.net into the search bar, and then... there came a loud thump at the door, causing him to fumble it.

Mouth gaping, he relinquished his fingertip grip on the screen, passed the phone into his other hand, and found that he'd posted a photo. It had been shared three times in five seconds.

'Dunn, open up. You're under arrest.' Came Steve's voice.

As Harold turned to digest Lisa's reaction, he found his movements hindered as though he was submerged in water, and discovered that she hadn't moved.

Another thump came. Not sharp like the last, but booming — a long, note, growing in volume, from a blow which rattled the door in its frame for several minutes.

As the sound faded, another took its place, a shrill ring, which increased in pitch to such a level, that Harold was forced to press his hands over his ears to subdue it. He felt himself growing very hot, and vomit curdled in his belly, threatening to shoot up past his throat at any moment. He freed a hand to wipe his nose, then discovered the action had stained his knuckles a rusty red, and that there was more of the stuff pooling down his chin on to his chest.

A black cloud hung at the window, obscuring the spotlight outside, and he couldn't hear the grumble of a 4x4 or the shout of a Camo Dude. The bangs at the door had ceased too, and for a second, there was stillness. Then, there came the metallic screech of un-lubricated gears grinding against one another, and blue light exploded into the room.

Agent Steve threw his right shoulder against the door, shattering the lock and swinging it inwards. He stepped into the room and moved left, with his pistol raised, while John stepped in behind him and moved right, and the other security personnel poured down the middle. Agents were usually the ones to shoot first in such situations, but rarely the ones who got shot.

Lisa Tsai sat up in bed and screamed.

'What the fuck is going on?' She said, clasping the duvet to her chest.

Steve blinked as the security bulbs flickered back into life outside and light pooled into the room. They moved in tandem, Steve checking the en-suite while John checked under the bed and inside the wardrobe. Both met back by Lisa Tsai, and each shook his respective head.

Someone flicked the light switch, and Lisa recoiled to find Steve leaning over her swirling a latex-gloved finger in one of the crimson pools on the bed.

'What is that?' Lisa said, knowing full well what it was, 'What have you done with Harold?'

'John, secure the room', said Steve, removing the glove and sealing it inside a polythene bag, 'and have someone run this. I want to know when you've confirmed whom it belongs to.'

John caught the bag and began hustling the animated Camo Dudes from the room. Once he'd closed the door, Steve ducked his hand into his pocket and removed a miniature black camera, and a postcard-sized piece of steel. He placed the steel on the ground at the foot of the bed, applied some pressure with his heel, and then stepped back as a 5-foot tripod, sprung up from the ground. He closed the drapes, dragged a chair over beside the tripod, and then secured the camera to the top.

As he settled himself and stared at Lisa from below the rim of his trilby, his tongue began to flicker between his lips. Many Agents around the base had been seen to do this, and the rumours as to why they did it were varied. Some said it was a tactic to unsettle those they spoke with, while others said that it was an obvious side effect of cloning.

He took a notebook and pen from his pocket, leafed through the pages until he found one that was blank, and then spoke abruptly, making Lisa jump.

'The time is 01.01 AM. The date is Thursday, September 5th, 2019. The location is Groom Lake, Nevada, United States, Codename: Area 51. The person being interviewed is Dr Lisa Tsai. The person interviewing is Agent Steve, 78383. The encounter is a definitive Class 4, and the subject was Professor Harold Dunn — still missing.'

Steve's gaze hadn't shifted from her face the whole time he'd been speaking.

'We're going to have a conversation, you and I.'

A thump in Harold's skull suggested consciousness, although this, combined with the tangy residue of wine that coated his tongue, could also suggest a hangover, and made him very reluctant to open his eyes.

He wondered how he had made it past security and back to his room in such a state, and then he tasted lipstick. He hadn't returned alone, he'd been with Lisa, who'd accompanied him back to share in a nightcap and some light-hearted mocking at the expense of the '#StormArea51 crew' from the bar, and then… nature had taken its course.

Sensing movement beside him, he smiled and opened his eyes a fraction.

What met them was not Lisa and caused him to yell.

'Stop.' It was an instruction that echoed through his mind in his own voice, but of which he was not the source.

He was alone, in a long oval room, lit by a single, bright white panel, which stretched the length of the ceiling to two triangular windows, where a star-speckled night sky was visible beyond.

Back above his feet, he realised he was naked, and that there was a thin black tube, running from the floor, up in between his legs. His right testicle began to ache, a sudden pain that intensified the second he was aware of it.

He yelled again, and rolled in invisible straps binding him to the table, and then felt something prick him in the spine. The pain vanished, and he dropped back onto the table with a clang. Agent Steve loomed overhead, lowering a pillow towards his face, tongue flickering like an earthworm on an electric fence.

'No… leave me alone.'

'Stop.' Came the internal voice again, and all faded to black.

CHAPTER EIGHT

'What do you want?' Lisa asked, and Steve made a note on his pad.

'Where's Harold? Is he in trouble?'

'Yes,' Steve said and made another note.

She stared at the figure translating her every reaction into text, and decided it was time she composed herself. Harold had apparently done something stupid during the night while she'd been sleeping. She guessed he'd wandered into a restricted area or stolen a file, but what business was that of hers? She barely knew the man.

'Can I get dressed?'

'Yes,' he said, making no note but keeping his biro poised, as she sat there with the duvet around her.

'Turn the camera off then.'

'No,' he said, but turned his chair, so that he was facing away from her.

Her eyes narrowed. He could still be watching her in his periphery. Who could tell what his eyes were doing behind those shades?

She swore, clambered out of bed and walked over to the en-suite bathroom, plucking clothes as she went.

'Door open, please, Dr Tsai.'

She got changed and splashed cold water on her face. Crimson eyes stared back at her from the mirror, crazed eyes, and look at all that bushy hair. What would she look like on the tape?

'You've nothing to hide,' she said, 'You've nothing to hide.'

'Quickly, Dr Tsai.'

She took a deep breath and with fresh conviction, she walked back into the room and sat down on the bed.

'Now just what in the hell do you want?'

His eyebrows appeared over the frame of his shades. 'Tell me about your activity with Professor Harold Dunn over the last twenty four hours.'

'I met him when he arrived at the base yesterday morning, about 11...'

Steve's expression gave away nothing that might support or vilify her statement.

'I showed him to his room and said I'd come back and collect him for lunch, then I went off to my own room, but when I came back, he'd gone.'

'Gone?'

'Yes, he went with you.'

'Did Professor Dunn mention what we discussed?'

Lisa paused, watching the hovering nib, choosing her words. She wasn't about to lose her job over some one-night-stand's reckless inquisitiveness, she would tell Agent Steve the truth. God, she sure knew how to pick them.

Agent Steve held up a finger before she could answer. 'I think we should take a moment,' he removed a rectangular machine from his pocket, which had a small monitor in the centre, and two circular pads attached to dangling wires.

'Your hand, please, Dr Tsai.'

She flinched and then allowed him to wrap the pads around two of her fingers. A red light glowed on the device, and her pulse rate appeared on a line graph.

'Let's continue,' He said, 'Did Professor Dunn mention the content of the aforementioned conversation?'

'He said he'd found some binoculars in his room, and took a good look over at Hangar 18-'

'He already knew it as 'Hangar 18'?'

Lisa glanced down at her pulse rate visible on the machine's monitor, prompting Steve to do the same.

'No, I think I told him it was called Hangar 18.'

He made a note.

'A-anyway, I told him it was beyond his clearance... he said he thought the A1 might have been down there but I told him it wasn't and then we just went to lunch. Then we... '

The finger went up again.

'Describe this lunch to me.'

'It was chicken pie, I think...'

His chin jerked up, suggesting that she'd misunderstood his question.

'Nothing happened at lunch, we just talked about his missile, the crazies that are always round the gate... Jasper pointed out the scientists from Hangar 18...'

'Jasper?'

'Dr Hennimore.'

Note.

'Who else was present?'

She gave him the names of her friends.

'Then what happened?'

'Nothing. We left.'

'You left with Professor Dunn?'

'Yes...I mean, no...'

His eyes flicked towards the screen.

'I was talking with Joe. Kowalski. Harold was right behind us.'

'You weren't looking at him as you left the canteen?'

'No,' she said, 'what did he do?'

He waved her question away. 'Continue.'

'Well, then he gave his speech on the A1 in Hangar 7. That was at about two-thirty pm, and then I went back on shift.'

'Where did Professor Dunn go?'

'He went back to his room as far as I know.'

'And then?'

'My assistant phoned me to say that Harold had left the base. He mentioned to me when I first met him that he might visit Vegas while he was in Nevada. I thought that he'd go get a hotel for the night and be back in the morning.'

Lisa felt herself becoming flustered as they approached the subject of the one-night-stand itself, and she was sure that the lie detector reflected this, even though Steve had now tilted it out of view.

'My assistant then rang me back ten minutes later, telling me Harold had been in an accident. Well, not an accident so much, he had blown a tyre or something and gone off with some of those crazies. It's well known they drink up at that bar in Rachel, so I thought I'd better go and check on him…

'

Suddenly Kowalski burst into the room and Steve jumped up to turn off the camera.

'Lisa, what the hell is going on?'

Agent John appeared with his hat and shades askew and grabbed Kowalski around the waist, yanking him back the way he'd come.

'Get off me,' he said, 'Lisa's a respected scientist, you've no right to treat her this way!'

Suddenly, the Camo Dudes were also piling back into the room, bellowing at the Agents.

'This is bureaucratic bullshit,' said their moustachioed leader, 'We run the security at this facility, not you! Tell us what's going on!'

The Agent pulled out his ID card. 'We're Agency. We are the authority in this situation!'

'Bullshit.'

The instant the guard's hand moved towards his belt, he found Kowalski flying towards him, and by the time he'd wriggled out from under the scientist, the two Agents were looming over him, guns drawn.

John slipped his gun back inside his jacket and heaved the man up.

'You're fired.' Steve said as John guided the Camo Dude back towards the door, dragging Kowalski behind him, 'As for the rest of you, anyone else who values their job should leave immediately.'

The mob grumbled towards the door again, some of them under the guise of helping their leader, and the door closed behind them.

Steve re-seated himself in front of Lisa who had not moved throughout the ruckus. It had been courageous of Kowalski to come to her aid, and she'd never thought him a courageous man.

'Now…' Steve said, turning the camera back on and glancing over his notes, 'Before we were interrupted you said you'd suspected Professor Dunn had gone to a bar in Rachel, following a puncture, and that you'd decided you'd go and check on him?'

'Yeah, he was at the bar. The Lil Al'le'inn'. ET-themed, you know it? Not my kind of place. The bartender was actually throwing someone out as I arrived, but Harold convinced me to stay for a few.'

'Whom was the bartender throwing out?'

'I dunno, I've never seen him around the gate before I don't think, but then again there's so many of them these days, what with the whole 'Storm Area 51' hashtag… '

'Describe him.'

His insistence on this subject took her by surprise. 'Oh, I dunno, skinny, about 6ft, long black hair.'

'Did he say anything?'

'I didn't really catch it… 'I was there; I was there!', I think. I can't remember.'

Steve made several notes and then nodded for her to continue.

'So we had a few drinks and then came back here.'

Steve looked at her.

'Then we had a drink and went to bed.'

Steve's pen hung poised.

She sighed. 'You know, together.'

He flicked back several pages and made a small mark. Perhaps ticking a fact as being correct.

'There, now, I've told you everything I know.'

The machine, in Steve's hand, gave a loud beep.

'I have. That thing's busted!'

Beep.

'What's your name?' He asked her.

'Lisa Tsai.'

'Tell me 'the Earth's flat.''

'What?'

'Do it.'

'The Earth's flat.'

Beep.

'I'm telling you the truth!'

Beep.

'God damn it.'

Steve put his pen down on the notepad, pulled out his phone, and dialled a number.

'Has he arrived yet, John? Oh, good. Send him in.'

The door opened, and a petite man entered, no taller than five-five, with round glasses, curly hair, and a grizzled black-grey badger beard.

'Hello,' he said, taking slow steps towards them, one hand fidgeting in the other.

'Dr O'Neill. I need you to ask Dr Tsai here some questions.'

Lisa stood up. 'Who is this? What's he going to do?'

'Calm, my dear,' said O'Neill, 'I mean only to hypnotise you. Please, lie down.'

He looked a patient man, but upon seeing Steve rise from the chair, he said, 'Come now… nothing to fear.'

She walked around the bed and lay down upon it.

You've nothing to hide, she reminded herself.

The hypnotist circled her then lowered his hand across her eyes.

'Try to sleep,' he said, 'And allow your fears and stresses to disappear. You're in your bedroom. There's no one else here. There's just the sound of my voice, which you find comforting and relaxing. You're going deeper and deeper, deeper and deeper. Allow yourself to let go completely. Deeper and deeper, deeper and deeper. You are asleep.'

O'Neill stiffened and lifted his hand, as Steve came round to his side. 'She's under.'

The Agent tore a scrap of paper from the notebook and handed it to him.

'Now, Lisa, can you hear me?'

'Yes,' she said, in a monotone.

The machine lay silent.

'What happened after you came back to Harold Dunn's room this evening?'

'We talked, had some wine, and had sex.'

'Ok, anything else?'

'I felt him get up in the night. He went somewhere for a long time and then he came back.'

'Where did he go, Lisa?'

'I don't know.'

He glanced at Steve, who whirled his hand.

'Where do you think he went, Lisa?'

She didn't reply.

'It doesn't work like that,' O'Neill hissed, balling up the piece of paper and tossing it aside.

'What happened next?'

'Something terrible,' she said, 'There was a lot of blue light in the room and this noise...'

'What did the noise sound like, Lisa?'

'Like... cars being mangled in a crusher.'

She shuddered and gave a single kick of her foot.

'We are overstretching the mind,' said O'Neill, 'She needs to rest for a few hours.'

Steve nodded without looking up, scribbling in his notebook.

O'Neill snapped his fingers, 'Awake.' and Lisa sat bolt upright and projectile vomited.

CHAPTER NINE

T he moment Harold's eyes opened, he recalled an Agent trying to smother him, and sat up. He found himself fully clothed, able to move, and with nothing attached to his genitals. Scanning the oval room he found no Agent, or any tenderness as he rubbed the front of his trousers. He was grateful for both of these things.

Questions began to race through his brain.

'What had they been doing to him?'

'Where was he?'

'Where was Lisa?'

'Hello.' Echoed a good impression of himself.

'Agent Steve?' Harold said, climbing down off the table and finding a metal floor, vibrating ever so slightly. 'Where are you? How're you doing this?'

As he spoke, the panels on the wall beside him separated, and his captor was revealed.

It was humanoid, in that it had a head, two arms and two legs, but its skin was light grey and hairless. It had a thin mouth, with no lips, and four fingers on each hand, with no fingernails. It had a bulbous head, twice the size of a human's, and two great, black ovals, through which it stared at Harold, unblinking. Harold stared back at Hollywood's Grey Alien, standing four foot tall, five yards from him, in a plain, white jumpsuit.

'Wha… this is a trick.' He said.

'It is not.' Came Harold's voice

'This is a hallucination. I was drugged. Steve?' His eyes continued to roam around the room.

'The drug we gave you was a mild sedative and the effects have long since worn off.'

Harold caught sight of the stars beyond the window again, and his mind began to race. He remembered Hangar 18… the craft… the thumps at his bedroom door and the explosion of blue light.

He jogged to the windows, and flung himself up against them. As his eyes rolled down he saw that he hadn't been simply looking out at a starry sky, he'd been looking out into Space itself.

His heart rate doubled and his breathing grew haggard as he turned and slid down the glass.

'Try to remain calm,' said his voice again.

'Stop that.' Harold said, jamming his hands over his ears. 'How are you doing that?'

Through the open door entered a second alien, an inch taller and leaner than its brother. He had a tighter jaw, which gave it a natural scowl.

'Telepathic,' said this second Alien, 'So that won't help.'

This alien also communicated in Harold's voice but in a gruffer tone. One Harold usually reserved for reporters or car insurance people.

'What do you want with me?'

'Firstly, I would like to introduce myself.' Said the original, pointing to its chest, 'My name is Nyn, and this is…

'Troni.' Said the other, 'And I prefer 'he' rather than 'it'.

Harold gawped at the pair. Could they read his thoughts or had this Troni just been making an assumption.

'We can read your thoughts.' Troni said.

'Fuck you!' Harold said, pushing himself to his feet. If he was in a ship full of these creatures, he was screwed. Hell, he was probably screwed anyway, but in his immediate situation he was much bigger than Troni and Nyn, and he could feel fear giving way to aggression. He balled up his fists, as he decided he might as well go out fighting.

'Just try it,' said Troni, taking a step forward, but Nyn slapped a hand on his chest and glared at him.

He turned back to Harold with a softer expression. 'We don't want to hurt you.'

'You were experimenting on me.'

Nyn shook his head. 'We were extracting some DNA for our breeding program. I apologise if you endured any pain, it varies in different humans.'

Harold stared, the words 'different humans' resonating with him.

'Oh, yes, we've been conducting extractions for about five years now, ever since we discovered the similarities between human and Zetan DNA, and you'll be pleased to hear that there's no scarring, no after effects we are aware of, and that none of our subjects ever remember a thing.'

'Zetan?'

Nyn looked at Troni, offering him the opportunity to communicate, but he was glaring off somewhere out to space.

'That's us.' Nyn said, 'We're from Zr2, a planet in the Zeta Reticuli system, almost 40 light years from Earth.'

Harold's anger was dissipating, replaced by wooziness.

'Come and sit down.' Nyn said.

The hand that curled round Harold's wrist, felt like one of the latex gloves that Helen had liked to wear on their anniversary. He shivered at the memory as gunfire rattled through his brain, but managed to suppress it.

'Another pervert,' said Troni, without turning to look at them, 'No wonder you like him so much, Nyn.'

'Apparently he is capable of talking to females,' said Nyn, his light tone slipping. 'No wonder you envy him so much, Troni.'

Troni turned and trotted over into Nyn's eye line.

'Some of us talk to females too much, don't we Nyn? Maybe we should show our new friend the subsequent dangers of doing so.'

The two Zetans stared at each other and then poured away with the rest of Harold's environment, like some great waterfall suddenly suppressed, and now he was somewhere else. There was grey sand under his feet and the vastness of space above him, and behind him stood a pair of fifteen-foot water tanks, metal gleaming in the starlight. He wasn't sure how he knew they were water tanks, he just knew, with the calm conviction one has when dreaming. Beside him stood Troni, glaring dead ahead. A giggle floated towards Harold, distorted, much like a radio being tuned in, and in the glare of the spotlight he saw Nyn up ahead leaning against the open steel gate, chatting away to a female of his kind. She had slight ridges above her eyes, and a narrower frame, but little else to distinguish her as female.

'That's right Nyn,' Troni whispered, 'Neglect your post for another tumble with 'Easy' Preesey.'

There came a clang above them, and Troni snapped out a metal rod, and shone a powerful beam upwards towards the canopy of the second tower.

'Nyn, why's your friend always so weird?' Came a squeaky voice, which could only have been the girl, Preesey…

'That's enough!' Nyn said sternly, and the room flung itself back up against Harold's eyes.

'It's the truth!'

'You have no right…'

'Sorry to interrupt.' Harold said, shaking his head as his eyes recoiled from the brightness of the room, 'But do you think you could hurry up with erasing my memory or whatever so I can get back to Earth.'

'Not yet.' Said Nyn, his tone softening again as he turned back to Harold, 'We require you for additional means, I'm afraid.'

'Additional… experiments?'

'No, we just want to talk.' Nyn said. 'Perhaps you'd like to rehydrate first?'

He tapped a compartment set inside the table and a blue drawer rolled out, containing hundreds of bottles of water. Nyn selected one and handed it to Harold. It was cold to the touch and sealed, and the label read Evian, from the French Alps.

Harold read that the expiry date was December 2020, and took a sip. It was refreshing and helped suppress a little of his nausea.

'So you found our ship.' Said Nyn. It wasn't a question.

Harold then deduced that he must be in a craft identical to the one he'd seen in Hangar 18, and that he was in the enormous dome on top, he just hadn't realised because of the illuminated section of ceiling.

'Yes, I saw it,' Said Harold taking a long draw from the bottle, and then replacing the lid, 'So... the US government knows of aliens? Of you?'

'Obviously.' Said Troni.

'We've made contact.' Said Nyn.

'Was it the Roswell Incident?' Harold said. 'Out of all the crackpot UFO theories, I always thought that one seemed to have the most truth to it — I mean, the news said it was 'a weather balloon?''

Nyn nodded. 'On the outskirts of our galaxy there's a great wormhole. Some younglings flew near — a game to see who'd go closest in their father's craft and it took one of them. They were the ones who crashed in your Nevada desert.'

'But you say your planet is only 40 light years away? The nearest wormhole to Earth is some 27,000 light years away...?'

'That's black hole. And that's only the nearest one *you* know of.' Troni said.

'There's a wormhole just five light-years from Earth actually, though very small.' Nyn said, 'They're like telescopes — big at one end, small at the other.'

Harold shook his head again. 'What caused these... Younglings... to crash?'

'It could be that they lost their nerve, or their systems failed coming through the hole. They were not experienced pilots.'

'Or they may have been shot down, Nyn, let's not forget that possibility.' Troni said, 'Maybe by humans... maybe by something else.'

'Like what?'

'We know nothing for certain.' Said Nyn, 'We are the first to travel through the hole since the Younglings and have only learnt all this in the years since we've been here.'

'So are you two like detectives?' Harold said, 'You've come to investigate what happened?'

The two Zetans glanced at one another.

'No,' Nyn said, with a hint of a sigh, 'We were charged with pursuing the Maitre.'

He didn't wait for Harold's next question.

'The Maitre are a parasitic race, who overpopulated their home planet, Megopei, and then began spreading to other planets. They'd claimed twenty-six planets for their colony, before the Universal Governance became aware. They were told they could keep the planets they had already colonised, because they were barren and no one else wanted them, but if they ever attempted anything resembling a hostile takeover, they would be punished by extermination.'

'And then they found us.' Troni said, 'And they couldn't help themselves.'

'They feared to attack us openly, fearing punishment at the hands of the U.G, so they hatched a plot' Nyn said, then shot a narrow-eyed glance Troni's way, 'As you've started the history tour you might as well show him the rest…'

Reality slipped again and Harold hung next to Troni on a ladder set into the side of a tank, the ground so far below, that the drop would surely kill him if he fell, though he knew he wouldn't. He realised he wasn't even holding the ladder.

'Those Younglings,' Troni muttered., 'I'll teach them to break in here.'

He pulled a white cylinder from his belt, bit the top off it, and flung it as hard as he could into the air. It spun towards six shadows grouped around the centre of the tank's canopy and burst with a flash of light that blinded Harold. Troni, however, had shielded his eyes, and Harold felt his surprise at what he now saw illuminated around the hole in the centre. It was not the Younglings.

'Maitre!' Troni bellowed and fired after the six blurs as they leapt to the next tank and slid over the edge. Harold spotted a steel barrel, with a little green liquid oozing over the rim, roll towards the hole, and plummet downwards into the water below.

Reality returned once more.

'That was an infertility toxin they introduced to our water supply. The water supply we were meant to be guarding, and maybe if somebody hadn't been so distracted…' Troni said, glaring at Nyn again.

'Troni,' Said Nyn, with a flap of his arms, 'who got us thrown out of the military and charged with guarding that damned treatment plant in the first place?'

'So what happened next?' Harold said, heading the pair off.

'They ran.' Nyn said, 'They rendered us infertile and they fled, straight through the same wormhole as the Younglings.'

'The cowards.' Troni said, his skin turning a darker shade, 'They knew that in open warfare we'd destroy them, with or without the help of the U.G.'

'We chased them through the hole and tore them to shreds with our cannons' Nyn said, 'But on the other side we found their battered craft, with no life forms on board, and the vast expanse of your planet beyond.'

'As a result of our, or should I say, Nyn's mistake, we're forbidden to live on Zr2 again until we expose the Maitre on Earth, that is, before they eradicate your species and our last means of reproduction.'

Nyn ignored the jibe this time. 'So now you understand our need to conduct as many abductions and extractions as possible. It's our only means of reproduction — the only way to keep our species alive.'

'I still think you have no right.' Harold said.

'We've permission from the U.G.' Troni said, shrugging.

'If your species was on the brink of extinction and you had the option to save it, wouldn't you do everything you could to do so?' Nyn said.

Harold didn't reply. He just sat and processed the information: Aliens existed... hostile aliens existed... those aliens who abducted humans were in fact the good guys...

'Your species *is* at risk, Harold.' Nyn said, 'Although the Maitre landed on Earth accidentally, the conditions are perfect for them. They are manufacturing your demise, and it is an added bonus for them that that will exterminate us too.'

'Two birds, one stone.' Harold said, 'Will they poison our water?'

'No.' Said Troni, 'Earth nations don't share a water supply — a selfishness that's worked in your favour.'

'Then how?'

'You humans love to antagonise one another,' Troni said. 'If you're not hoarding water or food you're building devices to threaten each other with. Devices you, personally, are all too familiar with, if that primitive network you call 'The Internet' is telling the truth about whom you are.'

'They've access to Nukes?' Harold said, squeezing the bottle between his hands.

Nyn nodded. 'Tension grows between your nations. Nuclear war could occur any day. So I ask you again — if your species was on the brink of extinction and you had the option to save it, wouldn't you do everything you could to do so?'

Harold gritted his teeth. 'What do you want from me?'

'We need you for our primary objective — to prove the Maitre are engaged in a hostile takeover,' Troni said. 'Revealing them to your own kind might accomplish that. Humans are so loud.'

Harold laughed in disbelief. 'Who do you think I am? Some politician... some activist? I breathe one word of this to anyone and they'll lock me up in a padded room.'

'You are a respected scientist and the face of Alien life on Earth.' Nyn said. 'See for yourself.'

This time it was different, there was no waterfall of colour, merely a blurring of the sharp angles around him, and the growth of a white rectangle in the centre of his field of vision. No matter which way he turned his head, the rectangle remained in place. He began to worry about the strain all this telepathy was having on his brain.

The screen flickered, and CNN anchor Claudia Thornton appeared, in all her blonde haired, red lipsticked glory.

'Our top story this evening: Do Aliens Exist?'

'Experts and fanatics alike were sent into a frenzy today when this image was shared online, allegedly from the top secret military base, located at Groom Lake, Nevada, codename: Area 51, which has been linked with extra-terrestrial activity since an alleged Roswell crash in 1947.'

Harold recognised the image as the one he'd shared from his phone.

'This 'alien craft', was posted on Stormarea51.net, allegedly by this man...'

The image of the craft shrunk and next to it swam up the photo from his Area 51 ID, and not one he'd have chosen to be broadcast on national television.

'… Professor Harold Dunn, the British, chief engineer on the controversial A1 nuclear missile project. We've been unable to reach Professor Dunn for comment but Tina Gower is with a man who claims he was drinking with him on the night the picture was posted. Tina?'

A young brunette, whom Harold did not recognise, appeared on screen, desperately trying to keep her hair under control in the breeze. Standing next to her was the fat, ginger leader of the Ufologists, his mop greasy and unmoving atop his pimply forehead. What had been his name again?

'Hi Claudia, hashtag Storm Area 51 was an online joke that sent the Internet into a frenzy last month. Yesterday, when the event was meant to occur, a crowd amassed and attempted to break into the base before being dispersed. I'm standing here with Gordon Bottomly (That's it!), outside the Lil A'le'inn, in Rachel, which is only twenty miles from Area 51. Mr Bottomly, you were unsuccessful in your attempts to storm the base, but what happed to Harold Dunn? You say you were drinking with Professor Dunn, on the night of his alleged discovery?'

'Yeah,' Said Gordon with vigour, 'Yeah, he come on down from Area 51 and blew a tyre. Those old dirt roads, ya'know? So he came back to the bar with us to find someone to help him.'

'How did Professor Dunn seem to you?'

'He was a nice fella, though I got the impression that he and his girlfriend thought our theories a little far-fetched. We're used to that though.'

'You say there was a woman with him? Was she from the base as well?'

'Yeah, we got that impression.'

'What was her name?'

'Lisa or Lucy. I'm not sure. Lisa I think, I'd had a lot to drink.'

'Had Professor Dunn had much to drink?'

'We all had.'

'What do you say to the critics who say that the photo of the craft shared by Dunn on his one-man-mission is clearly a hoax?'

'I say: Why would the US government close down the site if the photo were a hoax? Why haven't we seen or heard from Dunn or his girlfriend since? They've been black-bagged, or killed, or abducted by the aliens.'

The camera jerked away from Gordon and focussed on Tina Gower's darkening face. Harold wondered if she thought herself better than this story.

'There you have it, Claudia. Next, I'll see if I can track down the actual owner of Stormarea51.net for an exclusive CNN interview. In the meantime, back to you in the studio.'

Reality bled into the screen, and all regained its integrity.

Harold shook his head. 'They'll all still think I'm insane.'

'Some will.' Said Troni.

'Some will believe your story.' said Nyn.

'Can't you come with me? They can't very well call me a nutter if you're there, can they?'

Nyn shook his head. 'The cover-up of the crash in Earth year 1947 and your planet's domestic unrest has prompted the U.G to conclude human society is too primitive for the revelation. They've branded it illegal to communicate with humans outside of abductions... unless the Maitre's existence on Earth is conclusively proven to its peoples.'

'Yet, it's ok to be telling me all this?'

'Not at all,' Said Nyn, 'But the time we have for scanning random areas of the USA and Russia for Maitre is thinning, and so the time for a calculated risk has arrived. You are that calculated risk.'

Harold frowned. 'Hold on. What do these things look like? How come no one's spotted one yet?'

'They look big, slimy and horrible.' Troni said.

'They can mimic certain primitive beings... including humans. We suspect they've infiltrated both the Russian and US governments.'

'So what makes you think I'll be able to spot one?'

Nyn turned, walked over to the wall and pressed a square panel, which vanished to reveal a series of shelves. On each shelf was a sealed plastic tub, in each of which were different coloured pills. Nyn selected a tub containing pink pills, filled a vial, sealed it with a purple stopper, and then held his hand in front of the opening to make the panel reappear.

He returned to the table and passed the vial to Harold.

'Just one of these will force a Maitre to reveal itself.'

Harold waved his hands. 'Excuse me everybody, I know I'm probably a wanted criminal and also an infamous nut-job, but would you mind swallowing this magic pill the aliens gave me?' He rubbed his temples and screwed up his eyes.

'And you don't have long!' Said Troni, 'Your government has indeed been painting you as a... 'nut-job', was it? But the Maitre will still be rattled by your discovery and will be accelerating their process.'

'We have considered the most direct course of action,' Nyn said, 'We suspect the Russians will launch their warhead before the US – they are further along in their program – so there must be at least one Maitre in the Russian President's cabinet controlling all the variables. That's the one you should go after.'

'You're beaming me, a Brit, into Russia, to go and talk to the President... about aliens?'

'Negative,' Troni said, 'The Maitre also suspect the Russians will fire first, which is why they've positioned their Mothership there – completely legal providing they remain undetected by humanity – but they will blast us to pieces if we go anywhere near.'

A klaxon bellowed through the craft. Harold leapt up off the table and noticed that both Zetans had gone ridged and their eyes had closed. Leaning forward, he clicked his fingers in front of both of their faces, to no response.

After several minutes, in which he grew concerned that he might have to pilot the craft himself, they both jerked back into animation.

'The word 'Maitre' was just used on a radio frequency on Earth, in Nevada.' Said Troni, 'That's where you begin.'

CHAPTER TEN

L isa retched, as O'Neill held the plastic bin in front of her and rubbed her back.

'What did you do to me?'

'Unfortunately, I overstretched your mind a little, and this is the body's reaction. My apologies.' he said.

She looked up from the rim of the bin and watched Steve pop his notebook back in his pocket, and check his watch.

'Interview with Lisa Tsai, terminated 01.01 AM. Will recommence at 06.00AM.'

He took the camera from the tripod, but left the tripod itself where it was, then stood, walked to the door, and opened it. John was standing alone outside, having dispersed the mob.

'The results from the blood came back,' said John, 'It's Dunn's.'

'Thought so, but always best to check,' said Steve. 'Would you mind taking Dr Tsai back to her room to rest, then bringing her back here at 06.00? We'll keep Dr O'Neill here in Professor Dunn's room.'

'You can't do this to me.' Lisa said, getting up and moving over to the far wall, 'I've told you what I know. I am an American citizen. I have rights.'

'I need to make my report,' Steve said then looked back at Lisa.

Coming to a judgement, his hand re-entered his blazer,

and he handed John a plastic-topped syringe. 'Sedate her if necessary.'

John crossed the room, seized Lisa by the bicep, and stared her in the face. For a full minute, that's how they remained, her terrified face reflected in his shades, divided by the syringe lifted between them.

Then he did something shocking — he smiled. Never in her eight years at Area 51 had she seen an Agent smile, and it was not a friendly smile, it was a crocodilian grin.

'She'll be no trouble.'

As he moved her to the corridor, she caught a glance from O'Neill. One which warned caution.

They passed a few cleaners on their way to her room, their eyes moving from her, to John's raised ID, to the floor, or simply remained fixed on whatever they were scrubbing. Kowalski's yells still echoed through the corridors, from wherever he was being restrained.

John slammed her door behind them and let go of her arm, which tingled as the blood flow resumed.

'Get undressed,' he said. 'Then throw your mobile phone on top of your clothes.'

Lisa wondered how many more times she'd have to degrade herself like this, but complied with his request down to her underwear, where she paused,

He cocked his head and stared at her, like a barfly watching a waitress cross a dance floor. She had now rescinded her long-held belief that Agents were emotionless clones off a conveyer belt. This was a very different beast to Steve, one with emotions and impulses, and that made him more terrifying somehow.

John's tongue flickered, as he pocketed the syringe, and then produced a set of handcuffs.

'Over by the radiator.'

She moved before he seized the opportunity to move her himself, and tried not to flinch as the two steel bracelets pinched her wrists.

'Good girl, you're very brave,' he said, 'Want to see some magic, good girl?'

He jumped back theatrically and showed her his palms. 'Look, nothing in my hands…

He wriggled his fingers, shouted 'Abracadabra!', and lunged forward; an extended flick knife appearing at the end of his arm. She shrieked as it halted an inch from her right eye.

'Pretty cool, huh?'

She glared at him, unable to hold back the tears.

He left her, walked over to the bed, and attacked it with the knife, drawing clouds of feathers as he stroked it left and right, then he moved to the wardrobe and her chest of drawers and went at them with the same ferocity. She was unsure as to the purpose of the vandalism but chose not to ask about it. If he was attacking her things, he was not attacking her.

After he'd destroyed the room, he moved to her clothes and began to pick through them, with a tenderness he'd not shown to the rest of her possessions. He hooked her skirt on the end of his knife, and lifted it in front of his face, leering past it in her direction.

She averted her eyes and was alarmed by his close proximity when she looked at him again. There was a series of clicks, and the handcuffs slackened and were removed from her wrists.

'Can I get dressed now?'

'Of course you can,' he said, examining her mobile phone with interest.

She did so quickly and then decided that before he destroyed her phone as well, she might chance something unlikely.

'Can I call someone?' She said.

He looked up at her with surprise.

'My mother?'

He chuckled, and with a flick of his wrist, there came a loud twang just to the right of her head. She turned and saw her SIM card pinned to the wardrobe by the knife. As she watched, both pieces separated and tinkled to the floor.

He walked towards her.

'I'm a magician, Dr Tsai, and my speciality is making people disappear. Are you sure you want to call your mother?'

'No,' she whispered, as he wrenched the knife out of the

wood and folded it into his pocket.

'Very well,' he said, scooping up the flakes of plastic from the floor and taking her laptop from the bedside table. 'If you need anything, just shout: 'Agent John'. I'll be right outside.'

'I hope I never see you again!' She said as he opened the door.

He turned, reached into his pocket, and showed her the syringe again.

'We need you fresh for your next session with Dr O'Neill, so if you aren't asleep in ten minutes, that's when you'll see my friend and I again.'

He waggled the syringe.

'I warn you, he can be a bit of a prick.'

Chuckling, he closed the door and she threw herself down on her torn pillows.

How had this happened? One moment she'd been idling along with her normal routine and then, out of nowhere, came Harold bloody Dunn. She could very well go to prison for the rest of her life, and for what? A drunken tumble with an average-looking guy who couldn't keep his nose out of things that didn't concern him?

Her door swung open.

'That wasn't ten minutes,' she said, spinning around, and then froze as she saw the man standing there — Kowalski, with the bastard, John, splayed out in front of him.

'Joe? What the hell?' She leapt out of bed and threw her arms around him, 'How can you be here?'

She released him though her hands remained on his chest. There was a sour odour drifting from the damp rag, he held in his right hand. 'What did you do?'

'I had to get you out.' Kowalski said, 'Them keeping you here like this, it's barbaric. All because some creepy Brit went nuts and started posting conspiracy theories on the net. He's not even one of us.'

'He... what?' She said.

'The rumour is that he's posted some hoax photos, alluding to aliens he's found on the base. They tracked the phone, and when they came to arrest him, he'd run off, leaving you to deal with his mess apparently.'

Lisa processed the information and thought very hard about Harold Dunn, the man she hardly knew.

'How on Earth did he make it off the base?'

'I don't know,' said Kowalski, with a shrug.

'Agent Steve… he had some guy hypnotise me. I think I might have told him things I heard while I was sleeping. Maybe I heard Harold leave the room on some subconscious level?'

'So… the rumours about you and him are true?' Kowalski said, apparently unable to stop himself.

Funny, she thought, how even in such chaotic times, the staff of Area 51 still carried on gossiping as though all was normal.

She ignored him. 'The hypnotist is back in Harold's room, he might be able to tell us what the hell happened to him.'

'We should really get out of here,' Kowalski said, leaning back to look up the corridor.

'He is our way out of here,' she said, striding over to John and drawing his Glock from his belt.

Several minutes after Lisa and Kowalski had left the room, the first bubbles of red began to appear in John's nostrils. Then it overflowed and began dribbling from his mouth as well.

CHAPTER
ELEVEN

D r Henry O'Neill lowered the final two cards towards the top of his tower.

This work for the Agents wearied him and felt highly unethical, but he knew that the fee involved would be substantial and that the alternative to compliance was arrest. So really he had no choice. Maybe he would breach the prospect of retirement once he'd made those final two mortgage payments on his house, and certainly not midway through a job.

There came a series of frenzied knocks at the door.

'Alright, alright,' he said. Surely it wasn't Steve coming to send him back to work already? Barely half an hour had passed since he'd declared his subject needed to rest. Maybe there was something regarding his fee that Steve wanted to discuss.

O'Neill straightened his tie and opened the door. He was greeted by a gun.

'What did you make me say?' Tsai said, jabbing him in the forehead, 'Tell me what the hell's going on.'

'Steady,' said her accomplice, placing a hand on the gun, and taking it from her.

O'Neill stood there, rubbing his forehead, saying nothing. This man must have helped her escape. He recognised him now, he'd seen John bundle him out of Tsai's room earlier, as he'd waited to go in. What had happened to John? He wasn't O'Neill's favourite among the Agents - there was a sadistic streak in him – but he was still an Agent nonetheless, and he could not imagine these two getting the best of him. The only one of them O'Neill disliked more than John, was an Agent Kyle, whom he'd never met, but had seen the handiwork of. He'd interviewed an old employee, Dr Morgan Andrews, following a session with Kyle, and the damage to the man's mind had been extreme and irreversible.

'Come on, O'Neill, you can explain it en route.' The man said, waggling a finger at him. 'Take us to your car.'

O'Neill shrugged and decided there was no point in resisting. They'd never make it off the base anyway.

As he took a step towards the pair, he noticed that the gun, which looked a lot steadier in the man's hand than it had Tsai's, was a Glock. Didn't the Agents carry Glocks? Had this man killed Agent John?

He read the name on the man's lab coat as he passed him; 'Kowalski', the name didn't ring a bell.

'Wait!' Said Tsai, nipping back inside the room, and then reappearing holding Steve's lie detector and a blanket.

Resourceful. He thought.

The two pushed him through the corridors, swinging him around corners, this way and that, downstairs, heading for the visitor's garage. He was sure it was after three-thirty, Steve wouldn't be along to his room until six, and the corridors wouldn't get busy until seven, but it was inexplicable they met not one night owl. He cursed the laziness of the staff at Area 51.

He led them to his red Ford Fiesta (he knew better than to drive his Mercedes on the dirt roads) and they climbed onto the back seat, and slid under the blanket.

'Drive.' Came Kowalski's muffled voice, 'And remember; if you turn us in, we're going to prison for the rest of our lives, so I've nothing to lose by putting a bullet in you.'

O'Neill started the engine and rolled towards the garage door, which began to rise as he tripped the sensor.

Lisa found it stifling underneath the hairy blanket,

particularly with Kowalski breathing hot air on the back of her neck. Though she presumed she should not be irritated with the man who'd just saved her life, he probably even deserved a treat. With that thought, she inched her bottom back a few inches and nestled further into the curve of his body. Her anxiety gave way a little to excitement.

O'Neill showed his pass to the guard sitting up in the gate office, who ticked him off a sheet and then took a long drink from his coffee mug, keeping one eye on his Hustler the entire time. Still, O'Neill continued to stare at the guard, his pass still held aloft, eyes darting to the back seat.

'Go on then,' said the guard, and O'Neill was forced to accelerate.

Imbecile. He thought.

At the Restricted Area sign, he found three empty 4x4s and a dozen Camo Dudes, wrestling with a mob of Ufologists. They waved him past.

Fucking unbelievable.

Lisa chanced a peak from under the blanket as the chants of 'ET's welcome!' and 'Free Harold Dunn!' died away.

'Where shall we go?' She asked Kowalski, watching the rock formations become road signs as they pulled onto the highway.

'I rent a trailer up at the Lil A'le'inn, Rachel,' he said, drawing a glance of surprise from her.

'Hey, there's quite a few of us on that base who enjoy a certain celebrity status amongst those geeks, you know?'

Enjoying the moment of levity, she chuckled.

'You heard the man, O'Neill.'

Throwing the blanket off she stretched, feeling pleased as Kowalski tried and failed to conceal his erection.

They drove the rest of the way to Rachel without incident, and only a few people were pottering about in the parking lot as they pulled in beside Kowalski's trailer.

'Right then, O'Neill.' Lisa said, once they were safely inside the trailer and Kowalski had pulled the curtains, 'Tell us what happened to Dunn.'

'What do you expect me to say?' He said from the folded sofa bed, eyes drifting around the trailer, 'I only know rumours and what you told me when you were under.'

O'Neill spotted a gap in the curtains, which meant there was an opportunity for a signal to be made, at the right moment. Kowalski noticed his attention drifting and raised the gun to retain it. 'Better start talking.'

This time Lisa reached up and put her hand on the gun. 'No need for that,' she said, smiling, and pulled the lie detector from her pocket, 'Or should I say... no need for that... yet?'

CHAPTER TWELVE

As Lisa attached the pads to the slight fingers of O'Neill, she noticed how smooth his hands were, and cold, like rose petals. She found herself wondering how often he moisturised and then if he was gay. Glancing up at his face, she drew a minor flinch of surprise from the hypnotist and then gave her head a shake. It was not a time to get distracted.

'What is your name?' She said.

O'Neill rolled his eyes.

Kowalski jabbed him in the chest with the gun.

'Ouch… Henry O'Neill.'

'Tell me that you believe the Earth's flat.'

'I believe the Earth's flat.'

Beep.

'Excellent,' said Lisa, sitting down beside Kowalski on the couch, 'now, tell me what rumours you've heard about Professor Dunn and I.'

O'Neill rubbed the knees of his chinos and then calmly interlocked his hands. He might have been giving a lecture to a bunch of college students.

'The rumour is that you both went out drinking and then went back to his room.'

Despite appearing relaxed, O'Neill was choosing his

words carefully. The Tsai woman seemed reasonable, albeit a little impulsive, but he did not like the way the gun flexed in Kowalski's hand. The man did not appear dangerous at first glance, but exuded an aura of danger, given time to notice it.

'At some point in the night, Dunn left his room alone, then came back and posted online that he'd discovered evidence of extra-terrestrial life… in Area 51.'

He felt a little annoyed by their subdued reaction but then considered that. Kowalski would already have heard the rumours and informed Tsai, unless… Tsai had had something to do with getting Dunn off the base? Perhaps Kowalski and Tsai had murdered Dunn for some reason and created an elaborate cover-up?

'Under hypnosis, you stated three key points: A: Dunn left the room. B: Dunn returned to the room. C: There was a lot of blue light, and you heard a 'loud, metallic, grinding noise."

'Blue light?' Lisa said, her face creasing.

'So she dreamt about some blue light? So what?' Kowalski said, standing up, 'Dunn's probably locked in a cell somewhere getting tortured by your Agent friends. We've heard the stories. You're full of shit.'

Lisa again felt thankful for how personally Kowalski was taking her situation. Perhaps the Agents had burst into her room, stolen Harold away, and then erased the memory, and the blue light and grinding sound were all she had left of it.

'You doubt the machine?' O'Neill said, nodding towards the lie detector.

The pair said nothing.

'The facts, confirmed by CCTV, are thus: Harold Dunn entered Hangar 18 with a stolen ID, before returning to his room, then, minutes later, there was a flash of blue light, and Agents broke into his room and found only you inside.'

'There's CCTV in the rooms?' Lisa said.

'There's CCTV in every room on the base,' he said.

'Now shoot me if you wish,' He said, looking now at Kowalski, 'But what I've said will remain the truth.'

'Are you seriously suggesting that Professor Dunn was abducted by aliens?' Kowalski said.

'I'm suggesting nothing.'

'Blue light… metallic noises… Dunn, vanishing into thin air. You are suggesting…'

'I'm suggesting nothing!' The little man shouted, taking them by surprise. 'I'm merely repeating what Dr Tsai said under hypnosis. I'm a parrot, not a magic eight ball!'

Lisa stood up and went to the sink. As she gripped the cold porcelain, she stared through the gap in the curtains a challenge to the dawn sky. Was it true? Were aliens real? She felt Kowalski's hand on her shoulder.

O'Neill watched the action. Tsai did not respond to Kowalski's touch. Their affection for one another was not equal and he no longer suspected a joint murder plot. Perhaps Tsai really didn't know what was going on, and Kowalski was assisting her through mere infatuation.

How dull, though Tsai, the desperate paranoid, and Kowalski, the dangerous obsessive, still made for a turbulent blend.

He watched how Kowalski held the gun outstretched behind him, as he comforted Tsai, so if he made a dash for the door, Kowalski could pull the trigger on reflex and the bullet would still kill him. He thought about his mobile phone in his jacket pocket, which they'd yet to take from him, and prayed it wouldn't ring and alert them to its presence.

Had he left it on silent?

'Joe, do you know a guy from the bar called Andrews?' asked Tsai, elation lighting up her face.

'Sure, he lives over on Lot Seven.'

Andrews threw open the door on the second knock, releasing a pungent aroma of stale bourbon. He wore a lime green dressing gown, which looked as though it hadn't been washed for some time.

'What do you want?'

'Sir, my name's Lisa Tsai, I was in the bar the other night, and I heard you mention that you were familiar with Area 51.'

His eyes narrowed, and he folded his arms and leant against the door frame.

'You cops? Press?'

He looked past Lisa and saw the two men behind her.

'You,' he said, pointing to O'Neill, with his eyes wide, 'I know you. You're with them.'

He reached into the doorway and pulled out a baseball bat. 'You get away you hear?' He said, lunging at Lisa, who moved just beyond his swing. 'I got my rights.'

Kowalski revealed the gun from behind O'Neill's back, and Andrews stopped talking, weighing up the situation the best he could in his state of mind.

'He is our prisoner,' said Lisa, 'Sir, our friend is in danger, and we think you might be able to help us.'

'What can I do?' He said, eyes still on the gun.

'Our friend,' She said, 'He went inside Hangar 18, and now he's missing.'

Andrews almost dropped the bat. 'Inside, quick,' he said, hopping back inside the trailer, as though he were standing on something hot, then slammed the door and bolted it once they were all inside. He heaved a pile of clothes off of his couch and gestured for them to sit down.

Lisa couldn't tell if the couch was beige or if it had once been white and was now just really filthy. Regardless she lowered herself onto it as Andrews poured himself a tall glass of whiskey, without offering the bottle to anyone else.

'You're wasting your time here,' said O'Neill, 'I remember this fellow. He was some IT guy. 3D printed an ID card, coded it himself, and made his way into Hangar 18. Sub-par coding, it set all the alarms off, and he got himself caught.'

'I saw it, you bastard!' Andrews said, slopping his drink across the stained counter, 'I saw the ship! I didn't get no photo, but I wrote it all up.'

He turned to Lisa and Kowalski, 'I've got a photo to go with my article now though, haven't I? Thanks to your friend uploading it to my site.'

'It's your website?' O'Neill said, his eyebrows shooting all the way up to his considerably high hairline.

'You betcha, buddy.' Andrews said, with a little cackle, 'Your Men in Black friends might have shut down my website for the time being, but I got a dozen printouts of that baby before they did.'

He took a pink folder off the top of the microwave, and removed a piece of paper, which looked very white in comparison to everything else in the trailer, and then turned it over.

O'Neill was first forward to see the photo, though after several minutes, his expression cleared and he sat back down. 'Poor photoshopping. The blurring around the edges of the craft is a dead giveaway. Looks to be your standard of work, sir, if the rumours are to be believed.'

As Andrews hurled vulgarities at the hypnotist, Lisa digested the picture of black domed, stingray, hovering in the dark room.

Was that really Harold's photo? Was that an Alien craft?

'The Aliens got me too, missus', came a whisper, and she realised that Andrews had finished with O'Neill for the time being, and stuck his whiskery lips in her ear.

'Right after the Agents had me interrogated. I woke up in the middle of the desert. No memory of how I got there. That's when I wrote my article.'

Lisa turned to O'Neill, 'You hypnotised Andrews here once, you can do it again so we can find out more about what happened to him.'

'Simple: he was abducted, no doubt, by this...' O'Neill picked up an empty whiskey bottle from the counter and made a whirring noise, as he mimicked it hovering.

'Hypnotise him, or I'll shoot you.' Kowalski said.

O'Neill spun the bottle in his hand and replaced it on the counter. 'That I don't doubt,' he said, 'I think I'd enjoy a little browse through that head of yours, Dr Kowalski.'

'You never will,' said Kowalski, glowering at the little man.

'Let's not make any promises.' O'Neill said, 'I shall put in a request when the Agents catch up with you, providing they don't shoot you on sight, although I suspect they shall take you to see someone else first, someone Dr Andrews has already met.'

'Don't say his name in my house!' Andrews said, the glass shaking in his hand.

O'Neill shrugged. Hypnotising the drunk would buy him a few more minutes, while he waited for Steve and company.

'Come on then, let us take a canter over pastures old. You two get off the sofa and let him lie down.'

'What are you going to do?' Andrews asked as Lisa and Kowalski edged past him, 'I don't want you fiddling around in there for too long. I still get the headaches from the last time.'

'Nonsense, there are never any after effects,' Said O'Neill, 'I'm merely going to put you into a subdued state and access your subconscious. I suspect you're confusing your regular hangovers with something more sinister.'

Andrews shook his head, but drained his glass, and lay down.

'Allow your fears and stresses to disappear,' said O'Neill, any antagonism now absent from his voice, 'There's no one else here, just the sound of my voice which you find comforting and relaxing. You're going deeper and deeper, deeper and deeper. Allow yourself to let go completely. Deeper and deeper, deeper and deeper. You are now asleep.'

And he was, with a thin stream of dribble pooling onto the fabric of the couch.

'What's your name?'

'Morgan Andrews.'

'What state do you live in?'

'Nevada.'

O'Neill looked at Lisa for further instruction.

'Ask him about the aliens,' Lisa whispered.

'It doesn't work like that; you can't just go galloping in,' he said, 'Heck, you're as bad as…'

Then he thought better of what he was about to say and cleared his throat.

'Why were you let go from your job at the base, Morgan?'

Andrews' face twitched with discomfort.

'I went into Hangar 18.'

'What did you see in Hangar 18, Morgan?'

'A craft.'

'The same one Professor Dunn took a photo of?'

'It was identical.'

'What do you think happened to Professor Dunn, Morgan?'

'Maybe he's being tortured by Agents. Maybe he's been taken by them,' he said through gritted teeth, beads of sweat streaming down his forehead. He kicked out with both of his legs.

'Maybe we should stop,' O'Neill said, though as he said it, he was struck by a sudden curiosity. He'd always wondered what the infamous Agent Kyle did to people, down there in that dungeon of his, that made them like Andrews. He was overstretching the man's mind, but it wasn't a mind worth saving... besides, he smelt terrible.

'Is that what happened to you, Morgan, were you tortured?'

'Yes, after the second round of hypnosis they gave me to the blonde man,' he said, fists balling up, head digging back into the sofa, 'Afterwards, I came here and posted my story online, and waited for them. Five bullets for them, one for me. I was never going back to him... but it wasn't them who came.'

'Who was it, Morgan?' O'Neill said, 'Who came for you?'

Andrews' eyes flew open, and he screamed, arching his back, prompting them all to recoil.

'The blue light,' he said, in a hoarse tone, eyes wide and unseeing, 'The Greys.'

O'Neill snapped his fingers, but nothing happened.

'They took something from me. There was pain,' he said, grabbing his groin with both hands, 'And there was a word... an enemy.'

O'Neill gave up on snapping his fingers and began shaking the rigid, babbling man. He'd never been unable to wake someone before. He dropped him back on the sofa and began to slap him as Kowalski poured something out of a brown bottle onto a rag.

'Maitre,' said Andrews, spine slackening, and hands flailing against Kowalski as he fought to press down the rag, 'The enemy is Maitre.'

The screams became muffled and then stopped, and Lisa watched Kowalski roll the man into the recovery position, facing away from them. He was quite the man of action when it was required.

'Can we go now?' He said, 'Every Agent within a

thousand miles will have heard that screaming.'

Lisa nodded. 'We need to get to a computer and find out what Maitre means,' she said, 'Unless anyone's got a Smartphone on them?'

O'Neill was concerned he'd shaken his head a little too brusquely, though she didn't seem to notice.

'My phone and laptop are back at the base.' Kowalski said, 'Besides, the signal around here's sketchy at best. We'll find a computer in Vegas.'

She braced as she opened the trailer door, expecting to get peppered with gunfire the moment she did so, but the parking lot was deserted. She could hear no sirens, nor see distant flashing lights, excluding the action from the Lil Al'le'inn. Then it hit her. She didn't have an Alien database at her disposal, but she had the next best thing.

'Fancy buying me a drink?' She said.

'Are you crazy?'

'Look, that bar's full of people with heads full of this shit.'

Kowalski looked past her towards the bar, and rubbed his eyes, but nodded his assent.

'What about him?' He said, jerking a thumb at O'Neill, who watched them from the floor beside the sofa.

'We can't take him with us,' said Lisa, 'He might give us away.'

'You're right,' Kowalski said, and O'Neill felt gripped by an intense dread as he watched him dowse the rag again.

'Do not come near me with that stuff.' O'Neill said, 'I am an asthmatic and allergic to most sleeping medication. That stuff could kill me.'

'It's harmless,' said Kowalski, and held out the rag towards him.

'Stay away from me, I say,' he said, scooping up Andrews' glass and launching it at Kowalski. It missed and shattered against the wall.

'Alright, leave him be, Joe,' said Lisa, reaching out and gripping the back of Kowalski's shirt. She felt alarmed by the abrupt change in the hypnotist's temperament.

'But we can't set him free,' Kowalski said, glaring at O'Neill.

'No, we can't,' she said, 'What do you propose we do

with you, O'Neill?'

O'Neill felt himself sweating as he went to the kitchen and began rooting through the drawers. He felt like a fish that'd just hopped back out of the net.

'He must have some… aha,' he turned and showed them a roll of grey electrical tape, 'Tie me up, and tell the police where I am when you're ready.'

He tossed Lisa the tape and held out his hands, trying to keep the smile off his face.

She rolled off a long strip.

'The toxin would save time,' said Kowalski, still fondling the rag.

Lisa ignored him. She reckoned it was probably one of his own creations, rather than purchased chloroform. Scientists were always so anal about their own creations.

She tied O'Neill's wrists and feet and then slapped a strip across his mouth.

'When Andrews comes to and remembers what you did to him, you might well wish you'd accepted the toxin, O'Neill.'

She pushed him, and he toppled over onto the floor, where he laying groaning, long after they'd left. He was relieved to have avoided Kowalski's toxin, but he was not a young man, and the fall had knocked the wind out of him. Also, she was quite right about Andrews, what would the drunken loon do if he woke up and found him helpless on his trailer floor?

CHAPTER THIRTEEN

This time when Steve awoke, he found no alerts on his phone, which meant two things Dunn had not been found, and John had had no problems with Tsai. The time read four forty-three AM. He had slept for two hours, and his alarm was due to go off in two minutes. Such occasions pleased him, as they were a reminder of how much command he had over his own body clock. As he deactivated the alarm, he struggled to recall what the alarm tone even sounded like.

He rolled off the top of his bedspread and smoothed down his trousers. He'd slept fully clothed, still haunted by how close John had come to discovering him in a state of undress when he'd burst into his room the previous day.

As he poured lukewarm coffee from the pot, he set his phone down on the counter and called John on loudspeaker. By the time the phone had reached its fourth ring, Steve was staring at it, and no longer pouring coffee. He and his colleagues never answered their phone later than the third ring. It went to voicemail, and he redialled, setting down the coffee pot, and pulling his jacket off the door hook. The anticipation was overwhelming. The second the call went to voicemail again, he plunged the phone back into his pocket and flung open the door. He jammed his heels into his shoes as he raced down the corridor, slipped on a freshly buffered floor, tripped up some stairs, and then burst through the landing doors. There, protruding from room 205, were two motionless legs, ending in a pair of gleaming black Oxfords.

His heart thumped in his chest, as he trod forward, listening to his tongue flicker between his lips. The Glock tensed in his right hand, hungry for violence.

When he reached the doorway, he crouched, so that he'd have the edge on any assailant aiming for his head. He then turned into the room, his gun arm stuck out in front of him. The room had been processed clothes hung out of wardrobes and drawers, and the bed sheets had been cut to ribbons, but there were no signs of life. He shuffled forwards and pressed John's jugular, but found no pulse. Steve was not surprised most of John's blood seemed to be soaking into the carpet. He checked the wardrobe, under the bed, and finally the en-suite, and then holstered his gun and dragged John further into the room so he could lock the door.

How had she done it? That little bitch. He should have given her straight to Kyle instead of bothering with that namby-pamby O'Neill. Speaking of whom, he would have to go and fill the hypnotherapist in on what had happened.

His eyes rested back on John's body and all the dried blood around his mouth and nostrils. That much blood wasn't typical in the absence of puncture wounds. Again he asked himself how she had done it; ruptured his spleen, strangled him, poisoned him…? Those seemed the most likely causes, but there was no time for an autopsy, nor was there time to go and speak to O'Neill, as the pink of John's skin was already turning dark green, and taking on a much rougher texture.

Steve holstered his gun and dialled a number on his phone.

'Front gate.' Came a phlegm-laced monotone. Had the moron been sleeping?

'78383 Steve, requesting information,' he said. 'Who's left the base within the last three hours?'

There was the sound of rattling plastic wheels as the guard sat up in his chair.

'Oh, ahem. Just looks like… a… Dr Henry O'Neill, sir.'

O'Neill? Was he in cahoots with Tsai in some way, the treacherous old fool?

'I want total lockdown. Have the base searched for Dr Lisa Tsai, now. Do you understand?'

'Yes, sir.'

Steve ended the call, opened the door and peered out into the corridor. The early birds had begun to emerge, passing by the corridor's ends, yawning and scratching their heads, probably lusting after that first coffee of the day, the one which gave a person faith they could endure another twelve-hour shift.

As he hurried to his room to retrieve the necessary equipment, he was forced to remind himself that only he had the key to the Brit's room, but was unable to quell the prickle of fear that someone might gain entry, in his absence, and discover the now radically different corpse of John inside.

Back in his own room, he took a photo on his phone, of the waist-high bookcase, with its six thick volumes, and houseplant on top. Then he removed the books, and laid them strategically, so that the bookshelf could be lifted and placed upon them, without leaving fresh indentations in the carpet. Sally the Philodendron, was removed to his desk, with care, so that no soil fell on the mat. This protocol was one he'd engineered when he'd first joined the facility, and although he'd never trialled it, he had faith in its efficiency. Snapping out his flick knife, he slipped the blade under where the carpet met the wall, previously concealed by the bookcase, and then used his fingers to pull it the rest of the way to reveal a 5x5 metal square, set into the floor. Next, he spat a glob of spit onto the square, spit that began fizzing and steaming, and then dissolved, along with the metal lid, to reveal a hole in the floor. The pit contained a great many things, but it was the four silver cones and the two-and-a-half pound sledgehammer with the nine-inch handle that Steve required, and it was those that he placed inside the black case he kept under his bed. Then he reassembled the room, using the photo on his phone for reference. It took him several minutes to re-angle the bookcase correctly, and he worried over the position of Sally's leaves for even longer, until eventually he could stand it no longer, and deleted the photo, and fled back to Dunn's room. He stopped only once on the way, to steal a bed sheet from the maintenance cupboard.

As he turned the corner, back to the room, he expected to see a mob clustered around the open door, shrieking and poking at the corpse, but the corridor was still deserted. He unlocked the door, and entered the room, to find his friend unmolested, though now fully transformed.

He set down his equipment and prepared the body placing it flat, the hands by the hips, the feet together. Then he took the four cones and put them just beyond the edges of the pool of blood in which the body lay. As an afterthought, he took a condom from his wallet and stretched it over the smoke alarm. He'd picked up the trick from Working Mother, a publication he'd leafed through in some waiting room years ago. There had been an article by a Mrs Pennyporter, who'd surprised her son with a visit to his college dorm and caught him smoking weed, there had been a condom over the smoke alarm and a towel across the base of his door to stop the smoke escaping. 'Marijuana dealers try to trick our kids into burning themselves to death.' Mrs Pennyporter had said.

Steve licked his finger and rubbed a little saliva on each of the cones, which began vibrating in response.

'You'll be remembered, Grindl,' said Steve, as the vibrations grew louder, then each of the pods changed from black to blinding red, and then gradually returned to normal, leaving the room heavy with the stink of charred meat. He replaced the cones inside the case and wrapped the newly skinless skeleton in the bed sheet, then took out his gun and laid it within arm's reach.

He listened, and his tongue flickered, as he gripped the textured rubber handle of the sledge and then swung it down onto the skull. The crunch was loud, and his free hand hovered over his gun, but there came no sounds of investigation from beyond the door.

After a minute, he resumed, raining the blows down as quickly as he could and creating a lot of noise in the process, but speed was paramount. It took him thirty minutes to reduce the skeleton to fragments, then he tied a knot in the bed sheet, and laid it in the briefcase, along with the hammer and cones.

Before opening the door, he examined the room. There was a clean patch on the carpet but no corpse, no blood; no residue whatsoever.

As he stepped out into the corridor, he remembered the condom but decided to leave it where it was. It would throw Dunn's reputation further into disrepute if people began to suspect that he was a drug user.

CHAPTER FOURTEEN

The Lil A'le'inn was bustling with tourists all talking about similar things; phenomena they had seen or the phenomena they expected to see. Most had the inside scoop on the shady workings of the government, and all were, of course, being continuously monitored by the Men in Black. Some even claimed to be ex-Area 51 employees, who'd worked on alien autopsies and saucer test flights, but Lisa didn't recognise any of them. The only person she recognised was a girl, with jam-jar glasses, who was standing atop a chair, giving a sermon on the Plejaren, from Planet Erra — seven foot, humanoid creatures, of power and wisdom, who lived for thousands of years, maintaining the harmony of the universe. She stopped talking mid-sentence, when she spotted Lisa and Kowalski, gave a little shriek, and then swam towards them through the crowd, seemingly oblivious to their amusement.

'Lisa. How great to see you again. Stacey, remember? She said, grinning, and then nodded to Kowalski, 'Joe, pleasure as always.'

Lisa looked at Kowalski, who looked at his shoes. 'I told you, I come in here every now and again, didn't I? I like their stories.'

'Come and join our table.' She said, linking arms with

Lisa and pulling her into the crowd.

'I'll get us some drinks, I guess.' Said Kowalski and slouched off towards the bar.

Lisa took a seat amongst the Ufologists, and the fat, ginger guy leant over, 'Didn't expect to see you in here again so soon after last night. You Martian-dissectors can drink.'

'Oh, Gordon,' Stacey said, slapping his chunky arm, and just like with O'Neill's sexuality, Lisa began wondering what the story was there. Again, she shook her head, and forced herself to stay on the topic.

'I need some information on a type of Alien,' she said.

'Got a new one locked up in there, have you?' Gordon said, and turned to the three strangers at the table as Kowalski returned with the drinks, 'Lisa and Joe here work at Area 51.'

He was answered with variations of, 'Yeah, whatever.'

'No, they really do.'

'Ever heard of a Maitre?' asked Lisa, sensing that incessant interrogation might be imminent, should Gordon continue with his assurances.

An excited murmur ran through the group.

'Only one of the most bad-ass alien races out there.' Said Stacey.

'Really?' Kowalski said chuckling. Lisa wondered if it was Stacey's enthusiasm that amused him.

'Well, just plain 'bad', rather than 'bad-ass' is probably more accurate.' Gordon said, 'One of the most violent alien races in the universe. Parasites, really.'

'From the Megopei constellation.' Said one of the others.

'They can live for up to one-hundred-and-twenty years, roughly seven foot…'

'They've abducted more than five thousand humans…'

'Guys,' Lisa said, trying to digest all the information at once, but they were off, and there seemed to be no stopping them now.

Kowalski gave her a grin, which she returned. Despite their peril, the feverish game of nerdy one-upmanship was pretty funny. Then, she felt déjà vu — the situation was not dissimilar to her previous night, only with a different man — both found the nerds amusing, both wanted to sleep with her.

She stopped grinning, averted her eyes, and took a long pull on her beer.

CHAPTER FIFTEEN

O'Neill's abdominals, which he'd given no attention since his youth, burnt as he clenched, and then he jerked back to try and free his phone from his inside pocket. After failing for the third time, he lay flat, breathing through his nose, tingling with pins and needles in the parts that bore his weight. He rolled onto his other side and accidentally booted the counter. His eyes shot to Andrews, but still, the man lay motionless. He would have sighed with relief, had it not been for the strip of tape across his mouth, and that the broken tumbler he'd thrown at Kowalski was now almost impaled in his back. Then an idea struck him, and his fingers began scrabbling for a shard that might be big enough to be used as a saw. His fingers were slippery with blood by the time he'd located one, but he was pleased with it — the perfect length and dexterity to secure between his thumb and forefinger for the action. Rolling onto his back again, he watched his hands conduct the motion, dropping the shard a few times onto his front and having to roll over to pick it up again.

After several minutes of anticipation, he could take it no longer and wrenched the tape apart on the fifth attempt. He hissed, as the tape around his mouth tore off some skin, and then almost set about unwinding the tape around his feet before he stopped himself. Andrews might hear... it was better to saw through it. He picked up the shard again, made quick work of his final bond, and then made a silent dive for the door. Tumbling out onto the sandy lot outside, he heaved in a lungful of oxygen and was struck by indecision. What should he do now? Run back to the base, or hide and wait for backup?

The answer seemed obvious, and it came to him as he rushed back to close the trailer door, fearing that a breeze might wake Andrews. Sitting in a crop of bushes beside the trailer, he removed his phone and was relieved when it illuminated to his touch.

He had nineteen percent battery, forty-three missed calls, and seven texts. The phone had been on silent, he remembered setting it now, so that nobody could disturb him while he built his card tower. He did what the texts and voicemails of increasing hostility told him to do, which was to call Steve, who answered on the first ring.

'O'Neill?' Steve said, 'Where are you?'

'Lot 7, Lil A'le'inn, Rachel.'

Steve relayed this information to someone, and O'Neill heard the sound of a car door slamming, and the rev of an engine.

'We're moving to your location now. What happened?'

'Tsai and Kowalski came to my room and kidnapped me at gunpoint, made me drive here. Had me hypnotise that Andrews fella you brought in last year. You know, the other bloke who wandered into Hang...'

'Yes, thank you,' Steve said, in a manner that made O'Neill suspect that the Agent would destroy his phone the second the call ended. 'Are they with you now?'

'No, they tied me up in Andrews' trailer and went into the bar to talk to those Ufologists from the gate. Andrews is still in his trailer, they knocked him out.'

'You're sure that Kowalski and Tsai are still in the bar?'

'Yes.'

'Confirm Andrews' condition. I don't want him making trouble for us when we arrive.'

O'Neill bit his lip. 'I'd rather not if it's all the same, he wanted to...'

'O'Neill, I'll remind you that now we know where Tsai and Kowalski are, you are expendable. One might call you a 'loose end'. So if I were you, I'd think very carefully about how insolent you can afford to be.'

Steve said this in his best monotone, an indication that he knew he didn't need to add emotion to authenticate his threat.

'Ok, I'll call you back.'

'No need to hang up,' Steve said.

'Fine,' Said O'Neill, 'But you'll need to be quiet for a few minutes.'

Steve didn't reply, but O'Neill could still hear him breathing on the other end of the line, and the sound of his car bumping over the rough terrain. He also noted a lack of engine noise that would have been synonymous with a race to his location. The Agent wasn't rushing.

He peered through the thin branches of the bush. Save for the shapes moving to and fro in the bar windows, his immediate environment was deserted. Over the ruckus, he heard a hawk shriek in the distance, and could just hear the creaking of the wooden posts, holding up the washing lines. As he stepped forward, he tripped over a black cat, which had chosen that moment to chase a lizard from its hiding place. The cat squealed, but maintained its pursuit of the lizard, and scrambled below another trailer across the way. O'Neill swore, and stole to the window above Andrews' sink, to peer in through the gap in the curtains, though, try as he might, he still couldn't see the sofa from his position. If only the gap had been half an inch wider.

For a moment he considered lying to Steve, saying he'd entered the trailer and that Andrews had still been unconscious, but then he spotte nmd the CCTV camera on the roof of the bar and knew that the meticulous Agent would definitely check it, and then punish him for his dishonesty.

With a sigh, he picked a dusty rock from the ground and weighed it in his hand. It was heavy enough to do some damage, but not so heavy that he'd need to use both hands. Moving to the front door, he pressed his ear against the plastic and expected to hear a shout from Andrews inside, or from a neighbour behind him at any moment. Neither came, so he squeezed the rock, and went inside.

Andrews still lay prone on the sofa — silent, unmoving. Something about the scene unnerved O'Neill. It was no longer fearing Andrews might wake up at any second and beat him to death, it was something else. He took a few steps closer to the sofa and inadvertently stepped on the shard of glass he'd used to free himself, \which flattened with a loud crunch. He stared, and still, Andrews didn't move. He advanced some more, so that he was within a footstep of the sofa, ready to smash Andrews' head in if it was all a bluff.

He heard a distant voice and put the phone back to his ear.

'O'Neill? Are you still there?'

It was now as he leant over Andrews that he noticed his eyes were a little open and then he noticed the dried blood about the nostrils and mouth, and much of it staining the backboard of the sofa. He dropped the rock with a clunk and felt for a pulse.

'O'Neill?'

'Andrews is dead.'

'You killed him?'

'No. I think he's been dead this whole time. Must have had a reaction to whatever Kowalski gave him.'

'What are his symptoms, as you see them?' Steve said.

'His eyes are open, there's blood about his mouth and nose… a lot of blood.'

'Same as John.'

O'Neill took a moment to process the information. He'd been right, after all, Kowalski had killed John with the toxin, and he'd now killed Andrews, and he would've killed him too had Tsai not convinced him otherwise. She really must be ignorant of whatever agenda the man had.

'I want you to watch the bar and call me if Tsai or Kowalski leave the area. Is that clear?' Said Steve.

'That's clear.'

'I'll be there soon.'

O'Neill stepped back outside the trailer, as Steve terminated the call, and told himself that he needed to get away from the Agents and their bullshit once and for all, he was a hypnotherapist by trade, not a spy. Then he heard a slurred protest and spotted two familiar figures stumbling away from the bar's entrance and turning in his direction.

He dove for his bush and thought that he did not envy Tsai, in her condition, with only the murderous Kowalski to look after her. How had she become that drunk, that quickly?

CHAPTER SIXTEEN

Lisa became aware that she'd lost the ability to follow what the Ufologists were saying, but could not pinpoint exactly what the problem was. The room was ablaze with colour. Objects — chairs, glasses, tables had become dazzling shades of yellow and brown and white. People, themselves, were just fluctuating buzzing blurs, and everything felt so heavy. She felt her head lolling and planted her elbow on the corner table so she might catch it on her palm, but she missed, and her head struck something hard instead, then she was toppling backwards through the air, and hit the floor. There were a series of smashes.

She heard a man, a long way away, say 'She… go… now!' Then she heard Kowalski nearby, 'Busy day… exhausted… my trailer… few hours… be fine.'

'Joe… help me.' She said, as tears and snot dribbled down her face.

'She's ok.' She heard him say. Then she was back on her feet, and moving forward. She knew he was helping her. She needed to get a message to him about her condition. He must be as confused as she was.

'Joe… I'm not right… I feel…'

She felt his breath in her ear. 'Drugged. An Agent… in here… a trap. Give me… gun.'

She felt the pressure removed from her lower spine, as he pulled the heavy pistol from her waistband. Then a wave of fresh air hit her, offering euphoria as it washed over her skin, and cleared her senses. Unfortunately, the clarity was momentary, and the size of the parking lot made her head spin, and the few lights outside began to pop.

She felt something hard crash against her tailbone and knew she'd fallen over again.

'Get the car.' She said, frustrated by the exertion she had to place on her lips to get them to form the words, 'I'll be fine... in a moment.'

'No.' Kowalski said, and she felt the ground disappear from below her, 'We don't know what... given you. I've antidotes... medicine... stolen from... base... back at... trailer. Just keep quiet... don't... more attention.'

She gazed up at the blanket of stars, glistening on the black canvas above, saw something move. A UFO, perhaps? They were nonsense, weren't they? Or were they? She couldn't remember.

Suddenly, the air became stale, and she landed on something soft and springy. A door slammed, and through the haze, she saw Kowalski pull down the blinds, and then lift one to peer through. Other than that, he gave no indication that he thought someone was following them.

CHAPTER SEVENTEEN

O'Neill watched the gun tumble from Kowalski's pocket, as he struggled with Tsai, and scurried out to collect it as soon as the trailer door slammed.

The steel felt cool in his hand, heavy and powerful. He was ready now, for Kowalski, should he come back outside to look for it. A quick pop to the leg and Steve would be very impressed. Though having never fired a gun, O'Neill thought that maybe he was overestimating how good of a shot he was in his excitement. Better to be closer, he decided, and started to walk towards the trailer as his phone vibrated in his pocket.

'We'll be with you in two minutes.' read the text from an unknown number. Steve had done away with the other phone as predicted.

'They've moved to Lot 4.' He typed in response. 'Kowalski isn't Tsai's accomplice. He's done something to her.'

CHAPTER EIGHTEEN

'Have you got an antidote? You said about medicine?' Lisa said, feeling as though Kowalski had been standing at the window for a long time. Had he been or was she just imagining it? She had thought the effects of the drug were wearing off, it was easier to speak, and shapes were a little sharper, though she knew she was still hallucinating. She was sinking ever deeper into the bed.

'Medicine?' Kowalski said as he drew the latch with a click, 'You've already had your medicine. I popped it in your drink.'

She was confused by this, and by the laugh that followed, which did not sound like Kowalski. Her head felt like a boulder as her neck strained to lift it so she could look at him, and then the world came in to focus, and she realised she had not misunderstood him. The positive side effect of this, was that the fear which flooded her body accelerated the production of white blood cells in rebellion against whatever Kowalski had given her.

'No,' She moaned and tried to get up.

'Ah, ah, ah.' he said, and shoved her back into her original position.

His mouth chuckled, mere inches from her own, and then moved further south, past her face and onto her neck.

'I've always watched you, always wanted you,' he said, planting a wet kiss on her cheek, 'maybe they'll let me keep you for a toy once the work's over?'

'What are you talking about?' She said, pushing against his bony shoulders, 'Have you gone insane?'

He allowed her to push him away, and then stood at the end of the bed and began to undress. She felt very cold, despite her quickened pulse rate. She could hear her heart pumping away in her ears.

Pump! Pump! Pump!

'What the fuck are you doing, Joe?' She said, as he pulled off his boxers and threw them aside. She stared at his penis, flopping around, semi-erect.

He was her friend. No matter what was happening, he would not do the unthinkable.

'You're my friend.' She said, but he only howled in response and sprung towards her with such force that she was driven flat.

'No.'

Buttons pinged across the room as he attacked her clothes with vigour. He got the skirt away with ease but struggled to tear the shirt off her flailing arms.

She knew she was still too weak to fight him off, or even make a fist, so as his face came up over hers again, she spat in his eye.

'Monster.'

'Monster is it?' He said, chuckled with only a slight twitch of anger, and then backed off to stand at the end of the bed again.

'You have no idea.' He said, and then her friend Joe, was no more her friend Joe than he was one of her own species.

CHAPTER NINETEEN

S teve had lied to O'Neill each time he'd reassured him that he was rushing to his location, and was, in fact, driving very slowly towards Rachel, with a unit of soldiers rolling along behind him. He did not want the revving of engines, nor the screeching of tyres, to alert anyone to his coming, because, regardless of O'Neill's protestations of Tsai's innocence, he intended to kill her, as well as Kowalski, and probably O'Neill as well, for good measure.

When they finally arrived, and his black Ford LTD Crown Victoria rolled to a silent stop on the gravel outside the Lil A'le'inn, his army undid all his stealthy precautions in an instant with a slamming of doors and a thundering of boots, as they piled out of the jeeps. He gritted his teeth as faces began to appear at every one of the bar's windows.

'Secure a perimeter,' He said to those soldiers nearest, 'and you two come with me.'

He marched towards the bar, and then stopped to duck his face behind his hat as a group emerged from the doorway, their Smartphones held aloft.

'Deal with them. Destroy their phones.' Steve said, and the two soldiers manhandled the group inside, where a series of screams and crashes broke out. Anonymity, in a highly documented world, was paramount for an Agent, and Steve did not follow the soldiers inside until the din had stopped, and he was sure that no one was filming him.

He drew his gun as he ventured inside, and studied the two unconscious bodies lying between the toppled tables, and then the patrons beyond, crouching under the aim of the soldiers. He had expected more resistance. There was a little sobbing here and there.

'Listen to me.' Steve said, 'You will be shot if you don't. Do you understand?'

Brief, predictable silence followed, and then there were several whimpers of 'Yes.'

'You will close your eyes and not open them again until instructed. Do you understand?'

'Yes.' repeated the entire room.

'You will stand up remembering not to open your eyes. Do you understand?'

'Yes.' Came the answer and everybody climbed unsteadily to their feet.

'You will hold out your mobile phone to be collected. Do you understand?'

'Yes.'

He leaned close to the senior officer. 'Bring me their SIM cards, and then have a man go out into the desert and bury their phones.'

'Yes, sir.' The officer said, and Steve soon had a pocketful of SIM cards, in a little mesh bag.

'Keep them here.' He said to the same officer, and then lowered his voice to a whisper, 'Remember, blood equals panic, so sedate anyone who gets out of line.'

The man nodded, shouldered his rifle, and pulled a pistol from his belt. The other soldiers must've guessed Steve's command because they mimicked the action without waiting for instruction. Steve doubted anyone in the bar would recognise the pistols as dart guns.

'Get down on the floor.' Steve said, 'Anybody who glances up will be shot. Do you understand?'

'Yes.' The patrons mumbled as they clambered back on to the floor.

Then Steve turned and walked back outside, where he found a young soldier slapping and rattling his flashlight.

'Any sign of O'Neill?'

The kid fumbled and dropped the flashlight, then stood up in rigid salute.

'No, sir. We've men searching for him, sir.'

'I didn't ask you to search for him, I asked you to secure the perimeter. Has that been done?'

'Yes, sir. I think so, sir.'

Steve fought an urge to berate the boy further.

'Get the unit ready to follow me to Lot 7.'

'Yes, sir.' He,' he said and scampered off to find his commanding officer.

Steve stared at the boy then felt his eyes move down the row of lots. He tried to guess which might be Lot 7, without looking at the numbers on the mailboxes, a variation of a ritual he and John had enjoyed whenever they'd made house calls. He chose a pale blue trailer, about six doors from where he stood, for no other reason than that there was a cat, sitting in front of it, tossing the dead body of a lizard.

Mittens caught the suited man's eye, which seized her with such an intense fear, that she abandoned her prize and raced for home.

Steve ejected the clip from his Glock and reassured himself that it was full to capacity — fifteen rounds. He desired to return to the bar after dealing with Tsai, Kowalski and O'Neill, to kill a few of the patrons as well — maybe all of them — pluck free all those loose threads, though he knew it would be a waste of time and that his lust for blood stemmed from his grief for John. Even Tsai, Kowalski and O'Neill were worth questioning before they died. The gun shook slightly in his hand as he replaced the clip.

He felt the expectant gazes of the men assembled behind him and hoped that they were not all as wet behind the ears as the boy he'd ordered to assemble them. He reassured himself that the screening process to be stationed at Area 51 was rigorous. The boy was probably just an anomaly — some Major's nephew. Besides, each man held an M4 Carbine assault rifle, all one had to do with one of those was point and compress the trigger, then sit back and watch one's target disintegrate. He only hoped that the stupid boy's barrel would not be pointed his way when his stupid finger compressed the trigger.

His reverie was shattered by a scream, from the very trailer he'd guessed, and he held up a palm to steady the men as his tongue felt the breeze.

CHAPTER TWENTY

T he creature looked at least seven foot tall, and skeletal, with long appendages, but none so noticeable as the dripping twelve-inch erection which swayed in front of Lisa's face, like some hypnotic serpent.

'What do you think?' It rasped, in a voice that might have suggested laryngitis in a human.

Lisa screamed, which prompted the beast to flex its rope-knot knees, and propel itself towards her. It caught her around the neck with a clawed, four-fingered hand and threw her up against the ceiling.

When her eyes flickered open again, she focused on the small splatter of red on the white canvas above her. Then all disappeared, replaced by a long, hairless face, with two dark, triangular, pupilless eyes. A single nostril puckered in the centre of its face, omitting a sulphuric scent, and a slit of crimson maw parted below. It was smiling at her, smiling as it slithered over her and left her coated in cyan blue slime.

Then it folded its limbs and propped itself over her, like an arachnid over a paralysed fly, and spoke again. 'Very soon the human race will annihilate itself, and my species will populate the planet Earth. Everyone you've ever known, loved or fucked will be gone... and concerning the latter that's quite a lot of people isn't it, Lisa?'

He chuckled, deep and rattling, as she shut her eyes, and moaned. Her hands slipping against his coat of slime, as she tried to push him away.

'Oh, don't worry, Lisa. I told you, you're coming with me. I want to play with you forever.'

She went to scream again, but he jammed his four fingers over her mouth. This made her open her eyes, and she watched a long, maroon tongue, detach itself from its host, and topple onto her chest. She feared it might slither up to her face, and try to slide down her nose or inside one of her ears, but it had other ideas and began slithering in the opposite direction, the implications of which were even worse. Then, as she felt it slobbering over her navel, and she willed herself to lose consciousness before it reached its destination, there came a sudden knock at the door, and the tongue leapt back into the creature's mouth.

'Who is it?' It asked in Kowalski's voice.

'Agent Steve.'

It gave a guttural bark, which Lisa assumed was some vile curse in its native language, and scuttled off her and over to the door.

'What do you want?'

'I need you to open the door, Dr Kowalski. We need to talk about what happened to Agent John. Do you know he's dead?'

'You killed him?' Lisa said, realising that she should've already guessed this.

'Shut up.' Said the creature, moving to the window and pressing down a blind.

'Dr Kowalski, I will enter within the minute should you choose to ignore me. Is Dr Tsai in there with you?'

It stepped away from the blinds and cursed again. It began a deep bobbing pace across the trailer, like some gangly chicken. This display of anxiety gave Lisa a sudden burst of confidence, and she realised that she was now fairly lucid.

The creature, otherworldly or no, feared the Agent.

It stopped pacing, closed its jagged eyes, and began to shrink, its body contorting before her eyes. The untidy mop of brown hair was the first thing she recognised. It was turning back into Kowalski.

'Yes, I'm here,' Lisa yelled.

Her shout did two things, it prompted several responses from outside which confirmed Steve had people with him, and it made the half-Kowalski turn back into the creature again with a squelch.

'I told you to shut your dick hole, you little bitch, or I'll kill you!'

So the creature struggled to transform under stress. She couldn't allow him to re-adopt his disguise.

'Steve would only come here with serious people. You're never getting out of here alive.'

'Then neither are you.' It said, and once again tried and failed to turn back into Kowalski.

'Pathetic.' She said, and just as the creature swung round, hissing, coiled to lunge at her again, there came a crash, which rattled the plastic door in its frame.

'Stop!' Bellowed the creature.

'Open up.'

It thought for a second, then grabbed Lisa by her hair, and dragged her over to the door.

She felt a serrated claw against her jugular.

'Open the door,' It said, 'But keep the chain on. Tell him we didn't kill anyone.'

Her confidence had deserted her again, now that she was the only thin, fleshy barrier separating Steve from the killer of his partner. She thought it unlikely that he would feel any affectionate restraint, particularly if he felt her also responsible and braced for the impact of a bullet as the Agent's blank expression appeared in the crack, between the buckled door and its frame. Steve held his Glock level with her stomach, while a dozen laser sights scurried across her face. She felt the claw, at her throat, press through another layer of skin.

'We didn't kill anyone,' she said, hoping her monotone would make it obvious that she was being coerced. She really didn't like to say 'we'.

'Ask for a phone.' Said the voice in her ear.

'We'd like a phone.'

Steve's eyebrows shot up and then the corners of his mouth curled into the slightest hint of a smile. 'What's that at your throat, Dr Tsai?'

He moved his lips, right into the crack between the door and the frame, and then with his tongue flickering and his eyes rolling, he whispered, 'Could it be that I've caught you undressed and unarmed... Maitre?'

Lisa's face vanished, and the door slammed.

CHAPTER TWENTY-ONE

As the youth crept closer to Steve, trying to ignore the hisses of his Sergeant Major, he considered the trouble he was going to be in when he got back to the base, but his father was a senator, and that meant something to these people. Plus, if he could just see past the Agent, he might see Dunn's corpse, or perhaps O'Neill, Tsai, Dunn, and Kowalski, all in on the alien hoax together together, and that would make him the authority on the matter, amongst those of his own rank. He had advanced within five paces of the Agent and could see Tsai in her underwear. She was a hottie, even covered in all that blood and blue stuff. A quick shower and she'd be good to go. Then he spotted the serrated claw at her neck, the glistening blue limb it was connected to, and the great eyes in the gloom beyond, and then the door slammed.

'Oh my god, that was an Al....'

Steve swung his gun through the air so that the butt cracked the boy's nose and dropped him to the ground, where he lay gagging and wheezing. A few of the soldiers took a half pace forward and then stopped still when Steve pointed his gun at them. It should not have been much of a deterrent — a pistol against twelve automatic rifles, but killing Steve was not the problem, his organisation, which had the addresses of your family, was the problem.

As the men lowered their guns and shuffled back into line, Steve reached down and grabbed the boy by the ear.

'If you breathe a word about whatever you think you just saw, you and everyone you've ever met will expire on an offshore detention site. Is that understood?'

'You broke my fucking nose,' said the boy. 'My father is a senator.'

'What's a senator, to a man who has killed a President?' Steve whispered.

The boy rolled over and looked at the Agent, conspiracy theories and political history racing through his brain.

'Now, I asked you if you understood.'

'Yes… fuck…'

Steve lifted the boy by the front of the shirt and tossed him stumbling into the wall of men.

'Now, I am going to go into the trailer. You are going to wait out here. I want someone to time ten minutes – not the boy – and if you've not seen me by then, you will empty your guns into the side of the trailer and then grenade it. Is that understood?'

'Yes, sir.'

Steve scanned the faces of the men and saw several of them looking down towards their watches, a malicious tinge to their expressions. Irritating and privileged as the boy was, these soldiers were comrades, and he'd bet his last dollar that should he be tardy stepping back out of the trailer, they'd seize their justified opportunity to destroy it whether they thought him still alive or not. It was their grenades that were important though, for the obliteration of evidence.

He turned back to the door, tensed and then sprinted towards it. The fittings which connected the door to its hinges burst and the door flew back against something solid.

Steve slipped to his feet on the laminate and spotted the Maitre scrambling to catch Tsai's ankle as she leapt off the bed for the exit. It missed her, and she landed on the shattered plastic of the door and scrambled a bloody trail across the floor to the kitchen counter, where she managed to stand, and seized a knife. Steve kept his gun on the Maitre, which glanced between the two humans and the door.

Steve broke the stalemate when he remembered he was on the clock and lifted his phone to his ear.

Lisa heard a tinny female voice say, 'Bartonville Fruit and Veg, Illinois, can I place an order for you?'

'78383, Steve, 290391.'

'One moment, please, sir.'

Static hushed down the line and then a man's voice replaced the woman's.

'Steve?'

'I have a Code Green.'

'A definitive Code Green?'

'I have it at gunpoint. Lil A'le'inn Motel, Rachel. Lot 7.'

'Contain it. We're moving to your location.'

'Understood.'

Steve pocketed the phone, and took a two-handed grip on the gun.

'Take the bitch and leave.' The Maitre said.

'Both of you shall be leaving with me,' said Steve.

'I'll kill her.'

'Then it is just you who shall be leaving with me.' Steve said, 'You overestimate the value of this woman. Kill her, if it will please you, and save me the price of a bullet.'

'You fucker,' Lisa yelled, and, in an act of impulsive stupidity, threw the knife at Steve. It never reached its desired target, instead lodging itself in the Maitre, who'd made a dash for the door in the same instant.

It squealed and stumbled into Lisa, a real piggy squeal, and then tore the knife out. Lisa screamed as it raked its claws across the open wound on her scalp, and hooked them into her hair. Hoisting her to her feet, the Maitre held her parallel to the Agent and pressed the knife against her throat.

'You will wear every drop of her blood.' It hissed and began to carve.

Steve closed his eyes for a second, as the wave of warm blood splashed his face, but found himself confused by the bang and the sound of shattering glass that preceded it. He opened his eyes and saw Lisa trembling in a pool of that cyan blood, with the Maitre prone at her feet, a cavern in the back of its skull. Beyond the pair was a shattered window, the drapes slightly askew, and the face of Dr Henry O'Neill, with the Glock smouldering at the end of his arm.

Steve sniffed, then walked to the door and stuck his head outside.

'Sergeant Major, you and three men, will detain Dr O'Neill, he's behind the trailer, and the rest of you will return to base immediately.'

'Yes, sir!'

As the unit traipsed back to their trucks, three identical Victorias skidded into the lot, and eight Agents emerged, identically dressed in their black suits and trilbies, but not all wearing sunglasses. Steve hopped down out of the trailer as they approached, led by an athletic man, in his early thirties, with a tanned face and a shaved head.

'Steve.'

'Mike.'

'Where's the... oh,' All eight of the men peered past Steve into the trailer, 'It's dead.'

'Yes,' Steve nodded, and jerked his thumb at the beaten unconscious body of O'Neill as it was dragged past, 'He was hiding behind the trailer with a gun.'

'You didn't secure the perimeter?'

'I ordered it,' said Steve, catching the eye of the scowling boy with the broken nose, clearly peeved having been robbed of his chance for explosive revenge against his assailant.

'I'll call in for a clean-up.' One of them said, turning aside as the rest clambered up into the trailer.

As Steve stepped back inside onto the broken door, he saw his colleagues considering Tsai, who had managed to stop most of her bleeding with tea-towel bandages and now stood, fists clenched, and half-naked in front of the men.

'What's her status?' One of them asked.

'Human,' said Steve.

'Is she needed for interrogation?' Said another.

'Yes,' Mike said before Steve could open his mouth, and seized Lisa by the arm.

'No! Let me go!' She said as he pulled her through the group, and out of the trailer. Steve ambled behind her, as she was dragged across the lot towards the cars, grazing her bare feet on the large stones that littered the parking lot. She thought she saw some reluctance in his stride, maybe a touch of empathy in his otherwise neutral expression, but he did not intervene as she was dumped onto the ground next to O'Neill and zip-tied. She screamed into the dust and spotted three Agents dragging a blue tarpaulin towards Lot 7.

'Alien! Maitre!' she cried, 'Joe Kowalski is a Maitre!'

It was Steve himself who strode forward and kicked her unconscious. The graze made by his shoe was indistinguishable amongst all the other blemishes on her face — a tapestry of dirt and blood.

He looked at the Sergeant Major and the three men who'd apprehended O'Neill.

'If either of them dies on their way back to the base, bury them in the desert.'

Then, as he turned away, he saw the boy again, sitting in the front seat of the jeep.

'What is he still doing here?' Steve said, struggling to keep the irritation out of his voice. He wondered if the boy hadn't been messing around with his flashlight, he might have illuminated O'Neill sneaking round the trailer, and the Maitre might still be alive for interrogation. He had needed to find out what its business was on Earth.

'His Dad…' One of the soldiers said.

'I don't care who his Dad is,' said Steve, 'Take him away.'

'Yes, sir.'

As the Agent walked to his own car, the soldiers clambered on board the truck, and the radio began to crackle. 'Base to Unit 431, Report Unit 431, over.'

'This is Unit 431,' replied the boy, 'we've two suspects in custody, one seems pretty confused, keeps yelling 'Maitre', is that Mexican or something…?'

'Give me that,' said the Sergeant Major, snatching the radio.

CHAPTER TWENTY-TWO

T roni wafted his hand in front of a panel on the wall and coaxed out an array of blue symbols. Some of the symbols were not dissimilar from English, but most were jagged or curved in a manner, unlike anything Harold had ever seen. He decided that he should try to commit some to memory, as he never knew when he might need to recognise the language of the Greys again.

'We're Zetans, not Greys. Racist.' Troni said, without turning away from the symbols.

'Sorry… Zetans.'

'We call these signals holographics,' Nyn said, 'They're how we pilot the ship and handle communications.' He pointed at one that looked a little like a lobster. 'This one, for example, symbolises an incoming signal. Our system detects keywords, like 'Maitre', in certain areas of Earth, including Area 51, and we listen to them telepathically. That's what we did a moment ago, but we'll play this one for you.'

Troni spun the wiggling lobster on the end of his finger, and a human voice crackled through the ship.

'This is Unit 431, we've two suspects in custody, one seems pretty confused, keeps yelling 'Maitre', is that Mexican or something…?'

Harold was struck by sudden unease.

'Who were the two suspects? Was one of them called Lisa?'

'Did you hear any names?' Said Troni.

'No.' Harold said, 'But you might know something I don't.'

Troni glanced over his bony shoulder at him and tapped the side of his head.

'On this matter, you know as much as we do. On all others, we will always know something you don't.'

'There's another transmission,' Nyn said, reaching past Troni and scratching a YY symbol. 'A media broadcast.'

'Good morning, this is Claudia Thornton, you're watching CNN.'

'In the early hours of this morning military officials raided a trailer in the town of Rachel, Nevada, just hours after the disappearance of Professor Harold Dunn, a high-profile nuclear engineer who disappeared from nearby Area 51 after sharing a picture of an alleged alien craft online. We'll go straight to Tina Gower, who's live from the Lil A'le'inn. Tina?'

'Hello, Claudia, well the Lil A'le'inn was once again the location of extra-terrestrial controversy today, and with me, I have an eyewitness who's requested that she not be identified. Mystery Eyewitness, can you tell us what happened?'

'Yes, Tina, some friends and I were enjoying a quiet drink in the bar last night when these two people we know, Lisa and Joe, who work up at Area 51, came in. We have quite a few friends up there, you know, so we know more than you might think...' Harold recognised the voice of Stacey, the skinny Ufologist, 'anyway, they came in and started asking questions about a specific species of Alien.'

'I see. Then what happened?'

'Lisa came over all sick and Joe took her back to his trailer to sleep it off and then, next thing we know, one of the Men in Black, who are responsible for monitoring alien activity on Earth and shutting up eyewitnesses, burst in and had us all held at gunpoint. Then he went over to the trailer and started shooting.'

'Were any arrests made?'

'Yeah, they took her and some stranger, but they shot

Joe, Joe Kowalski.'

How do I know that name?

'What do you think prompted the raid?'

'I reckon they came to get an alien from one of the trailers, escaped from a lab at Area 51.'

'Did you see an alien?'

'No but why else?'

'Indeed.' Tina gave the camera a half glance, 'Which aliens did Mr Kowalski and his female companion... Lisa, was it... ask you about?'

'Maitre.' Stacey said, 'one of the most violent alien species in the universe, and she was shouting it as they hauled her away.'

'Lisa?' Harold said, recalling the Agents banging at the door seconds before he'd been abducted. What had happened to her?

'Send me back to Lisa, right now,' Harold said.

'We shall. I hope you're not too late,' said Nyn and nodded at Troni, who pulled four symbols out of the main mass - a horseshoe, a barrel, a number 8 and an 'LL' - all of which locked into a vertical line and flashed.

'Brace yourself,' said Nyn, as a light, flashed through the windows and the craft lurched, sending Harold stumbling across the room into the wall.

'You were warned,' said Troni, as Harold re-joined them rubbing his forehead.

Beyond the windows, the black and white canvas of space had been replaced by blue, mottled with wisps of grey. Earth.

'We suspect things are going to get quite busy up here, but if you need any help just post on the Storm Area 51 forum, and we'll assist where we can,' said Nyn.

'Assuming you believe in us now,' said Troni, and twisted an 'O' symbol.

Harold heard a familiar ringing noise, and the environment around him began to dissolve.

'Good fortune,' said a hazy outline of Nyn, and he felt the Zetan tuck something heavy inside his jacket pocket.

'Wait until you're at the other end to vomit,' said Troni.

Harold forced himself to vomit there, on the spot, as soon as he felt the grumble in his stomach, and heard a curse in some far-flung corner of his consciousness.

CHAPTER
TWENTY-THREE

L isa awoke in a blaze of light and found herself bound, gagged and tumbling out of a sack onto a concrete floor. The back of her head hit the floor with such force that she was almost knocked unconscious again.

'Now, now, Steve.' Came a baritone voice, some short way ahead of her, 'Where's your sense of foreplay?'

Her environment swam into focus, an underground hangar of some kind, with a roof of blinding light panels. Ten feet away stood Steve, talking to a squat, little Agent, with a mop of blonde hair and rosy red cheeks. Never had she encountered one like this guy. He looked like a schoolboy, in his Sunday best, on his way to church with his mother.

'She's all yours now, Kyle,' Steve said, walking over to the door, 'Kill her if you like, but first get her to tell you everything about her escape and what happened with the alien.'

'With the alien?' Kyle said.

'With the alien,' Steve said and slammed the metal door behind him.

A silence of three seconds endured, as Kyle stared far off into the distance, and then murmured. 'How interesting.'

He gestured to a steel chair in the middle of the room, 'Have a seat, Dr Tsai.'

Lisa remained where she was, still reeling from what Steve had said. He'd ordered her death, or at least declared his ambivalence regarding it. She'd trusted the Agent to save her from the Maitre, only for him to deliver her to whatever this boy-man was.

'Come now, let me help you,' he said, his voice very near to her, and she felt hands under her elbows lifting her, taking care to avoid the sack-hair grazes, and guiding her towards the chair. She slouched, and his smiling face appeared as he dropped into a squat.

'There, all ok now, huh?'

She looked at him. Was this the Good Cop to Steve's Bad Cop?

'Look at that face, all that beauty besmirched by the aggression of others,' Kyle said, reaching out and running a cold finger down her cheek, 'Where's the romance there?'

She glanced into his blue eyes and found no good in them.

He rose and moved past her so she was forced to turn the chair to watch him, if only for some sensation of control. Her eyes followed him to a bright orange beanbag, where he collapsed in a great rush of air and began to read a book. She strained her eyes but was unable to read the title in the glare of the lights. He sniffed and flicked the page with exuberance, then spotted her squinting at him.

'Do you think it's bright in here?' He said.

She nodded, and he produced a small remote from his pocket. The lights dimmed.

'Better?' He said.

She nodded again.

He hopped off the beanbag, like the toad off the lily pad, and hurried over to her.

She yelped as he tore the electrical tape from her mouth.

'Oh, I'm so sorry.'

She licked her lips and tasted blood.

'Are you ok? Is that better?'

She nodded.

'Darling, if all you're gonna do is nod, then this isn't gonna be the stimulating conversation I'd hoped for.'

'Sorry,' she said, 'It's better.'

'Would you like a drink? '

She shook her head.

'You're being rude again,' he said waggling his finger in front of her face.

'Sorry,' She said, 'No thank you.'

He smiled and then retreated to his bean bag. He held up the book. 'You read this?' He looked at the cover, '*The Lies of Locke Lamora*, by Scott Lynch.'

She shook her head, and upon seeing his displeasure, said 'No, I haven't.'

'It's a wonderful tale about a young scallywag, in this alternate, medieval reality, who makes a success of himself through deception. Through pretending to be what he isn't. But this crook, this liar, has just one ounce of morality, which is his bond with those he loves — people with whom he shares a common interest.'

He paused as though searching for the appropriate words.

'Do you ever tell lies, Dr Tsai?'

'No, I don't,' she said, which in itself was a lie, but she was hardly going to say yes, was she?

'Good, good.'

From his pocket, he took a small, bright orange, twin belled alarm clock, twisted the steel dial on the back. He placed it on the concrete floor beside him, where it began to tick.

'Three minutes,' he said, sitting down and picking up his book again.

'Three minutes until what?'

'Three minutes until I have to go to work,' he said, without looking up from the page, 'Unless you want to make things easy?'

'How do you mean?'

'There's no need for me to explain what I mean. From the context of our situation it should be somewhat obvious, and if it isn't, it doesn't matter, as all will become clear in…' He glanced at the clock, 'two minutes and twelve seconds.'

'What?'

'Hush now,' he said, 'Locke and I are on an adventure here.'

'I'll tell you what you want to know.'

His eyes found her again.

'Darling, I don't want to know anything, it's my employers who do… and dear Agent Steve, of course.'

'I'll tell you anything.'

He sighed, licked his finger, and folded the corner of the page inwards to mark his place. Then he placed down the book, and picked up the clock, pinching the dial to stop the ticking.

'Well, Dr Tsai, if you insist on distracting me from my book I suggest you keep up this lifelong tradition of honesty because I shan't find your lies nearly as entertaining as Locke's, I assure you.'

'You know about everything before the abduction?' Lisa said, sitting up in the chair a little.

She wondered how many more interrogations of this kind she was destined to endure.

'Of course.'

'Well, after the Agent put me in my room, I was only there a while and then Joe… who I thought was Joe… appeared and took me away.'

He tutted.

'An incomplete analysis.' He said, and placed the clock back on the floor where it resumed ticking.

'He also knocked out the Agent at the door — Agent John.'

'He killed Agent John,' Kyle corrected. 'What was the toxin he used? How did he administer it?'

'He poured it on a rag. I don't know exactly what it was.'

The clock rang shrilly and Kyle reached down to silence it.

'Guests, please would you join us?' He said, and the door opened, and three squealing sacks were thrown into the room. From these sacks emerged Gordon and Stacey, the Ufologists, and her friend, Dr Jasper Hennimore, mostly unmolested from the look of him.

Both Stacey and Gordon scrambled back over to the steel door as it slammed shut and pounded upon it, begging for their freedom, while Jasper approached Agent Kyle.

'What is the meaning of this?' He bellowed, then

softened upon seeing Lisa's condition, 'Oh my gosh, Lisa, your face. Who…?'

He swung round in anger as Kyle stood sharply, and was again struck by a sudden change of emotion, upon seeing the claw hammer in the Agent's hand.

'It's me you want.' Lisa said as Jasper retreated towards the hollering Ufologists, and Kyle dogged his footsteps, 'They're not involved. They haven't done anything.'

'I like reading.' Kyle said as Jasper backed up against the wall, 'but it's not my only hobby.'

Lisa spotted that Kyle's tongue was flickering, as he raised the hammer and swung it through the air.

The head of the hammer missed Jasper and crashed into Stacey's skull, releasing a spray of blood across the white wall. Kyle smiled as the blood ran down his face, and Stacey collapsed gurgling in Gordon's arms.

'You bastard,' yelled Gordon as Stacey convulsed and gibbered, eyes invisible behind lenses of blood. But the Agent seemed unperturbed by the insult, made his way back to his beanbag, and reset the clock.

'Joe told me the toxin put them to sleep, that's all!' Lisa said, 'A toxin of his own creation, he called it!'

'You really didn't know he was killing people?' Kyle murmured from behind his book.

'No,' she said.

He sighed, put down his book, and twisted the dial on the back of the clock so that the alarm sounded prematurely.

'I'm telling you the truth,' she said, as Kyle rose again.

'I know, I know.' he said and tossed Jasper the hammer and a polythene bag of nails from his pocket.

'Dr Hennimore, in that locker over in the corner you shall find a canvas. I should like it hanging on the wall, please.'

Jasper looked ever so briefly taken aback, and then hastened over to the orange locker. He shared a look with Lisa as he passed — a look that said he too understood that they'd have to play the psychopath's games if they stood any chance of survival. This gave Lisa a little hope.

Kyle was considering the Ufologists. As Gordon opened his mouth to say something, he kicked him in it, separating him for Stacey.

'Get up,' said Kyle, but Gordon continued to lay groaning, holding his face and staring at Stacey who twitched only slightly now.

'Get up,' repeated Kyle, lifting the man, three times his size, with ease, and shoving him over towards Lisa. His X-File t-shirt was a mess of snot and blood.

'Jumping jacks,' Kyle said.

'What?'

Kyle gave Gordon a slap with the back of his hand, which almost sent the man down again.

'Jumping jacks, now. Until I tell you to stop.'

With a whimper the big man began heaving his arms up and down and his legs apart, still looking back over his shoulder at Stacey, who'd since stopped moving.

Jasper had located the canvas – a picture of a satsuma on a grey background –but found the nails bounced back out of the wall when he hit them.

'For goodness sake,' said Kyle, flapping his arms with frustration and plodding over to him. He found a nail gun inside the locker and plugged it into a socket.

'I saw that — it says it's broken,' Jasper said, pointing to a white sticker on the handle.

Kyle chuckled, pressed the whirring nail gun into Jasper's gut and fired twice.

'No!' Lisa said, as Jasper fell to the ground, and writhed in the growing ocean of blood, seeping across the white tiles.

'Seems to be working fine to me,' Kyle said, picking up the canvas, and nailing it to the wall.

He stared at it in admiration, stains and all.

'Really more of a blood orange now, isn't it?' He said, and chuckled his way past wheezy Gordon, with his flapping bingo wings and armpit stains, and plonked himself back on the beanbag.

'Now, Dr Tsai, you were claiming that you weren't aware you were on a killing spree,' Kyle said, 'Continue.'

'We took O'Neill from his room at gunpoint... Agent John's gun... we needed O'Neill because he'd hypnotised me and interrogated me earlier, and we wanted to know what he'd found out.'

'I've heard the tape.' He said, 'Most intriguing.'

'We hid on his back seat under a rug and had him drive us off the base... to Rachel.'

'Oh, it's so simple,' said Kyle. 'So lovely.'

'In Rachel, there lives this guy, Morgan Andrews. I'd heard him claim previously that he used to work in Area 51 and that he'd seen inside Hangar 18. We had O'Neill hypnotise him, and he claimed to have been abducted by aliens...during which time he heard his abductors mention an evil race called The Maitre.'

'Oh yes, Morgan and I are good friends,' Kyle said, smiling as though recalling a fond memory. It dawned on Lisa that it had been him, who'd made Andrews the way he was.

Was madness the fate that awaited her too?

Gordon collapsed suddenly onto his hands and knees, his breaths coming raggedly.

'Then we went to the bar in Rachel, the Lil A'le'inn, to see if the Ufologists knew anything,' Lisa said, as Kyle took out his Glock and pointed it at Gordon's head, 'They told us about the Maitre, but then I started to get weird.'

'Were you drunk?'

'I had only had one drink. Kowalski poisoned me, but I didn't know at that point. I let him lead me back to his trailer and then he started to do things to me.'

She shivered, partly because of the chill in the hangar, partly because of the memory.

'He started to touch me, kiss me, tell me he'd always wanted me, and then he transformed. He became one of those Maitre.'

Kyle sat up, attention pricked for the first time since they'd been introduced.

'It said they were going to conquer the Earth but that it was going to keep me as a toy. Then Agent Steve kicked the door in and O'Neill shot it.'

'How are they going to conquer the Earth?'

'He didn't say.'

Kyle stared at her for a second and then exhaled, slumping and rubbing his eyes as though the moment had exhausted him. Then he remembered Gordon and shot him in the face.

'No! Fuck! I told you everything!'

Kyle shrugged, and walked over to Jasper who was hissing through his teeth, slowly pulling one of the nails out of his stomach.

'You've told me everything, Dr Tsai?' Kyle said.

'Yes,' she said, 'Please.'

He pressed the gun to her friend's forehead. 'It's still not enough.'

'You… are no different… to these monsters, you're hunting,' said Jasper, glaring up at the blonde man.

'Oh, Dr Hennimore, I'm far worse,' said Kyle, and blew his brains out.

Lisa screamed as the gunshot echoed around the room; pristine when she'd entered, now a bloody hell.

As it died in her throat, she raised her chin to face her own inevitable death, but saw that Kyle had moved to the door. It was open, and Steve was standing there.

Standing next to the conversing Agents was O'Neill. He had bruises to suggest he'd endured some rough stuff himself, though nothing compared to Lisa's suffering. He caught her eye in a manner that conveyed his sympathy.

'I'm done,' said Kyle, slapping a tape recorder into Steve's hand, 'It's all on there. She didn't have anything to do with the killing of Agent John. She thought the poison was a sleep toxin. The Maitre intended to take her as a slave and alluded to a plan for worldwide domination but did not disclose how they intended to do so.'

Steve looked at Lisa. 'Are you sure she's telling the truth?'

'I assure you, I was thorough.' Kyle said, 'I can spare another hour tomorrow morning if you're still in doubt, but I'm needed up in Washington in the afternoon. Tricky group of extremists are pleading the fifth.'

'Shouldn't worry,' Steve said, glancing at the gore around the room, 'She doesn't look particularly spoiled herself, but I can see you made good use of the leverage.'

'I thought I'd leave her mostly unmolested should you want her for anything else.'

Steve sniffed and drew his gun. 'I'd say the risk she poses to us now outweighs the value of her continued existence.'

'I thought you might say something like that,' Kyle said and then began to climb the stairs. 'Goodbye, darling!'

Steve walked over to Lisa and raised his gun. 'Goodbye, Dr Tsai.'

She closed her eyes, waiting for the gunshot, the last thing she'd ever hear, but instead heard a strangely familiar sound — one of grinding metal. She blinked a few times and there, becoming more solid, was a figure between her and Steve.

'Harold?' She said and slipped over towards the Brit, who caught her.

Steve watched their embrace, thin-lipped.

'We've been looking for you, Professor Dunn,' He said, 'Seems I might need Agent Kyle back here tomorrow after all.'

'No,' said Lisa, but Steve was already reopening the door.

Harold glanced at the corpses around the room, cleared his throat, and took some steps away from Lisa.

'If you mean to hurt Dr Tsai or I, I shall make a signal and have both of us removed the same way I entered. Try explaining that one to your superiors.'

Steve sniffed, the tongue came out, and he closed the door.

Harold offered Lisa the briefest smile of reassurance, then found the gun back in his face.

'Alternatively I could just shoot you.' Steve said, 'What's to stop from me doing that?'

Harold blinked a few times. 'You'd be single-handedly dooming the Earth.'

Lisa watched the two men battle, each wrestling to appear detached, while tumultuously involved in reality. Harold's eyes kept blinking, Steve's tongue kept flickering.

'I know about the Maitre. I know what they're planning. I know how we can take them down.'

'I assume Dr Tsai's life is the price of your cooperation?'

'Obviously.'

A single shudder ran through Steve's body, so brief that Lisa thought she might have imagined it, and then he tucked his gun away inside his jacket.

Lisa exhaled, escaping another brush with death brought

only brief reinvigoration, and exhaustion found her. There was also the matter of Harold, she'd hugged the bastard who'd dragged her into this mess. What did that mean?

'We both need to rest now,' said Harold.

'We all still have much to discuss, I think,' said Steve.

'We do,' said Harold, 'But not now, I need to sleep.

Both men stared at one another.

'One signal,' said Harold, and pointed up to the ceiling.

Steve grunted.

'Hold out a hand, both of you.' he said, and they obliged. Both felt the impact of the something he injected into their palms, and the sting of pain that followed. Harold stared at the globule of blood.

'Some kind of tracer?' Harold said.

'Yes,' said Steve, 'But it is also a remote poison capsule meaning I can kill you whenever I like.'

'How nice for you,' said Lisa.

'Three hours then you come to my office. Room 122. That's noon.'

'Fine,' said, Harold.

'You'll find some of your stuff in a bag at the top of the stairs. You've saved me the job of burning it, I suppose.' Steve said, 'And make sure Dr Tsai takes a shower if you insist on bringing her with you, I don't want blood all over my office.' Then he left them, stomping away up the stairs.

It took Lisa quite some room to cross the room, and by the time they'd reached the stairs, Steve had vanished.

Atop the stairs was a door, beyond which was an astonishing sight. They found a dozen or so Agents, some of them drinking coffee and conversing, sitting in cushy armchairs, tapping away on laptops, some just leaning against walls doing nothing in particular. Lisa found the normality of it all terrible, particularly as she faced it in her underwear — though the group barely afforded the pair a second glance.

Harold yanked a lone blue duffel bag towards them, and they retreated back into the stairwell. It was indeed her stuff, although what could be broken was broken. She changed into a sports jacket, jumper, jeans, and trainers, while he stood guard with the bag.

'Ready?' He said.

'Yes, ready,' she said.

They crossed to the door on the other side of the room without another word. Inside the bag, she found her ID, but when she scanned it, the bulb flared red, and the door didn't open.

An Agent putting coins in the soda machine, leant past them and swiped his own, and the bulb flared green, and the door slid open.

'Thanks,' Harold said, and the Agent responded with an exaggerated sneeze.

'Don't let your girlfriend offer me a tissue,' he said, 'I don't want to end up like Agent John.'

'I didn't...' Lisa said, feeling an immediate swell of indignation at the accusation, but the Agent had already moved away with his beverage. Harold tried to steer her through the door, but she shook him off and strode out herself. The windowless panel slid home behind them; unmarked and inconspicuous.

'What was all that about Agent John?' He said.

She shook her head.

'Ok, look do you need to see a Doctor? I mean a real Doctor? Is there a medical office?'

'Probably,' she said and turned the corner, 'it's this way.'

They shuffled through the corridors, and staff glided by, people she'd worked with, eaten with, drank with, for years. They all gave her same look and then carried on their respective ways without a word.

She experienced more of the same in the Medical Office. The doctor didn't ask how she'd come by the injuries and seemed to have most of the painkillers and bandages she required to hand, as though he'd been expecting her.

'A lot of patients to see,' he said as he ushered her back outside five minutes later. Harold sat outside in the waiting room, where one other person sat as far away from him as possible, engrossed in an upside-down copy of the New York Times.

Her ID wouldn't unlock her room either, so they located Harold's in the bottom of the bag, and managed to gain entry to his. Harold looked around the room as Lisa climbed straight into bed. He was perturbed by how pristine the room was, as though it had never been slept in, though more so by the completed card tower on the dresser. The sight of his cards in someone else's tower sickened him, and he beat them off the table into the bin.

Lisa listened to the commotion but did not roll over until she heard a tick, tick, tick…

'Steve said noon, didn't he?' Harold said, fiddling with a plastic orange clock, 'I just thought I'd set an alarm.'

'Is that yours?' She said.

'Nope,' he said, 'Never seen it before.'

'Then do me a favour and throw it out of the window.'

CHAPTER
TWENTY-FOUR

W hen Lisa awoke, she did so with reluctance. All that had happened was escapable through sleep, but already she knew it was too late. Her brain had spluttered into action, and there was no stopping it. Her head ached, her wounds stung, and worst of all, as she opened her eyes, she found Harold staring at her.

'So what happened to you?' He said.

Just like that, the inevitable moment had arrived, and although she felt a lust to hear everything he had to tell her, she harboured a reluctance to tell him anything of her own ordeal. Glancing over her initial interrogation under hypnosis, she began with her escape with Kowalski.

'Where is he now?' asked Harold, 'Was he one of those in that cellar I found you in?'

She shook her head and told him about the transformation.

'A Maitre?' Harold said, eyes widening, 'What did he do to you?'

'Nothing much,' she said, 'The worst came after O'Neill and Agent Steve showed up.'

'O'Neill?'

'He shot the Maitre.'

'I thought he was tied up?'

'We didn't do a very good job of it apparently. I think Kowalski was more concerned with getting me on my own.'

'Seems a pretty longwinded method for a kidnap,' said Harold, frowning in a know-it-all way.

'He couldn't rouse my suspicions until he'd disarmed me. I had Agent's John's gun most of the time, until the bar, that's when he saw an opportunity to drug my drink and then take it. I suppose he must've dropped it when he was carrying me back to his trailer and O'Neill must have found it.'

'Yeah, but after that, I would've thought Kow… I mean, the Maitre, would've wanted to get you out of Nevada, as quickly as possible. What was even the point in taking you back to his trailer?'

'I don't know,' she said, but her expression revealed much of what Harold suspected, and he didn't press the subject further.

'So Steve and O'Neill brought you and the Maitre's body back here? How did you come to be in that basement with all those dead people?'

'I was interrogated by an Agent I've never seen before.'

Harold shook his head, 'Did he torture you?'

'I wish he had,' she said, feeling tightness in her oesophagus, 'He hurt my friend Jasper… and those Ufologists we met, they've been on the news, he hurt them too. He killed them all. It was horrible.'

Harold almost put his arm around her and then chose to scratch his head instead, watching the sand swirl outside the window.

'What did you tell him?'

'What the Maitre said, that they'd force the human race to destroy itself and then take over the Earth.'

'They're mobilising.' Harold said, 'We might have less time than the Zetans thought.'

'The who?'

He told her about waking up on the spacecraft and having his DNA extracted, and about the aliens named Troni and Nyn, who sought to prove the Maitre were invading planets and, as a by-product it seemed to Lisa, save humanity from extinction.

'But what do they expect you to do?'

'Apparently I'm some international UFO authority now,' he said, 'The Zetans think the Russians are getting ready to fire their Satan missile and if they're going to listen to anyone it's me.'

Lisa frowned. 'Why can't they just come down and warn them themselves.'

'It's against some kind of space law. Extra-terrestrials aren't allowed to visit Earth, and there's no proof the Maitre are on Earth... not until now.'

The realisation struck him.

'We need to get to a computer. I need to tell the Zetans that we have a Maitre corpse, it may serve as sufficient evidence of their invasion.'

Both took the time to wash before they dressed, then hurried to the door, only to find an Agent on the other side, his fist held aloft as though he were about to knock. He smiled with amusement, a display of emotion Harold had seen in none of the other Agents.

'Dr Tsai, I didn't leave my clock in here did I?' He said.

Lisa took a step away from the door. 'That's who killed them. That's Agent Kyle.'

Harold looked from her to the cheery little man. 'What the hell do you want?'

'Running off somewhere?' He said.

'Steve said he'd kill us remotely if we ran.'

'Well, yes, if I don't catch you first. They usually offer me the option of a six-hour chase, and what I catch I get to keep.'

He winked at Lisa, and Harold stepped sideways to obscure his gaze. The Agent looked him up and down with blue eyes that had lost their charm, and now suggested violence; sudden, and unrelenting.

'We're going to look for a computer.'

'Nonsense,' he said, 'You've an appointment with Steve you're very late for. He's quite cross, you know? Come now.'

Harold looked around at Lisa, who'd composed herself and shrugged.

As Kyle lead them to Steve's office he chattered incessantly.

'And if you run and I catch you. I get to keep you in my workshop at home. It's quite a place, and a couple of spaces recently opened up for two subjects' eager to help me practice my art. Hourly experiences, minute-by-minute agony, and perpetual fear of the imminent suffering to come. Lovely.'

'I thought you had to be in Washington,' Lisa said, knocking him off his tangent.

'Efficiency, darling,' he said, 'Had them talking within the hour... and I did it online. Very efficient. Of course, I had someone there to assist.'

He came to a stop outside Room 122 and pressed a buzzer. There came the sound of an electronic lock disengaging, and Kyle opened the door for them.

'There will always be room for you both in my home from Hell,' he whispered as they passed, and then closed the door behind them.

'Well, he's not creepy at all,' Harold said, and then considered Steve in his office. The Agent sat behind a walnut desk, a bookcase behind him, and six monitors in front of him. His fingers were blurred as they danced over a long keyboard, where the letter keys were duplicated six times over. Harold realised he was typing several documents simultaneously.

After a minute or so, Steve's fingers danced to a stop, and his eyes found them.

'Take a seat if you like,' He said gesturing towards the two leather chairs in front of his desk, 'Though you're both fully refreshed by now, surely?'

They both ignored the jibe and watched him attach a camera to the top of a tripod — 'So, Professor Dunn,' He said, 'You claim you were abducted by aliens?'

Harold ran through his meeting with Troni and Nyn and the mission they'd tasked him with, pausing here and there to frown at Steve's inflexions and occasional bursts of typing.

'Maitre... Maitre....' Steve said, 'It's a word I keep hearing. What's a Maitre?'

'It's a type of parasitic alien who want to take over the Earth.'

'You know what a bloody Maitre is.' Lisa said, 'You recovered the body of the one Dr O'Neil shot. Kowalski.'

'And if you'd just let us use a PC for two seconds, I can send a message to the Zetans, and we won't even need to go to Russia or any of it. It'll be proof the Maitre are on Earth.'

Steve interlocked his fingers and closed his eyes as though thinking.

'Well?' Harold said.

'I'd imagine,' He said, reopening his eyes, 'That one dead Maitre would be insufficient proof of invasion for something like your Universal Governance or whatever you called it.'

'Well then… if that's the case, then maybe I do still need to go to Moscow, and your Agency needs to help me. The Zetans told me you know plenty about ETs, so I don't know why you're pretending you don't.'

Steve's tongue flickered. 'These Greys… '

'They don't like to be called that!'

Steve shrugged, '… are a delusion of yours. These Maitre too.'

He sat back in his chair. 'What happened, was that Dr Kowalski and Dr Hennimore went on a sabbatical. Dr Tsai was meant to go too, but unfortunately, since meeting you, she's contracted your weakness for alcohol and taken complete leave of her senses. Tell me, this alien ship of yours, the picture that's turned you into a UFO celebrity, did it take long to create?'

Harold stared at the man in disbelief.

'We know what you're trying to do.' Lisa said, 'But it won't work. How do you explain Harold appearing in that cellar you tortured me in?'

'What cellar?'

Harold stood up.

'You know, even though the Zetans aren't allowed to land they've made hundreds of abductions over the years?'

Steve remained unmoved.

'And during those years they've acquired certain souvenirs, bottles of water, clothing… guns.' From his jacket pocket, he pulled a pistol and jammed it against his own head, 'Like this 45. for example.'

'Harold, what the hell are you doing?' Lisa said, standing up as well.

'If you're just gonna fuck us around, Steve, I might as well concede defeat and blow my fucking brains out.'

Steve sniffed. 'What have I to gain from stopping you?'

'As I said, without me, the Earth is doomed. I'm the only one who knows how to force the Maitre to reveal their true identities, and that's why I'm the only one who can convince the Russian PM that he has alien hostiles amongst his main staff.'

'How interesting,' said Steve, 'although, what's to stop me booking you in for another session with Kyle tomorrow morning and getting the information that way? I doubt he'll need the full hour.'

'I told you, one signal…'

'But I thought you said you require a computer to send that signal?' Steve said.

Shit, thought Harold for a second, but his natural ability to lie, one that had got him out of many scrapes with women over the years, kicked in with the adrenaline.

'I need a computer to provide a detailed message, but the Zetans planted a chip in me that sends them an alert if I'm under stress. They'll know if you hurt me.'

'You don't sound too sure, Professor Dunn.'

'I am sure,' said Harold, in what he hoped was a convincing voice.

Steve licked his lips, and then let the tension drain out through his nose. 'Put the gun down. We'll get you into Moscow, but you're not going near a computer.'

Harold opened his mouth to argue, but Steve held up his finger.

'You might still be a liar. You might be trying to leak something online. You've heard my offer, so either take it or pull that trigger. That's all there is.'

Harold lowered the gun. 'I want to see it through, but first, I need to know what a Maitre looks like.'

'That can be arranged,' Steve said, 'Now wait outside — I need to make a call.'

He dialled as they made their exit, but waited until the door had closed before he punched in the last number.

'Bartonville Fruit and Veg, Illinois, can I place an order for you?'

'78383, Steve, 290391.'

'One moment, please, sir.'

He listened to the static until it was broken.

'Steve?'

'We need to go to Code Amber.'

There was an intake of breath.

'You're sure they're already here?'

'Dunn claims they've infiltrated the Russian government and that they're influencing Reznikov towards pushing the button.'

'I know what they're doing,' Said Majestic 1, 'They're trying to force the Earth into nuclear annihilation so they can take it.'

'Yes, sir. Dunn claims he knows how to uncloak the Maitre, so he's the only one who can sway Reznikov.'

'Kyle has been unable to extract this knowledge?'

'Dunn claims his allies have ways of sensing his distress and will rescue him.'

'Do you believe him?'

'No,' said Steve, 'But I didn't want to risk it.'

'Very well. Bring him here.'

'Yes, sir.'

'Steve. Why didn't his allies move him directly to Russia? Why drop him back in Area 51?'

'I think he came for Doctor Tsai, sir, the two have grown close.'

'Then why not simply abduct them both?' asked Majestic 1, and Steve realised it was a test.

The thought had been niggling him, but he had been unable to find the answer, and now he was going to have to admit that...

'I don't know, sir.'

Majestic 1 grunted.

'There's been an explosion of UFO sightings over Russia recently — flying saucers.'

'Oh,' said Steve, searching on his computers, 'Apologies, sir, I've been busy with Tsai and Dunn.'

'The skies around Russia are being monitored, and Dunn's allies probably thought it safer that he make the journey by Earth technology rather than theirs. Otherwise, it's unlikely they'd be unable to get safely in range.'

'Yes, sir.'

'Be cautious, Steve. Inside Russia or out. The Hostiles will have heard Dunn's story, and will be looking for him.'

'I'll take a weapon,' he said, and the line went dead.

Steve hung up and dialled the number for Agent HQ.

'Clearance?' was the greeting.

'78383, Steve 290391.'

'Go ahead, Steve.'

'I need someone to load the Rep9 into my car,' he said, 'And put Doctor Tsai and Professor Dunn on the clearance list for Hangar 18. We're going to see it.'

CHAPTER TWENTY-FIVE

Harold wiped the sand from his eyes, as they waited outside Hangar 18 for Steve to find the right ID. Curiosity had substituted much of the apprehension he'd felt on his last visit, or at least suppressed it for the time being. His hand found something sharp and flat in his pocket.

'Allow me,' he said, and swiped the stolen ID through the reader, grinning in spite of himself.

Steve's jaw clenched, and he and Lisa smiled at one another.

They followed him through the door and down the spiral stairs, to the Perspex cabin below, where a black soldier stood rigidly, a pistol visible at his belt.

'Clearance,' he rumbled, in an African accent.

Steve passed his ID through the hole, and the guard scrutinised it before passing it back.

'Very good,' he said, 'And you Sir? Madam?'

'They're visitors.' Steve said, 'Harold Dunn and Lisa Tsai. Check the system. They're on there.'

The guard did so and then busied himself printing temporary passes and slipping them into plastic holders on lanyards.

'Where's the book-worm?' Harold asked, but was ignored.

They moved down the hall to the elevator, where Steve accessed the retinal scanner. The doors obediently opened.

'How did you get past the retinal scanner before?' Steve asked as they entered. The doors closed. Harold's stomach threated to try and escape as the elevator began its rapid decent.

Harold could think of no reason for not telling him the truth. Besides it might gain them a bit of favor.

'I got lucky. As I reached the elevator, the doors opened and some scientists got out. I merely acted like I was irritated for having to way and marched in. Same thing happened when I reached the bottom.'

Steve grunted. 'We'll have to address that security lapse.' By the time he finished his sentence, the elevator had reached its destination and the doors reopened.

They followed Steve down the sloping corridor, towards the growing sound of buzzing speakers, which sparked curiosity in Lisa.

'Sounds like Woodstock in there.'

'Do you remember my photo?' Harold said as Steve ran his ID through the reader.

'You mean that's the…' she said but was cut short by the opening of the doors.

Beyond them was an ocean of scientists, swirling around a triangular cotton tepee. Those who emerged from the tee-pee wore blue uniforms to distinguish them from the other scientists in white. Over to their left, was the alien spacecraft — the source of the buzzing.

'I can't believe it,' she said and then noticed Harold frowning in her periphery.

'I mean, of course, I believed you, Harold. I just can't believe I've worked here all this time and this… this was down here the whole time.'

'You should see what it's like inside one of those,' Harold said.

Lisa shook her head, and then they both hurried to catch up with Steve, expecting the crush to part momentarily for him before closing again forever, but it didn't, and the Agent was forced to do just as much elbowing as they were.

These scientists are the real McCoy — the alien-dissecting, saucer-flying, crème del a crème of the base, Lisa thought, they're irreplaceable to the point of immunity from the Agents, and they know it.

Lisa cringed at the memory of her posturing in front of the nerds at the Lil Al'le'inn, then depression leaked in at the corners as she remembered Stacey and Gordon, and then Jasper by association.

'It's amazing,' she said to Harold over the din, pointing at the craft in an effort to distract herself.

'It's controlled by these projections they call holographics,' Harold remarked. 'They move them with their fingers, and they control flight, communications…'

'Are you two coming?' Steve said, from the tepee entrance.

'Yes… coming.' Harold said, and pulled her out of the crush by her hand.

It wasn't difficult to slide her fingers back out of Harold's sweaty palm.

'I don't know why, but even after my encounter with an extra-terrestrial, this makes it all real, you know? That craft over there has been to other galaxies and landed on other planets. It represents the science of a species far more advanced than our own.'

'Hmm,' Harold said, and he as looked down, wiping his hand dry on his trouser leg, and, cursing his excessive perspiration once again, Steve grabbed Lisa by the arm and whispered in her ear.

'It is a miracle you're still alive, Dr Tsai. A miracle that might be undone should you have any recollection of what you see down here.'

'Hey,' Harold said as Steve shoved her into the tee-pee.

'Just get on with it,' he said and held up the flap for Harold.

Harold glared at him as he passed, but Lisa understood the tenuousness of her existence. It seemed unwise to push Steve regardless of whatever leverage they thought they had. The Agent would already be plotting a way to get the ball back into his court.

Inside, the Maitre — Kowalski — looked even more

grotesque than she remembered.

Its corpse lay long and slimy, with lidded eyes, and pale skin, atop a padded grey operating table. The scientists wriggled around like maggots, though some of them had gathered, crouched behind a hole in the headrest so that they could study the bullet wound.

'Give us the room.' Steve bellowed over the hubbub, holding up his pass, which drew laughs from those who stopped what they were doing long enough to acknowledge him.

Steve took out his gun and pointed it at the crowd, which got their attention, and they parted to let two security guards stalk forward from the rear, their M16 Assault Rifles raised.

Harold and Lisa moved in behind Steve so that he would take the wealth of any bullets fired.

'Stand down,' Steve said.

Both soldiers laughed, and as all the scientists flocked from the tent, causing pandemonium outside, the taller of the two lowered his gun a little and slouched towards them.

Lisa noted that he was about seven foot and no stranger to the gym, but not remotely attractive, and his posture suggested he was just as arrogant as ninety percent of the other security guards at Area 51. Ninety percent of the scientists were arrogant too but in an intellectual kind of way.

He came to a halt in front of Steve and considered him down his nose, with his head lolling to one side.

Harold suspected the giant had decided at a very young age that he'd little use for intelligence when violence could get him whatever he wanted, and he was fascinated to see how Steve would handle such a man. Despite their deductions, both were astounded by what the man said to Steve.

'Who the fuck do you think you are, little man?'

Their mouths fell open, but Steve did not flinch.

'I'm Agent Steve.'

'And?'

'All three of us have clearance to have this tent to ourselves.'

The smaller guard, still about 6'7, removed an iPad from the satchel at his belt and began scrolling on it.

The giant sneered. 'What if I don't give a shit about your

clearance?'

'Then I'll kill you,' Steve said. He delivered the line in a deadpan tone that made the giant's size and strength seem irrelevant.

The brute's veneer slipped, and he lifted the barrel of his rifle until it was an inch from Steve's face. 'You think? You think you'd kill me?'

'If I kill you, nothing happens. If you kill me, my Agency kills all your colleagues, they torture your family, and the police find child pornography on your computer. After 12 months you're found raped to death in your cell.'

All the confidence was leaking out of the guard, his skin was almost as pale as the dead Maitre's. 'That the protocol?'

'That's the protocol.'

'Come on,' said the smaller guard, putting the iPad away, 'they've got clearance.'

Steve watched them leave, his tongue flickering between his lips, and did not react when the giant flipped him the finger before disappearing. He simply turned back to Lisa and Harold and gestured, 'Well, there it is.'

Lisa hung back as Harold approached the operating table. She felt she'd seen enough Maitre for a lifetime, so instead, she scanned the room for the source of a clicking noise. Was it some medical instrument? Perhaps it was the deterioration of the Maitre corpse? Perhaps it was merely her own ears popping.

'A Maitre,' Harold said, and then took his phone out of his pocket.

'What are you doing?' Said Steve.

'I have no signal,' Harold said, 'but I can still take a picture.'

'Stop,' Steve said pistol pointed at Harold.

'You can't shoot me Steve,' Harold said, and then the gunshot rang out, clearing the remaining scientists from the hangar outside.

Lisa added her scream to the others and watched Steve seize the M16, poking between the flaps of the tent, and yank the giant back inside. Both of the men clattered into Lisa, who stumbled past Harold, and landed on something slimy.

Harold stared at the smouldering wreckage of the phone in his hand, a 5 mm wide hole in the middle of the screen, and then became aware of the blaring of medical monitors. There was the back of a large head in front of him, pale blue with an angry red maw in the centre.

The Maitre wasn't dead. It had some kind of regenerative capability. It instantly sprung from the table and grabbed Lisa, then started dragging her kicking and screaming across the tent towards the entrance, where Steve and the guard continued to pummel one another.

The second guard rushed back into the tent, with confusion all over his face.

'Callum, what the fuck are you do…'

The rifle fired, in response to a hard tug from Steve, and the guard was thrown back the way he'd come.

Steve landed a headbutt to the giant's face, which changed with a sudden squelch into that of a Maitre, and the rifle was thrown free into the air.

'Hey, fucker!' Harold said as he caught it, and swung round to aim at Lisa's captor. His broken phone hit the tiles. He compressed the trigger.

He fired until the gun began to click. The tent had long since collapsed inwards, with him inside. He made his way out and tossed the weapon away, his whole body still rattling. Steve was limping across the empty hangar towards the Zetan craft, firing one shot after another.

Lisa and the Maitre were nowhere to be seen.

CHAPTER
TWENTY-SIX

Lisa was aboard the craft and knew she was seconds away from being kidnapped again. This time there'd likely be no rescue. She was disorientated, an old wound on her head had been reopened, and she felt herself fading as she struggled to stand upright in the shuddering craft.

Kowalski, whose real name sounded something like Kaggap, was wrenching holographics left and right, causing most of them to flash red and buzz, but do little else.

'Your brain still full of shrapnel? Hurry up,' said his associate, whom he called Ratigs, and was so massive in his Maitre form that he was unable to sit down in the Zetan chair, so was hugging the back of it instead.

'One, I've never flown a Grey craft before, Two, I've just recovered from a headshot, Three, your bitching isn't helping, Four, I'm trying, I'm trying…'

'Five, there might be more Agents coming. So try harder.'

Three holographics turned green, and both Maitre howled with triumph. Then the whole craft tilted back on its axis and lurched upwards with a metallic whir.

Kaggap/Kowalski turned around and grinned at Lisa.

'I told you I'd get you, you little bitch.'

CHAPTER
TWENTY-SEVEN

A s Steve reloaded, and Harold stood there feeling helpless, two cylinders rolled out of either side of the rising craft, and clicked into place.

'Duck,' Steve said, and dived to the floor, as the cannons punctured a hole in the concrete roof. Debris from dozens of feet thick concrete, along with dirt and grass, started raining down. Another blast followed and blue sky started peeing through the cloud of dust.

Harold wandered through the dust cloud, with stinging eyes and ringing ears, shouting wordlessly, until someone grabbed him by the fabric at his shoulder, and began to lead him upwards.

Steve dragged him to the elevator, which opened upon their approach. Moments later Steve and Harold staggered out of the building into a massive dust clouse. Outside, they found a crowd of scientists, staring transfixed at a craft, the likes of which they'd never seen, as it rose into the sky.

Harold remembered his own pistol and fired a few rounds up at the craft.

'Pointless,' Steve said.

Then a lick of flame burst from the shrinking craft, and it tumbled a few feet, before pulling up.

The scientists yelled, and some bolted, as Steve looked at

Harold's gun in surprise, then here came another metallic sound, and a second Zetan stingray whizzed by overhead.

'It's Troni and Nyn!' Harold said, 'it's Troni and Nyn!'

Two bolts of blue blazed across the sky, forcing the Maitre into an evasive cartwheel before returning fire. Their shots struck the desert metres away, sending up a plume of sand that scattered the crowd once and for all. As the battle progressed the Maitre continued to wheel in the sky, lighting up cars and buildings, while the Zetans stuck rigidly to an 'aim, fire, move' protocol.

Both methods seemed effective, but the Zetans had the advantage. There was a smoking wound in their craft, just below the glass dome, but the Maitre were a blinding blue and yellow blaze, taking tumbles which didn't look deliberate.

Then, as the Zetans circled to make another pass, the Maitre stopped shooting and reared backwards.

'They're going to shoot off into space,' Harold said, but the Zetans were already upon it, as though they'd anticipated the move. They tore up the belly with a bolt of plasma from a previously unseen cannon at the rear of their craft.

The Maitre hung in the air for a minute, then all the lights went out, and all fifty feet of metal began to descend towards Earth.

It struck the desert with such force that people, cars, and much of anything that wasn't bolted down, within ten miles, flipped over.

When Harold found his feet again, he spotted the craft wedged between two mountains of sand. The Zetans drifted overhead, towards the way they'd come. They looked to be losing altitude. They were crashing themselves.

'Come on,' Steve said, running towards his Victoria, which had escaped harm and was sitting between the upside-down husks of two sedans.

They revved off the tarmac, and onto the sand. Steve screamed threats of death at everyone he passed, while Harold attempted to compose himself. It dawned on him that it was unlikely Lisa would have survived the crash. The resulting anxiety had tight hold of him when they skidded to a stop beside the colossal mass of metal, but it did not prevent him from being first out of the car.

'Lisa,' he leapt onto the metal and felt the heat through his loafers.

As he ran, dodging clouds of acrid smoke and tongues of flame, he began to slip, as the rubber of his soles melted. If he fell off the wing, the drop would kill him, but if he slid down it, he might survive, just with life-changing injuries. With that in mind, it seemed an age before he reached the shattered cockpit, but when he did, he leapt right inside, down into the smog.

He landed on a base that trembled from the perpetual explosions.

'Li…' He managed before the smoke wriggled down his throat and gagged him. A Maitre lurched suddenly from the shadow, illuminated by a single ray of defiant sunlight. Its face was locked in a mute scream, and its skin dribbled off its bones like hot butter.

Harold considered again that Lisa was dead and that he too was now due the same fate, but then he fell on her. Rather, he leant on something soft, and it groaned like Lisa. Harold guessed she'd clambered atop the examination table and the invisible straps had been triggered, or the Maitre had incapacitated her there to keep her out of the way. Either way, it seemed it'd saved her life during the crash.

He pulled her arm, and she shifted, then was yanked backwards with a gasp of pain. Harold felt forward and found the straps, then they disappeared momentarily, then were back. He booted the table, and the straps deactivated long enough for him to drag Lisa free.

'Come… on…' he said, and hauled her up, staring up at the shattered hole in the dome above. They'd never get back up there.

After several seconds of blind staggering, and increased light-headedness, Harold thought he'd forgotten how to breathe and was almost ready to accept death, when some faint wisp of air danced across his cheek, and drew his eyes to a slash in the fuselage, beside a glowing blue panel. The other Maitre was there, working at a mess of fading holographics, though it was impossible to distinguish which of the creatures it was.

As they edged closer, it turned towards them, and Harold

saw that it had a gash in its face, and its right eyeball hung on a thread out of its socket.

They passed within its reach, as a red line ran through three of the holographics, and an alarm hooted deep within the craft.

'Your talk… in Hangar 7… was dull.' It said, and then they left it behind, tumbling down the sandbank to the ground below.

Kowalski, after all. He lifted his eyes to look at the craft, which gave a loud pop and then vanished.

'Where the hell's it gone?' Said Lisa, coughing beside him.

He threw his arms around her, and she hugged him back, and when they broke the embrace, she smiled at him. 'Thanks for saving my life again.'

They heard Steve mumbling as he struggled up the slope towards them. His Oxfords were unsuitable for such terrain.

'But seriously, where is it?' Lisa said.

'Implosion device,' Steve said, brushing some of the sand off his knees. 'It's shrunk to the size of an atom.'

'Clever way of avoiding detection,' Lisa said.

'Troni and Nyn…' said Harold, 'Steve, give me your phone. They were crashing.'

Steve surprised them both by handing over his phone without comment, and Harold made a new thread on stormarea51.net.

'Are you both ok? – J'

Steve and Lisa stared at him, as the minutes ticked by, but Harold kept his eyes on the screen of the smartphone, hitting refresh until the response appeared.

'Crashed. Come quick. Will send coordinates. - T'

'They did crash.'

'Any human exposure?' Steve said, accepting his phone back and reading what had been said.

'No.'

'Good. Let's go down to the car.'

Harold glared at the back of the Agent's head but followed him anyway. What choice did he have?

Steve started the engine and dialled a number.

As he ran through what had occurred with MJ1, he

flicked through channels on his dashboard television, until he found CNN. Tina Gower's face appeared on the screen, next to Area 51's Restricted Access sign.

'…That's right Claudia, I'm standing here on the border of Groom Lake, codename: Area 51, where witnesses say they just saw an alien shoot-out between to UFO occurred over the base. There are claims the loser crashed within the base while the victor escaped.'

Harold watched some pixelated footage of the two brawling crafts and thought all involved with the alien conspiracy would be grateful of its poor quality. Had either the lighting or the mobile phone been better, the Zetans would have found themselves in breach of the laws enforced by the Universal Governance. Then they'd have new problems by all accounts.

'They've got cloaking devices,' said Steve, guessing what Harold was thinking about.

Tina continued, as they bounced off the desert track and onto a road.

'Although this footage is far from conclusive, this is the third alleged extra-terrestrial occurrence around the secretive base this week, which is leading many of those involved in the Storm Area 51 movement to question — are aliens here? And if they are, what do they want from us? Back to you, Claudia.'

Steve turned off the TV and Harold realised they were on the North road, rather than the West, which would take them to Troni and Nyn.

'Where are we going?' He said.

'We're going to Bartonville, Illinois.'

CHAPTER TWENTY-EIGHT

B oth Zetans had been thrown from the craft and lay beside each other against a flat piece of sandstone. Their craft smoking behind them.

They'd skidded to a halt just a few metres short of the edge of the cliff, with jagged rocks laying in wait below, and canines hungry for flesh. They had been lucky in that sense, but that was where their luck had run out. There was a gash in the fuselage which made any kind of flight impossible, and the holographic console was visible through it, flickering on and off.

Troni looked down at the bloody, pink grazes beneath the torn fabric of his spacesuit and then turned to look at Nyn, who'd come off far worse. He'd been glanced by the plasma bolt that'd torn through the fuselage and had a grisly burn right up his left side. Troni could feel the heat emitting from it and see where the fabric of the spacesuit had fused with his skin. Nyn took a shallow breath and then attempted to stand.

'No time to rest,' he said, 'We need parts. To repair the hole. You fix the battery, and I'll go and get some from the base.'

He fell and landed face first in the sand, where he remained until Troni turned him over, taking care to avoid the burn. The two Zetans looked at each other, and then Nyn's eyes began roaming the sky — that strange alien sky, with its puffy clouds of gas, and its single sun.

'Nyn, I'll go get the medical kit, and we'll get you patched up.'

Nyn gasped, and with a pop, the side of his stomach burst open, and a torrent of blood poured out onto the sand.

'Nyn!'

Troni pressed a hand over the wound; the heat had vanished, and Nyn's whole body was icy, but Nyn batted his hand away. The pressure must have been painful and was ineffective against the blood loss.

'Help Earth...' Said Nyn, reaching up and seizing Troni around the neck, 'They can't defend themselves... without us... without you.'

Nyn coughed and Troni felt some blood hit his face.

'Some of them... will be bad... but Harold is... good man... a friend.'

Nyn released him, and he fell back onto the sand.

'Tell Preesy I killed three thousand Maitre... and stole all the Agents' shoes.'

Nyn closed his eyes and left Troni alone, so far from home, with the responsibility of saving their species and restoring their honour. He screamed a guttural sound, his first non-telepathic utterance for many years, which stung his vocal cords, and he ran to the hull and pounded it until exhaustion overwhelmed him and he fell back into the sand again. The ruckus would attract humans, but he didn't care. He'd never liked humans. It was humans who'd probably killed the Younglings at Roswell — maybe even caused them to crash with their archaic radar technology. Let them come, let them fight, let them die.

He looked at his motionless friend. Nyn would've told him to see reason. If he fought some antagonistic humans and lost, the Maitre would suck Earth dry and then return to a diminished ZR2 stronger than ever. They had to be stopped now, on Earth.

He stood up, retrieved Nyn, and brought him to the examination table, which had escaped the battle unscathed. If he got the craft running again, the table had functions to slow

Nyn's decomposition, until he got him back to ZR2, but if that was ever going to happen, he needed a patch for the fuselage and a battery. He might be able to salvage something from the other crash site if the Agents hadn't already stripped it.

He flicked a hand in front of the holographic panel, to no avail. He punched it, and it blinked into life. With effort and repeated acts of violence, he found the stormarea51.netand began typing. He needed Dunn's help.

CHAPTER TWENTY-NINE

'Fuck Illinois. What about Troni and Nyn?' Said, Harold.

'My instructions are to take you to Bartonville, Illinois,' Said Steve, accelerating all the time, 'Not to take you on a wild goose chase after those Zetans.'

His phone vibrated on the dash, and Harold grabbed it before the Agent could.

'It's a new forum post: 'Coordinates: 37.064539, -115.814144 – T.''

He shoved it in front of Steve's face.

'If he's sharing his location they must be in real trouble.'

'My instructions are…'

Harold dropped the phone and punched his gun into Steve's stomach.

'Here are your new instructions.'

The Agent gritted his teeth and hissed in a way that Lisa didn't like.

CHAPTER THIRTY

T roni let his legs dangle off the edge of the cliff, listening to the desert sounds. A lizard pitter-pattered across the sand behind him. A hawk screeched at him from the ridge adjacent. A plane droned overhead. He squinted up at the latter and wondered if he was, at that moment, being photographed. If not by the plane, then by some unseen drone or satellite. Was it all over? Had he already invoked the wrath of the UG for trespassing on Earth? Wouldn't that be ironic?

He understood the need for Trespassing laws, but he did not understand why Earth's governing agencies, specifically The Agents themselves, couldn't be honest with their fellow humans about the existence of so-called extra-terrestrials. What was the worst that could happen?

It was a stupid question. One which he already knew the answer to even if he pretended he didn't. Humans were self-destructive. In recent years they'd been keen to appoint leaders who cared more about facilitating division than eradicating it, all for the upkeep of a decadent monetary system. Another demand of this system was the perpetual burning of the Earth's natural resources, and it would be that that would eventually kill the human if the Maitre didn't do it first. He did not think the Human a particularly stupid creature, more arrogant. Yes, arrogant and resistant to new ideas. An extra-terrestrial would undermine the Earth's technologies and main religions — the rules upon which their societies' laws depended. To make humanity feel stupid would be a very bad idea. They were a race who always needed someone to blame for their issues, and only an extra-terrestrial would ever unify their prejudices.

He reminded himself he was saving them to preserve his own kind and suspected he'd need to remind himself a few more times before his fight was won or lost.

The groan of an engine broke his reverie. He spotted a car accelerating into the valley. They'd found him.

He scrambled back to the ship and emerged with his Rep9 Cannon. A long, plump-barrelled weapon, packing a thousand rounds of molten blue plasma — Troni's favourite. As a species, the Zetans thought themselves conservationists, almost pacifists, which is why the more conservative amongst them called Troni hot-headed, and the more direct called him psychotic.

While still in the military he had defended the same Water Treatment plant he eventually came to work for. That'd been during the first Maitre invasion and he'd shot hundreds of them in the back as they'd fled back to their saucers. That day had been the day he'd gained his reputation and was the day before he and Nyn had been expelled from the military.

Troni got down on one knee, and took aim at the black car coming to a halt in the valley below.

CHAPTER THIRTY-ONE

'Look,' said Lisa, and Harold scanned his eyes up the red sandstone to where she was pointing. Some sixty feet up was the stingray, sitting lopsided on a narrow cliff, beneath a cloud of billowing black smoke. Steve brought the Victoria to a halt, and they clambered out, shielding their eyes against the sun. Harold was sure he could see something crouching on the edge of the cliff, but it could just as easily have been a rock. Then he saw the sunlight glinting off something metallic.

Steve had spotted it too. 'It's armed,' he said, pulling out his gun.

'Put that away, you idiot,' Harold said, slapping the gun down. 'Nyn?'

There came no reply.

'Nyn?' He bellowed at the top of his lungs.

Then, very faintly, what he thought was the beginning of a headache became words.

'Do you… some cable… climb up?'

'Yes, please,' Harold yelled and then felt some concern that Troni had overestimated his climbing skills. Regardless, he walked towards the cliff face and sidestepped the tumbling coil of steel cable.

'I heard something in my head,' said Lisa, joining him.

'It was me, but it wasn't me. Am I going mad?'

'No,' Harold said, curious that Lisa had overheard their conversation. 'That's Zetan telepathy. It's how they communicate.'

Steve was counting the bullets in his Glock's cartridge. He had either not heard Troni, or Zetan telepathy was nothing new to him. Harold would've bet on the latter.

He clicked the cartridge back into the pistol and said, 'Shall we get on with it then?'

'Yes,' said Harold, remembering that speed was important, and let the cable take his weight.

There were a few tricky moments during the ascent, where Harold's muscles exerted a twinge or his boot slipped on some fluid sand. Lisa nearly toppled back into Steve, when a hiss came from a handhold, but found a different one at the last second and hurried on. Harold began to wonder if the Zetans' psychic ability extended to manipulating gravity in order to aid them.

When Harold reached the cliff, such was his exhaustion that he could not summon the energy to climb over the lip. Then he felt a hand on his shirt collar which pulled him up and over.

Harold lay there on his back looking up at Troni, covered in glistening patches of red, with a scattering of pebbles, hanging there in the ooze. He climbed to his feet and spotted a swarm of flies above a large patch of blood.

'A little help,' said Lisa, at Harold's feet.

Harold reached down and pulled her up, and there she stood beside him, staring at Troni with more suspicion than awe.

'Forgive her.' Harold said, 'Her experiences with extra-terrestrials thus far have been less than pleasant.'

Troni nodded, and then Harold heard the scraping of gravel and reached back for Steve's hand. The Agent took it, and Harold looked down at him, standing with his Oxford's flat against the rock, suit flapping in the wind. Here was the man who had brought pain to Lisa, Morgan Andrews, and likely many others, and, at that moment, Harold realised it was only his grip and will, that kept him operational.

'Harold!' said Lisa.

Steve met his gaze, sensing danger in the seconds that ticked by, and in the slackening of Harold's grip. Then he did something Harold had not expected. He smiled, a toothy grin that curled round right up behind his ears and gave Harold such a fright that he tightened his grip, and the Agent climbed up his arm and made it onto the ledge. Steve gave Harold a shove so that he fell back in the sand, and then yanked out his gun. The Glock was only offered to Harold for a second before he noticed Troni, and the cannon he carried.

'Hey, where did you get that?' He said his gun on Troni now.

'Wouldn't you like to know, freak?' Said Troni.

'Stop it, we don't have time for this.' Harold said, climbing to his feet, 'Troni, where's Nyn?'

Troni sighed and closed both sets of lids, (one horizontal, one vertical), and tilted his head towards the battered craft. Through the hole in the fuselage, Harold spotted the motionless corpse of the cordial Nyn on the examination table. There came a waft of something like foul eggs, and Harold knew it came from the wound on the Zetan's side. His grey-blue skin was pure white.

Troni walked past them, slung his legs back over the edge of the cliff, and began playing with a beetle that had scurried on to his knee.

'Troni, I'm sorry about Nyn,' said Harold, 'Is there anything we can do for him?'

'No.'

Lisa still hadn't quite gotten used to hearing Troni talk in her own voice inside her own head, but now some of the wariness was dissipating, and she felt keen to communicate with him.

Troni looked back over his shoulder at her.

She smiled. 'I'm Lisa. I've already thanked Harold for saving me from the Maitre, but I owe you a thank you, too.'

Troni shrugged. 'I don't blame you for what happened to Nyn.'

'I… what?'

'He can read your thoughts,' Harold said.

'The thoughts of all present.' Said Troni, glaring at Steve, then returned to his beetle only to find it'd disappeared down a crack.

'Is it salvageable?' Said Harold, eyes running over the rest of the wreck, 'It's in better shape than the one the Maitre stole.'

'Needs a new battery, and thick sheet for the hole.' Troni said, 'That should be enough to hold her back to Zr2.'

'What kind of battery?' Lisa said.

'You don't have the technology,' said Troni, 'Ruin or not, our only hope is that the battery on the other craft survived.'

'But that vanished, Troni, it's gone,' said Lisa.

She balled up her fingers and then opened them. 'Pfft.'

Troni waved his hand, climbed to his feet, and walked inside, then, after some crashing and banging, he reappeared with a sphere wrapped in a purple rag.

'What's that?' Harold said.

'Necessary,' he said, 'Shall we go find the other ship then?'

Harold looked at Steve, expecting some argument, but the Agent already had his hands on the steel cable and had begun his descent.

'Lisa, shall I go next? That way, if you fall…' Harold said, but Lisa had already swung herself off and started after Steve.

Then he felt Troni pass him and watched the Zetan take a running dive off the cliff.

Lisa screamed as the Zetan hurtled past her, and Harold made it to the cliff edge just in time to watch the Zetan slow mid-plummet. Then he drifted, spiralling down like a leaky balloon, coming to a comfortable landing beside the Victoria.

'How did you do that?' Lisa said, some time later, once they'd joined him.

Troni shrugged. 'Our bones and muscles weigh very little in comparison to humans, and our skin is thin, so we fall like you might see a piece of paper fall, using the air resistance to slow our descent. I spread my blood equally across my body to ensure balance and then pump it downwards at the end, so as to ensure I land on my feet.'

'That's amazing.'

'It's evolution,' he said, 'Much of Zr2 is covered in

molten tar, so the settlements are built high upon supporting beams. As younglings, we're taught to blood-thin, so if we do take a fall, we can drift to the nearest beam and climb back up. Nyn has… had… this clumsy friend called Cubisht, who falls at least twice a day. He'd have been Sarpank food a long time ago if he hadn't learnt how to blood-thin.'

'Sarpank?' Said, Harold.

'They look similar to some of the serpents you have here on Earth, and they live in the tar, and eat all the debris which falls from the cities. They're an excellent trash disposal resource. They'll eat anything.'

'Can we get this over with? We've got to get to Bartonville,' said Steve.

'Taking them home to be gawped at by the rest of the family?' Said Troni, but Steve's phone rang before he could answer.

'Yes, sir… no, there was a complication… all is fine… I've a Grey in custody,' he said, climbing into the car.

'Zetan,' said Troni.

'Custody?' Said Harold, but the Agent flapped and motioned from them to get into the car.

'I'm transporting him to the other crashed vehicle, then bringing Dunn and Tsai straight to you.'

'Inconvenience am I?' Said Troni, as Steve terminated the call.

'Always.'

'You two know each other?' Lisa said, and Harold had been wondering the same.

'Should I tell them, Steve?'

'Do it,' said Steve, 'everyone else be damned, I'll drive us into a ravine.'

Harold glanced at Troni, in the rear-view mirror, and thought he saw a flicker of amusement, then he glanced at Steve beside him, and thought he saw a flicker of something that was quite the opposite. Nobody pressed the matter further.

The late afternoon weather had turned muggy. They rediscovered the crash site bathed in light by four powerful spotlights, and teeming with scientists in yellow radiation suits. Parked beneath one of these spotlights was another Ford

Victoria, with its headlights ablaze.

Waiting for us? Thought Lisa, or perhaps just a reminder to the scientists that the Government is watching?

Military officials were also present en masse as their entrance was impeded by two stern-looking soldiers. One of them tapped the window with his automatic rifle and asked for ID. Steve passed it over, and the man read it and passed it back.

'Very good, sir, but I'm going to need to see ID for your passengers too.'

Steve's mouth fell open, 'How dare you? Let us by, right now.'

'I can't do that, sir.'

Steve leant out of the open window towards the young man and said, 'I ought to shoot you right in the heart', and then dropped his hand from the wheel to his lap.

The soldier and his comrade leapt back with their guns raised, but Steve had only reached for the button that opened the rear-passenger window and let them take the briefest glimpse, at the Alien in the backseat.

The insolent soldier swore, and his partner dropped his gun, and Steve took the opportunity to accelerate away, the window whirring back up as he did so.

He weaved in and out of the scientists and then pulled to a stop fifteen feet from the other Victoria, which rolled out and stopped parallel to them. A tall black man exited the car, and Steve got out to meet him.

'Agent Farouk.'

'Agent Steve.'

'I need you to arrange an ODPMC for Sergeant Ross Lewis over on the gate.'

He scratched his head for a second.

'Best arrange one for his friend too.'

'Understood,' said Farouk and whistled to a passing Colonel, whose eyebrows shot up into his hair. Harold got the impression that some of the soldiers weren't used to the Agents yet.

Harold and Lisa got out of the car and watched Agent Farouk wander away with the dishevelled looking Colonel.

'ODMC, what?' Harold said.

'An ODPMC,' Said Steve, 'Other Designated Physical or Mental Condition. A discharge.'

'He was only doing his job,' said Lisa.

'He'll swear never to tell anyone about what he saw, but he'll go home and tell his wife. Timmy will overhear from the top of the stairs and go to school and tell his friends. His friends will tell their parents. Who will tell their colleagues, and before you know it it's all over the news... unless, of course, the source has a history of being mentally unfit, and that is what I'm providing. That's me doing my job, now excuse me.'

He walked away from them, found a box and stood on it, with, his ID held aloft.

'My name...' He began, but nobody stopped talking, so he pulled out his gun and fired it into the air, like some maverick sheriff from the Old West. That got everyone's attention.

'My name is Agent Steve, and I outrank every one of you.'

He paused and studied the sea of faces to make sure they understood.

'Scientists, I need you to get in line and face my car over there,' he pointed towards the Victoria.

After a few seconds of silence, a great din rumbled up as the scientists discussed what was being asked of them.oli98.

'Military personnel,' Said Steve, and all the soldiers leapt to attention, 'Take aim at a scientist and prepare to fire.'

Each soldier levelled his rifle, though some looked at each other for reassurance that they were all doing the same thing. Then the scientists' chatter turned to panic, and there was much shouting, but they began to fall in line.

Steve nodded, staring down the line of faces.

'Scientists, turn around one-hundred-and-eighty degrees. Soldiers fall in line behind them.'

More scrambling and shouting as Steve's commands were obeyed.

'Scientists, you will walk forward twenty paces by my count: 1... 2... 3...'

The scientists felt the barrels of automatic rifles in their backs and began walking.

'Military personnel, you will walk forward fifteen paces by my count: 1... 2... 3...!'

The soldiers complied, and then all stood waiting.

'Scientists, if you look back my way you will be legally executed without trial.'

'Military personnel, if you suspect your target is attempting to look back or has looked back, you are ordered to shoot them. Is that understood?'

'Sir, yes, sir,' came the soldiers' chorus.

Farouk walked past them towards the two lines with another Agent; a thin, ginger-haired man.

'My colleagues will be monitoring you, soldiers. Failure to carry out my orders will result in your immediate expulsion from the United States Military. Is that understood?'

'Sir, yes, sir.'

Steve examined the spectacle a final time and then walked back over to them.

'Well, that was disturbing,' said Lisa.

'We have an alien with us. Would you rather they saw him and I had to shoot them all?'

'Why would they have to die?' Lisa said, 'Everybody's going to find out about aliens sooner or...'

Steve grabbed Lisa by the throat and pinned her to the car. Troni leapt out with his cannon raised and Harold put his arms between the Agent and Lisa, in an attempt to separate them, to no avail. Her face began to turn an unusual colour.

'If you ever mention that word again in this context, I shall book you in with Agent Kyle indefinitely. Do you understand?'

'Yes,' she said with a croak, tears streaming down her cheeks.

He dropped her and yanked himself away from Harold.

'And if your hands touch me again, Professor Dunn, I'll see you're separated from them.'

'What about me, Steve?' Said Troni, 'I think she has a point.'

'You'll get yours,' he said.

'I invite you to try, at your leisure,' said Troni, then retrieved the purple ball from the backseat and elbowed past

Steve. He pulled off the fabric, and revealed a glass orb, about the size of a lawn bowl, and twisted the top and bottom in opposing directions. It gave a burst of light that blinded them all. Once they'd manage to prise their eyes apart, they saw that the orb hovered above Troni's hand, as he walked the long burn across the sand. The orb hummed, and the light fluctuated, and then he tossed it into the air and jogged backwards.

Ten feet in the air, the orb extinguished, and there, smouldering on the sand, was the stolen stingray.

'Re-integrator,' said Troni, then pottered about until he found the orb again and rewrapped it. Then he put into the back of the Victoria.

'Are the Maitre bodies on board not proof enough that they're operational on Earth?' Said Harold.

Troni shook his head. 'The technology doesn't restore flesh. The bodies are gone.'

He climbed up the side of the craft, found a hole, and wriggled inside.

Whilst Troni searched, and Steve heaved a trailer off of a jeep and onto the back on the Victoria, Harold and Lisa sat on a rock and watched the scientists and soldiers, facing away from them.

'Why does it feel like we're the bad guys?' Said Lisa.

Harold looked up. The stars had begun to appear. 'I'm too nosy for my own good. Troni's got a temper, to say the least, and Steve's a total psychopath. If anyone here's a goodie, it's you.'

She smiled. 'Would a goodie jump into bed with a man on the first day of meeting him?'

'At least he was a handsome man,' Harold said, and she laughed.

'What do we do next?'

'I think Steve's taking us to Agent Headquarters. Hopefully, they can get me a meeting with the Russian President so I can warn him about the Maitre in his government, thus preventing nuclear war,' he rolled his eyes at the enormity of his task, 'I guess you could see about coming back to Area 51 after I leave?'

She nodded, though he could tell what she was thinking,

that the Agents might never allow her to return to a normal life again, let alone come back to work at Area 51.

He put his arm around her, 'I won't let them hurt you.'

She flinched, and he removed it again, 'What can you do?'

'Steve needs me to convince the Russians of the Maitre plot.'

'He can't do that himself?'

'I have a way... and I have Troni.'

'He has Troni too, for the time being anyway.'

Steve cursed as the Zetan threw a hunk of metal out the craft, which just missed his head

'He does not have Troni,' Harold said, and they both laughed. Steve stared at them.

After about twenty minutes and a lot of noise from both Steve and Troni, the Zetan threw down a metal sheet and then dropped to the ground with a long, white cylinder, which looked like one of those halogen bulbs, used in every office in the world.

'The battery is not damaged.' Troni said, and handed the cylinder to Lisa, 'Take it, and get into the car, and pass me the re-integrator?'

Lisa frowned at his abruptness, but got into the car and passed him the orb.

'You two load that metal sheet,' Troni said, and wandered back over to the craft, as Steve and Harold heaved the massive piece of metal onto the trailer. It made a screeching sound not dissimilar to the sound the Zetan crafts sometimes made.

They got into the car and watched Troni reactivate the re-integrator and toss it into the air. With a pop, the craft vanished again, and this time Troni caught the orb as it fell. He hopped into the backseat beside Lisa and wrapped it up in its cloth again.

Steve fired up the engine and yelled 'Carry on!' as they sped towards the checkpoint. There were two different soldiers there, neither of whom made any attempt to stop them. Lisa looked at Steve, and her glare intensified the lower his foot pressed on the accelerator. His driving was annoying Harold as well. In fact, Steve's whole attitude had annoyed

Harold since they'd met up with Troni. He seemed to have exchanged his cool professionalism for pure antagonism, and that made Harold wonder what the history was between the two.

'If you're going to kill us all with your driving then what's stopping me from shooting you now,' Harold said, poking him in the ribs with the gun.

Steve did not flinch.

'Every time you wave that pistol around, Professor Dunn, it becomes less convincing,' he said, 'And don't forget that I have one too.'

Harold swallowed and put the gun away and Steve sped up a little more.

The Zetan crash-site was were still deserted when they returned, and Troni scrambled up the cliff face with ease, the battery held under one arm.

'Must be easy when you know the fall won't kill you,' Harold mumbled.

After several minutes had ticked by he said, 'So is he going to throw down something to winch up the metal or…'

Then there came the familiar metallic grind, prompting them to slam their hands over their ears. Unpleasant as the noise was, Harold whooped as the craft scraped its way off the ledge and hung in the air above them, blotting out the dying embers of the sun. The blue searchlight shone out and found the metal sheet in the back on the trailer.

'Stand back,' Came Troni's voice, and the heavy sheet rose into the air and made its way up to the stingray.

Soon they saw orange flashes and the hole begin to shrink. Troni finished the weld within fifteen minutes.

'You can do my roof at home,' Harold yelled, and a bright blue Troni sprang up in front of them, fluctuating, and buzzing, like a TV with a bad signal.

'Stop the war.' It said.

'We'll try.' Harold said, 'What are you going to do?'

'I'll return Nyn's body to Zr2. Despite my exile, they'll allow it, and then I'll come back to assist you.'

He stared at Harold.

'Don't let Nyn's death be in vain.'

Harold shook his head, 'I won't.'

Then the hologram vanished, and the craft began to rise into the sky. Forty feet, fifty feet, sixty feet, and then it accelerated upwards, and the sky swallowed it.

They clambered back inside the Victoria and were grateful when they hit tarmac again, after what felt like an age of rocky, desert roads.

CHAPTER THIRTY-TWO

Harold strained to heave the bloated sandbags off his chest so he could take a breath, and choked, as something salty trickled into his mouth. He held up a blood-stained hand, past which he could see the highway, and the endless bodies he'd mistaken for sandbags, crammed in between the crash barriers and totalled cars. He vomited, and then felt immediate guilt, as the vomit dribbled into the open mouth of a little girl, no older than ten. Bones cracked as he walked, and crows cawed around him as they feasted on eyes, and necks, and innards. His foot caught in a toddler's harness, and he fell on top of a naked fat man, whose wealth of cold flesh slapped against his face. He flailed for the mangled crash barrier, caught hold of it and hauled himself through, tumbling onto the sidewalk. He crouched, deep breaths on the concrete, and then stood. Where were Steve and Lisa?

'Lisa,' he said and got a response, a shout from below the bridge. Pulling himself up over the side he spotted Steve, ten feet away, shooting one Maitre after another, as dozens more poured in towards him.

Bang. Bang. Click. Click. Click.

He threw the gun aside and picked up a metal bar, but the Maitre behind him snatched it and tossed it far back over the crowd where it landed with a clatter.

One of them dashed forward and slashed Steve across the stomach with a clawed finger. He retched and fell to his knees, and then they all piled on top of him, a pulsating mess of horror. Two of them backed out of the fray and began hauling at some bloody rope, and Harold realised that it was Steve's intestine. Beyond that was the battered Victoria, where Harold spotted eight Maitre gathered with one rutting up and down in the centre, then it fell away, and another took his place. They all rasped and leered, and then suddenly stopped and fell silent. They turned to look at him, up high on the bridge, and then stepped aside to reveal Lisa, pinned to the bonnet of the Victoria, naked, eyes closed, and lips bared over her teeth in pain. Harold flung himself back from the edge and fell over. A rocket streaked across the blood-red sky overhead, and he knew it was his A1, and below that, hanging by their necks at the end of steel cables, were Troni and Nyn. Their fingers pointed at Harold in lifeless accusation.

CHAPTER THIRTY-THREE

The Victoria bounced over a pothole and jerked Harold awake.

'Whebba, huh?' He said.

Steve didn't answer, and Lisa still snored beside him.

He coughed. 'Where are we?'

'Utah.'

He sat up in his seat, his t-shirt heavy with cold perspiration. 'How long until we get there?'

'Another day. Perhaps less.'

'Toilet stop?'

'The more stops we take, the longer it'll take to get there,' Steve said.

'Well either you pull over and let me take a piss, or we all deal with the result for the remainder of the journey.'

'Fine,' Steve said, and listed towards the hard shoulder, then swerved back in again, much to the honking derision of the drivers behind.

'What is it?'

'We are being followed.'

Harold glanced out of the back window into the night, but the few cars he could see in the rain looked inconspicuous.

'How do you know?'

Steve kept his eyes fixed on his mirror and didn't answer.

After about a mile of tension, he moved back onto the hard shoulder and turned off into a deserted 7/11.

'Go,' he said. 'Hurry up.'

Harold gave Lisa a gentle pat and asked her if she needed to use the bathroom, but she only yawned and rolled over. He gritted his teeth and stepped out into the drizzle. The act of inviting Lisa had not been selfless — he was nervous about his sudden isolation now he knew they were being followed. He felt acutely aware of everything around him — the howl of the dog, the creaking of the rusty 7/11 sign, and the rattle of the trash can lid as it rolled past.

He jogged over to the entrance and nearly had a coronary as he touched the handle and a nomadic motorcycle club roared past. The comfort of normality awaited him inside the store — cheap candles, sodas, and magazines, and a young fellow at the counter turning over a comic book.

He took a breath, picked up a Playboy and flicked through a few pages. What would the stuffy Agent say if he returned to the car with that? What would Lisa say, for that matter? He fought the urge to buy the magazine, and instead placed some jerky and a New York Times on the counter, drawing the attention of the pimply teenager for the first time since he'd entered. He still kept one eye on his comic book as he rang up the goods.

'Hi,' said Harold.

'Seven-fifty,' said the clerk.

Harold felt irritation as he handed over a twenty. Not only was shitty customer service always annoying, but this was also the first non-government employee he'd met for some time, and the guy couldn't even look at him. As the clerk waited for Harold's receipt to print and fiddled one-handed with his change, he tried to think of some cutting remark to make as he left the store. Then the lights went out.

'What the hell?' Said the clerk, in the darkness.

'Power cut,' Harold said, and stepped outside, pleased that the clerk couldn't read his damn comic book anymore. The elation was short-lived as he realised the forecourt lights had gone out too, along with the Victoria's headlights. He could no longer hear the engine ticking over.

e Harold and Lisa were waving their arms in the shadows as though they were shouting, but there was no sound, save for a repetitive swish-swish-swish. Like a helicopter, but without the grumble of an engine.

Harold looked up at the source of the sound, and an explosion of light sent him staggering back against the door. Above him, fifty feet of lights rotated, attached to something that generated such pressure that it made it difficult to stand.

There was a buzz of power, and a blue ring appeared on the lot, and the rotating lights began to rise. Harold watched the ring snake towards his foot, as grit and insects moved up the beam. A gunshot pumped him full of life again, and his eyes fell back to Steve, striding out of the darkness with his pistol aimed at the lights.

'Run,' his lips read, and Harold complied, rolling out of the wind tunnel, and running as fast as he could towards the grassy expanse to the left of the store. The swishing noise intensified, and the lights swirled faster, as the blue ring gained on him. He felt nausea and retched as he ran. Then the hair began to stand up on the back of his neck, and he felt sluggish, as though running through water, and then his foot swung down onto nothing, and he was airborne. The blue ring was upon him.

Lisa, now awake and running, lunged for his leg and clawed at his shoe, but he was rising too rapidly. He watched the shoe twist on the ends of his toes and then tumble down to the shrinking 7/11 below.

He looked up, and was able to see the bottom of the craft — it was circular and looked like stainless steel, though it was hard to tell with so many lights spinning around it. He could see a blue sheet, at the end of a short tunnel, at the end which were Maitre.

A boom filled the air, and Harold felt his stomach jump up into his mouth as the beam vanished and he plummeted ten feet. Before he hit the ground, it blinked back on around him and he slowed, and then began to rise again. Another boom and a blue bolt blazed past Harold and struck the saucer, sending it spinning over to the left and throwing Harold around with it. He watched his vomit disappear up the beam and hoped it would strike one of his would-be captors right in the face.

But who's shooting? He thought. Troni was halfway to Zr2 wasn't he?

Harold's eyes raked the skies for the stingray, but couldn't find it, and then he plummeted downwards again, and again he was caught. His eyes followed the flight of the next bolt, backwards, and illuminated in the shot was Agent Steve, with a long-barrelled cannon.

The bolt struck home again, and over the swishing, Harold heard honking alarms, and then they died away, as the saucer shot up into the sky away from him.

It was flying up and away from him, wasn't it?

He got his answer a moment later when his leg snapped beneath him, and his head was catapulted forwards onto the concrete of the forecourt, like a child thwacks a ruler, but it did not knock him out.

'You're alright, Harold, you're alright,' Lisa said, taking his head in her arms, as the pain intensified. Above them, the saucer had vanished.

There was a clang beside them as Steve threw down his weapon, and then he jabbed a syringe into Harold 's neck. Lisa wondered if it was the same incapacitating toxin which she had been threatened with. Then, as Harold's eyes rolled, Steve recapped the syringe, rose to his feet, and walked back over to the storefront, where the clerk was lingering.

'Where are you going?' Lisa said.

'That saucer will need to return to the Mothership to be repaired, but feel free to open fire if it I'm wrong. ' he said, eyes raking the skies as he walked.

Lisa looked at the cannon. It had a hole that your hand slotted into with a small trigger built in, and four crooked pieces of metal snaking along the sides. She had seen the gun before. It was the same as Troni's.

Steve pushed the gabbling clerk back inside the store and the door shut behind him. Lisa tried not to think about what the Agent was up to and instead looked down at Harold. He seemed so quiet, so peaceful, and she thought about everything they had gone through together. They had both been kidnapped and assaulted, physically and psychologically, by humans and aliens alike.

From inside the store, there was a yell and a gunshot, and then Steve strode back out into the lot carrying a towel and a roll of tape.

There's one person I'm getting no fonder of, she thought, as he reversed the Victoria towards them. A part of her expected him to run right over them, but he didn't.

He got out and crouched down beside her, prodding at Harold's leg, then placed one hand below his shin, and another above it, on either side of the break.

'We need to set his leg before we go any further,' he said, 'Lift his arms.'

As she gritted her teeth and complied, Steve applied pressure, and the parts of Harold's leg that jutted out, snapped back into place. Harold shuddered and murmured, but remained unconscious, and Steve taped the towel around his leg.

Together they got him onto the back seat, with Lisa having to climb across it to pull him in, and then as she went to sit beside Steve in the front, she almost sat on a disk, which he whipped out of the way at the last moment.

'That was close,' she said.

'No matter,' he said, and snapped the disk up into little pieces, 'It's only the security footage from the store.'

As they rolled off the forecourt, Lisa couldn't stop herself from glancing in through the store window, and there she saw the clerk slumped over the counter, an inky pool of blood gluing him to his comic book. Steve dropped a wad of notes in her lap.

'What's this?'

'I had to make it look like a robbery. Keep that if you like.'

She threw it in the glove compartment. 'Let's just get Harold to a hospital.'

'He was wrong to want to stop.' Steve said, as they re-entered the heavy traffic of the freeway, 'I warned him we were being followed.

'Yes, but it was you who pulled over, wasn't it? You're driving.'

Steve didn't answer, so she slumped in her seat and looked at the other drivers. Average human scowls, utterly devoid of extra-terrestrial terror. Then her eyes detected movement up above, something zipping amongst the clouds. A trio of somethings.

'Up there,' she said, staring wide-eyed, 'Look up there.'

'Three now?' He said.

'You knew? You aren't concerned?'

'They won't try anything on the freeway, too much risk,' he said.

Lisa sniffed. 'Guess I was pretty lucky back at the gas station that they only went for Harold.'

'How do you mean?' He said.

'Well, the evidence suggests they're after me too.'

Steve shook his head, and almost smiled. 'Don't flatter yourself. One Maitre took a shine to you, but that doesn't mean they're all 'after you', so to speak.'

Lisa frowned, and looked back out of the window, but saw no more Maitre.

'As for why Professor Dunn has been targeted, the Maitre use advanced parabolic microphones to eavesdrop on conversations, so it's possible that they overheard the discussion between the Grey and himself, and learned that he was integral to the plan.'

Lisa was somewhat familiar with parabolic microphones. The Feds were always using them to eavesdrop on Mobsters, on her True Crime documentaries. All it took was a handheld dish to funnel the sound waves, and an earpiece and the Feds didn't even need a court order like they would if they were planting a bug.

'Although, it's possible that they might want you for information. If they have been eavesdropping they'll know of your affiliation. Yes, yes, I think you are probably still at risk of abduction.'

'Great,' said Lisa, irritated that Steve felt he had to give her just cause for concern.

'Let me know if you want a toilet stop,' he said.

CHAPTER THIRTY-FOUR

Lisa opened her eyes and strained them against the daylight, then heard a snore from the back seat and saw Harold sleeping, his leg still strapped up in the towel and tape. She looked at Steve, sitting in exactly the same position, and wondered if he ever slept.

'You didn't take Harold to the hospital?' She said.

Steve glanced at her. 'No. In hospitals, there are visiting restrictions, and if I were to leave him unattended, with Maitre still on our tail, I would be sentencing him to death.'

'But what about his leg, he can't…'

'I'll get a Doctor to see to him when we get to Bartonville. He'll sleep until we get there,' he said, in a voice that indicated the conversation was over.

Harold snores grew louder, as they endured the next mile without talking, so Lisa flicked on the radio.

'Tensions rose with Russia today, after President Reznikov ordered all Russian patriots to quote: 'return to the Motherland', and any Americans, or allies of the US, to return home 'while they still have the option'. This action, along with the intensification of the nuclear arms race, has led some experts to predict that war is imminent. Peace activists call for discussion, while both governments continue to flex their muscles.'

Lisa turned off the radio.

Harold groaned, as he felt the stab of pain in his leg and it all came flooding back to him. He had a thumping headache too.

'Harold, you're awake. How are you feeling?' Said Lisa, looking back over her seat at him.

He shuffled up in the seat. 'I won't be running any marathons. Where are we?'

'Dunno,' said Lisa.

'Bartonville, Illinois,' said Steve.

'This is Bartonville?' Lisa said, staring out of the windows.

Harold understood her surprise and shared it. Bartonville turned out to be a tiny village, close-packed with leafy trees, which glowed emerald green in the sunshine. Up the road ahead he could see a park, with a pond that glimmered as though inviting a toe-dip, and then he heard giggling and spotted a group of children, no older than ten, playing with a Golden Labrador on the grass. It looked more like the setting for a Famous Five novel, rather than for a secret organisation of government assassins, but he supposed being inconspicuous was rather the point.

How he envied all the people he could see — going to work, going to school, or just going, in complete ignorance of how fragile their little realities were.

They swung a left and turned off the main road into a little street with a row of houses, and a grocery store with a sign over it that announced, 'Bartonville Fruit and Veg' in big green letters on a blue background.

Like all the other shops they'd seen in the village so far, it was a colourful yet simple operation, with two window displays outside — one filled with oranges and the other with apples. Outside, on a wooden chair, sat a bald-headed man, with thick grey eyebrows, who was watching the tall stems of wheat nod in a nearby field. It was hard to tell, but Lisa thought the man looked to be staring with determination, rather than with vacancy. He became distracted by the Victoria as it rolled to a stop in front of him.

'Stevie-boy.' The man cried out, stretching his arms

wide. 'It's been too long.'

'Jack, great to see you.' Said Steve with warmth that surprised both Lisa and Harold as they climbed out of the car – Harold doing so with a cane Steve bought when they stopped at a very crowded Truck Stop and a makeshift splint he fashioned using two pices of wood he found by the dumpster. Steve assured them they were safe, given the number of people at the truck stop.

'Aren't you going to introduce me to your friends?'

The old man chuffed on a rolled-up cigarette, not his first of the day either judging from the butts around his chair.

'Sure. This is Professor Dunn and Doctor Tsai.'

'Pleasure to meetcha,' he said, placing his coffee cup on the ground, and reaching out to shake hands with both of them. 'Excuse me if I don't get up. With my knees I can only afford to a few times a day, and with my bladder, I fear I've already exhausted my ration… god knows how I'm going to lock up the store tonight.'

All three of them laughed, but Steve's laugh had a sardonic edge to it, which prompted Harold to feel suspicious of Jack. Then he reminded himself that the guy was a friend of Steve's or the closest thing Steve was able to have to a friend, so he was right to be suspicious. As he thought all this, Jack's tongue flickered out of his mouth in Agent-esque fashion.

Harold' reaction caught the old man's attention. 'Well, looks like someone's been in the wars. Take a tumble, did we?'

Harold leant on Lisa's shoulder to take the strain of his leg, gritting his teeth against the pain only slighty dulled by the pain pills Steve gave him. 'I don't think I should be talking about it.'

'O-ho. Can't be trusted, can I not?' Said Jack, then leaned forward in his chair, 'Tell me, Harold, do you ever still think about that pretty little administrative assistant back in England?'

Lisa rolled her eyes and Harold stared at the old man.

'How do you know about her?'

'That's enough of the pleasantries.' Steve said, and opened the door to the shop.

'Steve. Lisa… Harold,' he winked, then took his tobacco and papers out of his cardigan, and began rolling another cigarette.

'How did he know about…?' Harold said, then changed his mind, 'Who was that?'

'The most dangerous man you've ever met.' Steve said, 'So I'd be very careful what I said about him if I were you.'

Harold looked at Lisa and was more annoyed by her lack of disgruntlement, at the hint of his promiscuous past, than he would have been by the presence of some.

The shop they were standing it was brightly lit, and had two long wooden troughs down the centre, with three smaller ones by both walls, all piled high with all manner of fruit and vegetable. Harold inhaled, enjoying the musty smell of the place, and felt himself calming. There were only two people in the shop, beside themselves — a pretty young clerk, who stood slumped over the counter, typing out a text on a pink phone, and a hunched, old man, who was examining a pear with distaste.

Steve walked over to the girl. 'My usual, please.'

'Golly, mister, you gave me a start,' she said sticking her phone in the back pocket of her jeans, 'Now, I'm sorry, but I've only been here a week, so you'll need to help me out with what your usual is.'

'Apples, grapes, eggplant, nectarines, tomatoes.'

'Sounds like a nutritious diet, you've got yourself there,' She said, as a cloud shifted outside, and sunlight poured into the store and made her unstained teeth and golden hair shine. 'I'll need the manager to give me a hand.'

She's twenty-one and perfect, Harold thought. Didn't she look darling in that oversized navy work shirt?

She pressed something hidden below the counter. Seconds later the manager appeared, though he looked more like a bank manager than a grocer, in a white shirt and black tie.

'Ahhh, Mister…'

Harold and Lisa looked up in tandem, both realising they had never heard Steve's surname before, but the man noticed their expressions and changed tack.

'… Sir, follow me, please. I have your order back here.'

He held up the plastic sheet which divided the store from the back room. Steve went first, then as Lisa made to lead Harold through, the little, blonde clerk stepped in his way.

'I hope we can find something for you too, sir,' she said, then puffed her lips, and let her head tilt to the side, her bright, blue eyes, raking Harold from his toes to his face.

Harold smiled at her, enjoying her air of mischief, then realised he was standing there by himself.

'Thanks,' he said, and hurried passed her under the flap.

Inside the dank warehouse, the musty smell of the store had taken on a mouldy quality. Lisa suspected an orange or something had fallen from one of the crates and gone rolling under one of the shelves to decay.

She glanced back over her shoulder and saw Harold hobbling towards her, mind elsewhere. Probably still in the jeans of the young girl. She recalled what the old man Jack had said about Harold's marriage and the secretarial indiscretion he'd alluded to. How had he known about that? How grimly predictable though that the man who'd saved her life was a creep like the rest of them. Harold passed her and slipped on a piece of skin, but she caught him before he hit the ground.

'Watch where you're going, you old pervert,' she said and heaved Harold up to his feet again.

'I wasn't... I don't know...' Harold said, but then the Manager chuckled and passed them.

'I wouldn't even think about it. She'd eat you for breakfast.'

'I wasn't...' Harold tried again but gave it up.

The Manager drew the bolt, atop a battered, green door, and then inserted a key and unlocked it. He fell back into character.

'Your order should be already down there. If you don't mind grabbing it yourself, I just need to make a call. If the door gets stuck on your way back up, give it a thump, and I'll come open it for you.'

Steve nodded, and the man scuttled off.

Once he'd disappeared, Steve opened the door and set off down some steel steps, which clanged in a manner all too familiar for Harold.

'Um, Steve. What about Harold?' Said Lisa.

He looked back and spotted her propping Harold up in the doorway, who was looking at the stairs with little optimism.

'If you just take his other arm, between us we can…'

Steve scooped both arms under Harold's legs, turned, and proceeded to carry him down the stairs like a child. Harold found the humiliation almost as painful as the broken leg, and did not enjoy the way the Agent's ribcage dug into him, nor the wheezing in his chest, nor the warmness of his skin. By the time Steve had puffed his way to the bottom, Harold was redder than he was, and Lisa failed to conceal a giggle, as she propped him back up again.

Steve seemed oblivious to all of this and began flicking through his wallet. Then he gave a little grunt when he found the appropriate keycard and swiped it through the grey reader on the wall.

Not your typical grocery store cellar, he thought as the door slid open to reveal a bustling office hall. Down the centre there was a long, turquoise carpet, and to either side were cubicles, containing whirring monitors and ringing telephones. Some of the workers compared notes, some talked into receivers, and some pointed towards the enormous interactive world map in the middle of it all. It was surprising no one heard the noise upstairs in the store, but then again, they'd been unable to hear it until the door opened, and they'd been right outside. It must be soundproofed.

As he hobbled after Steve, with Lisa's assistance, through the press of Agency staff, Harold stared up at the map. Little red lights blinked in different locations.

Are they all UFO incidents?

A heavy set black man, with a bald head and an uncompromising face stepped into their path so suddenly Steve almost walked into him. He glowered down at the Agent, two biceps bulging under his tight black t-shirt.

'Your ID, sir?' He said.

Steve's eyes thinned as they sized up his obstacle, tongue flickering. Harold and Lisa braced as his hand darted inside his blazer, but then relaxed again as the Agent produced his wallet. Harold thought Steve must have encountered similar protocol before but that he had little tolerance for sudden movements and big men who presumed they could intimidate him.

The big man laid Steve's ID card on a white square on an otherwise black iPad screen, which, after several tense seconds, shone green. He grunted and passed the ID back to Steve, who plucked it from his fingers with vigour that might have been mistaken for smugness, though the big man appeared not to notice.

'Put this on, please, sir,' he said, handing Steve a blue lanyard, 'Insert your ID card into the holder and wear it at all times, until you leave. Then you must return it to me.'

Steve grunted and moved on past, but the big man lifted a large palm to prevent Harold from following.

'ID, sir?'

'Not this again.' Steve said, 'He's expected by…'

'ID, sir?'

'I don't have any,' said Harold.

'What do you mean you don't have any?' The big man bellowed, silencing the whole office. 'What are you doing here?'

He threw aside the iPad which clattered off a filing cabinet and took a step towards Harold, who let go of Lisa and took a hop backwards. He felt that one punch from the big man might finish him off, but then Steve was there between them with his gun out.

The sound of ringing phones intensified around them, as all the calls went unanswered. Lisa backed over to where Harold leant against the desk, watching David and Goliath.

'What's your name?' Steve said.

'Charlie… and I don't think you know…'

'Ah, now Charlie, it's my turn to talk,' Steve said, with his finger held up in front of him, 'I don't know if you're new around here, or if all those steroids have completely eroded whatever excuse for a brain you were born with, but I've been an Agent for a very long time, and you will treat me, and my guests, with respect.'

The flippant manner in which Charlie returned Steve's

gaze, made Harold suspect that this wasn't the first time he'd been threatened with a gun, but there was still a lot of sweat visible on his brow.

'I don't know what you think your job is here... maybe to provide security... but your ultimate purpose, like everyone else in this office, is to support us Agents, and the support I need from you now is two guest passes for my companions and for you to tell MJ1 that Agent Steve is here to see him, as requested.'

'You can all go back to work now,' Steve said to the office, who snapped back to their duties, and the chatter drowned out the sound of ringing phones again. 'Well, what are you waiting for? Go and get your toy.'

Charlie backed away from the gun and returned with the iPad. Harold saw a crack in the middle of the illuminated screen.

'Have you broken it?' asked Steve.

'No,' said Charlie, a vein throbbing in his temple.

Harold spotted a redhead in her early thirties, twisting a lock of her hair as she talked on the phone. She wore a low v-neck sweater, and as his eyes drifted down the curves of her body he sensed her eyes finding him. He recoiled like a child caught stealing sweets.

But did she smile at me? Harold glanced back her way to discover two bright, green eyes staring right at him, her plump, ruby lips curled into a definite smile.

He was thinking how much he might like it here when a slap on his chest brought him back to reality.

'Ouch. That really hurt.'

He glared at Lisa.

'Stop perving for five seconds then,' she said.

Harold looked down at his chest where she'd slapped him and saw a sticker that read: 'Temporary Guest Pass.'

'He will see you now,' said the redhead, and Steve barged past Charlie who dropped his iPad and said something derogatory.

The girl smiled at Harold again as he passee, and this time there was no innocence in it.

CHAPTER THIRTY-FIVE

That's the Zetans' champion? Thought Valk, as the wimp smiled back at him. Pathetic.

Then the Agent, Steve, looked in his direction, and his tongue began to flicker. Valk knew the significance of this and returned to his keyboard.

A message popped up in the corner of his computer screen.

'He will see you now,' Valk said.

The Agent passed without looking at him. Valk breathed a sigh of relief and praised the potency of human perfume. The woman, Tsai crossed next, glaring straight ahead, and he understood why some of the others liked her. She had a fire in her. Then, finally, Dunn the Chosen One came, almost literally, as Valk gave him a smile.

Once they'd moved out of sight, Valk glanced around the office, then removed a black electronic pencil sharpener from the desk and a small screwdriver. He turned over the sharpener and twirled the four screws out of the bottom, then rolled a metal ball out of the base and onto his hand. He dumped the items on to his desk, save for the ball, which he began to twist until there was a division between the bottom and the top. After cranking it twelve times, it grew warm and began vibrating violently, so that he hurried it back inside the sharpener and replaced the bottom and all the screws.

His co-pilot. Punce, stared at him from across the room, as he moved all the items back into the drawer and closed it. He nodded, then both of them headed for the Fire Door.

Whistles and jeers sounded around the office as Charlie followed the lithe redhead into the stairwell that lead up the wall of the grocery to the roof.

'Treat her better than you treat that iPad, Charlie!' Was the last thing they heard, as the door closed behind them.

'We'll jump,' Valk said, climbing the stairs, 'The wheat field will break our fall.'

CHAPTER THIRTY-SIX

Lisa and Steve walked down the windowless, brightly lit corridor, to the oak door at the end.

'Aren't you going to help me?' Harold said, hopping along behind them and stopping to rest against the wall. 'My leg hurts like hell.'

'I don't want some perve putting his hands all over me,' Lisa said and strode off to wait by the door, with her arms folded.

'You're like children,' said Steve, and grabbed hold of Harold's arm. Harold was grateful he hadn't tried to scoop him up again but was unable to indicate his gratitude in his expression, because he was busy shooting Lisa the most violent glare he could muster.

Once they'd reached the door, Steve knocked once then opened it. The room contained a small wooden desk with a laptop on it and filing cabinets on either side. The rest of the room was sparse save for two glass tanks containing a multitude of crickets, locusts and moths, and pretty much everything Harold had never wanted to be anywhere near. Lisa appeared to like them, but seemed more mesmorized by the man, sitting behind the desk.

He was an old man, as old as Jack sitting in his chair out front, but that was where their similarities ended. He was neat, his hair trimmed close, and his skin was free from blemishes. He wore horn-rimmed glasses and a tweed jacket with patches at the elbows. He looked like a college dean.

'Ah, Agent 78383,' He said in a voice that was equally as jovial as it was authoritative, 'And the celebrities. Let me introduce myself, I am Majestic 1.'

Harold suppressed a scoff.

'Funny, Professor?' He said, with a warm smile, 'You may simply call me Boss, or Sir if you'd prefer.'

He gestured to the three chairs in front of his desk and said, 'Have a seat.'

'New staff?' commented Steve, sitting down and forcing Lisa to suppress her anger and help Harold onto the chair.

'A few,' Said MJ1, 'A new security guard and a new receptionist. Why do you ask?'

'They both caused me problems,' Steve noted, glancing sideways at Harold. 'In different ways.'

'Just a little wet behind the ears, but we'll soon have them up to scratch. You were gentle with them, I trust?'

His blue eyes fixed on Steve, and any warmth in them began to cool.

'I didn't kill them.'

'Well, that's growth 78383,' he said, and the sparkle was back, 'Perhaps the backs of your ears are starting to dry at last?'

Steve sniffed. His trademark for surliness.

MJ1 lowered his spectacles and took a long, hard stare at Harold's leg. 'That looks sore.'

'It aches a bit.'

He pressed a red button, on a panel, set into the top of his wooden desk, 'Janine, can you get a medic to come to my office, please?'

He folded his fingers and waited for Janine's response.

'Janine?'

He stared at the intercom.

'Maybe a little wetter around the ears than I thought?'

He picked up his phone and punched in a number. 'Hi, yeah, can you get a doctor to come to my office, please. A broken leg. No, not mine. Good. Yeah. Oh, and get someone to ring me from HR in about an hour. I want to have a word about the new staff. Ok, thanks,' he replaced the receiver.

'So, I wonder — how does it make you feel knowing aliens exist, Dr Tsai?'

'Small,' she said.

'Small indeed,' he said, and chuckled with his eyes closed. 'Small, yes, very small indeed.'

The door opened and a young man entered wearing a burgundy jumper and denim jeans, with a black duffel bag and stethoscope around his neck.

'Ah, Doctor, if you wouldn't mind?' he said, pointing towards Harold's leg.

The Doctor nodded, set down his bag, and removed a scalpel, which prompted Harold to inch back his chair.

'What's that for?' Harold said, unable to keep the anxiety out of his voice.

'Now, now, don't worry scaredy cat,' said the Doctor, held Harold's leg, and began to saw through the tape around the towel. Harold gritted his teeth against the twang of pain, drawn by the Doctor's grip, and heard Lisa giggle.

Once he'd removed the tape and towel, Harold's leg was revealed to be an ugly shade of purple, with a jagged lump protruding midway down his shin. The Doctor remarked that it looked like mouldy eggplant. After propping Harold's foot upon his knee, he leant back for his bag, but he'd left it just out of reach.

'Oh, nurse,' he said, looking at Lisa who'd giggled further at his eggplant remark, 'Could you pass me my bag, please?'

Lisa grinned and flickered her hair over her shoulder. 'Why, yes, Doctor. Of course.'

She lifted the bag, but lost her grip and nearly dropped it.

'Oops,' she said and opted to drag it closer to the Doctor instead.

'Phew, that's heavy,' she said, and settled back in her chair, fanning herself a little.

'You're stronger than you look,' said the Doctor.

'Some big equipment you're packing there. I can't wait to see it.'

'Ok, enough.' Harold said, making everyone look at him, 'I mean... my leg's starting to throb.'

Lisa smiled and looked away, while Steve massaged the

crease between his eyes. MJ1 just tweaked his eyebrow and watched them all with interest, his eyes flicking from Harold to Lisa, to the Doctor, and then back to Harold.

The Doctor lifted a glass cylinder, with an embedded LED screen out of the bag, rested it on the carpet and slid Harold's leg inside.

'Are you sure about this?' Harold said, looking around at Steve and Lisa. Lisa was picking a bit of sand out of her nail, and Steve looked passive. MJ1 craned his neck for a better look.

Harold looked back at the contraption and saw a red button and a blue button on the panel.

'Nothing to worry about,' said the Doctor, who then pressed the blue button.

There came a whirring sound and a ring of warm white light drifted up Harold's leg and then back down it again, before disappearing. On the screen appeared a green-lit X-ray of Harold's leg, where the specific damages were obvious.

'Clean breaks,' said the Doctor and then looked up at Harold with a smile, 'This might feel a little weird.'

He pressed the red button, and there was a higher pitched whir, and the whole cylinder glowed red and became very warm indeed. Just as Harold thought the hairs on his leg might catch fire, there came two stabs of intense pain with corresponding cracks, which caused Harold to yowl. He kicked the machine off to be free of the intolerable heat.

'Hey, careful with that,' said the Doctor, and lifted the machine, with all the care of someone lifting a newborn puppy, and placed it back in its bag with the other equipment.

Harold stared down at his leg and saw that all the purple had vanished — only clean, hairless, slightly smoking skin remained.

'Is it fixed?' Lisa said.

'Unbroken, yes,' said the Doctor.

'Doctor, you're a genius,' she said.

'Yes, but I owe some of it, in this case, to the equipment.'

'That'll be all,' said MJ1, who'd had enough of their banter, 'Thank you, Doctor.'

'No problem,' said the Doctor and opened the door, 'If

you ever need a check-up, Miss, I'm sure Steve here can give you my number.'

'Thank you, Doctor,' said Harold before Lisa could answer, and climbed back into his chair unassisted.

The Doctor smiled, nodded, and closed the door behind him.

'That was incredible,' Lisa said, 'why aren't hospitals using that thing every day?'

'The technology is too incredible for the general public, I should think,' said Steve.

Lisa frowned, opened her mouth to say something, and then closed it again.

'Nuclear war looks imminent,' said MJ1, getting them all back on topic. 'The Russian fleet is moored near US waters, and their submarines already lurking inside of it. Our analysts believe we could all be dust as early as this weekend, so just what the heck do you three intend to do about it?'

Both Steve and Lisa waited for Harold to answer.

'I suppose you know about my abduction?' Harold said.

MJ1 nodded.

'Well, the Zetans told me that the Maitre…'

He paused to see how much the terms meant to the old man, but his expression was neutral and hard to read. Harold guessed he already had some familiarity with the topics but didn't want to interrupt him.

'They told me that the Maitre are shapeshifters and that they've infiltrated both American and Russian government agencies, although we may have killed all the ones in this country already. I don't know. We've killed a couple… Anyway, I need to travel to Moscow so I can expose the ones over there to the Russian President. The Zetans think the Russians will fire first, so that's why I need to get out there and convince them not too.'

MJ1 sat back in his chair and scratched his chin.

'Why didn't your Zetan friends just beam you straight into Russia?'

'They would have had to position over Russia, sir, and that's where the Maitre mothership is. Too dangerous.'

'So instead they've made it my problem… how considerate?' He murmured to the ceiling and then sat up straight again. 'How exactly do you intend to expose these Maitre once you've gained your audience with President Reznikov?'

'I have an idea.'

'Care to share it?'

'I'm afraid not,' Harold said, and fingered the vial of pills in his pocket as MJ1's expression tightened.

'I could ask Steve to undo the good Doctor's work.'

'Steve already had a similar idea,' said Harold, exuding more confidence than he felt (he hoped). 'The Zetans will know if you harm me and they'll beam me out of here. Then we'll need to think of a different, riskier plan.'

MJ1 sniffed, in a Steve-like fashion, and considered that.

'You could be lying,' he said.

'I'm not.'

'But you could be,' he said. The seconds of silence began to tick by Harold searched for some reassurance he could offer.

'You can't afford to risk it,' said Lisa, and everyone looked at her.

MJ1 sighed. 'I suppose you're right, Dr Tsai,' he said, and Harold smiled at Lisa, who refused to look at him. He wondered if she was almost ready to start speaking to him again.

'The main issue isn't getting you into Russia, or even getting you the meeting with Reznikov, although that will be a slippery one. No, the main issue will be staying alive long enough to reach the Kremlin. At present Brits and Americans aren't welcome on the streets of Russia.'

'It can be done,' said Steve. 'We have an Agent in Russia.'

'Agent Shura,' said MJ1, 'who will likely be shot as soon as he delivers you to Reznikov. So, the question is, have you convinced me that it's in my interest to risk the death of my last Agent within the Russian government?'

He stared them down, one by one.

MJ1 might just order Steve to shoot them, and he would probably do it.

'I'll see Agent Shura is made aware of the situation,' said MJ1 at last. Harold felt the relief wash over him. 'Steve, you will handle their entry into Russia and their conduct thereof.'

'Yes, sir,' said Steve, standing and opening the door.

Back in the main office, Harold kept his eyes forward so as not to get caught out by the redhead — or more specifically, to not get caught out getting caught out by the redhead. He didn't even spot her in his periphery, so she was probably off somewhere in a corner, wondering about his sudden change of heart towards her. He suspected Lisa's mood was lightening towards him and didn't want to sour it again before a long flight to Russia.

Steve had his lanyard in his hand and his ID back in his wallet and was looking around. Then he shrugged and tossed the lanyard into a nearby wastepaper basket.

'Throw your stickers in there,' he said. 'I don't know where the fool has gone.'

Harold and Lisa complied and followed Steve through the door, back out to the stairwell.

The door rolled closed behind them, and the din was extinguished.

Steve pointed upwards to a wooden shelf, which neither Harold nor Lisa had noticed on their descent. The Agent took down three paper bags from the shelf and tossed one to each of them.

'What's this?' Said Lisa.

'Your groceries.'

As they climbed the stairs Harold realised the ache in his leg had almost disappeared.

Steve reached the green door and knocked.

'Ahh,' said the Manager, opening the door at once, 'Sorry to leave you so long, sirs and madam. That call just seemed like it was never gonna end. You know, some people... yak yak yak yak yak?'

Lisa thought he looked amusing as he went cross-eyed and made the chattering motion with his four fingers and thumb, but found Steve's flat expression to be the real comedy.

Eventually, perhaps processing Steve's response, the Manager sighed and said, 'Oh, good you found your orders. I'll see you out then. Follow me.'

On their way through the store, Harold again

endeavoured to keep his eyes from roaming but was less successful.

The clerk drew his attention with a wolf whistle, as he made to follow Steve out of the door, and said, 'Nice!'

Did she mean his miraculous recovery or his bum? Harold wondered as the door closed behind him.

It was around noon. The streets of Bartonville were busier. People passed by Jack in his chair, still smoking his cigarettes and drinking his coffee, without him giving a sideways glance.

As Steve bent to speak with him, Harold looked at Lisa sitting in the front seat of the Victoria staring ahead. Had she overheard the clerk? Was she pissed off with him?

He leant towards the half-open window. 'Look, Lisa, I'm sorry if…'

The explosion tore open Bartonville Fruit and Veg, sending a massive cannonball of rubble, fire, and fruit, across the street.

Lisa's head felt heavy with liquid, as she sat up in the car seat, and saw flesh littered about the street.

She looked at Old Jack's chair charred and smoking, with a blood splatter reaching away from it like a gigantic, red hand. Though, that aside, the chair itself had barely moved.

A groan came from outside the window. She peered down to find Harold had survived and was slumped against the door with a nasty cut on his forehead.

Then she heard the screams of the other people on the street, but they were a little way from the store. Their attention was not on the gore, nor the gigantic blaze where the store had been, but on the saucer rising from the wheat field.

'Harold!' she reached out of the window for him, but he wasn't there. Steve, coated in white dust and blood, was bundling him into the back of the car. Then he jumped in the front seat and hammered the engine, wheel spinning into flight, as a second explosion burst from the store.

'Steve!' Lisa said, pointing over her shoulder at the saucer, continuing to rise, and the mass of people watching it.

Harold spun round. 'Maitre!'

'I know!' Steve yelled, 'Let me think!'

He swung left, and the Maitre disappeared.

Harold took a proper look at him. The parts of his suit he could see from the back seat were tattered and thick with dust, and his face in the mirror was bleeding profusely from a dozen pieces of glass wedged in his skin. However, Harold knew most of the blood drying on Steve, had been the Store Owner's, Jack's, who he'd seen split into several pieces in front of him. An image that would take a lot of years and alcohol to repress.

The Agent wiped some of the blood from his eyes and Lisa could not be sure that he wasn't crying. His lips wriggled over one another like fish in a barrel, and he was blinking so much that she feared him incapable of seeing the road.

'Steve, are you ok?'

He pulled out his phone and jammed in a number. The operator could be heard from the back seat. 'We're sorry. We've been unable to connect your call. Please try again later.'

He dialled again.

'We're sorry…'

He roared and smashed his phone against the dash, then tossed it down it down between his feet.

Lisa touched his arm. 'Steve….'

He slammed on the brakes, so that they all rocked forward, and then spun around with his gun pointing at her.

'Damn Humans! Damn Zetans! Damn Maitre! Damn Dunn! And damn you! If you touch me again, I'll execute you both! Is that clear?'

'Yes.' They both said in unison, watching the sweat pour off the Agent onto the leather seats.

He pushed several bursts of air out through his nose, and then took off again.

Soon the sirens behind them began to fade into the distance, and they swung into Peoria International.

'Steve, stop,' Harold said, as Steve leapt out of the car and limped across the intersection, seeming oblivious to the cars that honked and swerved around him.

'Steve look at yourself,' Lisa said, as they caught up with him.

The Agent caught sight of himself in a window and slowed.

'You can't enter an airport like that,' said Harold.

Steve rolled his jaw, then turned and walked back to the Victoria, taking care to mind the traffic this time. From the trunk, he removed a suit, in plastic wrapping, from a pile of half a dozen., Then removed a hand mirror, a packet of face wipes, tape, some bandages and a small jar containing some kind of balm, from a green medical bag to a paper bag.

'Steve,' Harold said, 'Frankly you need to visit the emergency room.'

Steve slammed the trunk. 'When are you two going to understand that hospitals aren't an option? Particularly, now. If that saucer saw us escape, they'll be gearing up for another attack. We need to get out of the country as soon as possible.'

Steve opened the back door and threw in the stuff, 'I'll be five minutes. Don't talk to anyone,' he said, then got inside and slammed the door.

Lisa and Harold leant against the car, eyes searching the skies for Maitre.

'So that was messed up,' Harold said.

'Yeah, I know,' Lisa said, 'poor Steve.'

Harold looked at her with surprise. 'Poor Steve?'

'Yeah, all those people he knew. All gone in an instant.'

Harold shook his head. 'You're the last person I expected to feel sorry for him after all he's done to you. The man's a psycho.'

'He's still human,' Lisa said. The colloquialism seemed to hold more clout than usual, considering recent events. Harold nodded.

'I guess. What do you think happened back there?'

'They had a bomb,' Lisa said. 'They must have followed us in and planted it.'

Harold nodded. 'Or maybe there was a spy already in there?'

'That horrible man, Charlie was it? Or that redhead slut. Or the Manager?' said Lisa.

Harold felt himself blushing and decided to shift her focus.

'So what do you think will happen to the Agency now?'

'I suspect they'll rebuild.' Lisa said, 'Aside from the MJ1 and his staff, I reckon most of the Agents work out in the field. You saw how many of them there were at Area 51.'

'Makes you think though,' She continued. 'We've been so lucky so far, but what if they're tracking us somehow? What if there are Maitre posing as airport staff?'

'I doubt it,' said Harold. 'The Zetans gave the impression that the Maitre only infiltrated government agencies. I doubt they'd post one here on the off chance that we'd use the airport.'

'But what if one of the bombers took on the form of an airport employee and wandered in here to wait for us? That's possible.'

Harold was spared the task of having to come up with a response by Steve's re-emergence, in a new suit without a single blemish on his skin.

'Come on then.' He said, throwing them some wipes to clean their own cuts.

'How does he do stuff like that?' Harold thought aloud.

Inside the airport, Steve pointed them to a bench, and after telling them not to wander off, he walked to the head of a line of disgruntled would-be fliers and pulled one of the employees from behind the desk off to one side.

Harold tried to relax, but couldn't shake Lisa's suspicion a Maitre might be lurking somewhere inside the airport. He became aware of the suited man on the bench opposite, glancing over his newspaper at them, and of the woman leaning against the enormous potted plant by the escalator, sipping a Starbucks, and even of the child, eating a bagel, unblinking behind a pair of thick glasses. The Maitre could be any one of them.

'What do you think he's saying?' Lisa said.

Harold looked at Steve, who was talking at, not to, the shrinking male employee, and holding his ID up to the security camera.

'Probably some government trick to fast-track us on to a flight?'

A man with a striking blue tie emerged from a security door and joined the employee. He looked over Steve's ID, and Harold spotted his other hand transferring a brown envelope to the Agent's pocket. The employee, whom Lisa thought looked a little dishevelled, approached them and asked that they follow him.

They walked straight to the security line, where they were ushered immediately to the front of the line. This caused the queue's moaning to intensify, as three more people were allowed to cut in front. No doubt they were wondering what made them so special?

As they walked towards the gate, Steve took the brown envelope from his pocket, removed several items, and then held out two passports and two tickets behind his back.

Harold took them and opened one of the passports, the photo was of Lisa, so he handed it to her with one of the tickets. He opened the other and stared his own picture, and the name beside it. The name was Sam Russell.

'Before you ask, I don't know how he does it,' said Lisa.

The security agent merely glanced at their passports and tickets before waving them through. Steve walked at a brisk pace mumbling the flight was leaving soon. As they walked, Steve took the opportunity to look at the ticket. They were heading to Atlanta. To his surprise and pleasure, the tickets were first class.

They had no further issue boarding the plane. Harold and Lisa sat together, with Steve across the Isle. Harold asked Lisa which seat she preferred and she chose the aisle, which was fine for him.

After Harold had made himself comfortable in the seat, he checked his watch — twenty minutes had passed since their arrival at the airport. It had to be some kind of record.

'Bring me a whisky,' Steve said to the flight attendant as she passed. She nodded, her smile unaffected by his bluntness. 'Certainly, sir.'

Poor girl, thought Harold, she's probably used to it.

As he waited for his drink, Steve handed them four more tickets for the other legs to their flight.

At that point, Harold discovered the New York Times he had bought from the 7/11 the previous day, rolled up in his inside pocket, and the jerky too. He realised he was starving and could not remember the last time he had eaten.

After offering Lisa a stick, who refused, he ate all of the

jerky, then started reading the Sports Section, as Lisa stared out of the window, and Steve stared at the whisky he'd been given. Out of the corner of his eye, Harold could see the level of the liquid trembling in the glass, further evidence of Steve's condition. The calculated Agent was gone, replaced by this one, who seemed to be all aggression.

CHAPTER THIRTY-SEVEN

A s his craft passed Mars, Troni jabbed at his holographics and scoured them for any sign of the Hole. It had been a frustrating departure from Earth, the navigation equipment had been damaged in the crash, forcing him to conduct a manual search, which had so far born no clues. Space, after all, was a huge place, though he'd been sure it had been somewhere around the 'Red Planet'. He glared at it out of the window, wondering if any Martians had spotted him, though he knew he'd have been attacked by now if they had.

The transmission klaxon broke his reverie and made him jump. A broadcast found him.

'Good afternoon, this is Claudia Phillips, with some breaking news. A potential terrorist attack has occurred in Bartonville, Illinois, where beloved local grocery store 'Bartonville Fruit and Veg' exploded at around noon today, killing at least three people. Some witnesses claim to have seen a flying saucer briefly hovering over the scene before disappearing into the sky. This comes just three days after the reported UFO shootout above Area 51. Police say they've no suspects at this time but have asked that people keep their conspiracy theories to themselves, as these can be extremely upsetting for the families of the deceased. More as we get it.'

Troni leaned on his knees with his elbows, and wondered if the facts were accurate. He had expected the Maitre to take more time to regroup after the crash at Area 51 and had at least expected Harold and company to be in Russia before they made another move.

Agent Steve had mentioned he was taking Dunn and Tsai to Bartonville. Did that mean all three were dead? Was it all over?

As he posted a message to Dunn on Stormarea51.net a shudder ran through the ship.

Probably some damage to the stabilisers, he thought, or some debris bouncing off the hull.

He wandered over to the glass and looked outside. There was a lot of debris around Earth, but amongst it, some distance away, was a glowing blue orb, that seemed to be growing bigger, and bigger, and bigger…

He leapt over to the holographics panel and wrenched the ship out of position so that the plasma bolt just seared the left wing. A Maitre saucer whizzed by, turned and fired again. Troni span away from the bolt, rolled out the cannons, and accelerated around a cluster of mangled satellites to meet it.

'My go!'

He fired off a dozen shots, which prompted the Maitre into a spin of its own. This defensive action wetted Troni's appetite, and he whacked the boosters and hurtled after it, down towards Earth's moon. Grey dust and small rocks splashed across the windows as Troni pulled up level, just before he hit the Moon's surface. He found himself closing in on the Maitre. He poked the hologram for the EMP sting and roared in triumph to find it still operational. The Maitre saucer wobbled in realisation of the danger and began swooping this way and that, but as Troni expected, it was unwilling to move back into the exposure of Space. The Maitre saucers might be more manoeuvrable, but on an open stretch they were no contest for the speed of the Zetan crafts, and that was why Troni was laughing, as the sting edged ever closer — the needle to the vein.

He felt like some great hunter, about to pull down his prey by its haunches, but then the Maitre did something he did not expect.

'Is that a rear cannon? They don't have rear cannons!'

He dithered over whether to roll out the cannons again or to press on with the sting, and that was all the time the Maitre needed to let loose a shot, blast a hole through the repair patch, and send Troni crashing down.

CHAPTER THIRTY-EIGHT

Punce roared as the Zetan craft nose-dived onto the Moon, leaving a long scar of metal behind it.

'Now die, Grey scum,' said Valk from the cockpit, and turned the saucer one-hundred-and-eighty degrees so that they were facing the wreckage. He scanned it but detected no bodies, living or otherwise. He scratched his head, and examined the craft's mangled innards, floating away in every direction. He knew one of the Zetans had been killed near Area 51, but what of this one? Had it perhaps floated off? Their new saucer was meant to be a premium design, and the new weaponry had clearly come at the expense of the scanners.

Beside him, on the second joystick, Punce chattered away as he lined up the guns for the finishing blow.

'We're going to get something nice for doing this — some nice warm continent on Earth perhaps? I like the look of South America, Valk. Have you seen South America?'

'Quiet, Punce,' Said Valk, peering out of the window that ran right around the saucer, 'We should go make sure it's definitely dead.'

'Definitely dead? I'm about to blow it to bits,' he said, thumb hovering over the red button on top of his joystick.

Valk grunted and slapped his hand away.

'Ouch! What?'

'What if it's crawled off somewhere?'

'You think it survived a crash like that?'

'Call me a perfectionist.'

'I could call you a few things.' Punce said, rubbing his hand, 'Fine. Take us down then.'

Valk pulled his own joystick towards him and sent them on a horizontal trajectory towards the right of the crash site. Fifteen feet from the surface they came to a halt and Valk pressed the black switch that extended the landing legs. He felt Punce watching him with a glazed expression.

'Are you just going to stand there, or are you going to get the masks?'

Punce mumbled something as he searched the lockers, and then there came an enormous crash, as he emptied one in its entirety onto the floor. Despite Valk's attempts to ignore the cacophony, he gained a massive headache, unimproved by the selection of objects that'd bounced off his skull since Punce had started searching.

'Are you done?' He said and turned to see Punce sitting on the floor with a mask in either hand, junk extending from him like ripples on a pond.

Punce smiled. He couldn't understand what his partner was so uptight about. Yes, their mission in Bartonville hadn't gone as they'd hoped, but on their way home they'd blasted a Zetan craft, and it had to be the one that'd been aiding the rebels.

He threw his partner a mask and then pulled on his own. They produced breathable air for twelve hours, while also balancing their internal pressure. Their bodies, themselves, would generate an extra thick layer of slime to protect them from the Sun's UV rays.

Valk activated the transport beam, picked up his plasma pistol from its slot beside the console, and walked over to the flickering blue sheet.

'Where's your gun?'

'Umm…' Punce said and began scavenging through the junk again. Valk shook his head and dropped through the sheet. Down the beam, on the Moon's surface, his feet found cool dust-coated rock, which he hooked onto with s claws to

199

counter the low gravity.

After far too many minutes, he heard a grunt on his headset, and Punce landed beside him, a thin golden cylinder clipped to his arm.

'What's that?' Said Valk.

'It's my gun, Valk.'

'That's the rifle.'

'Yes.'

'The one that doesn't shoot straight.'

'It shoots well enough.'

'Where's your proper gun?'

'Don't know.'

Valk shook his head again.

'You see him?' asked Punce, taking a few steps out of the beam towards the craft.

'How could I see him at this range?' Valk remplied as hebegan walking.

Punce liked the rifle. It was a little temperamental, granted, but it had a nice kick, and it was the biggest gun on the ship. He jogged forwards after Valk and bounced up onto the craft, pointing the rifle through a massive hole in the window, but he couldn't see anything because his partner was shining a torch in his face.

'Get back down here. Don't you know anything? We'll secure the area first and make sure he's not outside.'

'Does it matter?'

'Yes.'

Punce shrugged and glided back down towards him.

'You take the right flank, I'll take the left.'

Punce set off around the nose of the craft, and Valk wondered when he'd think to turn his torch on, or whether the torch on the end of that ridiculous rifle still worked. No matter, that was his problem. Valk had a job to do.

He kept his body near to the ground and hooked his way forward, his pistol outstretched in both hands. Soon, he came across a large laceration in the fuselage, which looked like it might have been a hasty repair job. Shining the beam inside, he recoiled and almost fired, upon seeing the Zetan drift towards him.

'Punce. Come here!'

Punce was several minutes, and he didn't so much arrive, as run straight into Valk. He hadn't got the torch working.

'Ouch. You fool.'

'Look. Dead. Told you we got it. You worry too much. Dead, dead, dead.'

'Oh, silence,' said Valk compressing the little red button on the side of his mask, 'Valk-transmitting, come in Mothership.'

There was a brief silence before he heard Nilodost's whine, 'Repeat.'

'We were returning from our mission on Earth when…'

'You were waylaid? Might I remind you, Valk, that following your failed mission to assassinate your assigned three targets, you and Punce were ordered to return to the Mothership immediately? Yet you're still not here.'

'Be quiet and listen, Nilodost,' said Punce, 'When I see you I'm going to shoot you in the rectum with my plasma rifle.'

'As I was saying,' Valk said, 'We were returning from our mission on Earth when we encountered a Zetan craft. It's got to be the one that's been helping the Humans.'

'And we blasted it into oblivion,' said Punce, dancing hand in hand with the corpse.

'You saw it? You destroyed it?'

'We did. We did. We did.'

'And you've confirmed the body?'

'Yes. Yes. Yes.'

A pause and muffled voices.

'Leader Atherpock is impressed with your conduct. Your reception on board the Mothership will be a warmer one than it might have been. I'll send a probe to confirm your claim.'

'Why don't you go probe a Conjor, Nilodost?'

There was a brief sound of static as the link was severed.

'Fool,' said Valk, then ducked inside the craft to see how Punce was further molesting the corpse. It turned out he'd exhausted his macabre interest in the dead Zetan and had begun picking through the cockpit instead.

'Anything worth taking?'

'Give me a second,' he said, searching an alcove, 'There's

some Earth water.'

Valk had developed a taste for Earth water and would miss it when he was forced to resume drinking the rusty solution they had back home.

'Grab a few bottles, but hurry up.'

Zetan craft made his skin crawl, whatever condition they were in, so ugly, so clumsy. Sweat shells for Zetan scum. He looked back towards his own ship, a far superior machine, despite the scanners. The Zetan floated in front of him, and he reached out his pistol towards its face to nudge it away, but then its head exploded into a dozen gooey pieces, and gave him such a start, that if there'd been gravity, he might've fallen.

Punce was laughing, his rifle outstretched. 'I knew this thing still fired straight!

'You...' Valk began, but then the light of his torch caught on something green, that brought his attention back to the corpse. He caught the Zetan's hand, prised apart its fingers and found a little, green ball with a red hole in it.

'Now that looks valuable,' said Punce. 'What is it?'

'I'm not sure,' said Valk, rolling the ball between his fingers, then he gave it a squeeze and a flash of light burst from the hole. They both looked around at the Zetan projected on the wall.

Somewhere, from deep inside the craft, there echoed a croaky voice.

'I have not used my vocal cords for many years, but I'm glad to use them now, in the moments before you get here. After the incident at the Water Treatment Plant on ZR2, where some of your kind poisoned our water supply and then escaped to Earth, I wanted to fly off to Megopei and hunt you all down on your own soil... law be damned... but one Zetan kept me grounded... my only friend... stopped me from running off to fight a fight I wouldn't win...' A cough on the recording.

'I don't like this,' said Punce.

'... His name was Nyn and you killed him. I swore I'd bring his body home but I was too reckless, too stupid... but he shall at least, have his revenge, against you.'

The ball between Valk's fingers began to smoulder.

'Goodbye… Maitre scum!'

'No,' said Valk, and dived for the gap, emerging on the other side in a few dozen pieces.

Only after the shock wave had passed, did Troni wriggle up the slope of his crater, and shine his torch out on the scene. Twisted shapes like metal vultures hovered over the charred crust, where the craft had been. The bomb had been his own invention, something he'd made in his room back on Zr2. When Nyn had come home, he'd been unimpressed.

'Have you stayed in all night making weapons again? I swear you've got more bombs than the rest of the military put together. You really need to get out and talk to some girls.'

Troni had told him he spent too much time talking to girls.

'Girls don't get you blown up or arrested.' Nyn said, lying down on his bed, 'Girls don't get me blown up or arrested. Well, they haven't yet anyway.'

Troni shook away the memory and gripped his gun a little tighter. It was impossible that the Maitre had survived, but that was what they thought of him, and he had no desire to be caught out at his own game. What he needed to do was escape. The explosion would not go unnoticed.

With Nyn's voice urging him on, he scrambled over the rim of the crater and fled towards the Maitre saucer. Atop the beam, he threw off his helmet and dashed for the control panel.

'No holographics?' he said, 'A joystick? Infantile!'

He fiddled with some of the dials, then there was a jolt, and Troni turned to see a bolt of plasma disappearing into space.

'Weapons.'

He moved to the other console and pulled the joystick. There was a grind as the legs retracted, and then the saucer bobbed, as though in water.

'Ha,' he said and pushed forwards on the joystick. This prompted the saucer to dip towards the surface and splash a wave of dust over the windows. Troni cursed as he stood up, his head smarting from where it'd hit the joystick.

'Sorry, Nyn,' he said, looking towards their craft for the final time, then pulled the joystick towards him, and rocketed upwards.

CHAPTER
THIRTY-NINE

L isa sipped her gin and tonic, while the one-eyed, green tentacled, Kang and Kodos plotted world domination. The personal TV, built into the back of the seat in front, contained most of her favourite shows, and some of them, like The Simpsons, were over one-hundred episodes long, so she had plenty to distract herself with. She giggled as it was revealed that Maggie the Baby had been an alien all along, but then stopped when it reminded her of Kowalski.

Pre-Maitre, she'd spent a lot of time with him, which had made his big reveal all the more harrowing. She'd eaten lunch with him every day, taken walks with him, and even spent time with him on what might've been called dates, at bars and restaurants. He'd always been a little surly around others, a little possessive of her, but no more than some of the other admirers she'd met in her life.

Five years ago next month, she'd gotten the call telling her that her parents had died, and he'd sat with her through the evening, all compassion and understanding. All that time he'd been a monster in a human suit. She shook her head, turned off the TV, and glanced out of the window.

They were on the final leg at last... or too soon... regardless, they'd be there in four hours.

They'd only stopped twice in both Atlanta and then

Amsterdam, and both times Harold and Lisa had busied themselves with gates and tickets, while Steve had wandered off without comment, only to reappear right before boarding, stinking of booze. In both cities, they had to go through customs. In Atlanta, Steve again was able to flash his badge and get them to the head of the line. But in Amsterdam, they went through as regular tourists. But the line moved fast.

She thought about how his occupation probably left little opportunity for relationships with anyone outside the Agency, making those inside of it the closest thing he had to friends — and he'd just lost a whole lot of them.

Harold drew her attention with a loud snore. She considered what she knew about him. He was probably divorced, something to do with a administrative assistant perhaps, and he'd likely had more than a few lovers. He had just the right balance of looks, intelligence and cheek, rather than charm, to appeal to some women. Although, she did suspect him of being a misogynist. He eye-fucked every woman he met, and when he spoke to her, he seemed to be making a real effort to suppress his frustration at the way she was. How had he become that way? Maybe his mother had fucked her fitness instructor, and he'd lived out his childhood with a very bitter father?

This made her think about her own family. She was an only child. Her parents often joked she'd been left on the doorstep by the hermit from the hill, which explained her introversion growing up. While she stayed indoors studying, with the curtains closed, her parents were off on hikes and the like. She'd always been invited but went along far too rarely — something she regretted. One December they'd been eager to visit the snowy fells of the Lake District, in England. They took up base in Grenton, a small village in the North West her father had a fondness for.

'They'll do anything for you,' her father had said to her. 'You pass them on the street, and they can't wait to offer you something — a cup of tea, a beer, directions to where you're going. Heck, most of them will walk you there even if it's miles out of their way. Honourable people you see, with no tolerance for pretension. You look down your nose at one of them, you better be sure you don't get seen doing it.'

'Yes, Dad,' Lisa would say as her fingers scurried across the keyboard.

'Oh, sad-sack. Don't you know the story of how you came to be? Well, there used to be this hermit you see…'

'Dad, if I agree to come, will you not tell the hermit story?'

Then he'd laugh that great belly laugh of his, map book shaking in one hand, coffee mug in the other, and Lisa would smile begrudgingly.

It had been on that trip to England, as they'd turned a coastal bend, their car slid on a frozen patch of mud. She could remember her Dad heaving the wheel from side to side, her mother screaming, and then… darkness.

Lisa woke up in Grenton Hospital, a week later. She'd survived because she'd been in the back seat, but the front of the car crumpled like a crisp packet, along with her parents — some engineering flaw, prompting the car manufacturer to withdraw that model the following week. Lisa received a settlement from them, one that still gathered dust in her savings account. It seemed like dirty money. Blood money.

She heard Steve grunt, and fidget in the seat across the aisle.

'How are you?' she asked him, but he only sniffed and turned over.

'I don't think he feels like talking,' remarked Harold, with a stretch that invaded her personal space. It made her think he would not fare well on a visit to one of her father's working-class towns, with their old fashioned values.

'What will you do if we live through this, Harold? I'd like to go on holiday somewhere. Not Russia. I've always wanted to visit England actually.'

He shifted in his seat and licked his lips.

I didn't mean with you, you arrogant bastard, she thought.

'It's where my parents are buried,' she said, 'A small church in the North West.'

'Oh, I'm sorry,' he said, exhaling. 'Where in the North West?'

'Grenton, Cumbria. Heard of it?'

Harold grinned, 'Yeah, it's only about seventy odd miles

from where I'm from. There's a factory in Grenton, I visited it during my youth as an apprentice. Didn't get to see much of the town though, but I did have a nice pie…'

A wave of pleasure washed over his face.

'If you like pie, check out Blue's Pie Shop, next time you're in Grenton,' he said. 'I lived off those pies when I was there. Stuff of legend.'

'I'll remember that.'

The plane jolted, bringing a few murmurs of surprise.

'Ladies and Gentlemen, this is your Captain speaking, we're currently breaching the gap between Finland and Estonia, and experiencing a little bit of turbulence. It's just the strong winds that are often present on the Baltic Coast. Please fasten your seatbelts, it shouldn't last more than ten minutes. Thank you.'

There was another sharp jerk, which flung the last dregs of Lisa's drink into the air.

Steve sat up, the whites of his eyes turned crimson. 'What's going on?'

'Just a spot of turbulence.' Lisa said, 'We're near Estonia.'

Steve peered out of the perspex dome, where there was a thick layer of cloud, with the dawn sun just peeking through. A movement prompted his gaze to sharpen, and he noticed a glinting speck shoot straight up from below and out of sight.

'Not good,' he said, as the plane rattled some more.

'Ladies and Gentleman, if you haven't already taken your seats, please do so and please fasten your s… huh… what the hell was that…?'

The intercom cut out, which brought some shouts of alarm, and jostling, as the passengers fought to return to their seats. This light brawling grew heavier as more turbulence shook the plane, like a child with an ant farm.

Steve unbuckled himself and climbed over them into the aisle.

'What's 'not good'? You said 'not good'.' Harold said, reaching for the Agent's arm and missing.

'Do not put the masks on,' ordered Steve, and set off up

the plane, tossing passengers left and right as he encountered them. One guy saw him coming and gripped a seat either side of him in defiance — a futile one, it turned out, as Steve punched him on the nose and set him sprawling to the floor.

The Agent passed through the red curtain, dividing the cockpit from the rest of the plane, and found the flight attendant hiding.

'Sir, I'm afraid you'll have to go back to your seat.'

'I must speak to the captain.'

The attendant unbuckled her seatbelt and stood between him and the cockpit door.

'The captain can't see you now, sir. You'll have to go back to your seat.'

Steve cursed and dug his ID out of his pocket.

'I'm an Agent of the US Government,' he said. 'And if you want us to survive what's coming next you'll let me into that cockpit right now.'

The stewardess stared at his ID, and then pressed the intercom on the wall.

'Captain, I've a US Agent here. He claims to know about the… unique nature of our situation.'

A few moments later, a young man with a pale face and a sweaty mop of ginger hair opened the door and led Steve to the front of the plane.

'Well?' said Steve.

A moustachioed, grey-haired man, whom Steve took to be the pilot, pulling levers and flicking dials, said, 'We're hitting more turbulence than usual, we can't gain speed, we're losing altitude all the time, and the radio's out.'

Steve heard the engines splutter for a few seconds, and in that time the plane plunged several feet. It was then that the metallic speck whizzed past the plane again.

'There it goes again,' said his ginger co-pilot, 'I swear we've got Russian bogeys all over us.'

He looked at Steve.

'This is the last commercial flight into Russia for the foreseeable future, we're due to decommission after this. They should've called it sooner. Why didn't they call it sooner?'

'Calm down, Billy.' The captain said then turned to

Steve, 'But there is some cause for Billy's alarm — we're not going to make the shore.'

As the speck made another pass, Steve caught a blue flash and realised the saucer was using its abduction beam to pull down the plane. The plasma cannons would not look like an accident, he realised, too much evidence for the U.G.

At that moment he understood how the current Maitre attack had come to take place. They had scanned the ruins in Bartonville and discovered their escape. They'd discovered there was only one flight left to Russia and confirmed that Steve's Victoria was in the airport parking lot. After that, it had just been a case of finding and scanning the right plane. Had Steve the time or frame of mind to check the flights, he too would have discovered that this was the last flight and taken a different route into Russia. He cursed his own carelessness and decided that he couldn't afford to be a slave to his grief anymore. He caught a whiff of the alcohol on his breath and felt ashamed.

'What is that thing?' Said the co-pilot, as the flying saucer made a slower pass. Steve wondered if it had spotted him

'Gentlemen,' He said, 'You're looking at the pinnacle of Russian aerial combat technology, we've had intelligence on them for years but never seen one in flight.'

'It's impressive,' Said the Captain, 'Look at the way it moves...'

'Yes, it's very nice...' Steve said, 'They're armed with armour piercing gas canisters, which they could well fire into the main passenger bay at any second. The canisters contain a toxin capable of killing everyone on this plane in under a minute.'

Both pilots looked at him.

'Much cheaper to produce than your average sidewinder missile. We think they bought the idea from North Korea.'

As he talked, one hand unscrewed the oxygen line, while the other plugged in a golden cylinder.

'Hey!' Said the Captain.

'It's the antidote, just in case,' said Steve 'Now put on your oxygen masks and drop the ones in passenger bay.'

Both men looked uncertain, and the captain asked for

another look at Steve's ID before they complied.

'Make the announcement,' Steve said and left the cockpit, striding back to his seat and ignoring the passengers' enquiries for information.

'Seatbelts on,' he said, as they felt the nose of the plane drop.

'Ladies and Gentlemen, we are preparing for a water landing, please fasten your seatbelts, and put on your oxygen masks.'

The second the masks dropped, Steve saw Harold go for it.

'What did I just say?' Steve said, reaching up and tearing it out of the ceiling.

'But the captain...'

'Never mind, 'the captain'. I'm telling you to leave it.'

The sanity of the passengers descended on the same trajectory as the plane. He heard some of them praying to God to save them, others screaming about a terrorist attack, others phoning to say emotional farewells to their relatives. Some just screamed.

The stewardesses were back in sight, returning the wild to their seats and applying masks and life jackets.

'No thanks, we're fine,' said Steve, as the stewardess reached them.

'But sir, you must...'

'No thanks, go help someone else.'

The stewardess' mouth thinned, and her eyes grew sharp, as though she was suppressing something, then she buckled and said, 'Go fuck yourself then,' and moved on to the next row.

'Keep your feet flat and your head against the seat in front.' Steve said, 'We're probably going to die in the crash, but if we don't, then I can get us out of here alive.'

Steve watched Harold feel for Lisa's hand, and he kissed her on the cheek. She pulled away and did not reciprocate his smile.

He overestimates his power over women, thought Steve.

Then the nose of the plane began to rise again, and Steve imagined the Captain wrenching the controls back to pull them out of the dive. Outside, he could see waves on the horizon. He was running out of time to implement his plan, but much still depended on the behaviour of the passengers.

'Cabin crew and passengers, brace, brace!'

The stewardesses began their death chant — 'Heads down, grab ankles, stay down. Heads down, grab ankles, stay down.'

Steve listened to the screams, none of which were as crisp as they had been two minutes ago — an indication that all the passengers had their masks on. He dialled a number on his phone.

'Heads down, grab…'

The chant died, along with the rest of the din, and Steve heard the engines cut out. There was a sensation of weightlessness as the three-hundred tonne plane glided the last few feet towards the ocean.

'When we land, we're going to get very cold, very quickly, if we don't move fast,' said Steve, and then ducked his head between his knees, in the hope that they would both copy him.

The plane hit the ocean, and several passengers were flung from their seats, and luggage crashed out of overhead compartments. After some teetering and groaning, they drifted to something of a stop, and Steve considered the rock of the current.

'Everyone alive?' He heard Harold say, and it was then that he realised that even he had been lulled into inactivity by the trauma of the crash. He jumped up out of his seat.

'Belts off.'

Lisa managed it fine, but Harold 's fingers struggled over the straps, and he seemed unable to compress the button, despite the fact he was looking straight at it. Steve spotted the water seeping in at the rear door and shoved Lisa out of the way, and undid his belt for him.

'The pilot hasn't pressed the ditching button,' remarked Steve, as they sloshed up the aisle. 'The fuel vents are flooding with water, and we've got about ten minutes before this craft is completely submerged.'

'The other passengers,' Lisa shrieked, 'Why aren't they moving?'

Steve had hoped that the shock of the crash would delay

any questions until they were off the plane, but there they both were, already pausing to inspect the limp figures.

'They're all dead.' Steve said, and tried the door handle, which refused to budge, 'A saucer brought this plane down, they may all have seen it, and that's why they could never be allowed to go back out into the world.'

He gave the handle a wrench, and the door popped out like a champagne cork.

'A saucer? Are they still out...' Harold yelled, over the whistle of the wind, but was cut off by Lisa.

'You! The masks! The passengers — you killed them all?'

Steve ignored her and shivered as he rummaged in the groove beside the exit, and found that the lever he was searching for wasn't there.

Damn have we ended up on a flight with no life raft? What are the chances?

Then his fingers hooked on something, five inches lower than it was supposed to be, and an orange inflatable slide flopped outside and began unfolding.

Incompetent engineers.

'Listen to me, you fucker,' Lisa said, 'You're an evil son of a...'

Steve seized her and threw her out of the door without ceremony.

'Come on, Dunn,' he said, 'Make sure you stop before the end of the raft because if you hit the water, I'm not jumping in to save you.

Harold gulped as he stepped up into the doorway, his view filled with swirling, black murk. A bulb burst overhead and blew sparks. That was enough for Steve, who shoved Harold in the back, and sent him tumbling down the slide, nails scrabbling over the rubber as he forced himself to slow before the end.

As Steve prepared to jump, he heard a noise behind him, something in the depths of the plane.

'Help!'

He looked down the slide at the pair and doubted their loyalty should they discover how to detach the raft.

'Help!' Came the call again.

He spluttered in exasperation and set off back down the

plane with his pistol drawn, his toes numbing as his Oxfords filled with icy seawater.

He passed their original seats, the water level up to his shins, and just a few rows back, he found the elderly couple who had preceded them onto the plane.

'Please sir,' he said, 'Help my wife.'

Steve looked at the lifeless figure, in the pearls and green cardigan, beside the man. Her mask had not deployed, and he'd given her his. He'd unwittingly murdered his own wife.

'I can't.' he said.

The man's watery blue eyes sharpened. 'How is it that you are so calm, sir, in the face of all this horror?'

The man had no chance of survival — at his age he would go into cardiac arrest the second the water found him. No need to shoot him. Steve holstered his gun and moved back towards the doorway. He un-looped the togs tying the raft to the plane and watched it drop to the ocean. Then, as he edged over the lip and prepared to drop, he heard the man shout a final time over the roar of the wind.

'You did this, and God and I have agreed that you shall be punished for it!'

Steve thumped into the middle of the raft, just as the current caught it and dragged it a considerable distance from the plane.

All three of them spent the next few minutes in silence, watching the plane sink below the surface, then Lisa scrambled towards Steve and slapped him.

'Jesus,' Harold said, and pulled her behind him, as Steve raised a hand to his cheek and stared at Lisa.

'There were children on board. Children.'

Steve sniffed. 'Children have eyes and ears and memories and voices, too.'

'What do we do now?' asked Harold before Lisa could answer.

'Wait to drown.' Steve said, tongue flickering, 'Or to be eaten by sharks. Or to freeze. Or…'

A flying saucer whizzed by overhead.

'Or there's that, of course,' he said and pulled out his gun.

The saucer circled and drifted back towards them,

coming to a stop overhead.

All three of them stared up at their impending doom, knowing what to expect, but the sudden burst of blue light still prompted Harold to topple overboard. Steve reacted before he could be swept away and dragged him back onto the raft.

'Not the nicest way to go, Professor Dunn, would you prefer to be shot? Dr Tsai?'

They both looked at him with the same flustered exhaustion one might expect from two people faced with the decision of a bullet to the head or a lifetime or torture in outer space. The choice seemed obvious, yet neither of them had the strength to make it. Steve also felt conflicted, and soon he was robbed of the option, as total numbness spread across his body and the raft began to grow smaller and smaller and smaller.

They passed through the blue sheet and found themselves standing in a small circular room with only one exit. Harold announced their arrival to the rest of the ship by collapsing to his knees and letting lose a string of retches.

Steve held his gun steady, eyes on the door, waiting for the loping frame of a Maitre to emerge. Behind him, he felt Lisa edging inwards to use him for protection. A bit rich, he thought, after her harsh words below.

The minutes ticked by, and Harold's retches grew lighter, and then all began to hear the patter of hurrying feet on metal, growing louder, getting closer. Steve held steady until he was sure that the Maitre would turn into the room with its next step, then raised his gun, and fired two shots.

'Watch it.' Their respective voices in their respective heads commanded, and in the doorway stood Troni, staring up at the smoking bullet holes.

'Troni,' Harold said, and raced past Steve him to lift the Zetan into an embrace.

Lisa laughed, and Steve wished he'd aimed lower.

'Yes, it's me. Now put me down before I drop you back in the water.'

Harold lowered him to the ground and patted him on the shoulder.

'How are you…? Where's your…?'

'Did you crash that plane?' Steve said, quashing Harold's babble. He still had his gun out, and his finger felt hungry at the trigger.

How hard can it be to fly one of these? Steve thought, and then regretted it.

'Of course I didn't crash that plane,' Troni replied, 'But you would crash this ship in ten seconds without me, so don't even think about it.'

Lisa and Harold both glared at Steve as he tucked his gun away, but he pretended not to notice. Troni led them from the small room, down a long corridor, and into a bigger room, where there were two rows of straight-backed chairs with bristles, presumably to stop the slimy Maitre from sliding off. Troni headed for two other chairs, with curved backs, in front of the biggest window, with consoles in front of both of them.

'Joysticks?' Steve said.

'I know,' said Troni, with a pained expression.

Lisa looked at Harold who shrugged.

Troni sat down in one of the chairs and placed his hand on a lever. 'You might want to hold on to something.'

He pulled it, and Harold's stomach dropped down to his shoes, as they were catapulted into space.

'Bloody hell, Troni,' Harold said from the floor, rubbing the back of his head.

'Only one good thing about these Maitre rust buckets,' said Troni. 'Easy space access.'

He looked at them struggling to stand on bowed legs and drenched in Baltic Sea-water.

'So, you probably want to dry off?' Troni pointed towards five alcoves in the wall. 'Just step inside one and push the blue button.'

Harold and Lisa let Steve go first. He stepped into the alcove and hit the button. He attempted to appear unfazed as the glass slammed down and a rush of vapour enveloped him. He wasn't sure if he'd convinced them with his façade, but because he was first out, he was spared their reactions. He enjoyed seeing Lisa when the glass over her alcove ascended. Her hair looked as though it might have had birds nesting in it.

'What?' she asked as she noticed Steve staring

He pointed past her towards Harold's alcove.

'Harold, I did not tell you to push the green button,' Said Troni. 'I told you to push the blue. The green is Maitre moisturiser.'

Harold spat out some cold slime, as Lisa burst out laughing.

'Oh my god, I can't even…'

'How do I get it off?' Harold said, goo running down his clothes and pooling into his shoes.

'Double-press the blue button.'

Harold did so abruptly and was grateful when the glass slid down again and the whoosh of vapour muted Lisa for a while. This time when he emerged, his skin was lobster red, which disguised his flush of embarrassment.

'Officially it wipes you of any contaminants, but it warms you up as well,' said Troni.

'It also takes off a layer of skin,' Harold noted.

'Enough nonsense,' Steve said, tongue flickering. 'What are you doing in a Maitre ship?'

'Saving your incompetent self.'

'How did you come by it?' queried Lisa, before their bickering could resume. 'What happened to your ship?'

'Crashed — an unfortunate incident on your Moon.'

'Maitre?'

Troni nodded. 'I lost Nyn. His body…'

'How did you find us?' Steve said.

'I figured that if you'd survived the explosion in Illinois, you'd still try to make the journey, so I looked on your Internet and found that there was only one scheduled flight left to Russia. I arrived just in time to see you hit the water.'

'We were pulled down by Maitre,' Steve said.

'I guessed that. Any other survivors?'

Steve felt Harold and Lisa's collective glare again.

'Oh, the Agent did what he does best, did he?' Troni began, but his tone dropped a decibel. 'Probably just saved them from the inevitable anyway. The US and Russia will both claim that the downing of the plane was an act of war against the other. The Earth faces imminent nuclear annihilation.'

'You've learned this?' Said Steve.

'I know this,' answered Troni, 'Human behaviour is very predictable.'

'True,' remarked Steve, then he caught a whiff of something unpleasant, but familiar. A stench he'd not smelt for a very long time. What was it?

'Then what are we waiting for?' asked Lisa. 'Troni, beam us into the Kremlin and let's get it over with.'

'If I move close enough to beam you in we shall be spotted and destroyed, besides how do you think the Russians will react to three people appearing out of thin air?'

'They might think we're aliens and listen to us,' replied Lisa, folding her arms.

'They're Russians. They'll shoot you before your mouth opens.' Steve said, only half-listening,

'Nothing to do with their nationality so much as their species. All humans have a primitive urge to destroy things they don't understand.'

'Stop!' Steve said, making them all jump.

'What is it?' Said Troni.

'Did you sweep this ship after you took it?'

Harold and Lisa both looked at Troni whose vocabulary had lost its bite.

'I… there wasn't time.'

'What's going on?' Harold said.

'We're not alone on this ship,' Steve said and took out his gun again.

As Harold and Lisa stared around for somewhere a Maitre could be hiding, the Agent stalked forwards, eyes on the ceiling, though mostly unused. His tongue flickered, and his nostrils flared.

'I don't see anything,' Harold said, but even as he said it, he heard a faint scurry of claws on metal.

Steve stopped walking, and his head bobbed from side to side like an owl. Then he spun around and fired. The gunshot echoed throughout this ship, followed by a screech and then something resembling an ape fell from the ceiling.

As it wriggled on the ground, it began to look less ape-like. Its body was squat and hunched and black with fur, like a chimp. But its face bore a long snout and was flanked by floppy ears, which would have looked more at home on a canine. Its fingers belonged to nothing Harold had ever seen — They were widely spread and bald, with hooked claws at the ends, and oozing suckers underneath.

It sat up, shaking its head, violet blood gushing from a hole in its shoulder, and then shone a pair of gleaming red eyes in Steve's direction. It screeched and leapt, powerful back legs launching it as though off a springboard, and then the rest seemed to happen in slow motion. The beast curled back its lips to reveal two jagged rows of shark's teeth and would've torn Steve's face off, had the bolt of plasma not knocked it off its trajectory. It whimpered on the floor and tried to rise for another attack, but Steve was upon it and firing, and did not stop until his gun went click, and the beast's red eyes had dimmed to black.

Harold and Steve both turned expecting to see Troni standing there, but he was over by the consoles. It was Lisa who held the plasma cannon, levelled at the twitching corpse.

'Good shooting, soldier.' Harold said.

'Idiot, Grey,' said Steve rounding on Troni. 'Y ou didn't you sweep the ship!'

Troni bristled. 'I've never claimed to be perfect, but I'm closer to perfection than your lot.'

'Who just killed the Conjor and saved us all?' asked Steve, 'It wasn't you.'

'Nor was it you.' Troni said, pointing at Lisa. 'If it weren't for her, you wouldn't have a face right now, which on reflection might have been of advantage to the rest of us.'

'Enough.' Lisa said, 'What the hell is that thing?'

'That is a Conjor. Native to Megopei,' answered Troni approaching the corpse and examining the metal below the bullet holes in its head, 'Looks like it has been fitted with an audio-visual receiver, hence the redness behind the eyes.'

He straightened up and gave it a kick.

'The Maitre enjoy pets. If any of you survive capture and interrogation, that's an existence you might have to look forward to afterwards.'

Steve lifted one of the Conjor's hands, 'Conjors can hang from places for years at a time and can turn invisible at will.

Two traits which make them excellent spies.'

'How did you spot it then?' asked Harold

'They have a very distinctive smell.'

'I didn't smell anything,' Harold said. 'Anyway, if the Maitre have been watching us through that thing, they know we didn't die in the crash and they could be heading for us right now.'

'It's possible,' Troni remarked. 'But Conjor spies, like this one, are fitted with trackers, and that one's been sitting up here ever since I stole this ship and no Maitre have come to collect it. It was probably put in here originally to keep an eye on the two pilots, not the most competent pair, and has not been monitored recently.'

'We need to find that tracker.' Steve said, 'Get me a knife.'

'No need,' said Troni, 'All of you help me move it to an alcove.'

That task wasn't pleasant as the Conjor's fur was thick with blood, and Harold swore that it growled as he touched it.

'Hit the yellow button, and stand clear,' said Troni, once they'd wedged it in.

'Not you, Professor Dunn,' Steve said, and hit the button himself, whipping his hand out before the glass fell.

A fizz of steam engulfed the Conjor, and it screamed and threw a paw up against the glass.

'I guess it wasn't quite dead,' said Steve.

No more movements or outbursts came from the alcove, and after five minutes or so the glass slid up to let the steam out, and what remained was a contorted dog-ape skeleton, scraped clean.

'Just before, when I hit the wrong button, what if I'd hit that one instead of the goo?' Harold said.

'Then that would've been the end of your contribution,' Troni replied calmly. 'Don't worry, I'll know for next time that you're unable to follow a simple instruction.'

CHAPTER FORTY

The mood upon the Maitre Mothership was a jubilant one because Leader Atherpock was feeling jubilant. Although Valk and Punce had failed to kill the rebels Dunn, Tsai and Steve, they had succeeded in killing the remaining Grey meddler. Two of his favourites, Morkon and Pinnt, had killed the rebels instead.

He re-played the human news and watched the tugs and cranes attempt to lift the plane from the seabed. It landed in water that was only 100 feet deep, less than a mile from the shoreline. There were no survivors. Morkon and Pinnt were back at their posts within Reznikov's government.

Great reward awaited all four Maitre, post-invasion, which should be any day now.

From his desk atop the platform, he watched the analysts and strategists working at their stations, breaking now and then to engage in casual violence. Morale was high, and Atherpock was pleased, but then his eyes fell upon Nilodost, and his mood soured in an instant. Nilodost was a stunted creature, who stood at less than 6 foot, and was a suspected pacifist. Following the Zetan war, when it came to weapon analysis, Nilodost had claimed to have lost his gun, which led many to suspect he'd not used it at all and was therefore single-handedly responsible for their defeat. This was never proven, but the rumour remained, and Atherpock believed it. He would have turned down the position of Invasion Leader flat had he known he would have been lumbered with a coward like Nilodost. Even being in the same room as a suspected pacifist put an upstanding Maitre's reputation at risk.

What irritated him specifically about Nilodost today, was that he'd announced Valk's and Punce's Zetan hit, and then announced little else since.

'Nilodost!'

The fool jumped out from behind his station and ran to Atherpock's platform.

'Yes, Leader Atherpock.'

Murmurs of antagonism were already rustling through the banks of workers, as they focused on the unpopular Maitre.

'Nilodost, you puss-sac, where are Valk and Punce?'

'They're not back yet, Leader Atherpock.'

Atherpock felt his derision come quickly to the boil. Assaulting other Maitre was encouraged within their culture, through murdering one was considered a worse crime than pacifism, and that was the only reason Nilodost was still alive.

'I can see that, Nilodost.'

'He can see that Zetan Lover,' said someone in the back.

'Yeah,' came a collective shout. 'Zetan Lover.'

Nilodost stared at the floor.

'Where's the probe you sent? I need a report.'

'I'll just check, sir,' Nilodost said and ran back to his station. 'Oh, yes, I have it here....'

'Did I tell you to return to your station?' Atherpock said, and Nilodost was pelted with rebukes and small items, as he jogged back to the platform.

'Leader, yes, I have the probe.'

'How long have you had the probe? This probe will confirm the demise of the Human-Zetan alliance?'

Nilodost made a guttural noise.

'Answer the Leader,' said someone.

'I've had it for two days, Leader Atherpock,' said Nilodost. 'Forgive me, I've been so concerned with tracking the remaining Agents, I completely forgot...'

Atherpock pulled his plasma pistol from his belt and shot Nilodost, who fell sprawling backwards.

The attitude of the floor changed in an instant.

'The Leader killed Nilodost.'

'He killed another Maitre.'

'Kill the traitor non-Maitre — Atherpock!'

As a hundred plasma pistols were extended his way, he said, 'Wait.' and held up his palm.

Silence fell, and a low, steady groan could be heard, and Nilodost began writhing.

'He's alive.' One remarked.

'Good shot, Leader Atherpock,' said another.

'That'll teach you Nilodost, you incompetent pacifist.'

Atherpock breathed an invisible sigh of relief that his reaction had not cost him his life. His aim had clearly deteriorated during his absence from the field.

'Arko,' he said, and a sturdy, seven-foot worker, with a looping scar across his face, rose and crossed the room towards him. Arko hadn't been obliged to serve in the Zetan War, but he'd volunteered. As a career soldier, he'd killed two thousand beings from eighty different worlds. During combat with Zetans, he'd been seen to toss away his gun and eat several of the enemy alive. This action was considered admirable amongst his peers, but it had resulted in a heart condition, which prompted Arko's hands to shake so much so that he could no longer aim a weapon. He'd been honourably discharged from the military and applied for a place in Invasion Co-ordination, which Atherpock had been delighted to grant him. Arko trod on Nilodost's ankle as he approached the platform.

'Arko, do you know how to analyse a recognisance probe?'

Arko shrugged. 'With respect, Leader Atherpock, how hard can it be?'

Nilodost stopped whimpering for a second to gawp at his colleague's audacity, but Atherpock broke into a grin.

'Show us the footage.'

'Yes, Leader Atherpock,' said Arko, and slouched over to Nilodost's station. He laid several swipes across the control monitor, and the hole in the desk swirled open, and a metal probe rose from inside. Atherpock turned a dial on his desk and dimmed the lights, and the probe projected a recording on the wall, large enough for them all to see. The room cheered upon seeing the smouldering Zetan ship and then again as the probe swung left, and zoomed in to reveal Valk and Punce examining a dead Zetan. Raucous laughter rang out when Punce blew up the Zetan's head to make Valk flinch, and Atherpock squinted at the pair. Despite their killing of the Grey, they had botched the Bartonville attack, and would probably not know that Morkon and Pinnt had rectified their error. The pair had a reputation for not being the sharpest, much to Valk's chagrin, and had a tendency to go missing for long periods of time when they made mistakes. Knowing this, Atherpock had told Nilodost to be subtle about his rage when communicating with them, but the fool had probably alluded to it, just to try and make them squirm.

The probe zoomed in again, to try to see what Valk and Punce were looking at on the wall, and then Nilodost was granted some immunity. The room collapsed into rage, as the craft exploded, and to make matters worse, a lone Zetan was spotted hurrying towards the saucer.

Atherpock stared in horror, praying with all his being for some flaw in the Zetan's trickery, but nothing surfaced, and it left in the saucer.

'I want the view from that saucer's Conjor, now.'

There were several unintelligible shouts from the floor, as all ducked back to their stations before a lone shout echoed out. 'It's down.'

Atherpock roared, and head butted his desk.

'Play the Conjor's footage,' Arko said, and another projection was thrown up on the wall. It was from the Conjor, hanging down from the ceiling above the Zetan's head.

'Kill him.' Someone yelled from the floor, but everyone present knew that that was too much to hope for. Conjors, as a species, were almost as cowardly as Nilodost, unless threatened.

'Skip forward to incident!' Atherpock said, and there was some blurring, and then the feed resumed; a flash of blue, and then the humans appeared on the projection, drenched to the bone.

'The scum pulled them out of the wreckage.' Atherpock

said, 'They survived again!'

They all watched, and after several minutes the Agent spun around and stared right at the Conjor.

Startled, it scurried into another position, but the Agent's eyes never left it.

'Look at that thing,' Said Atherpock in awe, as the Agent's tongue flickered and it began shooting.

'Find that saucer, now.'

'Leader, there was an unscheduled pass of Moscow, Russia by a saucer just moments ago.'

'They're there.' Atherpock said, his fists trembling, 'Get Morkon and Pinnt to their location right now. I need them found before they reach the Russian President.'

CHAPTER FORTY-ONE

'What do we do now?' Lisa asked.

'The same thing we were going to do.' Steve replied, taking a clip from his blazer pocket and reloading his Glock. 'We find Agent Shura and get him to set up the meeting with Reznikov, then you tell Reznikov your story, and we all get shot anyway.'

'Feeling optimistic are we?' asked Harold sarcasticly.

'As established, I can't drop you in the middle of Moscow and expect to avoid detection,' Troni said. 'I'll drop you on the outskirts, then go and await your arrival at the Kremlin. If the Maitre still haven't realised I've taken one of their ships, I should be safe.'

'Fair enough,' said Harold. 'Keep an eye on stormarea51.net'

Troni nodded then scowled in Steve's direction. The Agent was the source of an irritating scratching noise, as he cleaned out the barrel of his Glock with a thin bore brush.

'You getting ready to wipe out another hundred people, psycho?' asked Lisa.

Steve shrugged, and put the brush back in his pocket.

'Grab a seat,' ordered Troni. 'And this time, hold on.'

Harold was the first to sit down — having had enough experience of being thrown around the inside of an alien craft. He wondered how visible the scars on his head would be if he finally went bald — if he even lived that long. Lisa and Steve sat down next to him, just as they plummeted back towards the ground.

The light pooled in through the windows as they slowed their descent. The stars began to become clouds.

'Hmm,' Troni said as he fiddled with a few dials.

'What's…?' Harold began but was cut short as the craft jerked to the left.

'Sorry, sorry.' Troni said, 'Still getting the hang of it.'

The saucer came to a gradual stop.

'Ready to go then?'

'We're in Russia?' Lisa asked.

'Of course,' said Troni.

'I guess so then.'

Troni lead them back to the circular room and pulled a lever by the door to bring the blue sheet buzzing into life, and the transport beam beyond. Through the translucent sheet, Harold thought he could see some fields or were they car parks? It was impossible to tell with everything tinted blue.

'Good luck,' said Troni.

'You're kidding, right?' said Lisa, also looking through the floor.

Harold was pleased that she had just as much anticipation regarding a drop down the beam as he did.

'No.'

'The first time I met you, when you sent me back to Earth, you teleported me,.' Harold remarked. 'Why's that option not available this time?'

'Maitre saucers don't have that capacity.'

'Are you lying? Or is this because I was deliberately sick on your ship the first time?'

'I knew it!' said Troni, flapping his arms, 'I told Nyn, I said…'

Troni stopped himself and straightened up.

'No, that is not the reason,' he said in a strained tone. 'We've come a long way since then, and unfortunately this is the only option.'

Harold sighed. 'Urgh, what do we have to do?'

'Just jump through it,' Troni said. 'Don't overthink it.'

'See you again soon then, I guess.'

He held out a hand to Lisa. 'Shall we jump on three?'

Steve gave him a push in the back and he dropped through the sheet.

'Really?' Lisa remarked, watching Harold drift down the beam, then hopped down after him.

Steve turned to the Zetan. 'Pretty sure you can teleport from Maitre ships.'

'I'm pretty sure too,' said Troni. 'But that'll teach the ape to be sick on my ship!'

The pair looked at one another, smiles hidden behind their respective scowls of contempt, and then Steve jumped.

CHAPTER FORTY-TWO

D roplets of perspiration splashed across the room, onto the high-finish of the oak desk, and onto the well moisturised faces of the men who stood around it. As usual, all the men seethed about this blatant disregard for their personal comfort, and, as usual, they maintained neutral expressions and said nothing.

Below the ripples of fat, the swinging arms had a firmness, which suggested that they'd once belonged to a prime physique, which had now deteriorated with age. The man they belonged too was in some denial about this, but was prudent enough to ensure the national media only caught photos of him with his shirt off and performing impressive feats of endurance, such as lifting fallen tree trunks at his woodland retreat or hanging one handed from mountain faces.

This current ritual was a weekly one and was to ensure his cabinet were reminded of his strength and dominance. It only stopped when the patches of blood on the white Everlast punch bag turned the colour of ink, and the gasps of genuine concern had begun. He was grateful he had just heard such a gasp, as his knuckles were really beginning to smart.

He threw a final haymaker, which produced an impressive cloud of dust and then stepped back to allow his servants to dress him in a silk robe and bandage his knuckles.

While he waited for them to wipe down his desk, he opened the long, pine box and withdrew a thick, Cuban cigar. The end of which he snipped with the solid, silver cutter he always kept in his pocket, should he ever need to snip a fingertip or expensive cigar.

'Is someone going to light this?' he asked, 'Hurry up!'

He had been smoking more cigars than usual of late, as an online journal had recently run an article claiming he had asthma. He quickly squashed the rumours, along with said journalist's head, but still, he felt the room was waiting with bated breath to see if he'd cough. On this occasion, though, he was able to suppress   and released an impressive plume of smoke. How disappointing for them.

The two cleaning ladies began packing the various wipes, flannels and sprays away, while the two cleaning men unhooked the punching bag and heaved it from the room. As Reznikov watched them, his advisors seized the opportunity to wipe their faces. Everybody knew what was happening, though nobody made a comment. It was all part of the dance.

After several minutes, the last cleaner left the room and closed the door behind her, a signal the business of the day could begin.

A broad-shouldered man with thick features and grizzled grey hair stepped forward, then paused to straighten his suit. His demeanour unsettled Reznikov — the man's straightforward manner of speaking had deserted him.

Reznikov took the cigar out of his mouth. 'What is it, Prime Minister? Come on, spit it out.'

'Mr President, a commercial airplane, the last scheduled flight into Russia following your executive order on Monday, crashed at 05.45 this morning. No survivors.'

'This is not a simple crash?' Reznikov asked, his eyes galloping across the faces of his men. 'As you all tremble like children around me — my fearless cabinet. Did it land on a hospital or something?'

'No sir, it landed a mile off the coast, but it's how the plane crashed... our divers have recovered some bodies. Seems the cabin and crew died of gas poisoning.'

Reznikov wafted his hand. 'So? Incompetent engineers...

what?'

Prime Minster Sedova turned to Director Klebin, a thin man, with fluffy black hair, and a long curved nose, which had earned him the nickname — Vorona, the Crow. He was also the Director of the FSB, so it was said that he had his beak in everything.

'Mr President, I deployed a diving team as soon as I learned of the crash. They found this in the cockpit.'

He slid a thin, nozzled canister, inside a polythene bag towards Reznikov, who picked it up and glanced at it. 'This little thing gassed a plane full of people?'

'One hundred and seventeen people, Mr President, yes. It contained a quantity of Sarin gas, thirty times more deadly than Cyanide, capable of causing death in three minutes. A North Korean favourite.'

'So that's who it is?' asked Reznikov. 'The North Koreans are behind this?'

'We're not sure, sir,' said Sedova, 'The terrorists would have had to gain access to the cockpit, which is not so easy these days. However, North Korea might have a lot to gain should a shooting war erupt with the United States.'

'Gunshots?'

'None, sir.'

'So it must have been the pilots?'

'We've done background checks on both of them. They're clean,' said Klebin, 'But we're checking their personal laptops.'

Reznikov was growing more irritable. Not only had these men brought him a plane crash, but they were prevaricating.

'Are you going to tell me what you think happened? Or are we going to continue to discuss what you think didn't happen?'

'The plane was split pretty much between Russian citizens and American citizens, with a few Dutch,' said Klebin. 'As I said, one hundred and seventeen people died… but the flight records show one hundred and twenty people boarded.'

'The escape raft was deployed from the door of the aircraft, so there is no question that at least one person survived the gas,' said Sedova.

'Perhaps they drowned in the storm last night. Otherwise, you would've found them by now, wouldn't you Klebin?' Reznikov said, his moustache bristling.

'Yes, we would've,' Klebin said with conviction. 'But we suspect they were picked up. A peculiar aircraft was spotted by some local fisherman nearby.'

'Peculiar, how?'

Sedova grimaced and revealed the reason for his discomfort. 'The fishermen say they saw a flying saucer, which beamed up three people from the middle of the sea and then shot up into space with them. There were reports, not an hour ago, of a similar craft passing over Moscow.'

Every man in the room snorted, except Igor Spalko, Deputy Minister for Emergency Situations.

'You've lost your mind,' he said.

'You will hold your tongue, Spalko,' said Sedova, taking a few strides towards the junior man. 'I am the Prime Minister.'

'You should not irritate the President with your hysterical conspiracy theories,' said Spalko.

'Enough!' said Reznikov bringing about an abrupt silence, which was broken only by Spalko muttering. 'It's a hoax, a stupid hoax.'

'Continue,' Reznikov said, looking from Sedova to Klebin. 'Who are these missing passengers?'

Klebin removed three enlarged passport photographs from his pocket and spread them out on the desk.

'Their seats are registered to a Mr. Jeffrey Davis, a Mr. Sam Russell, and a Miss Laura Tong. Russell and Tong, at least, are fake names. Their faces match those of Professor Harold Dunn and Doctor Lisa Tsai, a Brit and an American, who have been featured heavily on the US news of late after allegedly leaking evidence that there is extra-terrestrial technology at Area 51. They're wanted fugitives.'

'I see, and the other man.'

'His face does not exist on the Internet, but we tracked his passport all the way back to Peoria Airport, in Nevada.'

'An American Agent,' said Spalko. 'He must be. That is where their base is. Bartonville, USA. It exploded just the other day.'

'Klebin and I agree that he is likely an American agent,' said Sedova.

Reznikov rose and walked over to his window, turning his back to the men so he could think without scrutiny. He understood the presence of the Agent, likely some mission to assassinate him, but why the two fugitives? Particularly ones who were all over the news?

His eyes scanned the people bustling along the street below, searching for one of the faces from the printouts. How he hoped he'd spot one, so that he could leap through the plate glass window, commando roll, and subdue the assassins with his bare hands. Despite this aspiration, he saw no one familiar and was forced to re-address his office.

'Seems to me, comrades, that a US government Agent has crashed a flight destined for Russia, murdered everyone on board save for two suspects of interest and entered our country in some kind of new, high-tech Spy Plane.'

The room was silent, awaiting his plan of action.

'I want these passengers found. If you catch them airborne, I want them killed. If you catch them running, I want them killed. If they're arrested, then I want them brought in for an interrogation, which I shall conduct myself, and then have them killed. We will send a message to the US, and, in the meantime, treat this as an act of war. Arm the Satan.'

There was a collective gasp at this and an outbreak of murmuring. A minister, who'd not yet spoken, stepped forward. 'Sir, Mr President, are you sure that's wise? I mean we can't even be sure…'

He was cut short by a blow from Spalko, which knocked him to the floor.

'How dare you question the President,' he said, glowering down at the minister, lying on his back, with hands up in submission.

'That's enough!' said Reznikov, 'Those are my orders, and they will be obeyed. That's the end of it!'

The men in his office nodded, and the fallen Minister picked himself up.

'Of course, of course, I only meant…'

'You are all dismissed.'

As the room began to empty, he caught Sedova by the arm. 'You and Klebin will continue to investigate this. I want a motive. I want to know why.'

'Yes, Mr President,' Sedova said. Reznikov let him go.

When the door shut, the suppressed cough forced its way back up his throat with vengence. He was forced to dive for the inhaler he kept in his bottom drawer. He took a puff.

He was not going to let a lack of information prevent him from affirmative action like some damn liberal, but he would still like as much of it as he could attain.

'What're you up to, Pope, you fucking fool?'

CHAPTER
FORTY-THREE

Duncan Pope sat at his desk in his oval office and felt confused. There was an untidy pile of coffee ringed, jelly stained, policies in front of him, few of which he understood, and all of which antagonised his migraine.

For the hundredth time that day, he forced his eyes back to the opening sentence of one he'd thought simple, one of his predecessor's he'd passionately opposed. It was a healthcare policy that used federal and state funds to support insurance for impoverished people, he knew that much from the Media. Pope paid for health insurance so he couldn't understand why these people couldn't as well. If they didn't have enough money, they should work harder and get higher paying jobs. The issue was clearly laziness and lack of ambition.

His eyes tumbled off the document again and landed on a picture of his family. The fashion model wife, and the five obedient children, all staring up at their hero, him, grinning into the camera lens like the hero he was. This was during his campaign. Although he thought the red baseball cap clashed horribly with his blue, Armani suit, at the time, his team at the time had insisted he wear it, 'to make him look more like an Average Joe.'

He recalled the cap had played havoc with his hairpiece. As he glanced at his reflection in the window, he noticed that his head-scratching had dislodged it. In a sudden grip of anxiety, he leapt out of his chair and hurried over to the full-length mirror, fearful a cabinet member might enter at any moment, or worse, one of his administrative assistants.

He had hand-picked all of his staff during his first week of presidency, with most of the cabinet members being old business associates, tycoons like himself, whose companies would benefit from being at the exonerative bosom of inner government. Furthermore, he had taken a great deal of time picking his 'background dancers', as he liked to call them, most of whom performed for him at their respective interviews, while he'd enjoyed whisky and cigars. These were administrative assistants, filing clerks, cleaners, and HR staff — all beautiful women, and useful distractions when he or any of his loyal members of government should need one.

Boy, could he go for a distraction right now.

Hairpiece back in place, he patted his podgy stomach, taking note of the extra pounds he'd gained since his inauguration. Fastening the blazer of his five grand fat-displacing suit resolved the issuegiving him a broad impression. The hero was almost back.

He returned to his desk to complete the ritual — flicking open his wallet, which he always left lying on the edge of the desk so that its girth would catch the eye of visitors. Then he began to slide the hundred dollar notes out onto the desk — a little green armada, conquering the turbulent ocean of white documents beneath. His maid had done an excellent job of ironing his cash so each note slipped easily from their home. Once he had counted out the full twelve-hundred and confirmed that his maid had managed to go another day with indulging in the natural thieving impulses he suspected of her race, he again congratulated himself for deciding not having her repatriated back to Mexico with the rest of her kind.

Though there was something... something that was numbing the effect of his hero's ritual. It stuck out, on the corner of the third document down, a word that always made him twitch: 'Reznikov.'

His initial relationship with the Russian dictator had been excellent, considered by most to be the most positive Russian/American political relationship for a century.

On the day Pope announced he was running against the elite and put forward his radical aims, Reznikov rang him personally to tell him how much he enjoyed his stance on immigration. Pope naturally responded by congratulating him on the way he handled his media critics. Pope's campaign team had come up with a catchphrase 'Sham Story', which could be attributed to any news article critical of him to de-legitimise it, whereas Reznikov in his own country would just have the author assassinated. Pope felt that Reznikov's method would never work in America, but he admired the finality of it.

Once Pope's candidacy was underway, Russia had gone after his opponent, hacking her computer and disrupting her social media campaigns. There was even a rumour they infected the electronic voting machines with malware, though Pope didn't want to hear about that. As far as he was concerned, he'd beaten the elite to prove himself the best man in America, and probably the world, all by himself.

All of this assistance, those parts he acknowledged and those he didn't, came at a price. During the second week of his presidency, he'd received the call a Russian fleet had crossed into US territorial waters. He'd rung Reznikov, with genuine fury, and added vigour for the benefit of his cabinet, who had all been were present, but had been relieved when he was assured that this had just been identified as a quicker route to Syria, where the fight against ISIS continued.

Irked as he was by this, he assured his cabinet that it was just the cost of business, telling Reznikov that he was fine to continue so long as the liberal media never found out. The real boiling point came when the US Navy crossed through Russian waters on its way to North Korea, and appeared on every major news channel in the world, being promptly ejected by a flotilla of submarines. When Pope rang Reznikov to demand an explanation, the one he received was that he should 'learn his place in the world' and then no more than a dial tone.

A fortnight later the USS Mississippi reported she was being followed by a Russian submarine, and received instructions to hide in an alcove and wait for it to pass. Unfortunately, there was a radar glitch, which prompted the

Mississippi to emerge early and bump her bow into the Russians. There were no casualties, hardly any damage even, but all the headlines sung to the tune of 'US attack on a Russian Nuclear submarine', and demanded a presidential response. He made a speech lavish with threats, and although there was no official response, American politicians in Russia began to disappear, and the Satan 2 program was unveiled.

A frantic knock came at the door, and the handle began to turn.

'Wait,' he said and removed a small mirror from his pocket so that he could check the angle of his hairpiece a final time. Once satisfied, he straightened up the papers on his desk and linked his fingers in what he thought was a presidential manner. 'Alright, come in.'

Melvin Porterfield appeared around his door. He was the least imposing man in Pope's cabinet at a mere 5'9, with a receding hairline of greasy black curls, a non-existent chin, and a forehead you could screen a movie on. The man was a rat, and there were many rumours about him, none of which he'd clarify. One of them was that he was once indicted for fraud three times in one week, and each time he'd made bail so fast he was home before his dinner went cold. Another was that he was once caught in bed with three young prostitutes, and he'd secured a libel settlement, and the reporter's dismissal, before the poor sap had even made it back to the office with the pictures.

Pope, who often got over-excited at public appearances, needed a man who could tell him how to get out of anything, and that was why this skinny man was his Chief of Staff.

'Ah, Porterfield, you're looking paler than usual… the wife shacked up with the pool boy again?'

'Mr President, we've just received word — last night, at 22.45pm our time, the last scheduled flight into Russia went down. 117 dead, 52 of which were American citizens.'

'Holy… fucking… shit.'

Pope gestured to the seat in front of his desk, and Porterfield took it.

'Did the Russians shoot the plane down?'

Porterfield shook his head. 'In the photos, I've seen the

damage isn't consistent with a missile.'

'Then, a hijack?'

'Intelligence says the Russians are convinced the passengers and pilots were gassed, through their oxygen masks. They claim to have recovered a cylinder with traces of Sarin — very deadly.'

'Have any terrorist groups claimed responsibility?'

Porterfield grimaced, then placed his briefcase on the desk, and removed a copy of the New York Times.

'Do you recognise these people?'

Pope snorted, as he read the headline: 'Scientists abducted by Aliens'.

'Yeah, I heard about it. What? Are you gonna tell me ET's involved now?'

'Sir, the man's name is Professor Harold Dunn, he was chief engineer on the A1.'

Pope's amusement evaporated.

'The woman is Dr Lisa Tsai, a research scientist from Groom Lake, Nevada, Codename: Area 51.'

'Well?'

'Both of them boarded that flight, under fake identities, and neither of them were recovered from it.'

Pope rubbed his forehead and tried to concentrate.

'So you're saying that they're the terrorists?'

'There was a third person not recovered from the crash.'

Pope lay a grainy printout, on top of the newspaper. It was a picture of a tall, Caucasian male, with a shaved head.

'And who the fuck is this?'

'I don't know. Area 51 have confirmed that he's affiliated with them and that he's a US Agent, but won't say any more.'

'I'm the god damn President,' Pope said. 'They'll give me what I ask for.'

He snatched up the telephone. 'Mission Intelligence.'

Porterfield waited, as Pope drummed his fingers on his desk, in that compulsive way he always did when he felt like he was losing control.

'Yes, this is the President. Put me through to General Rowling right now.'

He jabbed the button for the loudspeaker and slammed down the receiver. Tinny elevator music filled the room.

Despite the severity of the situation, Porterfield struggled to contain his amusement as the drumming quickened and a flush appeared below the President's fake tan.

The music stopped, and a smoker's voice rattled down the line. 'Rowling. Mr President?'

'God damn it, Rowling, you keep your President on hold for that long?'

There was an audible wetting of lips.

'Apologies, Mr President, I've a new administrative assistant… she isn't aware that you're to be put through immediately.'

'If it happens again, buddy, I'm gonna bust someone's ass!' Pope said.

Porterfield shook his head. Pope still hadn't learnt the fundamental differences between business and politics. In business, you might well tenderise an inferior to ensure future compliance, but in politics, no one man was bigger than the government. And the military was one branch, in particular, it was inadvisable to throw your weight at.

Regardless, Rowling answered with an apologetic, albeit, slightly strained tone.

'I'm sorry, Mr President. I'll send her straight home once we're done here. What can I do for you?'

'This Agent of yours, the one from the plane that Porterfield's been trying to grill you on, who the hell is he? What can you tell me about him?'

The answer was immediate. 'Nothing, I'm afraid, sir.'

Pope floundered in his chair.

'Who the hell do you think you're talking to, Rowling? He works for you, doesn't he?'

'Sorry, sir. Kinda, sir.'

'So you've a profile on him?'

'Yes, sir.'

'Well as your Commander-in-Fucking-Chief, I demand you email it to me now.'

'No, sir.'

Pope's tan had completely disappeared now, and Porterfield feared, as he threw himself forward towards the telephone, that his hairpiece might hit him straight in the face, but it didn't, it just wobbled there, askew.

''No'? 'No?' Where do you get your fucking balls, Rowling?'

'It's beyond your clearance, sir.'

Pope scoffed in disbelief.

'I'm the god damn President.'

'Yes, sir. Like I said: regrettably beyond your clearance.'

Pope picked up the phone console so that it shook inches away from his quivering face. 'You are out of a job, Rowling. Hell, I'll have you thrown in jail for this...'

'Very well, sir.'

Pope roared and threw the console across the room so that it shattered the mirror.

Seven years' bad luck, thought Porterfield, as the blonde bull rampaged around the office punching things and swearing violent rebukes against Rowling.

Porterfield had witnessed him like this before, so he waited patiently for him to tire himself out, much like a parent would with a child. When he did eventually return to his chair, his voice had taken on a steely edge.

'What do you know about this man, Porterfield?'

'I've told you all that I know.'

Pope panted, the great shoulders rising and falling.

'So what you're saying is that these two nuclear scientists and a government agent have formed their own terrorist cell?'

'The Russians certainly seem to think so. They lost dozens of nationals too and have recognised our agent. The Russian media claim that the trio were ordered by us to hijack the plane and crash it into the Kremlin, disguised as a terrorist attack.'

'But that's nutso!'

Porterfield shrugged.

'So that's it, we're at war?' Pope said, his chin sinking into his hands.

'And they've already begun to move.' Porterfield said, laying down a satellite picture of several warships, 'Their fleet entered our waters an hour ago.'

He laid down another picture — one of three submarines in various stages of submergence. 'There's been three submarine sightings off the coast of Alaska less than six hours ago.'

He laid down another picture — one of a sprawling mountain facility.

'Increased activity of eighty percent around all their known silos, suggesting...'

'Nukes?'

Porterfield nodded.

Pope inhaled, puffing himself up to his full size.

'Mr Porterfield, I want the A1 armed and ready for launch, ASAP.'

'Yes, sir.'

'And I want the fleet deployed, and all military personnel on high alert.'

'Yes, sir.'

Porterfield stood, and crossed to the door.

'And Porterfield...'

'Yes, sir?'

'I want my administrative assistant in here now. Not the brunette... the blonde.'

'Yes, sir.'

CHAPTER
FORTY-FOUR

James and Lisa slowed to a comfortable stop before their feet touched the ground, and then felt themselves being nudged out of the light. Steve, on the other hand, found the beam deactivated, when he was still about six feet from the ground and splattered hard into the mud.

'Not nice is it?' asked Harold, 'You should try it from higher up.'

'You idiot!' Steve bellowed at the saucer, which was retreating into the clouds. 'You just wait.'

He wiped the worst of the mud off his knees and then set off at a good pace like he knew where he was going. Harold chuckled and then felt the chill of the breeze through his thin jacket and regained a straight face. He would have worn something more suitable if he'd known he'd be across the grey fells around Moscow, on a chilly September morning.

The farmers stared at the peculiar trio trudging across their fields and climbing over their gates, but none confronted them, save for one small group by a tractor who laughed and pointed. Steve's hand whipped inside his jacket, and he took a step towards them, but Lisa grabbed his arm. The agent looked down at her hand, and she removed it., Then he stepped through the fence into the next field. Those farmers would never know how close they'd come to death.

They reached a little town beside a river, called Zvenigorod, and discovered some architectural marvels — pure white churches with breath-taking domes and spires, and an enormous redbrick monastery.

'It's beautiful here,' Lisa remarked as they passed a bakery. An old woman feeding some pigeons smiled in her direction.

'Good morning,' Lisa said. The woman's smile transformed into a glare.

'Be aware,' said Steve, catching a glimpse of Lisa's surprise. 'The locals know they'll be rewarded for reporting that they've seen some Americans in Russia, so it might be prudent to shut up. Besides, its highly unlikely these peasants speak English.'

They quickly found the bus station. Steve went to the window and negotiated in fluent Russian but with a flawed accent and purchased three tickets. Fortunately the bus station, as most businesses in and around Moscow, took American credit cards. They are only too happy to get US money.

As they loitered around waiting for the bus, Steve's statement began to play over in Harold's mind. What if the bus driver drove them straight to the nearest police station? What if the large skinhead with the thumping earphones, leaning beside Lisa, was a nationalist who aspired to one day kill a Brit or a Yank?

When the little bus, which was in desperate need of a lick of paint and new brakes by the sound of it, arrived, Steve leapt into action and beckoned for them to follow him. They moved towards the bus. But upon arriving, he stepped back off the bus to let the other passengers on.

'What?' Said Lisa, but Steve ignored her and dropped his phone under the bus wheel while the driver was distracted, and then rejoined the line and boarded the bus. When the bus set off, there was a small bump signalling the end of the phone's life.

As they bounced along the road, and the snow-dusted hills rolled by, Lisa fell asleep, though Harold was unable to. In addition to attacks from the Russian public, he feared attacks from the sky, and that was where his eyes remained for most of the journey, save for a few times when he glanced sideways at Steve, whose hand had not left the inside of his jacket since they'd boarded the bus. Harold felt both reassured and further disconcerted that Steve shared his paranoia, and now he had the additional fear that Steve might accidentally shoot him every time they went over a bump. But he didn't, and they were soon pulling into Belorussky Station.

Steve barked at them in Russian.

'Will you stop that?' Lisa said. 'I don't speak Russian.'

'It means 'come on',' said Steve, as the other passengers began to gather their things, 'As in, 'hurry up'.'

Lisa and Harold followed him to the door and would've been separated the instant they stepped off, by the thick tide of morning shoppers, had Harold not grabbed Lisa's hand and the agent's sleeve.

'Find a payphone,' Steve said, as they made it out of the surge. He began to glance around the square.

Harold spotted a lamp, atop of a concrete plinth, some twenty feet away.

'I'll be back in a second,' he said.

'Harold, wait…' Lisa said, but he'd already thrown himself into the current and allowed it to sweep him downhill. Seeing the lamppost approaching, he threw his shoulder sideways to escape and split one guy's shopping bag in the process.

'Sorry,' Harold said.

The man cursed in Russian before he was swept onwards. Harold put one foot on the concrete plinth and held the cold steel of the lamppost with the other. His eyes followed the gesturing Russian, with floppy blonde curls, and boyish face. He was clearly a model of some kind, and much more handsome than Harold, so he was not sorry he'd ripped his bag. The angry Russian became indistinguishable in the crowd, and Harold spotted a tall, grey box with таксофон written on it, standing on the corner of a busy junction.

'Steve,' he yelled across the heads of the crowd.

The agent looked at him liked he'd just fired off a machine gun and elbowed his way towards him, with Lisa hurrying along the path he created. Harold was torn from the lamppost and dragged away from the crowd.

'We may have every spy in the Russia on our tail, and you want to climb up a lamppost and shout my name outside Belorussky Station?' He said.

'It's just… a payphone.' Harold pointed over the heads of the crowd, towards the junction, and realised Steve was holding the front of his jacket. 'Take your hands off me.'

Both men stared at one another.

'Let's go, shall we?' Said Lisa, touching Harold's arm, allowing her to lead him back into the crowd. Neither of them looked to see if Steve was following until they reached the phone box and Lisa let go of Harold a little too soon for his liking.

CHAPTER FORTY-FIVE

The blonde man sat on a low wall, waiting for the dial tone to end.

He was beneath a McDonald's sign about half a mile down the road from Steve, Harold and Lisa, and was wrinkling his nose at the bin overflowing with cardboard cartons, rotten burgers, and plastic bags filled with dog shit. He was careful to avoid the edges when he tossed his own torn bag inside.

Then the dial tone ended and was replaced by heavy breathing.

'I've found them,' he said and hung up.

CHAPTER FORTY-SIX

As Steve emerged from the crowd and walked towards them, they heard the phone booth door slam. A large bald man, wearing a black bomber jacket, denim jeans, and red Doc Marten boots had gone inside.

'Excuse me, sir.' Harold said, knocking on the glass and forgetting that he was not supposed to be speaking in English, 'But we were hoping to...'

The man faced him, switched the receiver to his other hand, and then slapped one finger up against the glass.

'Well...' commented Harold and Lisa rolled her eyes.

He felt himself flushing and knocked on the glass again and said, 'Excuse me, sir.'

Steve shoved him aside, wrenched opened the door, and said something Lisa imagined to be very rude in Russian.

The man turned to face Steve, looked him up and down and sneered. He lifted the side of his jacket to reveal a large hunting knife, strapped to his belt.

Steve lifted the left lapel of his blazer and revealed his loaded gun holster.

The man dropped his jacket, and the phone, and held up his hands. He edged his belly out from inside the booth, gave both Harold and Steve a quick glance, and Lisa a lingering up-and-down examination, and then slouched off down the street.

An angry female voice could be heard wittering away in Russian at the other end of the line before Steve pressed the steel button and silenced it. He began dialling, each number clicking like a suppressed pistol as he jammed it with his finger.

He noticed them staring at him and paused.

'Both of you go and wait on that bench while I make this call.'

'Ooo, secret is it?' Lisa said, and Harold laughed.

Steve stared them into silence then said, 'Go sit on the bench and don't wander off.'

Lisa stuck her tongue out at him and then led Harold over to the bench. He shared her annoyance at the passivity with which Steve had deflected her jibe.

They both slumped in their jackets on the stone bench and were unable to distract themselves from the perpetual cold by people watching. Lisa only half-heartedly tried to push Harold away when she felt his arm curl around her shoulder. After a minute or so he felt her dig him in the ribs.

Had she nudged him by accident? Was she merely fidgeting?

She dug him again.

'Ok, ok, I'll move my arm.'

'No it's not you,' she said, her eyes aimed across the street at the bustling crowd. 'It's him.'

Harold followed her gaze, and spotted a tall man in his late twenties, with a mess of scraggly, black hair, staring at them from the alley beside the off-licence. He wore a black ankle-jacket, with enormous metal studded leather boots, and certainly stood out amongst the crowd. Harold wondered how it had taken him this long to notice him.

Lisa lowered her eyes for a few seconds, and counted slowly to ten, then looked at the alley again. The man had been joined by another — a squat fellow, about 5'7, with purple Mohican spikes that made up the height difference between him and his associate. This man wore similarly large boots, some tight tartan trousers and some kind of rock band t-shirt, with only a few strips of the sleeve fabric remaining. He had two bulging arms, which dropped down as far as his knees and would've looked more at home on a gorilla.

The tall man pointed straight at them, and the shorter man's eyes followed his finger.

'Maitre or Government?' Lisa said.

'I'm not sure,' Harold said, 'But at least we've got our own one of the latter.'

He looked at the phone box, 'Steve!'

Steve made no acknowledgement that he'd heard him.

'They're coming,' Lisa said, and Harold saw them advancing across the road towards them.

'Steve! Steeeeve!' Harold said, hearing more than a touch of urgency in his own voice. He jumped up, with the intention of rapping on the glass, but Steve had finished his call and stepped out to meet him.

'How many times do I have to tell you not to shout my…'

He stopped talking as the pair approached the kerb, his hand diving inside his blazer.

The taller man spoke to Lisa in a tone of joviality, and with a big smile, which revealed two rows of bright yellow teeth.

'I'm sorry, I don't speak…' She said, and then the two men slapped their foreheads in unison and collapsed on each other's shoulders laughing.

'Foolish of us,' said the taller man, 'we know some English. You are Lisa Tsai, da?'

'And you are, Harold Dunn?' asked the smaller man, pointing a stubby finger at Harold.

'You are advised to keep your voices down,' said Steve, hand still in his pocket, 'and to tell me how you know those names.'

'You're their Mib?' The taller man said, as though it had just become clear to him.

'What did you call me?' Said Steve.

'Their Mib, their Mib, their… Man in Black, who follow them around. We see pictures of you too. stormarea51.net, you are all big stars. We are big fans.'

Harold breathed a sigh of relief and shared a smile with Lisa. The two men were common garden nerds. Harold wasn't sure why he felt surprised that their extra-terrestrial stories had reached Russia — Area 51 was the international cornerstone of Ufology after all.

'Let us take the selfie?' Said the taller man, taking a step towards Harold.

'Sure,' Harold said, as the phone went up in front of him, and he caught a potent whiff of B.O, and wondered when the man had last applied deodorant. For that matter, when was the last time he'd had chance to apply deodorant, and had he smelt like this to Lisa during their shivering embrace a few moments ago? His train of thought was derailed before the taller man could take the picture, by Steve, slapping down the arm holding the phone.

'No.'

The taller man glowered at Steve and rubbed his wrist, 'You should not be so angry at us. We are friends.'

'No, you're not,' he said, and moved so that he was right in front of the tall man, gun shoved in between the folds of his jacket.

The shorter man swore in Russian, taking several steps back. The taller man seemed to have run out of words and was just staring down at the gun digging into his ribs.

'Steve!' Lisa said. 'They're not doing anything.'

'You, dwarf, get back up here,' Steve said to the shorter man still retreating into the street. The guy looked ready to take off, friend be damned.

'If you run I will kill this man.'

The shorter man looked at each of them in horror, and then gulped and stepped back up onto the pavement. Harold wondered if those big biceps were just for show.

'Good. Give me your wallets, both of you.'

Lisa looked around, but no one seemed to have noticed the confrontation.

The two men reached slowly into their pockets and removed their wallets, perhaps fearing they'd be shot if they moved too suddenly. Harold suspected they were right. As they handed the wallets over, he noticed that one had the Nirvana logo on it, that bright yellow smiley face with its tongue out, and the other was a simple cotton and Velcro number, decorated with little multi-coloured cannabis leaves.

'Are you both children?' Steve said, scowling at the

wallets in his hand, 'Or have you driving licenses in there?'

'We have IDs,' said the taller man, 'But no driving licences.'

Steve shook his head. 'Children or not, I now know where you live. So if I spot anything online about you seeing us, I'll know where to find you, and next time there will be no conversation.'

He returned his gun to his pocket, turned to Lisa and Harold, and shoved them both in the backs to get them walking. His hand lingered on Harold coat, and he hissed in his ear. 'That's Strike Two for you now. We don't want to end up on the Internet.'

Harold wafted at the agent and actually came into contact with his face, drawing a gasp from Lisa and a look of shock from Steve.

'You can't threaten me,' said Harold. 'You fucking need me.'

Steve glowered at him, for a length of time which dissolved much of Harold's confidence, and when he spoke, he spoke as though he'd been suppressing something for some time.

'In the unlikely event we survive this little mission of yours, what do you think happens then? You and Dr Tsai go skipping off into the sunshine, to get married, have children, buy a little dog perhaps…?'

Both of them stared at him.

'What happens is your usefulness ends, and I take stock of all these inconveniences you've caused me.' He said, 'I feel like a street worker, watching a fat child kick over the leaves I've just piled, longing for the day Mommy Zeta isn't looking, so I can gut you with my rake.'

And there it was, something that had already been wriggling around in Harold's brain — a feeling there was no chance of survival, only a choice of executioner — the Maitre or Steve. The man would never be their friend, only ever an agent.

'Dude, we just wondered if we could have our weed back,' said the shorter man, breaking the silence.

'What?'

'In my wallet… keep the money… but I just wondered if

I could have my weed.'

Steve guessed that the shorter man's wallet was the Velcro one, and tore it open. A small polythene bag containing pressed plant matter fell to the pavement, and the short man swept it up with surprising speed, for a man of his gait, and retreated back across the street with his friend.

'Pathetic,' Steve said, pocketing the wallet and beckoning to them both as though nothing had occurred. 'Come on, we need to get moving, we're meeting Agent Shura at a Coffee House on South Main Street in about an hour.'

Lisa whispered Harold's ear.

'The second you've convinced Reznikov and everything, we get as far away as possible from that psycho. Agreed?'

'Agreed,' said Harold.

CHAPTER
FORTY-SEVEN

The Coffee House turned out to be a moderate, red-brick building, with a painted green front, and a huge sign above its windows that read 'COFFEEHOUSE – PUB.' It had a little outside seating, which Harold thought he might enjoy had it been under different circumstances, and at a different time of year. Lisa was more endeared by the interior, which turned out to be a literary paradise. Two huge bookcases stood on either side of the spacious room, with a smaller one at the far end, all polished to a high finish and packed with hundreds of her favourite Penguin Classics. Something was comforting about the string lamps hanging low from the ceiling, dousing the few tables in the middle of the room in a low, hypnotic glow. The other patrons had gravitated towards the comfortable candle-lit booths, by the windows, and that's where Steve led them.

Both Lisa and Harold cringed in anticipation as the Steve approached a young couple, but he did nothing terrible and acquired their co-operation with a yarn that he was with the Mayor's office, and the man himself was on his way down and had requested his favourite table. He placed a crisp, five-thousand ruble note into the man's hand, and the couple left the table. Harold wondered if Steve had been handed the money with their passports back at Peoria International, or if he always carried foreign currency.

As they sat down, the door tinkled, and a thin skeletal man entered in an all-black suit. He was bald and pale, with sunken eyes that found them sitting in the cosy booth. Lisa thought he looked like something that'd crawled straight out of Hell.

Steve was noticeably chilled by him too, and his hand dropped below the table as the man approached them. His tongue flickered, and so did the skeleton's.

'Bartonville… Fruit and Veg?' He said, in a voice that was almost a whisper.

'Are you an interested customer?' Steve said.

'I am,' said the skeleton, and extended five elongated fingers towards Steve, which he accepted in his broad palm.

'Agent Shura?'

'Yes.'

'Agent Steve.'

Steve turned to Lisa. 'Doctor Tsai, you'll need to move.'

He handed her a one thousand Ruble note and said, 'Go and get us some coffee.'

Lisa clenched her teeth as Shura slipped into her seat.

'And a vodka,' said Harold.

She gawped at him, as Steve slid the note into her hand.

Harold gave a half-smile. 'Well if you're going…'

'You can go fuck yourself,' she said and walked over to the bar.

On her way, she passed the table the young couple had relocated to and saw they were examining a picture of a plump, elderly gentleman on the boy's phone. She didn't need to speak Russian, to know the couple were probably deducing with some indignation that the skeleton, sitting with Agent Steve, was not the Mayor. She thought about alerting the agent but then decided against it. Let the couple rebuke him for his deception.

At the bar, there was only one other patron, shielded from the world by a large tabloid newspaper. His briefcase lay upon the bar, occupying the space her elbows would've perched while waiting for the return of the absent barman. The situation would've been irritating under natural circumstances, but in her current mood, the situation demanded an act of passive aggression. Someone needed to be called to account for their shit.

She cleared her throat, and the newspaper dropped, to reveal a tanned, freckled face, which broke into bright grin upon seeing her. His looping blonde curls made him look like a surfer, but the navy-blue suit, a premium brand and tight in all the right places, suggested otherwise.

'Um,' She said, 'Would you mind… my elbows… lean.'

He must have got the gist of what she'd intended to say, because he made a small exclamation, folded the newspaper under his arm, and moved the briefcase to the floor. As they smiled at one another, the barman reappeared and looked at her expectantly.

'Oh…' She said, leaning across the bar and arching her back as much as she was able, 'Two coffees, please.'

The barman nodded his understanding but then said something in Russian she did not understand.

'I'm sorry?'

'He wants to know if you want premium blend. Just one-hundred-and-fifty more,' said the stranger, and she caught him staring at her, but not at her eyes.

'No thanks, the cheap stuff's fine.'

The barman nodded again and turned away.

'English?' asked the man, reminding her that she was meant to be keeping a low profile.

She wondered what line of work he was in. Something in the media she suspected or maybe a model.

'American,' she said without reserve, now she'd already been detected.

'You are here on holiday?'

'Yes… just visiting,' she said, 'You… live here?'

Apparently the ability to string a coherent sentence together still eluded her.

The man snapped his fingers. 'Lisa Tsai?'

The hairs on the back of her neck stood up and her spine fused. 'Huh, do I know you?'

She chanced a half look over her shoulder to see if Steve was keeping an eye on her, but he was still engaged with Agent Shura, and the only attention from the table she had was Harold's, who did not look very happy that she was chatting to the attractive stranger.

'No, but...' He flicked through a few pages in his newspaper and then held up the worst picture of her she had ever seen. Her grim face was next to Harold's, staring into the camera, as a legion of flying saucers flew by in the grey sky overhead. The article was all in Russian, but it didn't look good.

'I like aliens too,' he said, and she relaxed. Just another nut, but definitely the most handsome one she'd met so far.

'Yes,' she said. 'I'm into loads of weird stuff.'

She winced as she said the words, but the man's smile broadened.

The barman placed the two coffees on a tray in front of them and held out a hand for the money, but as Lisa extended the note, she felt her hand prevented by the stranger's, 'put it on my tab.'

The barman nodded and headed back into his office. The stranger dragged his fingers the length of Lisa's hand and then stood, tucking his newspaper under his arm.

'Thank you,' Lisa said

He reached into his pocket, removed a glossy business card, and placed it on the tray.

'I have to go back to work now, but maybe you can thank me over dinner, tonight or tomorrow? My name's Petr.'

In another life, she would have ordered Petr to take her back to his home that instant and made him call in sick for work the next day. But that was hardly a possibility, so instead, she just said, 'I'll think about it,' and, with the deadliest smile she could conjure, she sashayed back to her table without a backwards glance.

Shura accepted his coffee without losing his train of thought. 'So Reznikov meeting is arranged. He thinks you world-famous martial artists come to teach him new fighting style.'

'Who was that at the bar?' Harold asked.

Lisa looked at Harold and liked what she saw a little less with every second that passed. They'd slept together, some act of drunken madness, but with excessive arrogance and mediocre looks, he stood no chance with her long-term, not while men like Petr still existed.

'Don't know, just some guy,' she said, sipping her own coffee, and sharing a smile with Petr as he exited.

Steve stared at her but did not ask where his coffee was, nor for his change. He nodded at Shura who began talking again. 'Reznikov is very paranoid man. You must talk quickly and not lie. He will know if you lie.'

'I'm sure I recognised him,' Harold said, snatching up the business card and examining it with distaste. 'What is he? Some salon owner or something?'

'Are you two listening?' Said Steve, 'He's talking to you.'

'Seems your girlfriend forgot her briefcase too,' said Harold nodding his head towards the bar, where the brown briefcase still remained, 'Look a bit slow in the head if you ask me.'

Lisa stood up, Petr was still visible, striding confidently up Main St, but she could still catch him if she hurried.

'Hang on,' Harold said, also staring out of the window, as Lisa headed out of earshot. 'I accidentally ran into that guy in the square earlier. I'm sure of it. Thought he was a prick then too.'

Steve and Shura looked at each other. Lisa tried to elbow her way through a crowd of students, who'd just come down from the upstairs area and were separating her from the bar. Steve plucked the card from Harold's fingers and laid it down on the table. The embossed motto was in Russian.

Shura read it upside down. 'It says; 'The Earth is Ours, The Earth is Ours…''

'The phone number is familiar,' said Steve, with his eyes wide. 'Hang on, it looks similar to a nuclear launch code… Shura?'

Shura had leapt to his feet and barrelled through the students with ease, despite the large stature of several of them in football sweaters.

'Lisa,' Harold yelled, as Shura hit her with the force of a football player himself, and sent her tumbling over a table, just as the briefcase exploded — flame, wood, and crockery, bursting across the café.

Harold felt something solid shatter behind him, and a whoosh of heat, as he flew through the air and then hit the ground. As the world rocked back into existence, his ears began to ring, and the pain came suddenly to his chest, lungs and throat. He was stricken by a fit of coughing. Cool air tickled his face, where he had expected heat, and he managed to sit up and saw a splatter of blood on the concrete. He'd been blown outside.

As he sat facing the crooked remains of the café, barely distinguishable through the black smoke, he wondered how many more explosions lay in wait for him and again considered that it was quite miraculous that he was still alive. It was then his thoughts turned to Lisa and he tottered up on to his feet. His body continued to ache and his limbs stung from his grazes, as stumbled towards the cloud, but he forced himself on and rolled over the windowsill. Tongues of the flame flickered here and there, but nothing else was visible. The ringing, at least, began to quieten, but now he could hear screams and the clatter of footsteps. He was barged into by someone escaping.

'Lisa,' he shouted, as he struggled to keep his feet, 'Steve!'

The din around him grew louder, the hollering, the crackle of burning wood, and sirens in the distance.

'Lisa!'

Then a little of the smoke cleared, and he spotted her, sitting in the corner, face stained crimson. Part of a torso, clothed in black rags, lay next to her, missing all its appendages, spraying a relentless jet of blood straight into Lisa's face, and mouth. She screamed wordlessly and gagged, as she lay pinned with between two tables.

Harold mustered his strength and kicked the torso aside. It was like kicking a sandbag, and he tried to grimace through the pain in his toe as he lifted Lisa in his arms. He heard her retch and tried to ignore the warmth of the liquid running down the back of his shirt.

Then as he began to feel woozy in the smoke, and his strength began to fail him, he heard Steve's voice in his ear and Lisa was taken from him. 'We need to move.'

The black shadow led Harold back to the front of the shop and through the window. The fresh air splashed over Harold like cold water, but dizziness overwhelmed him, and he sank to his knees, as sirens and lights blared all around him. It was every horrible date at a fairground he'd even been on. He hated the waltzers.

He felt a hand in his own, guiding him to his feet again, and found Lisa wild-eyed and bloody but almost back to her senses and seemingly unhurt. Steve jammed his palms into both of their backs, and they crashed through the mob of firefighters, police officers, and survivors, to the street beyond the mayhem. As they ran, two black cars raced out of a side street and screeched to a halt behind them. There came several shouts in Russian, and then one in accented English that said. 'Don't move!'

'Keep running,' said Steve, and then the bullets began peppering the street around them, pinging off lampposts and smashing car windscreens. As each of them anticipated the conclusive pound in their respective backs, a greasy head emerged from an alley and yelled, 'Hey, this way!'

Like a flock of sparrows, the three of them changed direction in unison and without communication. Jogging ahead of them was the long-haired stoner from the phone booth, and ahead of him was his Mohican'ed friend, with four other similarly unusual people, who'd begun sliding down through an open manhole one by one.

As Lisa skidded to a stop, dropped to her bottom and dangled her legs into the hole, Steve staggered to a halt and pulled out his gun. 'Stop, it might be a trap!'

Lisa's head disappeared into the darkness, as shouts came from the end of the alley.

'You stay here then,' Harold said and flung himself into the manhole, grazing his back and missing the first few rungs of the ladder. Steve glanced back the way they'd come and knew that their pursuers were close. He looked the other way down the alley and knew it was too far — he'd be shot before he reached the end.

He cursed and threw his legs down the hole, grabbing the metal lid as he went. As the manhole closed, the stench hit him and made him gag, a noise which echoed around the sewer. The agent gritted his teeth as he descended so he would not make any more noise. He cursed himself for managing their escape with agonising chest pain but then showing weakness in the face of a little excrement. He suspected he had a fractured rib, seventh one down on his right side.

He dropped the last couple of feet, and waited for a confrontation in the dark. None came. Then there were shouts in Russian overhead and the dull clang of boots passing over the manhole cover. Steve raised his Glock to the air, ready to shoot at the first glimmer of light, but it never came, and the noise faded to nothing, save for the drip-dripping of falling droplets.

Torches and smartphones began to spark into life around them, and they found themselves on a jagged concrete walkway, one of two, between which ran a shallow river of the worst filth imaginable.

'It stinks,' Lisa said.

'It does,' replied Harold, 'I even heard our all-powerful agent gagging up there.'

There came murmurs of agreement from the four strangers and the two stoners they already knew.

A frizzy-haired brunette, with horrific acne, spoke. 'You guys are in some trouble, huh?'

Harold was surprised by the quality of her English, particularly as it had a twang which made him suspect that she'd picked it up from American sitcoms.

'I blame you for this,' Steve said to Lisa.

'What was that?' asked the girl,

'I told you not to speak to anyone… and now we have no contact… no meeting with Reznikov…'

Steve swung and punched Lisa on the cheek, sending her toppling down onto the concrete.

Harold roared and lunged at Steve, who parried his blow and head-butted him in the eye, knocking him down beside Lisa. When Harold had clambered back to his feet, he saw that both the stoners had shoved Steve back against the wall.

'It is one thing to attack us,' said the shorter man, as his taller friend, took the opportunity to fish their wallets back out of Steve's pocket. 'But hurt a woman?' He waggled his finger. 'We make big problem for you.'

Steve recovered from their unexpected gall and pushed them both away.

'I could kill everyone here in under a minute if I wanted to.'

Lisa stood up and refused to touch her smarting cheek. 'Ignore Steve. The guy's a fucking asshole.'

'Will you get off me, Harold, I'm fine,' she said, as Harold attempted to wipe the worst of the filth off her, 'Who are you guys? Why did you help us?'

'My name is Rosa Petrov,' said the brunette. 'We recognised you from stormarea51.net

'You worked at Area 51,' she pointed at Lisa.

'And you were abducted by aliens,' she pointed at Harold. 'Weren't you?'

The sound of a collective inhale was audible, as every nerd filled his lungs with funky oxygen, awaiting Harold's reply. His first instinct was to look at Steve for a permissive expression but then decided against it.

'Yeah... I was.'

Rosa gawped and murmurs of scepticism rippled through the group. Maybe they'd just wanted the opportunity to hear it for themselves before the government caught up with Harold and silenced him forever.

Predictably, Steve got in his face. 'Are you insane?'

Lisa was watched a fat boy of about seventeen, with thick-framed square spectacles, edge forward and begin whispering in Rosa's ear.

'And you... we know who you are... Agent Steve,' said Rosa.

Steve scoffed and paused in his rebuke of Harold. 'No, I don't think so...'

'Boris here knows you.'

'So you know my name's Steve,' he said, looking in disgust at chubby, snotty Boris. 'She literally just said it,' he jabbed a finger at Lisa.

Boris shook his head and began whispering again, this time for an extended period of time in which Harold became bored. Remarkable, he thought, considering their perilous situation.

'I haven't got time to watch you two whisper love poetry to one another,' Steve said.

'He says it's your face he recognises...' Rosa began and

then frowned and wiped some spit out of her ear. 'He says that on May 15th, 2009, he was eating his dinner with his mother in some hotel in Niagara Falls … and he headed back to the room because he wasn't feeling well. But when he went in to the lobby there were two men there, dressed as you are now.'

She turned to Boris and asked something in Russian. Boris nodded and whispered some more.

'From the English he understood at the time, he heard the staff tell the two men the previous hotel manager and another employee had indeed reported seeing a triangular shaped craft passing by the hotel several months previous, a craft which had spotted them. They disappeared the following night after relaying their claim to some private UFO investigators.'

'He says one of those men was you and that you whispered something to the new manager which disturbed him greatly. The manager spotted Boris watching, pointed to him, and said something like… 'Even in front of a child?'

'To which you replied 'Of course, in front of anyone.' And then as your hand moved into your jacket, your phone or your colleague's phone rang, and you both exited immediately without answering it.'

'Was the other agent Agent John?' Lisa asked.

'Who's Agent John?' Rosa asked. Both she and Boris stared at Lisa for further clarification on this.

'He's no one,' said Steve, shooting more daggers at Lisa, 'This is nonsense. It wasn't me this fat boy saw.'

Boris scowled, ducked his hand in his pocket and held up a piece of a paper. A captioned CCTV picture of two men in dark trench coats and black hats.

Steve's jaw clenched visibly in the faint glow.

'Is not you… in the back?' Boris asked in a timid, high-pitched voice, laced with thick accent.

'Actually, let me see,' he said and held out his hand. 'Maybe I can clear this up for you.'

Boris looked at Rosa who shrugged and then waddled forward and extended the document to Steve, who whipped it out of his pudgy fingers and began tearing it to pieces.

'Hey,' said Rosa staring forward, as Steve tossed the bits into the shit stream.

'It wasn't me after all, and now I've cleared that up.'

'That image is on the internet you know,' Rosa said. 'We can print another, no problem.'

'Enough,' Steve said. He turned to Lisa and Harold, 'It will be all clear up there now, so get back up that ladder.'

Harold shrugged and put one hand on the rung.

'Wait,' said Lisa, watching the Agent who was fixed on the group of Russian teens. 'Why don't you go first, Steve?'

Steve looked at her, and his eyes narrowed, confirming her suspicions. If she and Harold went first up the ladder, the second they reached the surface, they would hear gunshots below.

'Guess we're not in that much of a hurry, huh?' She said.

'Safer down here anyway,' Rosa said, smiling and looking about the place in a manner that made Lisa suspect this group spent a lot of time in the sewers. 'Harder for the government to track you via your brainwaves.'

Lisa and Harold looked at Steve, expecting an eye roll or something, but the Agent was back in stoic mode. Harold decided that this either meant he was thinking, or that he was about to do something.

He was indeed thinking, thinking for the hundredth time about the consequences of killing Lisa Tsai and Harold Dunn, then killing the nerds as well. However, they were his only source of light, and if they fled they'd take the source with them. Some of them would escape, and then there would be loose ends.

His tongue flickered, as the group continued to discuss the spotty girl's ridiculous notion about brainwave scanners.

Furthermore, Reznikov would never trust his account without Dunn and his Grey.

But what was to stop him killing Dunn and Tsai, meeting Reznikov, and then pulling in the Grey by posing as Dunn on the forum?

There was the telepathy. Now that the Grey and Dunn had communicated telepathically, could it be sensed by the other if one of them died? Would the other simply abandon hope and doom the Earth that way?

No, it was safer to keep the annoying pair alive for the time being. Of course, Reznikov might have them killed the second he met them, or the second after he met the Grey. The plan was hardly foolproof by any means.

'So now you need to speak to the President?' asked Rosa recapturing Steve's attention.

'Yes, we're here to prevent nuclear war invoked by a parasitic race of alien shapeshifters called Maitre,' Harold said, and couldn't help but grin as more eyebrows rose. He suspected their trust in him had dropped another notch and wondered if it was because they were jealous that he'd been abducted and they hadn't. Perhaps it was more likely that he merely sounded ridiculous, though several of them spoke as though they were familiar with the term 'Maitre.'

'Well, in the meantime...' Rosa said, sounding sceptical herself. 'My house is just a few blocks away. You can have some tea and take a shower. Give you time to plan your next move.'

Lisa straightened up, sensing movement. It was some innate response, some process of evolution prompted by the week. The tunnel seemed to have grown darker and the faces of the strangers around her grew gaunter.

'What... what if they're Maitre?' she asked, her voice barely above a whisper and looking at Steve. 'What if we've run straight from one trap into another?'

'Well done,' said Steve, taking a cautionary sniff of the air, then looking as though he regretted it. 'You're gathering some wits at last, although, if they were, we'd already be dead.'

'We're not Maitre, even if some of us often behave like we're from another planet,' Rosa said and gestured towards the two stoners, who wore expressions of surprise.

Bit rich coming from her, thought Lisa.

'Vlad,' said the taller man.

'Alex,' said the other. 'your resident aliens.'

All except Rosa laughed.

'Come to mine. You're both welcome,' she said and launched a glare Steve's way.

Harold suspected that Rosa, for all her aesthetic flaws,

might carry a rapier of fierce integrity. One she unleashed without a moment's notice, on appropriate moralistic battlefields...He found that intimidating...and somewhat sexy.

Harold sighed and turned on a smile. 'Unfortunately he's the cross we're forced to bare.'

Steve rolled his eyes.

'Ok then, all of you, follow me,' she said, and began down the tunnel with her group in toe.

Harold hustled, flanking the nerds to fall in beside Rosa. 'So, how come you know these sewers so well?'

'Like I said, government brainwave trackers...I try to avoid travelling on the surface level when I can.'

'Do all of you move about this way? Does it not get a bit smelly?'

'A few of them are sceptical of the government brainwave theory. It's me who uses them most. I don't even really notice the smell anymore.'

Lisa walked just behind the pair, listening to Harold flirt with the girl.

Why did she even care? Was it perhaps because she'd seen Harold look at the girl with derision when he'd first met her, and now he was speaking to her like she was some angel?

Rosa spotted Lisa's expression and stumbled on something invisible.

'Whoa.' Harold caught her.

'It nearly got a hell of a lot smellier for you then,' he said.

Rosa screwed up her face with such effort that her acne became a crimson spider web.

She looked down at his hand, still on her arm. 'Do not touch my body, ok?'

The group halted, and Harold began to feel anxiety creeping up into his chest. This wasn't going as planned at all.

'I thought you were going off the edge. I just wanted to...'

'Then let me fall. I do not need your help.'

Her eyes followed his hand as it dropped away, and then found Lisa.

'Dr Tsai, I've seen your face in the media. Do you do your own make-up? You always look so pretty.'

Lisa returned her smile, half glanced at Harold's appalled expression and then accepted the girl's skinny arm.

'Yeah, I do it myself.'

'Dyke,' said Harold, under his breath, and fell in line behind the group.

Their sewer parade continued, over the moist flagstones, until they reached another ladder. Vlad and Alex stopped and fell into a discussion with one another.

'What are you two doing now?' Rosa asked from the front.

'Little business,' said Vlad, tapping his nose and winking, and then followed Alex up the ladder. Most of the group chuckled, Rosa tutted, and they all set off again.

It was after half a dozen footsteps that a gust of cool air swirled up the sewer, bringing a welcome hiatus to the stink. It made Lisa shiver, so she looked back over her shoulder, and spotted the near-forgotten Steve in the flickering light, watching Alex and Vlad climb the ladder.

'What is matter?' asked Rosa, prompting Steve to look their way.

'No,' Lisa said. Steve said nothing.

'We don't have time,' she mouthed.

Steve listened to the manhole cover close overhead, tapped a rung of the ladder, then set off on his amble at the rear of the group once again.

He must know she was right. They were on a timetable, and he must fight his impulses. They will need to figure a way to escape this monster once they have saved the planet.

CHAPTER FORTY-EIGHT

V lad watched as the patty wriggled on its bed of bubbles, which popped and reformed, popped and reformed, with a hiss. Its goodness slithered up his nose, exorcising the lingering odours of the sewer. Somewhere, externally, someone spoke, but he was unable to hear them over the growl that rumbled deep inside of him.

There came a slap on his back, and someone said 'Yo.'

'Yeah?' he said, blinking and dragging his hair back over his forehead.

'You weak bastard,' said Alex. 'How baked are you?'

'Na, I'm fine, it's just those burgers, man, they smell fucking good.'

Alex looked at the burgers being worked by the owner of the cart and felt his own world dissolve around him. His brain pulsed in request of grilled meat.

'Do you two want a burger or are you just going to stand there?'

They both fell back into semi-conscious reality and began fumbling inside their pockets for change.

'Yeah, yeah, two burgers,' said Vlad.

'You're buying mine?' asked Alex.

'No, both for me. You're fat enough.'

'Fuck you, skinny boy. Who just scored more dope?'

Alex held up a polythene bag, plump with green herb.

'Fine… give this fat pig a burger too.'

The balding man dumped the charcoal brown patties onto buns and passed all three to Vlad. Both youths looked at the yellow finger smudges where he'd handled them.

The cart owner spoke before they could. 'Pay me then get the fuck away from here.'

'Pay this,' Alex said, and gestured to his groin, and then, by some unspoken agreement, they both ran, stumbling away from the man and his cart.

'You punks!' The man roared, running several paces after them before breaking down into a wheeze, with his hands on his knees.

'You junkie fucks! I'm calling the police!'

Alex and Vlad ran down the next street and collapsed onto the first bench they came too.

'Fuck, he said he'd call the police,' said Vlad, looking around as though he expected a dozen cops to dive on them at any moment.

'Wer fur. Dunf furder,' said Alex.

'What? I don't speak burger.'

Alex swallowed. 'We're fine. Don't worry.'

'Speaking of the police… how much trouble do you reckon we're in for helping those three alien freaks?'

Vlad stared at his untouched burgers, his mind racing. There was still a crackling haze in his chest and throat. It was good weed.

'Are you going to eat those?'

Vlad threw both burgers at his friend's chest. 'How can you be so calm?'

'Because you're just paranoid,' he said, and then tossed the bag of herb Vlad's way, as he ploughed the burgers in between his dripping cheeks.

Vlad attempted to pluck the little bag from the air as it came his way but missed by some distance, and it struck him on the chin.

'Fucker.'

He removed the kings from his pocket and began the procedure.

'Do you think that man…Harold…really got abducted?'

He said.

'Yeah, of course. You've seen those pictures?'

Vlad thought about the pictures as he placed the cigarette paper on his lap and began to sprinkle chunks of herb inside of the valley. Once satisfied everything was level, he took a tailor-made cigarette and squeezed it over the skin until a thick layer of tobacco lay atop the herb. Then he lifted the lips of the skin between his fingers and thumbs, rubbed them together to condense everything, and then twisted one inside the other.

'Yeah but are the pictures real?'

'Sure they are. Otherwise, why would he and the girl come all the way here from America?'

Vlad licked the lip of the roll-up, stuck it against the outside, and then twisted the hollow end off into a stiff spiral. He considered the overall motive of the mysterious trio, which elevated his fears over their own involvement, and made it easier to concentrate on disintegrating the spiral with his lighter. He placed the cone in his mouth and took a long pull so that the end crackled like burning bracken, and the saccharine smoke glided down into his lungs. Then he was hit by what he considered to be a very important thought.

'Hey... what if they are the aliens?' He said, passing the spliff to Alex who took a thoughtful drag.

'I hadn't thought of that... maybe they're setting up a stronghold on Earth to fight those other killer aliens they mentioned.'

'Maybe,' said Vlad, plucking the joint back out from between his friend's lips.

'What if they had some alien showdown back at the café?' Said Alex, 'What if they left some weapons there? We should go take a look.'

Vlad looked at him, with bloodshot eyes. 'Are you insane? It'll be crawling with cops. What if they recognise us from earlier?'

'Bullshit.' Alex said, accepting the joint back, 'We had our backs to the cops ninety-nine percent of the time. What if...we get our hands on some alien hardware? We'd be famous.'

'Famous and in prison.'

Alex shrugged, his enthusiasm for anything leaking away a little more with every puff.

'If we go take a picture of it… we can at least tell Rosa we left to go do something constructive. It'd save us another anti-dope lecture.'

Vlad nodded. That held some appeal to him.

'I guess… let's finish this, then decide.'

They finished the joint and then fell asleep leaning against one another.

They woke ten minutes later. After a thorough debate on which of them was the homosexual, they headed for the café, only just remembering to avoid the street with the Burger Man on it.

As they crossed the manhole cover they'd dropped down an hour or so before, Vlad felt very nervous. He looked at Alex and saw that he was sweating even though it was a chilly night.

'Are you sure about this?' he asked.

Alex shrugged. 'Depends, it's this or another lecture. You know the score.'

Vlad sighed, trying to remember why they hung out with Rosa, and nodded.

They both crept to the end of the alley and poked their heads out.

The café wasn't smouldering anymore. It had become a rotted mouth, with teeth of charred wood and broken brick. In front of this mingled a dozen plain-clothed police detectives, identifiable by the badges at their belts, and beyond them stood a line of uniforms, holding the press at bay, who were chattering away like chimpanzees.

'So, genius, what do you think the chances are of us getting close enough to seize some alien weaponry?' Vlad said, gaining himself a thump in the side.

'Fuck you, you agreed…' Alex said but was interrupted by a loud screech of tires. Two headlights were hurtling towards them down the alley. Their only protection was the pile of oozing bin bags, which was obscuring them from the driver.

Vlad turned to flee but found himself yanked back by his jacket.

'Don't go running out there, you idiot, they'll blow you to bits. What if they recognise you?'

''We had our backs to them earlier. How would they recognise us?' Vlad said, but Alex was already leaping to pull down the end of a fire escape.

CHAPTER FORTY-NINE

P innt slammed on the brakes, and snatched up his plasma pistol, as the two youths scampered up the side of the building.

'Leave them,' said Morkon, also watching the youths illuminated in the headlights.

'But they saw us.'

'They saw two men driving a van.'

'Yes, well, maybe I'd enjoy the target practice,' said Pinnt, flinging the stubby plastic gun back into the door pocket.

'As would I,' Said Morkon. 'But not with the entire national press around the corner.'

An hour or so ago, they'd been informed that Tsai, Dunn, and Agent Steve, had survived the plane crash. Morkon contested the freezing waters of the Baltic Sea would have finished what the crash hadn't if the late Valk and Punce hadn't let the Zetan escape to rescue the trio of humans, but Leader Atherpock, their lifelong friend and mentor, was furious with them, and now they were under pressure to put right their mistake. As a result, Morkon was nervous, and Pinnt was tetchy.

Both Maitre stepped out of the van, Pinnt carrying a black box, which pulsed within his fingers.

'You're sure that thing's trained?' Morkon said as he prised up the manhole cover.

'Yeah, yeah. He's a big wimp.' Pinnt said, setting down the box and patting it.

'What if it fails? What if it escapes?'

'Then we're in trouble, but if we aren't seen to be doing something to catch Tsai, Dunn and Steve, we're in trouble anyway, aren't we?'

He helped Morkon drag the cover aside.

'I've trained him well. He'll do the job,' he said, then stuck his head down the manhole, and instantly regretted it for the smell, but thought he could hear the echoes of footsteps on concrete some way away.

He sat up and breathed in the clean air.

'I don't envy you at all,' he said to the box. 'But I need you to go down into those sewers and kill any humans you find, then come straight back here. You shouldn't need more than an hour.'

He squeezed the box by the sides and then stepped back as it grew, larger and larger until it dwarfed the van. A growl rumbled inside.

'Now… I won't let you out if you don't behave,' Pinnt said.

A plastic tube snaked out of the side of the box and slithered down the hole. It was a sign that the Brorg knew it was about to be released, even if its master threatened otherwise, and it understood what it had to do.

'Hurry up,' Morkon said, glancing left and right.

Pinnt took a plastic panel from his pocket that had three coloured buttons.

'Red releases the main restraints,' he said, and there came a loud buzz from inside the box, and then the screech of serrated claws on metal.

'Amber releases the secondary restraints.'

A thump, as something heavy threw itself against the wall of the box, and another, louder growl.

'Humans are coming,' said Morkon, spotting torch beams over by the pile of bin bags.

'And green… is go.'

There was a ping, and like an antelope down a serpent's

neck - an antelope with claws, teeth, and venom more deadly than any serpent on Earth - the Brorg squeezed down the tube and landed with a splash in the sewer below.

'Happy hunting, beastie,' said Pinnt, squeezing the box so that it sucked up the tube like a piece of spaghetti and began to shrink again. He was answered by a bellow from below.

'Shut up, someone will hear!' Morkon said, pulling the cover back over the manhole.

Pinnt rolled his eyes, popped the box into his pocket, and got back into the van to wait for the Brorg's return.

As Morkon opened his door, a gunshot shattered the glass, and he turned to spot three cops jogging up the street towards them.

'Hey. They can't shoot us, we're government officials,' said Pinnt.

'Just get us out of here. We'll come back for your pet later.'

CHAPTER FIFTY

James heard a rumbling.

'Is there a subway near here?' he asked Boris, but the fat boy didn't answer.

There must be, he thought, it sounded like there was a train coming right up behind them.

He became nervous as the rumble increased and the other members of the group began looking around with confused expressions. They were regulars down here, and it was not a sound with which they were familiar.

Lisa stopped.

'What's wrong?' asked Rosa, coming to a halt with the rest of the procession.

Lisa shone her torch behind her on Agent Steve, who was standing, listening, waiting, and casting a long silhouette in the beam. She could hear his tongue flickering the way it did.

'We should keep moving,' he said suddenly and set off towards them at pace.

'What's going on?' Harold said.

'Keep moving!' He said and shoved Harold and Lisa into motion.

Then, just as they got going again, they all jumped at a new sound, but it was only the Dr Who theme tune.

'Ah,' Said Rosa, fumbling with her phone.

'Turn that off,' Steve ordered, driving the group. 'How have you even got a signal down here?'

'Little device, I make,' she said. 'Alex?'

Her eyes widened, and she pressed the phone closer to her ear. She said something that suggested disbelief.

'Did you say 'Extraterrestrials'?' Steve said and snatched it from her. 'Speak.'

Several seconds of animated babble came from the phone before Steve dropped it.

'Hey,' Rosa said, stooping to retrieve the phone, and then rising again slowly as she realised the rumble had stopped. A sweaty, sulphuric gust washed over them, diluting the stench to which they'd grown accustomed, and in the darkness were two triangles of crimson that stretched almost from floor to ceiling.

'Run!' Steve bellowed, and pushed through the group, so that he was in the lead. A high-pitched squeal from the beast unstuck the rest of them, and they were soon hot on the agent's heels. As they jostled with one another, some leapt to the ledge on the other side of the sewer, while others splashed down into the shallow stream of shit. All the while, the repetitive splashing footfalls grew closer.

Lisa had been squashed to the rear of the group, next to a skinny boy, with pale skin and large teeth, who sounded out of breath.

'Just keep going,' she urged just as a slim, purple tongue, snapped around the boy's waist and whipped him out of sight. A crunch ended the boy's scream and prompted Lisa to barge past the waddling Boris.

The tongue shot through the group a second time, causing them to skip as it flicked, this way and that. The end almost curled round Harold's shoe for a second but was unable to take hold.

'Shit,' Harold said, kicking his shoe off as it began to sizzle and corrode. He would have fallen, had the guy behind him not given him an inadvertent shove, and kept his momentum going.

'What is it?' He said, catching up to Steve in front.

'One big, hairy lizard,' said Steve. 'Far more dangerous than any predator on Earth.'

'Great.'

'Pray you get the teeth… otherwise it'll pull you into its

stomach and digest you alive.'

'Great.'

'It's a Brorg,' Rosa said by Harold's ear, and he realised it could have been her who'd crashed into the back of him.

'How do you know?' Steve said, but she didn't answer.

They turned a bend and found their surroundings striped with moonlight, as they passed below a series of grills.

'The Maitre developed them years ago for flushing their enemies out of bunkers and things,' said Steve. 'Like a ferret down a rabbit hole.'

Harold felt his childhood asthma resurfacing — the tightness in his chest, the nausea, and he found his footsteps even more uneven. He began to think of the grills as checkpoints. If he could just make it to the next one…

'Can we… outrun it?' he asked.

'Depends how old it is,' Steve replied. 'Our best hope is to separate at a fork and hope it goes after the other group.'

There was a guttural sound and a glob of purple spit flew by and struck the ceiling thirty yards ahead, which collapsed in a cloud of dust and shale.

'Alternatively, if it's just caved in the whole ceiling up ahead, we all die now.'

'Bullshit!' Rosa yelled and snatched Steve's gun from his flailing arm.

'What are you doing? Are you crazy?' he asked, but she'd already ducked aside, into a thin alcove in the wall.

They reached the pile of rubble and began the slippery ascent up the slope, to a hole at the top. Lisa thought it looked big enough for two thin people, but not big enough for one Boris. However, she was never to find out because the boy was upended by the snout of the beast and flung down into the river. He shrieked as the tongue whipped out and lashed off one of his trouser legs, and much of the skin beneath it.

Then the Brorg raised its head to observe the rest of the party and slouched forwards into the collective torchlight to stand over the boy. Its head was flat and snakelike but covered in a black fur, making it almost invisible in the dark, save for the two, fluorescent red eyes. It growled, studying the group one by one, then turned its attention back to the fat boy below it. It opened its mouth and revealed that it had two tongues, which rolled onto the floor and began to swim up the disgusting river towards Boris. The beast was playing with its food.

Then a gunshot echoed through the tunnel, and prompted the Brorg to make a sound which discombobulated all and made them flounder down the slope, their hands pressed over their ears in attempt to suppress the noise. After three seconds of agony, Harold forced his eyelids apart and saw the Brorg thrashing around, tongues whipping like out of control fire hoses, as it tried desperately to make a U-turn in tight confines of the tunnel. Then came a second shot, and the Brorg collapsed into sudden silence. Its tongues slithered back into its mouth, and its red eyes extinguished.

Boris fainted into the river, the splash prompting his friends to rush to his aid.

Steve wandered over and took a glance at the boy's leg, which was a deep crimson, with patches of yellow.

'It's stopped corroding,' he remakred. 'But he'll probably still lose the leg to infection, regardless of all the spare skin he has for a graft.'

Several of the group yelled insults at him through tears.

He shrugged and turned to Lisa and Harold, who were powdered white from the shale and striped brown from the river.

'Back to the surface,' he said, wiping just a few flakes of dust from his suit. 'They'll be tracking the Brorg and will be along any minute to find out why it's stopped moving.'

'But it hasn't stopped moving,' Lisa said, her torch illuminating the Brorg's hackles which were bristling. Several members of the group screamed, dropped Boris, and set off back up the shale pile. Then Rosa appeared between the beast and the tunnel roof, and toppled down its body, bringing herself to a stop before she landed in the sewage.

There were exclamations of relief to see her. Those who had fled came back to Boris, looking rather sheepish.

'How did you do that?' asked Steve, eyeing the girl like a dog eyes the new baby in the house.

'We know our stuff, you know?' She said, hopping off the beast and onto the ledge. 'I read about Brorgspontos.

They've sacs on their back, and if you put a bullet in one, well, it's like me kicking you in the balls. Shoot one twice and you induce a massive heart attack.'

She pointed the gun at Steve's groin. 'I wonder how many shots to give you heart attack?'

Steve grabbed the barrel of his gun and took it from her. 'Where did you read this?'

'The internet,' she said. 'All kinds of users post on there.'

Steve mumbled something about 'checking IP addresses' and holstered his gun, as Rosa checked on Boris' condition.

'I'm sorry about your friend.' Lisa said, 'The one who…' She looked at the Brorg, and Harold remembered the skinny boy who'd been taken.

The group ignored her, grieving in their own respective ways, as Rosa walked over to the ladder.

'I will call Alex and Vlad to bring car and rope for Boris,' she said to the group, then looked at Lisa. 'I will come to surface with you now to find out where we are.'

Then she began to climb. Lisa shoved Harold off the ladder before he could fall in behind her.

Harold frowned as Rosa heaved aside the manhole cover and let the light flood in. But then he decided he wasn't bothered as he preferred Lisa's bottom anyway. He would have been in even less of a hurry to climb the ladder, had he known his face would only be inches from a woman's bottom for a minute, before it became inches from the barrel of a Russian rifle.

CHAPTER FIFTY-ONE

It poked against the back of his skull the second he emerged. Lisa and Rosa were zip-tied on their knees, tight-lipped, flanked by two soldiers.

Amongst them was a short man, wearing a brown trilby, crinkled white shirt and black shoes, pants and tie, none of which looked expensive. He wore a police badge at his belt.

The detective took his cigarette out of his mouth, and held up a finger to lips.

'Hush,' he said, and waggled his finger to let Harold know it was ok to proceed up out of the sewer.

'What's going on?' asked Steve, alerted by Harold's pause.

The detective shook his head and pressed his finger to his lips again.

'Police!' Harold said, so that a soldier rushed forwards and yanked him roughly out of the hole.

'You get out here now, agent,' said the detective. 'You drop and we'll toss some grenades down after you.'

Everyone watched the hole with bated breath, as Harold zip-tied and given a few kicks, then Steve emerged, dropping to his knees before they could force him.

'How did you find us?'

The detective crouched down and blew a stream of

smoke into his face.

'Anonymous tip-off,' he said, revealing yellow teeth with blackened grooves.

Steve looked around at Harold, Lisa, and Rosa.

'As I said, they noticed the Brorg had stopped moving. They gambled that we'd take the first ladder out of there. Lucky.' He said.

'Is he one of them?' Lisa said, staring at the detective, who was listening to Steve with a curios look on his face.

'No, he's a pawn.'

'What was that?'

'I said that you're a pawn,' Steve said, looking up at him, 'you're being used.'

'Oh… by whom?'

Steve didn't answer, and the man laughed, revealing those horrible teeth again.

'Ah, the mysterious agent from America. Never says anything. Well, I'm sure I can get you to open up to me.'

Then his eyes shifted to Rosa, and he frowned.

'Who are you?'

'She's no one,' Lisa said.

'Who are you, girl?'

'Rosa Petrov,' she said, eyes drifting towards the open manhole. Her friends had sensed the danger and were being quiet.

'A native?' He said, then took out his phone and dialled a number. He spoke in Russian then shrugged and put his phone back in his pocket.

'Dr Tsai was telling the truth… you are no one,' he said and nodded to the soldiers. They began dragging her by her arms towards the hole.

'What are you doing?' Lisa said.

Rosa began kicking her feet and shouting in Russian, but then another soldier whacked her on the forehead with the butt of his gun, and she fell silent. They stood her, swaying on the spot with her eyelids flickering, then one of them prodded her with the end of a rifle, and she plummeted out of sight.

Screams rang out from below, which drew the soldiers closer to the manhole, and then a blue sphere dropped from the sky and exploded.

Several soldiers road the plume of smoke into the sky and then came down into the flames that chased them.

Out of the desolation lumbered the detective, waving a pistol, and kicked them all to their feet.

'Get up! Get up! Get up!'

He pushed Harold and company towards the line of police cars at the end of the alley, bundled them into the back of one, and then accelerated away, just as the fire engines swung onto the main street for the second time that day.

As the detective gabbled into his phone and careered round corners, Harold leant closer to Steve.

'What the fuck just happened there?'

'It was a trap.' Steve said, 'They tipped off the police, so that they'd hold us there, while they lined up a plasma mortar. They rushed it though, worried the police were just about to discover the Brorg perhaps.'

'Jesus,' said Harold, 'Lucky for us they went for a look.'

'Yes, we'd be dead otherwise. We were fortunate those Russian kids made all that noise when the girl landed on them.'

Lisa listened to the pair, thinking about Rosa, Boris, and the rest of the UFOlogists who'd helped them. The group had done nothing but try to help them since they'd arrived in Russia, and had paid dearly for it.

All three of them realised that the detective had stopped talking and was listening to them.

'You know, I saw the fire from your bomb, go down into that sewer. Your friends were killed along with my men,' he lit a cigarette and blew a poof of smoke. 'My men died happy, knowing that fewer terrorists are threatening our country.'

'You think that was us?' Lisa asked.

'That wasn't us,' Harold stated.

'Say nothing more. It's pointless.' Steve said, then began speaking quickly, in a low voice. 'When they interrogate you, say that you weren't involved in the attack. Say that you're US defectors, and you need to see the President. Say anything else, and we'll all be tortured to death. Is that clear?'

'Shut the fuck up,' ordered the detective. 'What are you saying?'

'Is that clear?'

'Clear,' said Harold.

'Clear,' said Lisa.

'I said 'shut up, shut up, shut up!'' Said the detective, punching the dashboard, 'I shall have it all from you soon enough. I shall have it all.'

CHAPTER FIFTY-TWO

The detective made several more animated phone calls as he tore around corners before they arrived on an industrial estate. He swung the car into a parking space outside a white building.

Across the lot, a haggard Jack Russell watched them, as his human scavenged in the skip for anything of value that might be exchanged for a hot meal. The Jack Russell's name was Niko, and he was guarding his territory. He was a very good boy.

Steve, Lisa, and Harold listened to the detective as he made another phone call, then a fire door in the side of the building beside them opened, and a dozen or so men poured out.

'Remember what I said,' said Steve, before the door opened and he was yanked out of the car. Harold and Lisa were close behind. All three of them were lifted by their zipties and carried into the building.

Niko the Dog sniffed and watched a plane fly overhead.
***

Harold was at the rear of the procession. He watched as Steve was dragged into one room, and then Lisa was dragged into another.

He was dragged into a room of his own and plonked

down at a metal table, in a straight-backed wooden chair. He feared for Lisa trapped in the room with the strange men and kicked the table leg in frustration.

'You pricks,' he said, as the four men filed out of the room. The front three jeered, but the one at the rear turned and walked back to him.

He had blue eyes and brown stubble across his head and most of his face. Harold could see muscles tensing in his jaw — a jaw that looked like it might have been broken before.

'What you say, American?'

'I called you a…'

The man punched him so hard that his lip burst, and he clattered off the chair, which shot across the floor.

There came a scream in the next room, and Harold wondered if Lisa had screamed because she'd heard the racket, or because she was receiving similar treatment.

The man bent over him.

'Call me, prick, American fuck? You're prick.'

Then he kicked Harold so hard in the stomach that he feared he might never retake a breath. But, eventually, blustering and coughing, he did.

'Enough.'

He looked up towards the door and the detective stood there. Although he had changed into all clean attire, it was still in need of an iron. Harold's assailant picked him up and dumped him back in the chair.

The detective settled himself in the opposite chair, set a tape recorder down on the table, and then pressed the button. He took out a cigarette packet, lit another cigarette, and then slouched, staring at Harold with low-lidded eyes.

'Professor Dunn… I see you on the news. You are the alien man?'

'I'm…' Harold said, and then hesitated. '… A US defector. I need to see the President.'

The detective's eyebrows shot up beneath his trilby.

'You are not Professor Harold Dunn?'

'I'm a US defector. I need to see the President.'

'Why are you in Russia, Dunn? What were you doing down in those sewers?'

'I am a US defector. I need to…'

The detective lunged across the table and grabbed hold of Harold by the front of the jacket.

'You are an American spy. A terrorist. Two explosions in one day. It is you. And you bring down a plane. What were you aiming for? The Kremlin? Tell me!'

'I… am… a US defector. I need to speak to the President.'

There came a knock at the door, which prompted the detective to throw Harold back in the seat. He shivered, only partially from the cold in the room.

'That will be the car battery I asked for,' he said, smiling and flicking aside the cigarette butt. 'How long do you think you can hold out for, huh? I told you I would get it all from you.'

As the detective answered the door, Harold saw the other man roll up his sleeves and stare at him with those crazy, electric blue eyes. He was in some real trouble now. Would Troni know somehow and rescue him? The Zetan had to act now before he was tortured. Harold did not think he'd ever be the same otherwise. He couldn't take it.

There came raised voices from the door and then the detective punched the wall.

'What's going on?' Harold said before he could stop himself.

The detective glared at him and then walked back.

'It seems you've got your meeting with the President, Mr. Terrorist,' he said. 'But by the end of that meeting you're gonna wish you stayed here with my car battery and I.'

Then he walked around and heaved Harold to his feet.

'Oh, what the hell?' Said the detective, and head-butted him between the eyes.

As Harold stumbled back, the room spiralling, the other man rushed forwards and punched him in the face as hard as he could, sending Harold sprawling back into the corner of the room, where he whacked his head against the wall. He blinked as blood dribbled into his eyes, and then he was heaved to his feet again and led out of the room.

Next thing he knew, his hands were freed and he was being thrown into the fire door. Out he stumbled into the car park, where Lisa and Steve were waiting for him. Both looked dishevelled but otherwise unharmed.

'Look at you,' Lisa said with a gasp, and began trying to clean his face with her sleeve, then regretted it. 'What the hell happened in there?'

'More importantly, what did you say?' Steve said.

Harold did not feel able to answer either of them and instead listened to the growing chop, chop, chop of helicopter blades. Sure enough, a black helicopter appeared around the side of the building and set down in the lot.

As Harold allowed himself to be led to the helicopter, he watched a homeless man sleeping, propped up against a skip, with a little dog in his lap.

How's he sleeping in the midst of all this chaos? Thought Harold, then decided that the man was faking it. It must be an 'I don't bother you, you don't bother me' philosophy, which seemed to be working.

Niko the Dog watched them board the helicopter and knew that he had protected his human and scared them away. He was a very, very good boy.

CHAPTER FIFTY-THREE

L isa looked at the purple-green bruise glowing on Harold's cheekbone and thought about how violent her life had become and what still lay in store now they were on their way to meet Reznikov. She consoled herself by thinking that this was, at least, the definitive hurdle — to convince the Russian President that aliens were real and that a certain species had infiltrated his government and were manipulating him into exterminating mankind.

It did not remain a consoling thought for long, so she distracted herself by looking outside. This brought discomfort too, because although she felt an unsuitable excitement at being on a helicopter for the first time in her life, given the circumstances, she kept expecting a bolt of blue to come tearing through the clouds at any moment.

She looked at the detective puffing away on his cigarette and the blue-eyed man with the bruised knuckles beside him. Were they Maitre? No, they'd had opportunities to kill them. Maybe the pilot? Perhaps he'd crash them into the building in some Maitre martyrdom, although, come to think of it, she was yet to meet a Maitre or hear of one, capable of such selflessness. She thought them egotistical beasts.

Her eyes found their way back to Harold again. He'd wiped away much of the blood and was now rubbing his hands together, in some attempt to clean them. His anxiety invoked resentment in her. What right had he to be upset? She'd far greater experience of institutional torture than he had.

That's one accolade I'll leave off my resume, she thought, and then felt ashamed of herself for her derision towards the Brit.

He glanced at her, and she smiled. He gave her a weak smile back and then winced.

The helicopter lurched, and her shoes began rattling against the steel floor.

As she felt her fondness for helicopters deteriorating by the second, she looked out of the window again and saw a white-bricked, green-roofed building coming towards them. They circled a gold-tipped tower of crimson, then touched down on the lawn.

'The Kremlin,' Steve remarked.

'What's the plan?' Harold asked, still fidgeting with his hands.

'There isn't one,' Steve said. 'It's up to you now, Professor Dunn. You alone said you could convince Reznikov and now our fates rest solely in your hands.'

Harold began wiping his face again. Then Steve leant in very close to him and looked him in the eye.

'And if I didn't believe you could do it, I'd have killed you by now.'

'In a strange, horrible way, I think that's the nicest thing you've ever said to me,' Harold said, inhaling as he checked that the vial was still in his pocket, and then exhaling when he found it. God, imagine if he'd lost it.

'Fucking homo bullshit,' said the detective, and his colleague sniggered.

Outside the helicopter, two rows of three men marched towards them, with a senior officer standing at the forefront. His uniform was emerald green, and he had a bushy caterpillar of hair above his top lip and another above both eyes. He barked, hound-like, and a young recruit broke away from the detail to pull open the helicopter door. The recruit raised his hand to Lisa, and she and Harold flinched away in anticipation of the strike, but the hand hung there, at her midsection, until she accepted it and climbed down from the chopper. The man then offered his shoulder to Harold, who accepted it, feeling the violence of the blades on the back of his neck. Steve declined the man's help and hopped out unassisted.

The man led them over to the six-foot-five, barrel-chested General, whose small black eyes examined them from beneath all the hair. Then his moustache bristled into a professional smile, and he nodded for them to follow him. Harold liked the man, even if his affection did seem habitual, rather than genuine, and he didn't doubt the man would kill them in a heartbeat if ordered to.

There was a clatter of boots that made Lisa and Harold look round and they saw the soldiers, marching in time behind them. Then they heard a shout and saw the detective jogging up behind them.

'Wait,' he wheezed, puffing away on the cigarette like a steam engine.

The general had also spotted the man and was registering an expression of confusion, then he barked an order, without breaking pace, and faced forward again. The three men at the rear of the procession, turned and bounced the detective off the front of their rifles, then began driving him back towards the helicopter.

'I was supposed to take you to him myself,' said the detective. 'But he's going to fuck you so bad! You're so fucked!'

Harold flipped him the finger, and then grinned as the man's scarlet face disappeared back on board the helicopter.

With a bellow that made Lisa and Harold jump again, the general sent two men to heave open the double doors of golden wood, which towered over them at ten feet tall.

Lisa began to have bitter thoughts about the crumbly, grey paint of the White House, as they moved on through the beautiful building. Every table, window, chair was carved in some ostentatious fashion that spoke of history or value, or both. Every person they passed had character, fearsome or beautiful. There was not one person who failed to make an impression on her. This was a regime where the officials could handpick who they worked with without fear of causing some moral uprising. Moral up-risers were assassinated without subtlety, and the media reported the stories as it was instructed. It had been a macabre culture that had fascinated and horrified her for a long time.

She wondered why the models and brutes that parted to let their small army pass did not look in their direction. Were they so used to seeing dirty, stinking rebels being marched to the president for judgement? She didn't enjoy this thought as it trivialised their credibility even more, in some way.

After what felt like many miles of gold and red carpets, and interesting people, Harold's and Lisa's necks began to ache from swivelling and their feet from the walking. Each breathed an internal sigh of relief and terror when they reached a red door, with bronze letters, they knew spelt 'President' in Russian.

The general knocked, then opened the door> gesturing them forward, like a father encouraging his child through the school gates for the first time. Then he turned on heel and walked away. Harold was sorry to see him go. He'd seemed somehow reasonable, despite them sharing no conversation.

Inside the room they found a dozen men — tall, small, fat, thin — All wearing grim expressions, though none so ferocious as the two who stood either side of the great bear in the centre. Harold thought he recognised one of them from the news but could not recall his name, Steve, on the other hand, probably had read files on them both.

The man on the left, five-foot-eight and built like a brick, was Igor Spalko, Deputy Minister for Emergency Situations. A man who'd only come to the forefront of Russian politics in the last two years, handpicked by the President after orchestrating the assassination of no fewer than twenty-five rebel journalists and recovering several photographs which showed senior members of the cabinet in compromising positions with some questionable individuals.

The man on the right was Bogdan Klebin, a six foot, hooked nosed, fluffy haired man, with a build as light as his file. The Crow was the director of the FSB and a man who conducted himself with the utmost discretion. Very little was known about him, though there was a rumour that he had personally bugged President Pope's desk, entering on a guided tour and then slipping away, under a velvet rope and past three lines of security, to do so.

Reznikov himself beamed at them, slouching back in his leather chair, to reveal several more inches of a stunning, navy blue suit, with solid gold buttons.

'Ah, the Aliens are here. I'm a fan.'

The room chuckled, as Reznikov spun a laptop for the trio to look at. It was stormarea51.net, and the forums were rife with gossip about Lisa, Harold and the Steve, who were in fact aliens and had been sent to Russia to save mankind.

Hopefully, partially correct, thought Lisa.

'Or are you terrorists?' he asked. Any lingering laughter died. He leant forward and clicked a button on his laptop so that it played footage of a plane being dredged from the sea. The silence was palpable. Harold tried to disguise his trembling hands by stashing them in his pockets.

'Did aliens abduct your voices too?'

'President Reznikov...' Steve said, taking a step forward, but a gun being cocked behind him, disrupted his train of thought. It was a greying man, built like a linebacker, and Steve knew him too. He was blunt, uncompromising, and right-wing. His name was Fyodor Sedova. Steve had not heard the Prime Minister enter the room and noted how comfortably the silver Smith and Wesson sat in his right hand. Maybe he was ex-KGB?

'Yes, Agent? Or is it Steve? Or is it Agent Steve?' asked Reznikov. 'Was there something you wanted to tell me?'

Steve shrugged and faced Reznikov again.

'President Reznikov, Professor Dunn is about to tell you something remarkable. It will sound like lunacy, but it's the single most important piece of information you'll hear in your life.'

'Such an introduction for Professor Dunn. Hey, where's my grand introduction?' the president said to the room, which began chuckling again.

Harold gulped, 'Sir, Mr President, a few weeks ago I was on a visit to Area 51 and discovered a craft...'

'You don't need to tell them that!' Steve snapped.

'Silence,' said Reznikov.

Steve felt the barrel of the revolver thump into the back of his head, and when Reznikov spoke, his tone was sincere. 'Sedova, you kill him if he speaks again, but don't get any blood on my desk.'

Sedova collaborated something in Russian and stepped to the side of Steve. Some of the ministers began jostling to avoid the potential spray of brains.

'Go on, Professor Dunn. What sort of craft?'

'It was black, shaped kinda like a sting-ray, with a glass dome on top.'

'America's new stealth bomber, perhaps?' asked Reznikov, chopping down the end of a golden-brown cigar, which he placed between his lips.

Lisa watched Harold lick his lips. Reznikov was offering a thinly veiled illusion of camaraderie, but all this was just foreplay. He knew who they were and wanted the 'A' word out of one of them.

'It was an alien craft,' she said, as Reznikov placed another cigar in his pocket and then shut the box.

The collective snort came at once from the room, and Reznikov's head turned towards her. It turned like the turret on a tank, the protruding cigar stopping level with her.

'Ah, Dr Tsai,' he said puffing away, with a strained face which made Lisa suspect suppressed laughter, or less likely, a suppressed cough. 'You worked at the base for some time?'

'Yes.'

'So you were already familiar with this alien craft before Professor Dunn turned up? I believe he was only there for a brief time?'

'No. I didn't have clearance for that section.'

'But Professor Dunn did?'

'I found an ID and snuck in there one night,' Harold interjected.

'Looking for your A1?' Klebin said, tipping his beak forward and grinning out from beneath it. 'I should very much like to discuss that with you.'

'You will discuss that at length soon enough,' Reznikov said flapping his hand. 'Continue your story.'

Harold gulped. He had not considered that they might torture him for information on his A1.

'Well I found the craft and posted a picture of it to a site, stormarea51.net. Then later that night...' He paused, for what he hoped was dramatic effect, 'I was abducted by aliens.'

The snorts turned into a full flurry of laughter, from all except the two men on the President's shoulders.

'The President is a busy man,' said the Brick, his hand tightening into a fist.

'Relax Spalko.' Reznikov said, rubbing his hands together and grinning, 'Let the man talk. I'm always watching this stuff on YouTube.'

Harold sighed, feeling like he was at school, giving a feeble excuse as to why he hadn't done his homework.

'The aliens who abducted me were Zetans,' he said, and then added, 'who look a lot like the grey aliens you see in movies,' which he regretted.

'The Zetans warned me about this evil race called the Maitre who have come to Earth to exterminate us.' He couldn't look Reznikov in the face, and felt more juvenile with every utterance. 'They're shapeshifters. They've infiltrated your government and the US's to try and start a nuclear war that will kill us all.'

'They want the Earth for themselves,' Lisa said.

Reznikov looked delighted, staring at them, one to the next. 'So what you're telling me, is that my wanting to kick President Pope in the ass, is not because he is an arrogant moron, it is because I have a spaceman in my ear?'

'We're rational people,' Lisa said. As the laughter began again she added, 'too rational to blindly argue that President Pope is not an arrogant moron...but you do have infiltrators in your cabinet.'

Reznikov leapt up suddenly and began jabbing at his ministers with his cigar.

'Where is he? Who's the spaceman?'

He laughed himself and turned spinning the cigar through his fingers, sending ash tumbling to the carpet.

'Why come all the way to Russia to tell me this? Why not seek out the aliens in your own government first?'

'It's public knowledge that you intend to fire soon,' said Harold .

Reznikov stopped laughing, walked over to Harold and stood in front of him, narrow blue eyes pressing into his brown. The man's build was formidable for a man at the wrong end of his fifties and Harold found himself looking away.

'Why bring down the plane?' he asked.

Harold opened his mouth to speak, but only a croak came out.

'We didn't,' said Steve.

'What did I tell you?' Said Reznikov, pointing.

'We didn't,' said Lisa, 'it was the Maitre. They have these beams on their saucers.'

'This is nonsense,' said Reznikov, stubbing out his cigar in the ashtray, 'you are all liars.'

'No,' said Lisa.

'This is poorly thought out backup plan, in case you got caught for the attack on the plane. A plan to delay the launch of the Satan.'

'No.'

'Shut up, bitch,' said Spalko, striding towards her, with the back of his hand raised in front of him in threat.

'Get them out of here.' Reznikov said, turning his attention to some papers on his desk, 'I want to know everything about that A1.'

'I can prove it,' Harold said, finding his voice at last as they manhandled him out of the room.

'The President's made his decision,' said Klebin, one of the men with hands on him.

'Wait,' Reznikov said, and the crowd of men parted so that he could see them. He waggled his finger at them, and they were brought back over to him.

'Go on then, Dunn,' he said, 'Prove your aliens are real.'

The crooked eyebrows were aloft again with amused curiosity, but the blue eyes contained only a milligram of patience. It was do or die time.

Harold reached slowly into his pocket, which drew Sedova's revolver back to his head, and produced the vial of blue pills.

'Your aliens are hiding in there?' Reznikov said.

'A bet with you — I bet that if you get everyone in this office to take one of these pills, then you'll see yourself an alien. They force them to take their true form. I know there's a Maitre in here.'

'Who searched these people?' Spalko said but got no answer.

'And I suppose you expect me to take one of these mystery pills too?' asked Reznikov.

'No sir,' replied Harold, endeavouring to keep his gaze this time, 'If you were a Maitre, the world would be in ruins already.'

Reznikov smiled, took the vial from Harold and held it up to the light.

'Fifteen pills,' he counted, unscrewed the top, and poured the contents into his hand. 'One for each of my men... and one each for you three.'

He extended his hand. 'Swallow.'

Harold accepted the pills from Reznikov, handed one to the Steve and Lisa, and then flicked his own down his gullet.

Reznikov prowled over to Lisa, who did the same, and then over to Steve, who was examining his pill.

'Do you doubt your own companion, agent?' asked Reznikov.

'This is the first I've learnt of these,' Steve said, his tongue flicking out so that it almost touched the pill.

Reznikov nodded, reached over, and took the gun from Sedova.

'You will eat it, regardless.'

Steve looked at the gun, shrugged and swallowed.

Harold felt a tingly sensation but little more, save for a sweet aftertaste on his tongue.

Reznikov stood, the pistol at his side, a clock ticking away somewhere. Lisa shivered, eyes searching the room for Agent Kyle, waving merrily from the back somewhere.

'Interesting,' Reznikov said, then turned to the room. 'Each man, here, form a line.'

'Sir, you can't be serious?' asked Spalko, eyes wide in disbelief.

'I am serious,' he said, 'I want to see an alien.'

'Sir, but if it's poison…'

'Do not question the President,' said a minister with a black eye, gulping down a pill.

'I'm happy to risk it, Spalko,' Reznikov said, dark lines accenting his grin.

There were some worried murmurs around the room, as the men stepped forward and took a pill, each eyeing the gun in Reznikov's hand before they swallowed. The Crow, Klebin, loitered at the rear of the room.

'Why are you not in line, Klebin?' asked Reznikov, dropping a pill into Spalko's shaking palm, who was red in the face at being forced to perform in the drama.

'This is madness,' said Klebin, 'Those pills could be a slow-acting poison, we could all die a week from now.'

Reznikov patted Spalko on the shoulder as the big man swallowed, and then walked over to Klebin.

'Consider this an act of faith,' Reznikov said, almost completely obscuring the slighter man as he stood in front of him. Just Klebin's determined face could be seen staring back, his crooked nose a hair's width from the plum in the middle of Reznikov's face.

'Or I have another option.' Reznikov thumped Klebin in the chest with the gun.

'This is not necessary.'

'This is your last warning,' Reznikov said, 'you have five seconds.'

Klebin stared at Reznikov, then at the pill in his hand, the gun in his other, and then back to Reznikov.

He began to shudder. Lisa heard the flicker of Steve's tongue, and then a pungent sulphuric aroma filled the air, causing some of the men to cough, their eyes to water, and some of them to scream 'poison' in Russian. Then there came a shriek which no human could ever have made.

Reznikov stared at what had been Klebin, the uneaten pill dropping to the floor as his palm shook, in awe of the tall, aqua-coloured creature in front of him, dribbling slime all over his hardwood floor.

'Maitre don't deal well with stress,' Harold said.

A moment later, Spalko became the second Maitre, and reacted with speed, barrelling into the men by the door and smashing through it. The action brought the rest of the room back to life, and the hollering and firing of guns began. Reznikov fired a shot into Klebin's shoulder, as the Maitre kicked him away, and crawled across the ceiling into the corridor.

'Don't let them go,' Steve said, scrambling to his feet, but Reznikov was already after the pair bellowing and firing wildly.

When they caught up with the President, he had run out of bullets but was still hurtling down the corridor, now slick with violet blood and slime. He leapt for the trailing leg of one of them, missed by some distance and crashed into a filing cabinet, but was staggering back to his feet and reloading his gun by the time they reached him.

'Don't let them get outside.' Harold yelled to no one in particular, 'They'll be beamed up in an instant.'

CHAPTER FIFTY-FOUR

'I told you, we should have shot them down in the helicopter,' said Pinnt, as he bounced into a administrative assistant, sending a stack of files into the air.

'Oh, yeah, more plasma fire in broad daylight, one of those a month is enough don't you think?' Morkon said, ducking a gunshot and clattering through the door into the stairwell.

'The plasma mortar was your idea.'

'The Brorg they were about to find was your idea. I had to take the shot then…it was necessary damage prevention.'

They hopped down five steps at a time and listened to the footsteps thundering along the corridors above them.

Just four more flights, Morkon thought, then hopefully we'll be teleported before we're shot.

'Oh-ho, you don't now think blasting that helicopter might've been 'necessary damage prevention'?' Pinnt asked, slicing a young minister up the middle that'd wandered out in front of them.

'How was I to know about those pills?' Morkon asked. 'Can't believe Reznikov force-fed us them anyway. I was sure he'd just chuck them in a torture cell.'

'Damn it,' Pinnt said hearing the humans reach the

stairwell, and vaulted the banister, as bullets began to rain down from above. Morkon landed beside him, and they both raced down a passageway. Morkon recognised where they were. The door ahead was a side exit, which would take them out into the grounds. Fifteen feet... ten feet... as they slowed down for the door, it opened and beyond them stood a line of soldiers, who dropped to their knees and raised their rifles.

'Left,' said Morkon, and barrelled into Pinnt, sending him sideways through the only other door, as eight guns fired and missed.

They came to a halt inside the room, as two dozen more barrels turned towards them, but these were not the barrels of guns, they were the barrels of cameras. It was the world's press, assembled for President Reznikov's address at six. Silence fell upon their entry, before the sounds swelled and then exploded into an ocean of noise and flashes. They fired 4 shots a second, and video cameras closed in, forcing them back into the corridor.

'It's done,' Morkon said, and then his head exploded, sending a wave of violet blood over the journalists in front of him. Pinnt just had time to pirouette on the spot, before he too, was shot in the head. Then Reznikov, Lisa, Harold and Steve, slid to a halt outside the pressroom.

The Russian president took a step forward and stood over the corpses with his revolver and second cigar, smoking simultaneously. Just one reporter reacted in time to snap that image, an image that would become iconic, and make his fortune.

Then the soldiers at the exit broke out in fresh commotion, and the trio followed Reznikov out into the sunlit grounds of the Kremlin, with the press hot on their trail.

Outside, the soldiers stood in a huddle, pointing up at the sky, where something hung. It was far away and hazy in the sunlight, but everybody recognised it as a flying saucer.

CHAPTER FIFTY-FIVE

Reznikov bellowed for jets and Sedova relayed the order into his cell phone, as Harold, Lisa, and Steve, waited in anticipation to see how the saucer would react.

Harold felt a buzzing in his ear, and began working his finger deep inside, to try and reach the itch.

'It's moving,' said one of the soldiers, and Harold saw that the saucer was indeed getting closer, and as it did, he felt the beginning of a headache, and the itch in his ear grew even more severe.

'Are you alright?' Lisa asked him, noticing the way he was trying to dig his brain out through his ear, and that was when he heard it, faintly, in his own voice.

'Tell them not to shoot, you fool. It's me.'

'Troni,' Harold said.

'Huh?' Said Reznikov.

'It's… the saucer… it's a Zetan. One of the good aliens I told you about.'

Two fighter jets roared overhead, past the alien craft, and began to arc back into a firing position. Reznikov looked from Harold to craft and said nothing.

Harold clenched his jaw and stepped in front of the President, and Sedova raised his pistol behind him.

'You're the first President to shoot an alien… be the first to make peace with one.'

Reznikov stared at Harold, who refused to look away this time, then nodded and took the phone from Sedova.

He gave the order, and stared up at the sky, then smiled as the two jets pulled out of formation. He handed the cell back to his Prime Minister.

The saucer descended to a dozen feet above the ground in front of them. People were pouring into the streets surrounding the Kremlin yelling, and pointing, and taking pictures, savouring a pivotal landmark in human history. A chance to say 'I was there.'

Then, four long legs unfolded from beneath the saucer and it landed, there for them all to see — with its gleaming silver hull and black dome.

They gasped as the blue beam burst from the base and flattened the grass below. Then the alien descended. He was very small, and grey, and not dissimilar to the aliens they'd seen in the movies.

'Hello, Troni,' said Harold .

'Hello Harold,' Troni replied.

Then Harold got down on one knee and hugged the Zetan, who patted Harold on the back a few times, but did not return the embrace with any enthusiasm.

Harold chuckled and released him, then looked at the press being held back by Reznikov's men, and the President himself standing a little behind Lisa and Steve, puffing away on his cigar.

Troni set off towards Reznikov, and Harold saw Sedova lurking nearby with his gun. Harold caught his eye and shook his head, and Sedova shrugged and lowered the gun, but did not put it away.

'This is the President of Russia.' Harold said, 'The leader who allowed me to test the pills. The leader who allowed you to land.'

'Sugar pills,' Troni said.

'Sugar…' Harold said, gawping at him, 'Sugar pills? You gave me nothing but sugar pills to save the world with?'

'The Maitre didn't know that.' Troni said, with a tone of amusement, 'They don't do well with stress.'

'One of them didn't even need to eat it,' Lisa said.

'I suspected as much.'

'I can hear…' Reznikov said, tapping the side of his head, 'My own voice… but…'

'Yes,' Lisa said, 'He's a telepath. Can be quite confusing when he's talking to multiple people but you get used to it.'

Reznikov nodded and extended a hand to Troni who reached up and shook it, a human gesture Harold was relieved to see the Zetan had had the good sense to reciprocate.

'Please, ask your cameras to come forward, I have some things to say.'

Reznikov nodded and snapped his fingers at Sedova, who hurried over to loose the press. Within the minute, Troni was staring down the lengths of a dozen microphones and cameras. He turned away and looked at Lisa.

'Perhaps you would speak for me if I told you what to say?'

Harold and Lisa both looked at him with surprise.

'Don't look at me like that, Harold,' he said. 'I want the world to know 'I come in peace' not 'come I peace in.''

Harold felt offended, but folded his arms and said nothing. After all he'd done for Troni, and he was giving the grand speech to Lisa!

She stepped forward and cleared her throat, and half of the media swung towards her.

'The alien, whose name is Troni, will relay his message to me telepathically,' she said. 'And I shall speak for him.'

'The aliens killed here today…' She began, then looked at Troni, who was looking at Reznikov for confirmation. The President nodded. '…Were of the species Maitre, who were trying to instigate a nuclear war so that they could repopulate the Earth with their own kind. I am not a Maitre, I am a Zetan. Someone who has seen their planet attacked by this scum.'

Troni paused again, as though choosing his words carefully. Harold realised that the critical point had been reached.

'When the Maitre attacked us, they poisoned us and made us infertile, so the only way we could reproduce was by harvesting the DNA of other species…like humans.'

A buzz broke out amongst the members of the crowd who could speak English and then more as it was translated to the people who didn't.

'We've abducted some humans. It's true. I will not lie to you. Though we did it only so our race could survive. Those humans did not suffer and were returned to their lives on Earth mere hours later, with no memory of their respective incidents.'

'I might also remind you, that if it weren't for the Zetans, we'd all be on the brink of extinction right now.'

Harold looked at Troni, who shrugged and pointed at Lisa.

Some of the murmurings began to subside so that Lisa's voice could be easily heard again.

'We could not approach you openly for your DNA, the human agencies aware of our existence thought that your society was too un-evolved to accept it, which prompted our governing body to make Earth-landing illegal. But I assure you that my race think that now is the time for communication. Now there is a need for us to unite against intergalactic threats like the Maitre.'

Silence fell. Harold listened to the blood thump in his ears. Lisa was looking at Troni, waiting for more words, but the Zetan looked like he was running short. Things were clearly not going as he'd hoped.

Then Reznikov stepped forward, and the cameras and microphones swivelled to face him, the world listening intently for his next words.

'On behalf of the Russian government of Earth, I offer the Zetan race our friendship. If they can better equip us for dealing with these extraterrestrial hostiles, then we, in turn, can provide them with the DNA they need, so that there will be no more need for abductions.'

Troni nodded and shook the President's hand a second time.

'On behalf of the Zetan race, I accept this offer,' Lisa relayed. 'And now I must return to my own planet with the news.'

He turned, stretched his arms, and let a long smile creep

around his face.

'Who will hopefully send a more eloquent ambassador to speak in front of your cameras,' said Lisa, then spun around and slapped Troni on the arm, as the crowd chuckled. 'What do you mean 'more eloquent'?'

'I meant a more eloquent transmitter-to-speaker, obviously,' Troni said, rubbing his arm. 'No need for violence. Don't want to start a war do you?'

'Just try it spaceman,' she said, and then broke into a smile.

'I say again — the Zetans have our full support,' said Reznikov.

'Then you shall cease any plans for terrestrial nuclear hostilities, and contact President Pope to discuss the best way to unite against a Maitre attack,' Lisa relayed aloud for the reporters to hear.

Reznikov fidgeted at this and glanced down at Troni.

Harold watched his mind wrestle over what was more daunting — an extraterrestrial attack, or an amicable conversation with Duncan Pope.

'Another attack is likely?' he asked.

'Inevitable,' Troni said. 'I'm speaking from experience.'

Reznikov sighed and nodded, then shook the Zetans hand a final time, and set off back to the Kremlin. Sedova ordered the soldiers to move the press back again, and then hurried after the President, gabbling into his cell phone again.

Lisa, Harold and Steve, walked Troni back over to the saucer.

From inside the beam, he plucked a blade of grass, sniffed it, and then let it drift back inside.

'Thank you,' he said. 'Without you, both of our races would have suffered at the hands of the Maitre.'

'Ditto,' Lisa said, tears streaming free at last. 'Thanks to Nyn, as well.'

Troni nodded, and they observed a few seconds of silence.

'Will the U.G command an attack on the Maitre now?' Harold said, unable to restrain himself any longer.

'I doubt it,' said Troni. 'The Maitre will already have their ships halfway back to Megopei. They will claim the

Maitre on Earth were rogue, exiled many years ago.'

'Bastards,' Harold said.

'But we foiled them,' said Troni. 'We saved a planet from them, and that is no small feat.'

He stepped back into the beam, and then seemed to have an afterthought.

'Reznikov's Maitre will have a saucer nearby. Find it and study the technology, as you will need it when you face them again.'

'I will check that you've been studying,' he said, and then smiled. 'You shall see me again.'

He stared past them both and they turned to see Steve, standing a few feet away with his hands in his pockets.

'I'm sure I'd even be content seeing you again, Lizard Boy,' Troni said, laughing as he disappeared from view.

As Harold watched the tongue flicker out of the agent's mouth, he was reminded of a drunken evening in a bar in Rachel, when a girl with jam jar glasses had told him about reptiles in human suits.

www.blkdogpublishing.com